CLAIM
DENIED

By

John Avanzato

KCM PUBLISHING

A DIVISION OF KCM DIGITAL MEDIA, LLC

CREDITS

Claim Denied by John Avanzato

ISBN-13: 978-1-939961-43-3
ISBN-10: 1-939961-43-2

First Edition

Publisher: Michael Fabiano
KCM Publishing
www.kcmpublishing.com

KCM Publishing
a division of KCM Digital Media, LLC

Books in the John Cesari series by
John Avanzato

Hostile Hospital
Prescription for Disaster
Temperature Rising

Cheryl

Always by my side

Table of Contents

Acknowledgements

A special thanks to my friends for their advice and time.

Russel Harris

Dr. Marianne Arseneau

Ed Kirwan

Annemarie Kelly

Dr. Karen Deacon

Tandee Certo Jones

Leslie Baxter RN

Lois McMichael

Nancy McGowan

Peter Lutz

Shelley Pletcher

Preamble

In the fall of 1777 the Revolutionary War raged across colonial America pitting brother against brother, father against son. It was as much a civil war as a rebellion against England which was increasingly seen as a tyrannical foreign power. Although the Americans had seen some success on the battlefield, they were undisciplined and mostly on the run trying to avoid open-field battles with the world's greatest military. Valley Forge, the low point for the Americans had not yet taken place but they had much to be thankful for. They had managed to avoid annihilation time and time again, thwarting and frustrating the British high command.

British General John Burgoyne known as Gentleman Johnny devised a plan to divide the colonies in two halves. He felt that if the British forces could isolate the northern, more rebellious, colonies from the southern colonies their resistance would eventually collapse. Arrogant and overconfident, Burgoyne held the colonials in contempt and generally saw the upcoming hostilities as a walk in the park. He even wagered a friend that he would return victorious within a year.

The grand plan was to divide the colonies via a three-pronged attack. The western forces, under the command of Barry St. Leger, were to progress from what is now Ontario through western New York, following the Mohawk River, and the southern forces under the command of Henry Clinton and William Howe were to progress up the Hudson River valley from New York City. The coup-de-grace was to be delivered by the army under the command of Burgoyne proceeding southward from Montreal. The three armies were to meet in the vicinity of Albany, New York, severing New England from the other colonies.

The western and southern forces never arrived and Burgoyne's army, bogged down by logistics, desertion and constant harassment by marauding bands of colonials eventually surrendered in its entirety at Saratoga in the first weeks of October, 1777. It was a crushing defeat for the British and marked a major turning point in the war. Following Saratoga, Burgoyne returned to England in disgrace to defend his conduct. In retrospect, Burgoyne's greatest blunder was underestimating the American spirit and will to fight against all odds.

When the Americans eventually won their independence, there was great bitterness and finger pointing in parliament, and some never gave up the idea of re-conquering the colonies...

Claim Denied

John Avanzato

According to the Department of Labor more than 200 million medical claims are denied each year.

Prologue

The twin engine turboprop Cessna rocked and rolled in the turbulence created by the sudden storm that had overtaken it. The two passengers gripped their arm rests, white- knuckled and frightened. The older man, in his seventies, looked out his window as rain pelted the small aircraft and bolts of lightning lit up the night sky. The Cessna was an older model built two decades ago and had seen much use in its lifetime. It was sturdy, reliable and easy to handle and he had picked it up at a bargain price as turboprops were no longer fashionable. He had chosen it tonight because of the short runway they would be landing and taking off on. Jets simply couldn't handle it.

Looking over at his son, he found him ashen and dangerously close to passing out from stress. The younger man was in his mid-thirties, tall and lean, built for polo rather than rugby. His father worried about his son's fortitude and his perverse desires. Would he be capable of running an empire? They had taken off from a small airport just outside of Las Vegas, where for a couple of hundred dollars people didn't ask too many questions or demand that you file a flight plan. Which was good because he intended to be back in his room at the Bellagio by dawn and would prefer no one be aware that he had even left Las Vegas. He had even paid a whore a thousand dollars to spend the night in his room and had spiked her drink so that he would make it back before she woke. Alibi set, he had taken off into the night to do the deed. The flight was just over three hours and for the most part had been comfortable. It was the last hour, when the unscheduled storm blew in, that had made their lives so uncomfortable but they were now within just a few miles of Napa Valley and would be starting their descent.

The trip had taken on sudden urgency and thus was worth the risk. The old man had learned through his sources that several new antitrust laws were coming down the pike in Congress that might interfere with his broader business initiatives. Apparently those drunkards who represent the people had finally woken up to the notion that one man owning multiple pharmaceutical companies, hospitals, and health insurance firms might not be in the best interest of the collective good. Still, the laws they were considering, he was told, would not penalize or breakup conglomerates established prior to the passage of the law itself.

He snorted at the stupidity but nonetheless, the news did indicate a need for him to pick up the pace a bit. The law might pass tomorrow, next month, or never. Such was how democracies worked. Then a stroke of good luck came his way. The CEO of Unicare Corporation, the second largest health insurer on the East Coast and third largest insurer in the United States, had decided to take a weeklong vacation with his wife visiting the wine country of northern California. Unicare was the missing piece in his desire to obtain total control of the healthcare puzzle and he wanted it desperately.

Negotiations had been ongoing for the last six months between McCormick Enterprises and Unicare. They had not been going well. Talks had come to a standstill and had broken down completely for a variety of reasons, but primarily it seemed that the CEO of Unicare simply didn't like him on a personal level. He had offered the man twenty percent more than the company was worth plus a hefty signing bonus that would allow him to buy a small Caribbean island as well as keep him in caviar, champagne and yachts all the rest of his life. He was perplexed and more than just a little annoyed at the man's rebuff. And then came this unpleasant news about legislation to protect the people and so forth. It was time to act and to act decisively. He would not let himself be caught with his pants down like Cornwallis at Yorktown.

Two weeks ago, the CEO of Unicare had stopped taking his calls, but that was okay because he had an ace up his sleeve. The head of the board of directors was a slimy chap who ate too much and drank too much. He liked fast cars and faster women and he needed money—lots of it— to fuel his lifestyle. Private discussion with him had revealed that he was all for the sale of Unicare provided that he was taken care of to the tune of a one hundred million dollar golden parachute. If the CEO could be persuaded to go along, then he promised to deliver the board lock, stock and barrel.

But what if the CEO couldn't be persuaded? You're a smart guy, he had said, figure it out. Let's just suppose that the CEO doesn't show up for work one day. Guess what happens? That's right, I'm next in line and will be appointed acting CEO until a new one is found, but as acting CEO I think it is in the best interests of the shareholders to sell the company. Grease a few palms here, grease a few palms there, and it shouldn't take more than a month or so to set the wheels in motion.

It wasn't an ideal way of doing business, the old man mused, but not entirely without precedent. And this was America after all, the birth place of unscrupulous business practices. Besides, with what he had planned, this would be considered child's play so he shrugged off his concerns. He and his team had harangued over what to do about the recalcitrant CEO for weeks when he had fortuitously learned from the CEO's hacked email account about the West Coast vacation and his plans crystallized.

Several years back he had purchased a winery right on Rte. 29 in Napa as an investment property and to gain some credibility in the States as a major player. The fact that a famous

Hollywood director was practically living in his back yard added to the allure of the purchase. At the time of the closing, he hadn't met the man and couldn't tell you even one movie he had directed, but he soon discovered that after a few drinks, the garrulous director became the life of any party.

The winery, he had been told, was one of the oldest in Napa Valley, established in the mid-nineteenth century. It had risen to prominence in the 1930s and 40s when it had rivaled the French in the superb qualities of its Cabernet Sauvignons. Apparently, Napa Valley was ideally suited for this particular grape and ever since that discovery California vintners had been giving the French indigestion. That thought made the old man smile. Between the French and the Americans, he wasn't sure who he despised more. A reversal of fortune caused by several years of bad harvests, in combination with loss of enthusiasm on the part of the original owner's descendants for winemaking, had plunged the winery into decline and in the 1960s the family sold the business to some nameless, soulless corporation interested only in quick profit. Within a decade, the vineyard's reputation had been run into the ground and its grand old name had become synonymous with cheap wine sold in boxes for people who couldn't tell the difference between wine and wine coolers.

Then, in the 1990s demand for high quality wine returned as palates developed greater sophistication. It became fashionable for the rich and famous to buy wineries and build homes all along the valley. As box wine sales plummeted, the corporation decided to get out of the wine business. They had put the vineyard up for sale just as the old man arrived on the scene. He didn't know anything about making wine but he had hired the best vintners, sommeliers, and grape growers money could buy. His goal was to restore the winery to its glory days and after five years he was well on his way. His high-end Cabs were selling like hot cakes for two hundred dollars plus per bottle and last year's vintage had received a near perfect score of 99 from *Wine*

Spectator. Lavish dinner parties in the winery's cellar tasting rooms were the talk of the town and where there is one famous movie director there are usually more, not to mention a plethora of actors, actresses and their entourages.

In the back of the vineyard, away from the main winery, he had built a modest estate, no more than twenty-five thousand square feet. It was attached to the winery by an underground tunnel which led directly into the wine cellar so when the parties got out of control he could beat a hasty retreat, frequently in the company of a young Hollywood starlet, sometimes two.

Another two hundred yards behind the estate, a solid half mile from the main road, he had carved out amidst the vineyards a fifteen-hundred-foot landing strip for the Cessna. It was recommended that the minimum takeoff runway should be twenty-five hundred feet but unexpected difficulties with the rocky terrain had thwarted his construction efforts. He could have overcome those difficulties with even larger engineering machinery and additional building permits but felt the price of increased local scrutiny and publicity too great.

Rather than abandon the project from what he thought was its ideal location, he instead stripped the plane down so that it weighed almost two hundred pounds less than when he had purchased it. Then, he had hunted extensively for a pilot with balls and experience with short runways until he found an ex-cocaine smuggler, who had been dodging radars, bullets and DEA agents for twenty years, languishing in a tequila-fueled haze on a beach in Tijuana. The Cessna was better than any plane he had ever flown and the runway was larger than any he had ever landed on or taken off from in his life.

The old man had learned to be secretive. He wanted to come and go as discreetly as possible, away from prying eyes, and in this regard, he had succeeded. People rarely knew when he was at the vineyard. The plane now circled slowly over the landing strip lit up by a series of lanterns placed strategically on either side of the runway. It was 2:00 a.m. on a moonless night. In the driving rain almost a half mile from the road, he assessed that it was unlikely anyone would notice their arrival.

When he had caught wind of the CEO's vacation itinerary he had set the wheels in motion and so far things had worked out according to plan. A gilded invitation to the CEO and his wife to attend a dinner party at this up-and-coming winery, to be attended by many West Coast elites, was too much to resist. To sweeten the pot, the invitation had also indicated that there would be a charity auction to benefit the homeless. When the wealthy partied hard in the States they generally liked to assuage their guilt by pretending it was all for the benefit of others, an observation he had made since taking up residence here and a sentiment which seemed to be unique to America. The filthy rich elsewhere couldn't care less what others thought of their extravagant lifestyles. At any rate, the CEO had taken the bait, and now was sitting snugly in his tuxedo in one of the cellar's stone-walled wine tasting rooms.

The plane touched down uneventfully and everyone breathed a deep sigh of relief to be on terra firma. As they deplaned, they were greeted by two large men in rain coats with oversized umbrellas and a completely enclosed golf cart to shuttle them to the house.

"Good evening, Mr. McCormick. I trust you had a comfortable flight."

"Hello, Jacob. We had a terrible flight and we're bloody well lucky to be alive. Isn't that right?"

He turned toward the younger man for a response but his son was leaning over retching. He just nodded weakly in agreement.

Once in the house, they dried off, entered the basement tunnel and proceeded toward the winery. "Did they give you any trouble, Jacob?"

"The man blustered and threatened a little but stopped when I separated him from his wife. She's not too far away in the cellar and he's under guard in the tasting room."

"Good. Does he know what's going on yet?"

"If he does, he hasn't let on."

"You haven't hurt him, have you?"

"No, sir."

"Well then, no point in wasting time. Let's get to it. I'd like to be back in Vegas by sunup."

The vast subterranean wine cellar was a maze of tunnels carved into rock. It was dark, damp and cool. The walls were lined with old wooden barrels, some quite large, up to eight feet tall lying on their sides, hundreds, maybe thousands of them. The smell of grape juice perfumed the air, permeating their senses and clothes. As they approached the corridor leading to the tasting room in question they passed a woman sitting on the floor, her hands bound behind her back and a strip of duct tape across her mouth. She was beautiful and blonde, about thirty years old, wearing a long and very expensive evening gown with high heels. Well, one high heel anyway. She must have lost the other on the way here. Her eyes were wide with fright and she had been crying, causing her mascara to run. She whimpered at the sight of the newcomers but they walked by almost as if they hadn't noticed her. She was that unimportant.

Entering the room nonchalantly as if this were just another ordinary, mundane business meeting, he took a seat opposite his captive and nodded at the man who kept guard. The CEO's eyes went wide when he saw the older man. He exclaimed, "You? What's this all about?"

"Now, now, Jonathan. Let's keep our voices down, shall we? After all, we are civilized, aren't we?"

The CEO was forty-five, athletic, with a full head of salt-and-pepper wavy hair. He was used to getting his way and right now he was outraged. "Civilized? You call this civilized?" He jangled his wrists handcuffed to the chair arms. "Where's my wife?"

"Charlotte is being well cared for. I assure you on that score and you know exactly what this is about."

Confused, shocked, and then indignant at the sheer gall of it all, the CEO arched his eyebrows in astonishment as he understood. Angrily, he said, "Unicare? You've got to be kidding me! You kidnapped me and my wife to coerce me into signing over Unicare? You must be fucking crazy. Well, the joke's on you, you slimy English prick. It doesn't work this way. I don't have the authority to sign away so much as a single damn secretarial desk let alone the whole company. For God's sake, you moron, it's a multi-billion dollar corporation with thousands of shareholders."

The old man shook his head. "No need for name-calling, Jonathan, and of course I know you don't have that kind of authority. All I want is for you to sign a letter of intent: that after months of negotiations you have of your own free will and with careful deliberation come to the conclusion that it is in the best interest of the company, its customers, employees, and most of all its shareholders to allow Unicare to be acquired by McCormick Enterprises, and that it is your intention to present to the board of trustees a timeframe for this transaction that would be most beneficial for all the involved parties."

The CEO laughed sarcastically, "Now why would I do that? And what good would it do anyway? No one would believe that pile of horse shit."

"Let me worry about what people will believe or not believe, and why will you do it? Hmm. Jonathan, I want to be reasonable, and most of all I don't want anyone to get hurt." He let that linger in the air for a moment before continuing. "I've offered you a great deal of money, much more than I should have, but at this point negotiations have come to an end and you have to understand that refusal is no longer an option on the table."

The CEO gulped ever so slightly at the not-so-subtle threat. It was difficult for him to accept that a man of his station in life was no longer in charge of anything, perhaps not even his own life. He wondered where his wife was. With much less defiance in his voice he said, "I want to see my wife. I need to know that she hasn't been hurt."

Grinning, the older man said, "There, that's much more sensible and you will see your lovely wife as soon as you do as I ask."

"Fuck that. I want to see Charlotte now."

"I'm sorry that you're having trouble understanding me, Jonathan. Perhaps this will help." He turned to Jacob. "Please open the briefcase on the table."

McCormick and the CEO were sitting across from each other at a long ancient wooden table in a thirty-foot-long rectangular room, lined from floor to ceiling by wine racks. Jacob, who had been standing discreetly off to one side, brought a leather attaché case to the table and snapped it open. The old man reached in and retrieved a set of papers, placing them in the center of the table with a Mont Blanc fountain pen on top. He then reached back into the briefcase and came out with several unusual items which caught the attention of the CEO. There was a small plastic bag with white powder in it, a syringe, and a rubber tourniquet. He placed these on the table next to the papers.

The CEO looked at him and he looked back. He said, "These are your options. You and I can sign these papers and Jacob, who is a public notary, will co-sign them. How I use them is my business. I have here a cashier's check for one hundred thousand dollars in travelling expenses and two tickets to Tahiti for you and your wife. In anticipation of your cooperation, I have taken the liberty of placing twenty-five million dollars in an offshore account in your name. You should be able to live like a king there. I don't care. I just don't want to see or hear from you again."

"And if I refuse this generous offer?" He looked suspiciously at the other items.

The old man lifted the plastic bag up so that the CEO could see it better. He said, "Do you know what the latest rage is across the country these days?"

The CEO shook his head.

"Heroin. Can you believe that? The scourge of the 60s and 70s is making a massive comeback. Purer, cheaper and twice as deadly—it's back. Drug overdose from heroin is becoming so commonplace that almost every police officer in every city and small town is required to carry Narcan with him in case he comes across an OD in the field. If you don't sign the papers, you and your lovely wife will be found slumped over in your rental car in a ditch somewhere with needles stuck in your arms, but the best part is that you will both be badly bruised with many broken bones, presumably from the accident, but you and I will know better, won't we?" He winked at the CEO whose eyes grew wide as he turned a ghastly shade of white.

He hissed, "You son-of-a-bitch, limey bastard."

"Don't make me angry, Jonathan, or I might let my boys play with your beautiful wife first."

The CEO gasped at the thought and sighed deeply in defeat. With no cards left to play he asked, "You'll let us go if I sign?"

McCormick smiled broadly and replied cheerfully. "Of course. I'd rather not complicate my life any more than it already is. As soon as you sign the papers, Jacob will drive you and Charlotte directly to the airport to catch your flight. He will stay with you until you board. You can buy new clothes and essentials when you arrive in Tahiti. Your bank account number and password will be emailed to you in exactly twenty-four hours once I am sure you have arrived without any sudden change in plans."

The CEO let out a deep breath and then looked up suddenly. "We don't have our passports."

"All taken care of, Jonathan." He reached into the briefcase and tossed two passports across the table at him. "You really should have invested in a better security system at your house in Boston, and saving your passports at the bottom of your wife's unmentionable drawer? Really? Pretty obvious, don't you think?"

The CEO suddenly looked exhausted and weak.

"Where do I sign?"

Chapter 1

I looked at the cat and she looked at me. She didn't like me very much, stemming from an accidental stepping on her tail incident a few weeks back. She was an ordinary house cat, fluffy gray coat with streaks of black. I guess she was cute for a cat. Her name was Button and right now she was eyeing me suspiciously. I put my index finger across my lips imploring her to be quiet. She inched forward another step on her belly and was about a foot and a half away. Any closer and I would have a problem. I was very allergic to cats and could already feel my nose starting to twitch and my eyes water. This would be the wrong time to start sneezing and Button damn well knew it.

Studying the bottom of the box spring, I willed myself to ignore her as I listened to Kelly and Omar argue by the doorway. He was supposed to be away on a business trip but had decided to come home a day early and surprise her. Boy, did he do that. Right now, they were heatedly discussing why she was wearing nothing but a thong and camisole in the middle of the afternoon while the twins were asleep in the other room.

Tough question.

From my vantage point under the bed, I had a great view of her calves. She had beautiful dark brown skin and very sexy legs which just moments ago had been wrapped tightly around my neck. Thank God when she heard Omar come in the front door, she had the presence of mind to take off her high heels and throw them into the closet while I crawled under the bed. Seeing her in black heels might have pushed him over the edge. Women didn't walk around their homes half-naked in stilettos. Only in my dreams.

She said, "I just bought this outfit yesterday and wasn't sure if I really liked it so I was trying it on again. You know, getting ready for you to come home, Omar. So what do you think? I'm so glad you came home early. So what happened, by the way?"

That's my girl. She was good and his accusatory tone disappeared as he explained that things had gone more smoothly with his client than he had anticipated and that he was able to wrap things up early. He was a partner in a large accounting firm and had been in Connecticut the last two days. They must have been kissing as things got quiet and I watched her get on her tip-toes next to him. I turned and saw that Button had come a few inches closer. I was tempted to push her away, but was afraid she'd make noise if I startled her. Her eyes turned into slits as she studied me as if I were a mouse. I didn't like the look in those cat eyes.

Bodies fell onto the bed above causing the mattress to bounce and when I turned back I saw feet and legs intertwined, dangling over the side. Oh, brother. Things were starting to heat up as I heard Omar whispering passionately how much he wanted to make love to his wife and I settled in for a long day.

Kelly realized she needed to slow things down and said, "Oh darn, I think I just heard one of the girls crying. I better go check. Why don't you get out of your suit and clean up? You didn't even shave today."

He said, "I didn't hear anything."

Just then I sneezed.

Omar exclaimed, "What the hell was that?" He jumped off the bed and got on his knees lifting the bed skirt.

Kelly panicked. "Please, Omar, it's not what you think."

"Shit! There's a naked white man under our bed and you're telling me it's not what I think. You come out of there, Cesari. We're going to have this out once and for all."

The bus lurched to a stop in front of the main entrance to Saint Matt's Hospital, jolting me from my daydream. That was the last time I saw Kelly socially. Damn that cat. I knew she did that on purpose. I just couldn't prove it. I hoped she was in somebody's sesame chicken by now. That would be true karma. Shortly after that incident, approximately three months ago, Kelly filed a restraining order against me in order to mollify Omar and save her marriage. Unbelievably, she retained Cheryl Kowalcik as her attorney to serve me the papers. Cheryl was another ex-girlfriend of mine, blonde and bitter, skulking around Manhattan and she gleefully took the job, even volunteering to personally serve me the restraining orders. To add to my humiliation, she came to a noontime medical staff meeting to confront me with the news in front of my peers. I shook my head thinking about it. That was a dark day for sure.

Once in the lobby of the hospital I waved my ID at the security guard and made a beeline for the basement. It was 8:05 a.m. and I was behind schedule.

I entered the basement conference room, nodded at several people, poured myself a cup of coffee from an urn on a nearby credenza and sat down next to an attractive Chinese woman in surgical scrubs. Helen Ho was an orthopedic surgeon on staff at Saint Matt's, and she specialized in sports medicine—and breaking my heart. I'd been trying to get her to go out with me for weeks, but she seemed to take great pleasure in turning me down. I would have settled for casual sex but apparently that wasn't an option.

"Hi, Helen, how's the world of orthopedics?" I whispered, adjusting myself in my chair. We were in conference room C in the basement of the hospital. I looked around and saw all the usual suspects representing their respective departments.

"It's fine and you're late again, Cesari."

"I was dreaming about you and didn't hear my alarm go off."

She just shook her head.

At the other end of the table, the medical staff secretary was in the middle of reviewing the minutes from the last meeting. A curmudgeonly woman in her late fifties, Terry Konklinberg took no prisoners and even less shit from anyone on the medical staff. A Saint Matt's employee since she was eighteen years old, she rightly felt entitled to a certain amount of respect and right now she wasn't feeling the love from me. I was ten minutes late and she gave me the hairy eyeball.

"Did I miss much?" I quietly asked out of the side of my mouth to Helen.

"Shhh."

I sipped my coffee and smiled, black and sweet as always. I loved using that line and I loved black women. Win-win. All hospital committees were a colossal waste of time but quality assurance meetings like this one were the worst: extremely boring, tedious, and always dangerous because you never knew if you were the one who was going to get thrown under the bus. The task at hand was to review specific cases for deficiencies in care provided by nurses, doctors and other hospital personnel. The big joke in modern healthcare was the concept of team. We were all equal members of the team until something went wrong. Then it was all about the doctor. All of a sudden no one wanted to be on the team any more.

Peer review like this was total bullshit anyway. On paper, the idea was to ensure that the practice of medicine at our hospital was in line with community standards, but the main reason for all the meetings was to keep the state of New York off our backs so the hospital could keep collecting fat checks from Medicare and Medicaid. The government could give a rat's ass about quality of care. All they wanted was documentation that we held meetings about it. You could die from a mild case of constipation but as long as we documented our efforts to adhere to guidelines for treatment, the state could care less. Alternatively, you could save someone's life against all odds and have your license suspended because you forgot to sign your name in the right place. It was all about conformity.

Helen leaned over as the secretary finished talking. "I guess you didn't get the memo?"

"What memo? And did I ever tell you that you look really hot in scrubs? I mean it. I don't say things like that to every girl."

She chuckled quietly. "Shut up. The memo that said this meeting is about the GI department, and don't you have a girlfriend?"

I tried not to show alarm. I was notorious for not reading hospital memos and notifications. I looked around the room. We sat around a long oval table: six physicians, four nurses, two administrators, and the secretary, who was sitting next to the chief of staff, a sixty-year old hematologist named Arnold Goldstein. He thanked the secretary and cleared his throat.

"Dr. Cesari, so glad you could make it."

"My apologies for being late, Dr. Goldstein."

He cleared his throat. "Yes, well, we have a long agenda so we might as well get started and address the GI problem."

GI problem?

I was one of ten gastroenterologists on staff here at Saint Matthew's Hospital on Third Avenue in lower Manhattan. We performed over thirty thousand outpatient procedures per year and brought in tens of millions of dollars in revenue to the hospital and yet every time someone called a meeting they prefaced it with the "GI problem." These meetings were painful and so the guys in my department rotated monthly who attended. That guy did his best to fight off whatever accusations were made against the group and then reported back to the others.

"I was unaware that there was a GI problem, Dr. Goldstein."

He shuffled through some papers in front of him until he found the one he was looking for. While he did that, I wrote "*My loins ache for you.*" on a napkin and slid it over to Helen, giving her my best c'mon-I'm-a-nice-guy smile.

Goldstein said, "There have been so many GI-related issues this month that I decided to devote the entire meeting to addressing them. In addition to the usual patient management concerns, which we will get to, several egregious patient complaints directed toward members of your department have recently come to light. Three formal complaints in the last two months to be exact."

"What do you mean by formal?" I watched Helen smile, shake her head, and roll her eyes as she read the note. She was adorable.

"They took time out of their busy lives to not only call in their grievances but to write letters to the CEO of the hospital, and in those letters they threatened to call the state if no disciplinary action was taken against the physician in question. Is that formal enough for you?"

I raised my eyebrows. You had to be pretty angry to do something like that. "Yes, so what happened?"

Goldstein looked pretty smug. "Well I'm so glad that you're impressed, Cesari. One patient complained that she had unusually severe pain during her colonoscopy and that your colleague Dr. Sharma was very unsympathetic, and I quote, 'He is a heartless bastard and I hope he rots in hell.' The second case was an eighty-eight-year-old woman who claims that one of your other colleagues, Dr. Compton, was inappropriate because he asked her if she was sexually active."

"What's inappropriate about that?"

"Nothing, but her main reason for the consultation was rectal pain and she interpreted the question as suggesting that she engaged in anal sex."

"Yeah, so what? It's not totally unreasonable."

"Except for one thing. She's a board member here at Saint Matt's, a major contributor to our foundation, and the widow of one of the more prominent Presbyterian ministers in all of New York. She hasn't been with a man since 1999 and your fool of a colleague asked her if she's been having anal sex. For crying out loud, Cesari, don't you GI guys believe in tact? Even if she was, you don't think a woman from that generation is going to say that out loud. At any rate, she says and I quote, 'He is a pervert and I can't believe that it is acceptable medical practice to query decent God-fearing women about such things.' Now granted, these cases leave room for the possibility of misinterpretation but nonetheless we here at Saint Matt's take all patient complaints seriously." Arnie looked exasperated and took a sip of water.

Helen slowly slipped the napkin back to me and I glanced down at it. *Not if you were the last man on earth.*

"The third case is the one that shook us up the most. It's a letter from the wife of a fifty-year-old Albanian immigrant, named Jetmir Konstandin, who died recently from colon cancer. She says his treatment options were never clearly explained to him and that because of improper documentation, his claims were denied by the insurance company. He could not afford out-of-pocket payment for his care and so chose to die at home without treatment. He paused for effect while I discreetly drew a frowny face on the napkin and slid it back to Helen.

I asked, "Improper documentation? On what basis is she making that claim?"

"On the basis that her husband is dead and she has every right to ask questions."

"Look Arnie, if she wants to sue, let her sue. I don't see what another frivolous lawsuit has to do with this committee."

"Calm down, Cesari. It serves no purpose to impugn her motivations for the accusation. You know the drill. The woman filed a complaint and we have to dot all the i's and cross all the t's, so don't get your panties in a bunch. Now, the problem is that the patient's insurance should have covered everything if even half of what the wife says is true. According to her, we misrepresented his care either through negligence or gross incompetence or both in our recordkeeping."

"I'm not sure where this is heading. Arnie?"

"Well, as outlandish as it sounds, she seems to think that somehow her husband's medical record was switched accidentally with someone else's. In short, due to some ghastly error in documentation on our part, her husband was denied lifesaving care and is now dead. She didn't need to say it out loud but obviously litigation is on the table or perhaps worse, as a mistake of this nature would undoubtedly make headlines."

I took a deep breath and scanned around the room. All eyes were on me. "Fine, so what am I supposed to do besides say I'm sorry?'

"Well, I'm glad I finally have your full attention, Cesari. Maybe now you and Dr. Ho can stop passing each other love notes. The wife is very serious about her complaints and demands that some explanation be forthcoming to her satisfaction. All she needs is to convince a lawyer that her case has some merit and since her husband is dead, after all, she may have a point."

"Yeah, but people die from cancer all the time."

"He didn't die from cancer, Cesari. He committed suicide rather than become a financial burden on his family."

I was taken back by that news as was everyone else in the room. He continued. "Do you see now why this has the potential to escalate out of control if not handled correctly?"

I paused, thinking about it. What could I say? "Who was the doc involved?"

"I thought you'd never ask. It was your pal, Anthony Macchiarone."

Jesus. *Tony Macaroni,* as we called him, was a really nice guy and very attentive to details. Probably one of the least controversial guys on staff. "What does Tony have to say about all of this?"

"Not a whole lot that's been helpful. Like many of your people, he seems to have developed short-term memory problems under direct questioning."

Nice ethnic slur Arnie.

"I find it very difficult to believe that Tony could make a mistake like that, and was that last part really necessary?" I liked Arnie but he could have an acid tongue when it suited him.

"Relax, Cesari, that was a joke so call off the Sicilian hit men, all right? I agree about Tony but we need to convince Mrs. Konstandin that we are doing everything we can to investigate her complaint one way or the other. To that effect, we are going to pursue two parallel investigations to prevent the possibility of being accused of white-washing this thing. We would like to keep this in-house as much as possible for obvious reasons. If any of the competing hospitals caught wind of this they would have a field day with it. They might even alert the state anonymously. As a gastroenterologist, you are in the best position to understand the nuances of what happened. Therefore I want you to review the record, interview Tony and Mrs. Konstandin, and then submit a formal report with your conclusions before the next meeting. Make sure your report is as thorough and as unbiased as possible. None of this Cosa Nostra protect-my-brother stuff."

He was a regular riot today. I asked, "Will she speak to me?"

"She insists on it. She is very adamant in her claim that a mistake was made and that we are the ones who made it. Terry here will provide you with her contact information." He nodded at the secretary next to him.

"Who will be doing the parallel investigation?"

"That's for me to know and you not to. The hospital will be engaging the services of an independent auditor and hopefully both reports will exonerate Saint Matthew's and Dr. Macchiarone."

"Or at least Saint Matthew's anyway."

"Exactly."

Fuck. He just put me in charge of a witch hunt and Tony was the witch.

Chapter 2

After the meeting, I walked with Helen up to the operating room. I liked the way she moved, slinky and sexy. I made sure I stood an inch or two behind so I could get a good look without being too obvious.

She said, "Do you have to stare at my butt like that all the time?"

I looked away quickly, embarrassed. "I'm not sure what you're talking about, and I don't have a girlfriend, by the way."

She cocked her head and smirked. "Really? What happened to the stripper?"

"That's not fair. She was an exotic dancer, not a stripper, and now she's studying classical piano. Things didn't work out. That's all." She was referring to Myrtle Rosenblatt, aka Cocoa, whom I had dated a few months ago, a former pole dancer who was now enrolled in Juilliard.

"Well, that's too bad. Maybe you should try Craigslist."

I wasn't one to give up easily. I've met girls in the past who were immune to my charm, but they were few and far between. My basic strategy with the more difficult types like Helen was to tire them out, so I asked, "Did you really mean that about me being the last guy on earth?"

She paused in front of the door to the women's locker room while she thought it over for a few seconds. "Okay, Cesari, maybe that was a little harsh. I'm sorry. I guess if you were the last guy on earth and I was super crazy horny and there was a paper bag lying around I could put over your head, I would consider it." She must have thought that was real funny because she started giggling.

Wounded but not down for the count, I pleaded, "But Helen—I think I love you." When it came to sex, whining was a perfectly legitimate battle tactic. Besides, bagging a woman doctor would do wonders for my ego. In my world, that was the holy grail of sexual conquests.

"Where's your pride, Cesari? I can't believe you're begging."

"I'm not begging, I'm cajoling. There's a subtle difference. Besides, it's pretty obvious I can't live without you."

"Oh, please. Why do white guys lose it around Chinese girls?" she asked.

This was news to me. I had never taken a poll on the subject. "Is it the sushi?"

She shook her head, exasperated. "Sushi? You are such an asshole. I can't believe it."

She turned to enter the locker room but I put my arm in front of her, resting it against the door jamb. I said, "I was joking."

She looked at my arm and then into my eyes. Our lips were inches apart. "And just what do you think you're doing?" She knew very well what I was contemplating. I contemplated it all day long.

"I was toying with the idea of kissing you."

She smirked as her eyes darted back and forth to make sure no one was watching. She whispered, "I don't think you have the balls."

Ouch. I looked from side to side. It was risky kissing another physician right there in a public hallway. God knows how much gossip that would generate if someone were to walk by at just the wrong moment. She had cajones, I'll give her that much. She called my bluff and I hesitated.

Footsteps caused me to withdraw my arm and free her passage. She smiled, "Ha, I didn't think so." She disappeared into the locker room before I could come up with a witty response, but at least she was smiling. Well, that was mildly humiliating but it seemed to me I was making progress. Deep down I think she liked me, sort of.

I went into the men's locker room, changed into navy blue surgical scrubs and proceeded off to the endoscopy room to begin my day: ten colonoscopies in a row, scheduled at half-hour intervals, followed by hospital consults, paperwork, phone calls and five or six cups of coffee. Tomorrow it would start all over. Somewhere in the chaos, I would forage for food, take bathroom breaks, and figure out a way to review that case Arnie had given me. I was too busy to worry about the fact my personal life was an absolute train wreck and that I hadn't had sex in weeks—months, unless you counted an office fling with a secretary.

I had ex-girlfriends all over Manhattan, starting with Kelly, the beautiful but very married African-American nurse on the west side with the restraining order on me. Then there was Cocoa, and finally, Cheryl, a midtown lawyer who hated me so much that she dreamed of one day opening the *New York Times* and reading my obituary. Worst of all, was that I had a muscle-bound, mobbed-up friend named Vito Gianelli who considered me his best bud. No matter how much distance I tried to put between him and me he managed to narrow the gap faster than I could pull away. We grew up together in the Bronx, and he couldn't seem to get past all that male bonding we did as kids. There was something about taking turns cracking people over the head with baseball bats that made guys feel close to each other.

I entered the endoscopy room and was greeted by my nurses. "Good morning, Dr. Cesari."

"Good morning, Debbie, Christine. How's everyone today?" The patient was semi-reclined on the stretcher, looking relaxed.

"We're fine. Just waiting on you." I looked at the clock. I was only five minutes behind schedule. That wasn't bad at all considering I'd just come from an eight o'clock meeting.

"Hello, Mr. Carson. I'm Dr. Cesari. Remember me? Are you ready for your colonoscopy?"

"Hi, Doc. Of course I remember you. I'm old, not demented. Now let's get this over with, I'm hungry." He was approaching seventy and we had been to this rodeo together on several prior occasions. I knew him pretty well.

"All right, let's do it then. Please roll onto your left side and face the video monitor and we'll get started." The room was a twenty-foot square and seemed small with the stretcher, video equipment, crash cart, sink and cabinets.

Debbie said, "Not so fast, Doc. You need to have him sign his consent first and then we need to do the time-out." She handed me a clipboard with a generic consent form and a pen.

I took them from her and handed them to the patient. "Please sign at the bottom, Mr. Carson, where it says patient signature."

He looked at the piece of paper, squinting and rubbing his chin. "What am I signing, Doc?"

"It's the consent form that says I explained to you in great detail how you might die as a result of today's procedure. Just sign at the bottom please."

He raised his eyes at me. "I don't remember you saying that. Don't I get a chance to read it? Can somebody hand me my glasses?"

Christine reached under the gurney into a bag with his personal effects and handed him what he asked for. He placed them on and sat back, settling in for a relaxing read. I looked at the wall clock and then at the nurses. Modern healthcare and surgical practices didn't allow for such delays, but to deny the patient his right to read his consent form would have been a cardinal sin, so we waited patiently.

I said, "It doesn't say anything different than the last five times you had this done."

Halfway through, he looked at me and asked, "Yeah? I don't seem to remember any of this. Why do you wait until the last minute before you give this to the patient? Is it because you don't want them to know what they're getting into?"

"It's not my decision, Mr. Carson. New York State has mandated that all consent forms have to be signed, dated and timed within seven days of the procedure. Since most people like yourself are scheduled weeks, sometimes months in advance, the only way we can meet New York State guidelines is to have you sign the consent on the day of your exam. I know it seems odd but we have no choice."

"So what's all this mean? I can't sue you if something goes wrong?"

I chuckled. "Not at all, Mr. Carson. In fact, that's the beauty of it. In a court of law, this piece of paper is meaningless other than to prove we didn't drag you in off the street against your will. Informed consent is supposed to be a meaningful discussion with the patient concerning his care: why the procedure is necessary, what are the alternatives, and what are the risks. Technically, this should be done in a nurturing environment that is geared towards the patient's ability to understand, and then the patient should be allowed ample time to digest the information, and of course, ask as many questions as they wish. Any good lawyer would point out that these conditions where you already took your bowel prep and are lying naked with an IV in you are extremely coercive and therefore this is not a true informed consent discussion."

He looked puzzled. "So what's the point?"

"The point is that there are too many bureaucrats running healthcare these days who don't have a clue as to what real doctors and nurses do. If you think this is stupid, wait until we do the time-out. Just remember how many times you've already told someone your name and why you're here since you arrived an hour ago, including these same nurses."

He shook his head and signed the consent. "I trust you, Doc."

Debbie said in a loud, attention-getting voice, "Time-out everybody. Okay team, we have Mr. Joseph A. Carson, here for a colonoscopy today with Dr. Cesari because of a history of colon polyps." As she barked the ritualistic time-out, the other nurse grabbed his wrist pretending to study his ID bracelet.

"Mr. Carson, could you please tell us your date of birth?" Debbie asked.

He looked at me as if he thought we were all nuts. "May 15, 1945."

Debbie asked, "Is that correct, Christine?"

Christine studied his ID and responded. "Yes it is."

"And what procedure are you expecting to have today, Mr. Carson?"

"Are you guys kidding me?"

"Could you please answer the question, Mr. Carson?" Debbie asked again politely.

"A colonoscopy, of course."

Debbie loved her time-outs and threw everything she had into them. "Mr. Carson has a history of high blood pressure and diabetes. He last took his insulin twelve hours ago and his blood glucose this morning at eight a.m. was 240. The doctor was made aware. He has no medication allergies but states that he is not sure if he is allergic to bananas. Therefore we are using appropriate latex allergy precautions because of a potential latex cross sensitivity. He denies a history of obstructive sleep apnea but his wife says he snores so we will also take those precautions. Once again, the doctor was made aware."

Mr. Carson looked at me very concerned. "What's going on here, Doc? I'm starting to feel like I fell through the looking glass."

I chuckled. "You and me, pal. I apologize but we're just following New York State rules and regulations. It's like this everywhere now. I'm sorry, Debbie. Please continue."

She looked dismayed and hesitated.

"What is it, Deb?"

"You interrupted the time-out, Doctor. Technically, I'm supposed to start all over from the beginning."

I looked at the wall clock. It was going to be a long day. "Do what you have to do, Debbie." So she started over.

Don't ever get between a nurse and her paperwork.

I finished the last case at 2:00 p.m. and wandered over to my office on the third floor of the hospital to chat with my secretary, whom I shared with three other gastroenterologists. Her name was Julie and we had been bad once at an office party not too long ago. We did have one minor relapse a week later but had been good since. Several other secretaries were aware of the tryst and we were still trying to live it down, especially since Julie was engaged. How these other women had found out was beyond my understanding. Julie and I were alone at the time and she swore she hadn't told anyone. Somehow women always knew who was doing what to whom and they were now keeping a close eye on the situation in hot anticipation of further indiscretions. There was literally nothing women enjoyed more than being the first to get the scoop on someone else's dalliances.

28

She looked at me uncomfortably, glanced around, and smiled when she thought it was safe. You couldn't get more jumpy. "Good morning, Dr. Cesari."

"Good morning, Julie. How are you today?" She was in her late twenties with light brown hair and a great figure. She was neither gorgeous nor homely but attractive in an ordinary sort of way. She took good care of herself and dressed well. I could smell her perfume and I liked it.

"I'm good. It's been busy. One of the other secretaries called in sick so I've been helping out." Her eyes darted furtively back and forth.

I looked around to see who was within earshot and lowered my voice. "You know, Julie, it's okay to look directly at me. It might even be less suspicious."

She blushed and laughed. "Oh, my God. Am I that obvious?"

"You might as well sew a scarlet letter A on your top."

She covered her face with her hands, chuckling. "Oh, brother. What am I going to do?"

"C'mon, Julie. You have to get past it. Water under the bridge, you know? It's over and done."

"Is it?"

"Julie, c'mon. I thought we both agreed it was a mistake?"

She appeared to calm down a little. "I know. It's just that I—think about you—about that night and the other time. You know?"

I let out a deep breath and smiled. "I do know what you mean and I think about you too, but we can't. You're engaged to be married, and we have to put it behind us, okay? It never happened." I stopped short of saying *so get it through your head*.

She nodded. "I know you're right, but I can't help it and I feel so guilty."

Okay, I needed to change the subject fast before things started to spiral out of control. The last time we had this conversation she almost jumped across the desk at me.

"That's a beautiful locket, Julie." She wore a gold locket around her neck in the shape of a heart.

"Thank you. My parents gave it to me for my eighteenth birthday. I keep their pictures in it. Want to see or is that too hokey for you?"

I smiled. "Not at all. Show me."

She opened the locket and presented it to me. I leaned over to get a better look.

"That's really sweet, Julie. Which branch of the military was your dad in?" I asked noting his uniform. They looked to be in their late twenties.

"He was army and served in the first Gulf War. He was a gunner in an M1A1 Abrams tank."

"No kidding?" I really was impressed.

"Yeah, he's a really cool guy. You'd like him, Mom too."

She smiled seductively. "They live in Queens. I could take you to their apartment. Of course, they're on vacation right now in Florida but they wouldn't mind if I gave you a private tour."

Ignoring the obvious invitation, I cleared my throat. "So, how's Thurman?" She lived with her fiancé, Thurman, a 275 lb., thirty-year-old body builder on the New York police force.

She pouted, knowing I had just changed the subject. "He's fine. He had today off so he's down at the gun range practicing again. Apparently, he's the top gun in his precinct again this year and will be competing in the city wide marksmanship contest coming up in the fall. If he wins, he may be eligible for the nationals. He always says, '*Remember, Julie, your gun is your friend.*'" She said the last part in a mocking deep voice as she rolled her eyes.

Great.

I said, "He enters a lot of contests. Didn't he win some sort of bodybuilding thing last year?"

"That's powerlifting. He's a powerlifter, not a bodybuilder. He says bodybuilders are sissies and narcissists." Again in the mocking voice she said, "*Powerlifters are real men, Julie, like Viking warriors,* and yes, he came in second in the New York State finals for powerlifting. I think he squatted 600 lbs. or something. I don't even know if that's a lot and I don't care."

It was a lot.

Great.

Fooling around with a 275 lb. pound, sharpshooting New York City policeman's girlfriend could shorten one's life expectancy significantly. "Well, that certainly is interesting, Julie. Say, do you know if Tony is available?"

"I'll check." She picked up the phone and buzzed him. When he didn't answer, she stood up and walked down the hall to his office. She wore a short, tight skirt and had a great ass. I could watch it all day long and I chuckled because I had, too. That's why we were now in this peculiar situation we found ourselves. It was at a coworker's retirement party right here after hours six weeks ago. Two martinis, romantic music, an empty office and now we couldn't even look at each other without blushing. Of course, I couldn't blame the second time on alcohol. That was pure unadulterated lust on top of the break-room table three days later. You might call that a follow-up visit.

She returned, smiling coyly. "He said to go right in. He's in between patients and has a few minutes. He was just on the phone and that's why he didn't pick up."

"Was he really on the phone?"

She knew I liked to watch her rear end and she frequently trumped up reasons to let me. She smiled. "I'm quite sure I don't know what you're talking about, Doctor."

31

"I bet. Well thanks anyway, Julie, and I'll talk to you later. If anybody's looking for me, tell them to page me overhead. I have some consults to do that should keep me here till five or six."

I waved goodbye and headed down the corridor thinking about her and that night. She really was wild when she let her hair down but I had to throw her off the scent permanently and quickly, before this thing exploded. I had been to this dance once before. I knew how volatile it could get, and cops weren't exactly known for being understanding when it came to guys bending their girlfriends over their desks. I sighed, shrugged it off, and hoped she wasn't going to be a problem as I let myself into Tony's office. I found him sitting behind his desk staring out the window down at Third Avenue.

"Hey, Tony. How's it going?"

He stood up and we shook hands. "Not bad, Cesari. What about you?"

"I'm good, thanks." I took a seat in one of the consultation chairs in front of his desk and he plopped back down in his soft leather wing-back.

"So what's going on, Cesari?"

"The usual bullshit. I just wanted to give you a heads-up. It was my turn to represent the GI department at the Professional Executive Committee meeting this morning and one of your cases popped up for review."

"Which one?" he asked, unconcerned. Doctors these days were used to having their decisions questioned and second-guessed. Somehow, playing Monday morning quarterback with healthcare had become a national past time in this country, and God forbid if you questioned the benefit of it all. Now that was a good way to get in trouble fast. If you wanted to survive, you'd just go to your committee meetings, sign your reports and keep quiet.

I crossed my legs and relaxed back. "Well, Tony, it seems that one of your patients, a fifty-year-old Albanian immigrant named Jetmir Konstandin, died not too long ago. I haven't had a chance to review the particulars yet but Goldstein gave me the short version. It's pretty serious, so I thought I'd let you know. Do you remember the guy?"

He scratched his head. "Not really. Vaguely, maybe. Goldstein called me about him a couple of days ago but I've been so swamped with work I haven't had a chance to review the record yet. I see hundreds of people every week. You know that. Give me a second and I'll pull his chart up right now. He turned to a nearby laptop and punched in a few keys. "That's Constantine with a C?"

"No, it's Konstandin with a K."

"K?"

"Yeah, I'm guessing that's the Albanian version of Constantine. I'm surprised you don't remember him. He probably had an accent."

"C'mon Cesari, we're in Manhattan. Everybody has an accent."

Good point. I watched him as he played with the keyboard. Tony was thin, of average height and build with thick, black hair and an olive-skinned, southern Italian complexion. I was bigger and stronger but we could have been related. We had discovered that our great grandparents had come from the same small town in Sicily and had immigrated to the U.S. within a year or two of each other back in the 1920s.

He studied the screen carefully and said. "Yeah, here he is. Let's see, I met him for the first time almost a year ago. He underwent a negative screening colonoscopy and was fine. His labs were all normal and I never saw him again. I really can't say that I remember him though. I must see thousands of cases like this every year. So what's the problem? Goldstein was kind of vague when he called."

"Like I said, I haven't had a chance to see his chart yet, but he died a month ago and his wife filed a complaint about his care. Apparently, he had metastatic colon cancer despite his negative colonoscopy."

"Really? Fuck." He let out a deep breath. Missing a cancer was a gastroenterologist's worst nightmare.

"Yeah, so they want me to look into things and file a report. Shit happens, so don't lose sleep over it, all right?"

"So why is the committee reviewing this case? Sounds like a straightforward, either-I-missed-the-cancer-or-I-didn't kind of case. That's what I have malpractice for."

"Well, it's a little more complicated than that. When his condition took a turn for the worse and he needed extended homecare, the insurance company denied their claim on the grounds that his medical condition didn't warrant it based on your records. No one in this day and age can afford things like that out-of-pocket so the wife naturally got upset. She demanded to know why his claim was denied and the insurance company blamed you. After reviewing his chart, she is insisting that his records were either doctored or misrepresented and she is being quite vocal about it, even threatening to go to the press. This is where it gets a little fuzzy and I'll need to roll up my sleeves because I don't quite get what's going on. The bottom line is that the hospital wants to make sure we didn't screw up and forward the wrong records to the insurance company."

"Well, I don't know what to say. Either he had cancer and I missed it or it was a rapidly growing tumor that developed after his negative colonoscopy. The second option is hard for laypeople to understand, but in either case, you don't have to postulate foul play. Besides, it seems like much to-do over nothing. I don't mean to be unsympathetic but we all got to die of something. Why can't people just accept that?"

"That's true, Tony, and I think that most people do understand that, but I also think that people should be allowed to die with dignity and without their families being sent into poverty by exorbitant medical expenses for which they thought they had insurance."

He nodded. "I didn't take you for a bleeding heart, Cesari."

I chuckled. "Trust me, I'll never be accused of that, but I learned right from wrong a long time ago and it's got nothing to do with politics. I understand that Mrs. Konstandin may be in denial and emotionally distraught but it doesn't mean she doesn't deserve to be heard. Besides, if I have to choose between a grieving widow and a greedy, multi-billion dollar insurance company, whose side do you think I'll take?"

"Fine, but what's this mean for me? Is she accusing me of malpractice or worse?"

"I haven't spoken to her yet so I can't be sure where she's coming from, other than she believes there has been a flagrant miscarriage of justice and that you're at the center of it all. However, I'm sure it won't be long before some lawyer or family member encourages her to sue. I mean, you can easily see how this would look to the public. The greedy doctor was doing so many cases so fast that he must have missed the cancer or failed to document the chart properly. No one cares that there is an accepted miss rate even in the best and most methodical of hands. Even harder to comprehend is that there might not have been an obviously discernible primary lesion to find and cure in the first place. No, the bottom line here is that a guy died from a disease he was sent to you to find and you didn't find it so there it is. Let's just keep our fingers crossed on that one. For the moment, however, she seems primarily irritated at the insurance company for failing to provide the financial support she needed for his care which ultimately led to his death."

"The cancer led to his death, Cesari, not the insurance company's lack of financial aid."

I grunted. "Maybe. His medical costs for nursing care, special beds, IV lines, parenteral nutrition, antibiotics, oxygen, etc. were estimated to be just over twenty thousand dollars per month. As the saying goes, the only thing more expensive than living in Manhattan is dying in Manhattan. He was a janitor at a local public school and his wife works as a maid in the midtown Hilton. They simply couldn't afford it. She came home one night after working a ten-hour shift changing sheets for happy tourists to find the love of her life lying in bed with a self-inflicted gunshot wound to the head. He held a Colt .45 in one hand and his wedding photo in the other. You getting the picture Tony?"

He was shocked. "Holy shit. You've got to be kidding!"

"Do I look like I'm kidding? This is bad and I haven't even scratched the surface yet, so you'd better brace yourself."

He slumped back into his chair, suddenly looking very small, and let out a deep breath. "I will."

I stood to leave. "Okay, I know you have work to do so I'd better go now but I'll stay in touch. If there's anything else you can remember give me a call, okay? I'd like you to review the guy's chart a bit more carefully and we'll get together in the next few days so I can formally interview you. Goldstein wants a complete and thorough investigation and as such, expects your full cooperation. By the way, he doesn't believe you or anybody else did anything wrong but one can easily see how this might appear if it looks like we swept it under the rug."

Tony looked apprehensive. "Should I be worried, Cesari?"

"That depends."

"On what?"

"On whether you believe our prisons are filled with innocent people or not."

"Great."

"Just saying."

Chapter 3

I lived in a spacious loft on the corner of Sixth Avenue and Waverly Place in Greenwich Village just a short block away from Washington Square Park. The building was a modest-sized, three-story brick structure built in the 1940s. It now housed a Polish meat market on the ground level and storage space on the second. I had the entire top level to myself. It was much bigger than a single guy needed and I was getting hosed with the rent but I needed the room for my dog, Cleopatra, a five-year-old, 250 lb. English mastiff. The scent of kielbasa perfumed the entire building and had the same effect on Cleopatra that catnip had on a cat. We both liked pierogis as well so from a food point of view we were quite content. As I fumbled for my key, I heard her whine with anticipation on the other side. The door slid open and she leapt up to meet me, almost knocking me down as she licked my face. She had a gigantic head, typical for her breed, which made her appear not only ferocious but twice as large as she really was. But despite her enormous size she was a big baby. She cried all the time and wanted to play constantly—and I loved her.

"Hi, girl. Yeah, I know I'm late." With her standing on her hind legs, we were face to face so I grabbed her and kissed her back. She was too big to ignore or leave alone so I paid a college kid from NYU to walk her and keep her company for an hour or two every day while I worked. I checked her water bowl, saw it was full, and grabbed a bag of dog food, filling the empty dish next to it.

I said, "Sorry, sweetheart, but no kielbasa tonight."

As she ate, I stroked her head and chatted her up in my best baby voice, which she loved. A couple of years ago she had saved my life from a hit man who had made the mistake of misjudging her gentle disposition. He had paid for that miscalculation with his life. To say that I had a somewhat checkered past was an understatement. I had been in and out of the mob in various roles since my childhood in the Bronx when I had fallen in with the wrong crowd. By wrong crowd, I meant my pal Vito Gianelli. Having finally extricated myself, I lived a mostly neutral although somewhat tension-filled existence just a few blocks from Little Italy, where running into old "friends" was always awkward and extremely uncomfortable. I never knew who was going to see me as a potential threat and decide the world would be a better place for them if I suddenly stopped breathing.

I poured myself a bowl of Frosted Mini-Wheats with skim milk and sat in front of the TV to watch the news and enjoy my dinner. Halfway through the doom and gloom, my cell phone rang. It was Cocoa. I really liked her but she had a very powerful uncle, Leo, who forbade me from seeing her. I didn't usually buckle to things like that but he made a very persuasive argument that she would be better off without me. It also helped that he had caught me with a stolen handgun and promised to turn me in to the police if I didn't stay away from her. I got lucky in the sense that he didn't know the stolen handgun belonged to a dead federal agent. I was unlucky because he still had the gun in his possession, hidden away somewhere just waiting for me to make a wrong move. I've been waiting for the other shoe to drop on that one for a while. I toyed with the idea of not answering the call but couldn't help myself. I was drawn to her like a moth to a flame and suspected I would end up the same way—burnt to a crisp.

"Hi, Myrtle."

"Hi John, and please don't call me Myrtle, you know I prefer Cocoa."

"But you're not a stripper anymore." I teased.

"First of all, I was an exotic dancer not a stripper. That's so old-fashioned. Secondly, Cocoa has been my nickname since I was a kid, remember? I liked Cocoa Puffs a lot. I told you all about it and besides, I prefer it to Myrtle and you already know all this, so stop."

I smiled. "Oh yeah, I remember now, but I kind of like Myrtle. It's classic, but if it's Cocoa you want then Cocoa it is. How are you?"

"I'm fine and what about you?"

"I'm trying to keep a low profile. Know what I mean?" Cocoa called me at least once a week despite the fact that I dumped her unceremoniously several months ago after her Uncle Leo had threatened me. I was older than her and used that as the excuse. She didn't buy it for a minute. Sometimes, I answered her calls and sometimes I didn't. It depended on how strong I was feeling. She was very beautiful and had a dynamic personality which was very hard to resist.

"Yeah, I know what you mean. How's Cleo?"

"She's great. We were both just finishing up dinner when you called and I was going to take her for a walk in the park."

"Really?"

"Why do you sound so surprised?"

"Because it's a beautiful night and I was thinking of taking a walk there myself."

I groaned inwardly. "Cocoa, do you think that's a good idea?"

"What, taking a walk? Walking is the best exercise. You should know that, you're a doctor."

"That's not what I meant. We can't get back together. I'm too old for you."

"What are you talking about? Who wants to get back together? I just said I'm taking a walk in a public park, so calm down. Geez. Besides, I'd love to see Cleo again. How about I meet you there in fifteen minutes, all right?"

I hesitated and then said, "See you in fifteen."

The park's proximity to the loft was the other main reason I accepted the unacceptable rent. Trying to maintain a reasonable lifestyle for a large dog in Manhattan wasn't easy or cheap but she was worth it. Besides, our nightly romp in the park was a riot as she wagged her tail, sniffed the air and tried to say hello to everyone we passed. Some were put off by her size and sidestepped us, and others were helplessly drawn to her friendly demeanor. When the park was overly crowded, I put a muzzle on her to calm people down, but not tonight.

I spotted Cocoa sitting on a bench and she stood up to greet us. God, she was gorgeous: five foot four, wavy, shoulder length, reddish-brown hair and big brown eyes. She had a perfect figure and luscious lips. It was late June and she wore a yellow top and short shorts, highlighting her tanned and toned dancer legs.

"Hi, Cleo. How's my girl?" She leaned down to hug Cleo, who licked her face enthusiastically. She didn't have to lean far because Cleo's head was almost up to her chest.

I said, "Hi, Cocoa. Nice flip-flops."

"Thanks." She let go of Cleo's head, and threw both arms around my waist, pressing her face into my chest. "It's been a long time."

She lifted her face up to look at me and I leaned down to kiss her on the forehead which caused her to pout. She wanted a real kiss and pulled my head down until our lips touched softly and I felt a bolt of electricity shoot through me. I looked into her eyes and said, "It hasn't been that long, only a couple of months."

"Well, it seems like forever to me. C'mon, let's sit." She grabbed my free hand and we walked back to the bench she had been sitting on. Cleo lay down in front of us contentedly people-watching. The park was busy with strollers, cyclists, roller bladers, musicians and soap box politicians.

Cocoa said, "Thanks for agreeing to meet me. I didn't think you would."

"You don't have to thank me. We're friends, aren't we?"

"Right, of course," she said wryly.

I didn't respond to her sarcasm so she continued, getting straight to the point. "I miss you, John."

I nodded slowly. "And I miss you, Cocoa."

"Then why …?"

I sighed. "Cocoa, we've been through this already. It just wouldn't work out. It's really better if you find someone your own age."

"Stop it. I didn't understand this silly discussion the first time and I still don't. I'm twenty-five years old and can make up my own mind who I want to date. Besides, you're only ten years older than me. It's not like you're in your sixties."

I sat there quietly, trying to picture what it would be like trying to keep up with her in my sixties. She had almost unlimited sexual energy and it was hard enough as it was.

"John, please tell me what's wrong. Help me to understand. I just can't believe it's because of our age difference. I've been through this a million times a night in my mind and I just don't get it. One minute we're having a great time and the next you won't even have lunch with me. Was it something I did? Is it because I'm Jewish?"

41

I chuckled, grabbed her hand, kissed it, and then looked into her eyes. "Don't be ridiculous. You didn't do anything, and you're perfect just the way you are. I wouldn't change a thing about you. Besides, do I seem like the kind of guy who would let religion get in the way of a little hanky-panky?"

She liked that and smiled. "No, you don't. Then what is it? We got along so well. We really fit together."

"It's not you, Cocoa, it's me."

She rolled her eyes. "Oh please, that is so cliché." I saw tears forming at the corners of her eyes.

I was starting to feel really bad and took a deep breath. "Cocoa, I want to tell you, I really do, but I just can't." Uncle Leo would have me drawn and quartered if I did. Maybe meeting with her like this wasn't such a great idea. "I think I should go, Cocoa."

She gripped my hand tightly and looked me in the eye. "Please don't. That would really be cruel."

I sighed and nodded, and we sat there in silence for a few moments looking straight ahead. Finally, she said, "Was it Uncle Leo?"

She caught me completely off guard and I hesitated before responding. "Why would you say that?"

"I don't know exactly, but he seems awfully interested in you. He calls me at least once a week and always asks if I've heard from you. Plus, he thinks he's being clever the way he casually works it into our conversations. At first, this seemed normal, but it's been three months and now it just seems odd. And as I think about it, he was the only one in my family who wasn't upset for me when I told them you dumped me. In fact, he seemed rather smug, and ever since, young lawyers from his firm have been calling out of the blue to ask me out. It seems a bit contrived if you know what I mean."

I didn't say anything but my facial expression must have given me away.

She picked up on it and said, "It was him, wasn't it? What did he say to you about me or us? He's like that, very opinionated and very controlling. I know he is. I've heard him say some very unkind things about Italians too. Was it that? If it was, I will kill him. You might as well tell me because now I'm going to ask him."

"Whoa, whoa, whoa, cowgirl. Take it easy." I grew noticeably concerned. "Cocoa, please don't say anything to him. It will only make things worse."

"Worse? For who? What did he say to you, John? He has no right to interfere in my life like this." She was getting upset and rightly so. I knew I shouldn't have agreed to meet her.

I let out a deep breath, very conflicted about what to say. "You have to promise me that you won't confront him if I tell you."

She was indignant. "I'm not going to promise that."

"Then I can't tell you."

She pouted and squinted her eyes. Thinking it over she reluctantly said, "Okay, I promise."

"He found out about the gun."

"What gun?"

"I brought a gun to your house, remember, when your parents were in Europe a few months back. It was in a duffel bag which I slid under your parents' bed. A lot happened and I forgot it there. Your uncle found it and through his contacts in law enforcement was able to identify my fingerprints on the weapon and that it was stolen."

"Oh God, the Sig Sauer .357, I remember it. And then what? Continue."

"Please don't make me say it."

"I need to hear it."

"He ordered me to break up with you or he would turn the gun over to the authorities."

"He blackmailed you into dumping me?" I saw anger cloud her features.

"He felt I was a bad influence and—maybe he was right."

I watched her carefully as her face darkened and she began to scowl. "I am going to kill him."

"Cocoa, please. You can't say anything to him. He still has the gun, and I really did steal it. I know it was all in self-defense but that would be difficult to prove. He's a big shot attorney and has powerful friends in law enforcement. I wouldn't stand a chance."

"I'm going to kill him but first—I'm going to kill you."

"What?" I was taken aback by that. "Me? I didn't do anything. I'm the victim."

She punched me in the arm. "I've been crying myself to sleep every night for months just because you're afraid of going to jail?"

I didn't know how to respond to that. "Jail isn't anything to sneeze at, Cocoa. I've been there, and your uncle assured me that I was looking at a minimum of five years—easy. And he didn't even know that the guy I took the gun from was dead."

She punched me again and again and then started crying. "How could you not tell me the truth? I've been so brokenhearted."

I bowed my head. "I'm sorry. I didn't know what to do."

"You're a coward."

"I'm not a coward. I just didn't see any way of fighting back. He had all the cards."

She sat there quietly, as she collected herself, digesting it all. Then she suddenly stood up. "C'mon."

I stood up with her, and Cleo came to attention as well. "What?"

"We're going back to your apartment."

"We are?"

"Yes, I have a lot to get out of my system so I hope you're not tired. Let's go. I'll figure out what to do about Uncle Leo later."

Somehow, this didn't feel right or very smart. I let out a deep breath. "I don't know about this, Cocoa."

"You live in that loft on Sixth Avenue above the Polish meat market, right?"

I nodded. "How did you know that?" I had moved there after the Uncle Leo incident and hadn't told her. For that matter, it just dawned on me that I hadn't told her which park I would meet her in so how did she know?

She said, "What difference does it make?"

I stared at her, wondering if she'd been stalking me. It wouldn't have been that difficult to do, just wait for me to come out of work. I wasn't that paranoid that I routinely checked for people following me. Besides, I had no right to complain, I'd been stalking my other ex-girlfriend, Kelly, for months too. The world was filled with people stalking each other.

"Are we dating again?" I asked.

She laughed and slipped her arm through mine.

"I didn't know we stopped."

Chapter 4

At 2:00 a.m. the cell phone on my night table rang loudly and I fumbled to answer it, trying not to wake Cocoa. I was exhausted. She and I had gone at it vigorously for two solid hours before I pleaded for mercy—and sleep. I had dozed off about an hour ago thinking that if I were sixty years old, I'd probably be in the emergency room right now with chest pain. In my haste to find the noisy, vibrating phone in the dark, I knocked the small lamp off the night table and it tumbled to the floor with a crash.

Cocoa said, "What happened?"

I whispered back. "Sorry, it's nothing. Go back to sleep."

As she rolled away onto her side, I resettled the lamp and answered the phone. "Tony, what's going on? It's two in the morning." I stood up and walked into the living room.

"I need to talk to you, Cesari." He sounded upset and his voice quivered.

"I assumed that's why you called, Tony. Now what is it? I have to work in the morning."

"It's about that guy, Konstandin. The patient you asked me about today."

"Are you serious? At two a.m., you suddenly remembered something about him? Why can't this wait?" I replied in a hushed, annoyed voice.

"Just come over to my place, will you? I want to show you something in person. It's too hard to explain on the phone."

"Are you insane? For Christ's sake, Tony, I have a house guest. What am I supposed to do? Just leave her?"

"I'm sorry, Cesari, but it's important and I'm worried about what it means."

"You have got to be kidding me!"

"I'm not kidding. Please come over. You remember where I live?"

I was pissed. "Yeah, on Jane Street by Greenwich Avenue, apartment 4A. This had better be good, Tony. I mean it."

"Thanks, I'll put on coffee."

He hung up and I splashed water on my face to wake up and then threw on a pair of jeans and a cotton shirt. Cocoa was sound asleep again and I gently shook her, whispering. "Hey, I have to go out. I'm sorry."

She looked at me sleepily. "Out? Where and why?"

"A guy from work just called. He's got some sort of problem he needs my help with. He lives nearby in the West Village. It shouldn't take that long. I'm sorry for waking you again, but I didn't want you to be alarmed if you woke up and didn't find me here."

"What kind of problem could he have that couldn't wait till morning?" she asked, half-asleep but now curious.

"I don't know but he sounded like he was pretty stressed out, so I'm going over to check it out. He's a good guy so it must be serious. I'm sorry, okay?"

She rolled away from me. "Be careful and hurry up back. I like morning sex too."

I left her, went down to the street, and caught a passing yellow cab over to Tony's apartment on Jane Street where he buzzed me in. He lived in a modest single bedroom unit with a kitchen and nice-sized living room. I had been there several times socially. He wore blue jeans and a T-shirt. He looked a bit disheveled and his hair was a mess as if he had run his hands through it many times. I smelled alcohol on his breath and saw a half bottle of Jack close by.

I said sternly, "All right, so what's the crisis?"

"Thanks for coming, Cesari. Have a seat and I'll show you." We sat on his sofa with a laptop propped open on the coffee table in front of us. There were piles of papers and charts strewn about next to it. I glanced at the screen and saw that he was logged onto his medical records.

"What were you doing? Catching up on your records at this hour?"

"Yes, always. It never ends. You should know that. There's not enough time in the day to do all the paperwork we're expected to so I usually bring home my charts every night to finish up. The more electronics they put in place to make things easier, the worse everything becomes."

I nodded in full agreement. Government intrusion into healthcare had turned highly trained physicians into data entry specialists who now spent as much time punching laptop keys as they did talking to patients. Why? A good question to which there was no easy answer. Part of it was data collection to study health trends, part was documentation of services provided for billing purposes, but a large part of it was the firm belief on the part of the government pinheads that all progress is good progress. A lot of techies believe that we should do things simply because we can, like upgrading from Windows 7 to 8 and then to 10. Look how great that was.

Tony continued. "Well, I was doing my medical records and started thinking about that guy, Konstandin, so I thought I'd review his chart in greater detail like we talked about. By the way, would you like a cup of coffee? I just made a fresh pot."

I glanced at the bottle of Jack on the table, took a whiff of his breath again and said, "Sure, but only if you have one with me."

"Sure." He got up and walked into the kitchen. "Sugar or cream?"

I said, "Black and sweet."

He returned with two mugs and handed me one. I took a sip and immediately felt a caffeine jolt. "Nice coffee. French roast?"

"Of course. Well, anyway. I pulled up the guy's record. This morning when we spoke I honestly couldn't remember him from a hole in the wall. You know how it is when you only see some guy once or twice. We're all moving so fast these days and doing so much."

He was right and I offered no argument. "So what did you find out?"

He turned the laptop toward me to see better. "That's the record I saw when you came to the office. The one that shows he had a negative screening colonoscopy and was asymptomatic."

I looked at the colonoscopy report with him. Since the exam was negative and the patient was asymptomatic there were no follow-up office visits. "Okay, looks pretty standard."

"Yeah, except for this." Using the mouse, he clicked and scrolled until we came to the page with the patient's billing information. There in bold letters and numbers was the code Tony personally submitted following the patient's colonoscopy.

I watched with him. "So, what am I looking for?"

"Are you blind, Cesari? The billing code I submitted for his colonoscopy. I submitted it as a colon cancer not as a screening colonoscopy."

I must have looked confused so he continued. "Don't you get it? After his procedure, I had to submit the diagnostic code in order to get paid and I said he had colon cancer. That means

I knew he had colon cancer when I saw him and so I billed it like that but my report says he was fine. I must have fucked up the report. If that report went to the insurance company, then of course they would have denied his treatment."

Puzzled, I said, "I guess I don't understand. So you knew he had cancer, screwed up the report and he was denied further care on the basis of that report? That doesn't make sense. Wouldn't he have called you back and told you there was a problem with his insurance?"

"You're asking me what an Albanian immigrant would do once he got caught up in our massively screwed up and complicated healthcare system? You've got to be kidding. I can't even get my own heartburn medications without being denied two and three times."

I nodded. That was a good point. A lot of people didn't understand their healthcare rights and frequently didn't exercise them. He might have simply taken a classic fatalistic approach and assumed there was nothing any one could do to help him, but we were jumping to all sorts of negative conclusions now. Tony was tired, probably a little drunk and extremely pessimistic.

"Okay, Tony, so he had colon cancer and you screwed up the report."

"Even worse, Cesari. We're assuming I did the report wrong but told him the correct diagnosis. I can't be sure of that either. It's possible I told him that he was perfectly fine." He hung his head dejectedly and I saw a tear form in one eye. "And now he's dead because of me. The poor schlep didn't have a chance one way or the other."

I thought about that. Many—maybe up to half—of patients with colon cancer at the time of diagnosis were asymptomatic, so if Tony told him he was okay, he would have accepted that until the cancer had spread and it was too late, but what were the odds of that? I let out a deep breath. "Geez, Tony, let's go over this. Tell me again. How do you think this might have happened?"

He sipped his coffee and said, "I've been thinking about it and to be honest, it wouldn't be that hard. We have about five to ten minutes after each colonoscopy to do our reports before moving on to the next case, right? In that five to ten minutes we have to do the report, go speak to the patient and their families, answer any phone calls and deal with any nursing issues there might be. If I was distracted I might have momentarily gotten confused about whose report I was doing. I know it's a lame excuse but it's the only one I have. This is even worse than malpractice. For God's sake, the guy killed himself. When this comes out, I won't be able to get a job as a dog catcher in this town."

He was starting to shake and tremble. I said, "Okay, Tony, stay calm. It's a little hard for me to believe that even if you did the report wrong you wouldn't have at least verbally said something to him and his wife after the procedure. You know like, *please make an appointment to see me in a week to discuss the biopsies.*"

"Who knows? Maybe I did and maybe I didn't. If I was in a rush and had the wrong report in my hands all bets are off. Like I said, I can't be sure. I can only tell you what I documented." Tony held his face in his hands in defeat. "According to the nursing records, when we were done he was totally zonked from the sedation and probably wouldn't have remembered anything anyway. Besides, he didn't speak any English and the hospital didn't have an Albanian interpreter. He came for his exam with a friend who just barely spoke English himself. Normally, I would have followed up with a personal phone call to a patient with cancer but it happened the day before I was heading out of the country on vacation and I probably had a lot on my mind. By the time I got back I just forgot. To be honest, even now, I don't truly recall him or his exam. I couldn't swear one way or the other what I really found or said that day."

I looked at him sympathetically. "Okay, I know this looks bad for you, Tony, but maybe there's another explanation."

"Sure there is. I'm a fucking criminal. That's the other explanation."

"You're not a criminal. At the worst, you made an honest mistake. That's all."

"Right, like anyone will believe that. Funny thing though. Like you just said, if I found a cancer, you would think that there would be some pathology reports from biopsies but there aren't."

I thought about that. "That is interesting. Unless you couldn't reach the tumor for some reason and didn't take any biopsies. That wouldn't be that unusual. Is there any chance that the note is correct but the billing code wrong?"

"God, I wish that was the case but the guy really did have colon cancer so that scenario doesn't make sense."

He was right. "I don't want to add to your list of things to worry about but is it possible that you simply got his name mixed up with another patient? Because if you did, then there might be some other report saying that somebody who is perfectly fine is dying of cancer. God only knows how that might impact that person's life."

Tony groaned. "I hadn't thought of that. This report is from almost a year ago. Oh, God. I hope nobody overreacted. I'll have to back track to the date I saw this guy and review all the other notes from that day to see who I might have diagnosed with cancer. Hopefully, nothing happened and I can just amend that report if I find it."

"Do you do all your notes immediately after seeing a patient or do you let them carry over?"

He sighed. "Depends on how tired or busy I am. I've been known to let them slip for a day or two or three."

"You better check your op-notes for at least a three-day period just in case his chart got mixed up with one on the following days. Look, Tony, the more information you can provide me on what happened the better off you'll be. A lot of people are going to want to understand something that is very difficult for anyone outside of healthcare to grasp. The other thing you should do is call the insurance company and ask to review the records that were submitted to make sure they match up with what you have."

"That makes sense. I'll do that first thing this morning. Are you going to call the insurance company as well on behalf of the hospital?"

"No, I don't have any legal grounds to review their records because this is an internal audit but you do since it was your chart they used to deny the claim. I'll review whatever they give you. I'm also going to speak to Mrs. Konstandin about what happened."

"Are you going to tell her about this?"

"I'm not going to lie to her, Tony. She's been through enough but I'll see if I can dance my way through without pointing fingers."

He nodded dejectedly. "I'm so fucked. I can't believe it."

"What about a surgeon or oncologist? Do any of your notes suggest you referred him on to another specialist such as a surgeon or oncologist?"

"That's a good point, Cesari, but there's no record of any referrals. This doesn't make any sense."

"Look, it's late and you're exhausted. We'll work on this some more tomorrow. Why don't you try to get some sleep, okay? No more booze tonight. You're depressed enough and if you come in to work exhausted or hungover you're just going to increase the possibility of another mistake. It happens all the time to physicians. They get preoccupied with a case that went bad and then make even worse decisions because they're not concentrating."

"Yeah, I know you're right. Well, thanks for coming over and I'm sorry for freaking out."

"Hey, I don't blame you. Try to relax, all right. I'll let myself out."

He looked at his watch. It was 3:30 a.m. "You can stay here if you want. The sofa's pretty comfortable."

"Tempting, but I don't live that far away and like I said on the phone earlier I have a house guest but thanks anyway." I looked at him as I turned to leave. He didn't look like he was going to be all right but I was tired and he was a big boy. For better or for worse, he was going to have to deal with this like a grown up.

Chapter 5

The next morning, I woke up late and found Cocoa in the kitchen having coffee. She said, "I hope you don't mind me making myself at home."

I smiled, gave her a kiss and poured myself a cup. "I would have been disappointed if you hadn't." She wore one of my cotton dress shirts she had found in my closet and had only fastened one of the middle buttons. Yum.

"So how'd it go with your friend last night?"

"My friend will be fine, thanks. I'll fill you in later. I'm running behind. I'm sorry I can't stick around and reminisce about how great it was to hold you in my arms last night, but I have to walk Cleo and then get to work. You're welcome to stay as long as you like. Have classes started at Juilliard by the way? We didn't talk about it."

"Relax, and have your coffee. I can walk Cleo for you. That will help you save time. I was going to wake you but you looked so comfortable and no, school hasn't started yet. It begins late August. Right now all I do is study theory and practice every day on the grand piano they have available for enrolled students."

I furrowed my brow. "Juilliard's in midtown, in Lincoln Center, isn't it? That's quite a hike every day."

"Yeah, it is but I don't mind. I practice in my head during the train ride."

I nodded. That sounded like a neat trick. I didn't play an instrument and was kind of intimidated by people who were musically inclined. "Do you think you can handle Cleo? That would be a great help. It would save me at least twenty minutes or so."

She made a face. "Yeah, I can handle her, but I'll need a key to your apartment to lock up."

I hesitated. That was smooth. She's back in my life one night and we're already doing the key thing. On the other hand, I never wanted her out of my life. She smiled as she read the ever-so-subtle hesitation in my face but I reached into one of the kitchen drawers and handed her a spare key, then sat down to finish my coffee. I said, "Don't lose it."

"Don't worry."

Cleo had come over and placed her head in my lap. I hugged her and wrestled with her head. "Ready to eat, dog?" She gave a little jump and a woof as I filled her bowls with fresh water and food.

"By the way, Cocoa, I have a college kid come by once a day to walk her for me. Her times are variable but she usually swings by late morning or early afternoon just so you should know."

"What's her name?"

"Bridget, why?"

"I'll stick around and let her know that you won't need her services any more, assuming that's all you've been paying her for."

I let the accusation slide and she continued. "I've got tons of free time until school starts and can practice at my own pace. This place is huge. I could even rent a piano and practice here. Then Cleo won't have to be alone at all. In fact, I think I'll do that."

56

Wow, she was good. I said, "I'm sure Uncle Leo won't mind at all."

"He's not going to find out, and I'm going to take care of him anyway so don't you worry. I just need to figure out how."

I was extremely concerned and asked sarcastically, "Why would I worry?"

"Because you're a coward and you're afraid of him."

"Was that nice? Maybe we should just leave the Uncle Leo thing where it is. You know, let sleeping dogs lie."

"Not a chance. I'm furious at him."

Great.

I sighed. "Well, thanks for taking care of Cleo. I'd better get going. I already paid Bridget for the week so I think we're all squared away there."

"All right, I'll see you tonight then."

"Sure thing. I'll call later." I leaned over to give her a quick kiss and as she put her arms around my neck the shirt she wore splayed open revealing her large, firm breasts. I held my breath at the sight. Man, I could get used to this in a hurry. The thought crossed my mind to take her back into the bedroom. She smiled as she caught me admiring her. I willed myself to calm down and headed out to work, finding myself in the lobby of Saint Matt's in less than fifteen minutes. Five minutes after that I entered the GI department.

"Hi Julie, I'm sorry I'm late. How far behind am I?"

"Good morning, Dr. Cesari. You're lucky. Your first patient cancelled and your second showed up late so you're doing just fine. They just put her into the exam room a few minutes ago. There's fresh coffee and bagels in the break room if you're interested. One of the pharmaceutical reps brought them in."

"Thanks, I'll check it out as soon as I get myself organized."

I went into my office, turned on my laptop, donned the white lab coat I kept on a hook behind my office door, made sure I had my stethoscope and rushed to the exam room to see my first patient.

Pausing in front of the exam room door to collect myself, I knocked politely and let myself in. "Good morning, Mrs. Darnell. How are you today?"

She was a seventy-five-year-old woman, short and thin with gray hair, but in fairly good health for her age. There were some issues with osteoarthritis and acid reflux but she was generally okay. Looking through her record, I saw that her last office visit was over a year ago and her last colonoscopy was five years ago. She was found to have polyps and diverticulosis.

"Not good, Doctor. I've been sick to my stomach for weeks. My primary care physician, Dr. Kamil, says I need another colonoscopy and I think so too."

"Hmm, that may well be the case, but why don't we talk about it a little? Can you be more specific about what you've been feeling? Are you having any pain?"

"Of course. I hurt every day, everywhere and I'm always tired."

"Hmm, I meant do you have any abdominal pain?" I had closed the laptop and jotted down a few notes on a legal pad while we spoke. I was a little old-fashioned and felt it was rude to stare at a computer screen while talking to someone. Maintaining eye contact with the patient was a better way to build trust and gain confidence.

"Yes, that's why I'm here. For the last few weeks, my stomach cramps up and then I have wicked diarrhea."

"How many times a day does that happen?"

"Three, sometimes four."

"Any fever, vomiting or rectal bleeding?"

"I'm very nauseated and have no appetite but no vomiting or fever."

"Have you been travelling or taken any antibiotics in the last several months?"

"I haven't been travelling but about a month ago my dentist put me on Augmentin for an infection. I'm much better from that. Why?"

"Well, it's very common for people to develop secondary infections as a result of being placed on broad spectrum antibiotics such as Augmentin. The antibiotic negatively affects the bacterial counts in the colon. This results in an imbalance between some bacteria which are good and some that are bad. The net result is that one of the bad bacteria known as Clostridium difficile, or C. diff, can become a problem and cause symptoms such as you have. This is quite common nowadays and I think that's what may be going on."

"It's common, you say?"

"Yes, very."

"Then why didn't my doctor tell me about it?"

"You'll have to ask him."

She looked at me sideways. "Are you trying to protect him?"

"From what?"

"Never mind. So, what's next?"

"We'll send off stool samples to test for the infection and I'm going to place you on another antibiotic today to begin treatment, but right now I'd like to examine you, if you don't mind?"

"A colonoscopy now?"

"No, no. I just want to listen to your heart and lungs and press on your abdomen. Routine and mostly to make sure there's nothing more serious going on that might require more urgent intervention."

"Oh, sure."

I helped her onto the exam table and she thanked me.

"Am I still going to need a colonoscopy, Doctor?" she asked.

"That is a very good question. Some people would say that anyone your age with a change in bowel habits regardless of whether there is an infection or not should have one just to make sure there is no cancer. The government and insurance companies would love for me to tell you that at your age you don't need one, because they're the ones paying for it and they claim that the odds of me finding anything serious are quite low, thus making the procedure an inefficient use of limited resources, but it's not that straightforward."

"It's not?"

"No, it's not, because you're a human being, not a statistic, and I'm a physician, not a government bureaucrat. My job is to take care of you, not to save the government money. If they don't want to pay for your colonoscopy they should tell you so themselves and then pass laws shielding the physician from claims of malpractice. Instead what they do is intimidate physicians into not ordering tests with threats of financial penalties or by placing so much red tape in our way we become exhausted and give up. Then they wash their hands of it and leave us out to hang legally if something goes wrong."

She looked at me sympathetically. "Are you going to be okay, Doctor?"

I chuckled. "Yes, thank you. It's very frustrating that people are trying to manipulate my decision making and they think I'm too stupid to understand what they're doing. My obligation is to take care of you to the best of my ability and if the government doesn't like it they can put handcuffs on me." I placed my stethoscope on her back. "Now take a deep breath and let it out."

"I think you should do the same, Doctor."

So I did. "Yes, just like that and again."

"How's it sound in there, Doctor?"

"You're going to live."

She laughed. "I think I'm in pretty good hands."

I nodded and smiled. "You better believe it."

"Well, I'm glad you're on my side. So, am I going to get a colonoscopy or not?"

"Of course you are. I have bills to pay."

We both chuckled and after I finished my exam I brought her to Julie to schedule her colonoscopy and other tests. I returned to my office and as I dictated her note, I started thinking about Tony, and how he might have screwed up his medical records. As he said, if you were really busy and distracted, it wouldn't be that hard especially if you waited until then end of the day when you were tired and had piles of charts in front of you.

I looked at my laptop screen. There were thirty names in a row from top to bottom on my schedule today. If I clicked on the wrong name and didn't notice it, I could potentially complete the entire record without realizing it and then save it and move on to the next. By tomorrow, it would be ancient history. Most mistakes like that wouldn't have had such dramatic consequences but his patient had cancer. Poor Tony. He was right. He was definitely fucked.

It was the perfect storm. Normally, he would have told the patient right then and there, after the colonoscopy, that he had cancer or some euphemistic equivalent. You never like to use the word cancer right after an examination. Many people would simply freak out. You have to break it to them gently. *Well, we found a tumor in there, Mr. Smith. Not sure what it is. We'll need to see what the biopsies show. Try not to worry too much. You're going to be fine.* That would have been closer to the real conversation, but the language barrier with Mr. Konstandin may have prevented any meaningful transfer of information, in addition to the fact that the guy was very groggy from sedation.

61

The morning wore on like that until about 11:30 when I took a breather waiting for the last appointment before lunch. I was thinking about calling Cocoa and smiled inwardly. I really did like her. She had a very bold and assertive personality which took some getting used to but was quite endearing once you did. It made me happy just thinking about her but she was a loose cannon for sure. I hoped she didn't do anything rash with her uncle. She didn't know him the way I did. He wouldn't hesitate to give her lip service about how sorry he was and then I would just disappear into the criminal justice system or worse. On the surface he was a respected Philadelphia trial attorney but deep down I knew he was connected. If he couldn't get me one way, he'd do it another.

As I reached for my cell phone, I heard Julie scream through my closed door. I leaped up and ran into the reception area. She was by herself staring at the overhead TV in the empty patient waiting area.

"Julie, what happened?" On the screen was the local news showing some guy in a white lab coat on the ledge of a building. He was holding onto an angled flagpole for support. He looked tiny as the oversized flag swept back and forth in front of him.

She stammered, "Look, look—oh, my God ..."

I studied the screen carefully. The guy's face was too far away to make out but the caption on the bottom read that we were looking at the front of Saint Matt's.

Shit.

"That's the flagpole on the tenth floor outside Goldstein's office. Do we know who it is?"

Julie was crying now and on the verge of hysteria. She nodded but didn't say anything so I repeated myself. "Julie, who is it?"

As I stared at the screen, the camera gradually zoomed in and focused on the guy's face and I held my breath. It was Tony.

Jesus!

I ran into the hallway and spotted a throng of people at the elevators. The noise level was high as everyone chatted excitedly trying to figure out what was happening. The crisis was in full swing. I found the stairwell and bounded upward two and three steps at a time. I had started on the third floor and by the time I reached the tenth I was thoroughly winded and paused to catch my breath, but not for long. My adrenaline was surging and I was pumped up. I rushed into the hallway and saw another crowd of people. I noted that law enforcement and medical personnel hadn't yet arrived. I fought my way through the mass to the office door everyone was standing in front of. It was Goldstein's office. I asked no one in particular, "What's going on inside? Why is everyone out here?"

"The door's locked and no one's seen Dr. Goldstein."

"Step aside," I commanded, and they parted like the Red Sea.

I took a two-step head start, then launched a massive kick at the door just below the handle and watched it splinter and cave inward. The office was empty. The window behind Arnie's desk was wide open and a gentle summer breeze swept into the room. I ran to the window and stuck my head out scanning around. Tony was ten feet to my right, perched on an eight-inch cement ledge, clutching the flagpole.

"Tony, what are you doing?"

He looked at me. He had been crying and looked disheveled. His hair was unkempt and he hadn't shaved. He obviously hadn't taken my advice to get some rest. "I fucked up, Cesari. I didn't even refer that guy to surgery. I did absolutely nothing for him. Even worse, I told a guy with cancer that he was fine. I killed him."

"Tony, you didn't kill anyone. You made a mistake. It's the business we're in, man. You're a good doctor. Everybody sooner or later screws up. It's the nature of what we do. Nobody's perfect. You're overtired and taking this too personally." I looked down and saw several ambulances, fire engines and police vehicles pulling up next to the news vans. The crowd had swelled and was blocking traffic in all directions.

"After you left last night, I called her up. I know I shouldn't have but I did."

"Called who, Tony?" Keep him talking.

"Mrs. Konstandin, his wife. I apologized to her for my mistake. I told her everything. I wrote it all down and left it on Goldstein's desk so the hospital's off the hook."

"Okay, Tony, I get it. You feel bad but you don't need to overreact like this. Why don't you come in and we'll talk it over. You're not going to make anyone feel better by doing this and you're certainly not going to bring him back."

"I don't know about that, Cesari. I think it will make Mrs. Konstandin feel a whole lot better. She told me that she hoped they would take my license away and throw me in prison. Did you know that he had two grandchildren and one on the way?"

"Tony, she was upset. You can understand that. Her husband died. You need to take a couple of weeks off to collect yourself. Things won't seem as bad after a good night's rest. You know what? I'll take some time off with you. We can go to Bermuda or something? You know, sit on the beach, have a couple of drinks, meet some chicks. A couple of studs like us won't be lonely for long. Does that sound good to you? It sounds good to me."

He wasn't listening and started unwrapping the rope that tethered the flag to his end of the pole. I looked down and saw the EMS people deploying a huge air mattress with a bullseye in the center. "Tony, what are you doing?"

"I'm sorry, John. I'd love to go on vacation with you but I don't think that a couple of piña coladas are going to help me."

I gingerly climbed out onto the ledge with him just as EMS and police entered the office behind me. I leaned back against the building and held my breath as I balanced myself on the narrow ledge, trying not to look down. A little-known Cesari secret was that I was afraid of heights.

"Go back Cesari or we're both going to die."

"No one's going to die, Tony." I peeked downward, not sure whether I really believed that. "This is unnecessary and you need to understand that." As I spoke, I clutched the wall with my hands behind my back and inched toward him.

A cop stuck his head out the window. "Hey, guys. How's it going out here?"

I liked his casual, I've-known-you-forever tone. "Hello, officer. My friend and I were just talking about coming back in. Weren't we, Tony?"

Glancing over at Tony, I saw that he had freed the rope from its cleat and was tying it into a slipknot. Fuck, he wasn't taking any chance of landing on the air mattress.

The cop called out to Tony. "Hey there, Buddy. Whatever's bothering you, I'm sure we can talk it out without having to scare all those people down there. What's your name?"

Tony didn't answer as he placed the newly-made noose around his neck. I looked at the pole and wondered if it would support his weight. I said, "Tony don't, please."

"Don't move another inch, Cesari. This is the only justice possible for what I've done. An eye for an eye. Isn't that what the Bible says?"

Oh, God. The first thing they teach you in crisis intervention is that when they start quoting scripture at you, you're pretty close to the end. I was still five feet away. "It also says that if you ask for forgiveness it shall be granted."

"I don't deserve to be forgiven." He looked at me. He was crying. "Tell my mom that I love her."

"Tony, no ..."

He jumped off the edge and plummeted, dragging the large flag with him. The rope was still attached to the far end of the pole, so when he reached its limit, it tautened and jerked him back upward, bending the pole as he swung to and fro, his legs kicking in the breeze. I had never witnessed a scene like this before. A man dangling by the neck attached to an American flag attached to a metal flagpole. I didn't have much time to think it over and acted impulsively. As he swung, his momentum brought him within a few feet below me. Without thinking, I leapt off the ledge after him like a sky diver, hitting him like a truck going through a stop sign. I wrapped my arms and legs around him tightly. The extra weight and force of the impact were too much for the pole, which snapped. We were sent hurtling toward the earth where we just barely landed on the edge of the air mattress and tumbled onto the cement sidewalk. The crowd roared its approval at the drama.

We were immediately surrounded by emergency medical personnel and other city employees. Tony was barely conscious and gasped for air but had a strong pulse. He was still alive and that was all that mattered. The medics placed his neck in a cervical collar and he was hustled to the emergency department.

Protecting Tony during the fall I struck the back of my head on the cement sidewalk sustaining a lump the size of a golf ball. I was fuzzy and momentarily disoriented but without serious injury. The EMS people looked me over and suggested I go to the emergency room for further evaluation but I declined. After a few minutes my head cleared and I felt fine. The police debriefed me and let me go back to my life. The reporters were a different matter. They hounded me all the way to the elevators in the main lobby of the hospital. I couldn't blame them. I mean, how often do you get to see two guys in white lab coats jump off a building together?

*****

In a boardroom on the eighty-seventh floor of the Freedom Tower in lower Manhattan, two well-dressed men sat in a plush office, riveted by the drama as they watched Cesari jump off the tenth floor of Saint Matt's live on TV.

The older man, approaching seventy-five, with perfectly coiffed silver hair, puffed on a cigar and sipped Bulleit whiskey from a Waterford crystal glass. He reflected on the fact that the only good thing that ever came out of Ireland was its crystal and the only contribution to world culture of note from the colonies was bourbon, unless one counted America's recklessly promiscuous women. Rutherford Cecil McCormick was a self-made man descended from the landed aristocracy of old England. His people had squandered their wealth and good name on wine, women and assorted other depravities but they had never lost their pride. Beginning with his grandfather, they had slowly climbed their way back up the food chain and were now poised to let the world know they were ready to resume their rightful place in the halls of the high and mighty. He liked to refer to his current project as the British Invasion Part II. He would succeed where Cornwallis, Howe and Burgoyne had failed.

He turned toward the younger man, his son, and in a voice dripping with sarcasm asked, "Duncan, would you care to explain to me what I'm watching?"

Thirty-five years old and strikingly handsome, Duncan Ronald McCormick was being groomed for greatness. He replied, "It would appear that one of the physicians at Saint Matt's went over the deep end and caused another to go over with him. A double suicide is not unheard of in the annals of the mentally ill, and this is Manhattan, after all. Alternatively, maybe they both just realized they were Italian."

His father looked at him sternly. "Your famous sense of humor may have served you to good purpose in the fencing club at Oxford, Duncan, but I assure you this is no laughing matter. Saint Matt's is a test hospital for our new system and I'd rather not have all this extra attention while we work out the kinks. So, once again, who are these two?"

The younger man sighed deeply. "Sorry, Father. Of course, you're right. The one who jumped first is one of five physicians at Saint Matt's we've been testing our latest protocol on. I don't know anything about the other one other than what the news announcer just said—some bloke named Cesari. This island appears to be crawling with Italian immigrants. It makes one wonder what all that fuss is about at the Mexican border."

"Does today's drama have anything at all to do with that Konstandin case?"

The younger man furrowed his brow in thought. "Unlikely, but Konstandin's wife as you know has been stirring up quite a commotion with the claims department at Unicare. I've personally made her several offers to try to settle her down but apparently she's one of those types who believe in justice and has filed a complaint against the doctor at the hospital. That's the one who just tried to hang himself. She is also contemplating a lawsuit against us. It would seem a bit of an overreaction for the chap to jump off a building at this juncture but these Yanks can be so awfully melodramatic. I really don't know him that well or what kind of coping skills he has but from what I just saw, my guess is he doesn't cope well at all with stress."

The older man chewed on his cigar a bit and asked, "What about our exposure?"

"None, we set everything up perfectly. There is no way of tracing any of this back to us. The program doesn't leave even the tiniest digital footprint. The only real drawback at the moment is that I have to be in relatively close proximity to the target for it to be effective, but I'm close to solving that problem."

Rutherford Cecil McCormick sat back in his chair somewhat more relaxed at the news. "Duncan, do you have any idea how much money this will make us if it works?"

"We already have millions so is it safe to say billions, Father?"

"More like trillions, Duncan."

"Blimey, Father. You don't say?"

"I do say, so you better not screw this up, lad. I want your assurance that you have this situation under control. You do whatever it is you have to do to keep this Konstandin woman quiet. What is it the Americans like to say? Oh yes, make her an offer she can't refuse. Bad publicity right now would make our investors extremely skittish, understood? And while you're at it, find out what the bloody hell is going on at Saint Matt's that is making doctors there jump out windows."

Chapter 6

O n the third floor, Julie and a mob of doctors, nurses and other hospital staff cheered my arrival. Most of the women were crying. I waded my way through, shaking hands and acknowledging their gratitude. Julie threw her arms around me, so overcome with emotion she could barely speak.

I said, "I think we should cancel the afternoon. What do you think?"

"It's already been taken care of. Most of the patients have been calling in anyway on the assumption that they were going to be rescheduled. You're the talk of the town. Is Tony going to be okay?"

"Not clear yet. I'm going to go check on him in a little bit."

"What about you? We all saw you hit your head on the sidewalk on TV. It looked awful. I couldn't believe it when I saw you stand up after that."

I instinctively rubbed the lump on the back of my head. "I'll be all right. Probably will get a massive headache before the day is over. Right now, I just need to calm my nerves and get my cell phone. I left it in my office."

"Speaking of phones, they've been ringing nonstop for the last hour and not just your patients. The girls at the hospital's switchboard say that everybody in the city wants to know who you are including the network and cable news stations."

I thought about that. "You know what, Julie? You might as well cancel tomorrow as well. It's going to be a media circus for the next few days anyway and I think I should just lay low until things settle down. Everybody's going to be wild, even the patients, and I just don't see how I'll get anything done."

She nodded. "You mean especially your patients. They already think you're a hero."

I laughed. "Thanks. By the way, does anyone know where Dr. Goldstein is?"

"He called. He saw it all on TV. He was at a conference in the midtown Hilton and is on his way back right now. He told me to tell you to stay put and do not, I repeat, do not talk to anyone in the press."

I chuckled at that. "A little paranoid, isn't he?"

She smiled and looked around furtively. The crowd had disappeared out of earshot back to their desks and offices. She leaned toward me and lowered her voice. "He ought to be. You're famous now, and to think, I had your seed in me."

Oh, brother. Alarmed, I looked around hastily. "Hey, take it easy. We're at work and I got enough publicity."

She growled playfully and I went into my office. My cell phone was on my desk. It revealed a bevy of missed calls and text messages, including three from Cocoa, so I started there.

"Hi, Cocoa."

"Oh, my God, I saw the whole thing on television. That was amazing. Are you all right? The news kept showing you hit your head on the cement over and over. It was terrible. I had to turn it off."

"Sore, but I'll live. Where are you?"

"I'm still at your apartment. Bridget came and I told her about the new arrangements. She was disappointed but okay. She wasn't what I expected. Didn't seem like your type. Kind of nerdy."

I chuckled. "Will you stop it? She's just a kid."

"She's twenty-four years old. That's only one year younger than me. We had a little chat."

"She is? Well I didn't know that, and it doesn't matter so just stop."

"Anyway, Cleo's been walked, fed and cuddled all morning. I should get that lucky. By the way, I rented a piano. They'll be delivering it this afternoon. I hope you don't mind."

I'd forgotten what a chatterbox she could be once she got going. "Well, I'm glad you're getting along with Cleo and the piano is fine. How much is this going to cost me?"

"Seriously? I don't need or want your money. I got plenty of my own and if I need any more I'll squeeze it out of Uncle Leo." She laughed at that. "He has no idea what he's started with me."

That made me grin. "Boy, remind me not to piss you off."

"Damn right about that. So what happened with that guy? Was he the friend you went to see last night?"

"Yeah, that was him."

"I guess your little pep talk didn't help?"

"Apparently not. It's extremely complicated and I'll fill you in tonight. There's a lot going on right now. How about a nice dinner out? I've been eating cereal every night and could use a real meal, and besides I think we should celebrate our reunion."

"That would be great. How about seven?"

"Sounds great."

"Okay, as soon as they deliver the piano I'll go home and change into clean clothes. I'm still wearing the same underwear from yesterday."

I groaned. "I didn't need to know that, Cocoa. You know, girls should try being a little more mysterious like in the old days."

"You want mystery? I'll give you mystery. You can guess whether I'm using birth control or not."

I laughed. "Okay, not that much mystery. Besides, I scare easy when it comes to that. Look, I've got to go now. I've got about ten or twelve calls to return."

"Bye."

As I left my office to go check on Tony, Julie stopped me, handing me a piece of paper with a name and number on it.

"What's this?" I asked.

"He called before. I forgot to mention it. He said he's a lawyer."

"Great." Nothing alarmed and irritated doctors more than calls from lawyers.

"Sorry."

"It's okay. Look, if anybody needs me, I'll be roaming around the hospital. Right now I'm going down to the ER to see Tony."

"Got it, boss."

As I walked to the elevators, I glanced at the name on the paper, Esha Deshmukh. Fuck, what kind of name was that and what did he want? Probably wants to sue me for mistreating the American flag while I was saving Tony.

The emergency room was in total free fall as always: overcrowded, understaffed, noisy and now, in addition, full of police and reporters. The excitement of Tony's near death experience hadn't worn off yet and probably wouldn't until they got some newsworthy answers. Fortunately, the reporters were kept at bay by the police and hospital security. I skirted the masses and snuck into Tony's room, where I found his nurse, Annie, and the ER physician, Mike, tending to him. My heart sank as I saw that Tony was intubated and now completely unconscious. He was in a neck brace to immobilize him.

"Hi guys, how's he doing?"

Annie waved politely and Mike nodded in my direction while he wrote something on a clipboard. He was a broad-shouldered guy who exercised regularly, ate a lot of yogurt and loved gin martinis. He wore blue surgical scrubs and sported a scruffy beard. Finishing his note, he turned toward me and smiled. We had spent many nights together in the ER taking care of critically ill patients. "Hey Cesari, I was wondering when you'd show up. I missed it all on TV but I heard you've been upgraded to superhero status. I want you around when I decide I can't take it anymore."

I nodded. "Thanks, but what about Tony?"

"Hmm, not too shiny at the moment but he may be all right. He didn't quite crush his larynx when he jumped but he came close. It's severely bruised and edematous. That's why he's intubated. We almost had to perform a tracheostomy. His cervical spine is the big problem. Most people think they're going to break their neck and die instantly when they do what he did but generally that's not what happens. Usually they just die slowly from strangulation. In his case, there was just enough force on impact to herniate several cervical discs and the MRI showed bleeding along his spinal cord. There's a great deal of swelling right now and it's too early to tell if he'll ever walk again. We're admitting him to the ICU and the neurosurgeons are on the way. I guess if he makes it, the shrinks will get their turn with him. So there it is in a nutshell. I'm sure he'll live but whether he's going to be happy about it is another story."

"Thanks, Mike. Let's keep our fingers crossed."

"So why'd he jump?"

"It's a long story, Mike, and I really shouldn't go into it here."

"You're right. Anyway, I've got to keep moving. This place is a zoo as always. Nice talking to you, Cesari, and once again, great job."

He left the room and I walked up close to Tony while Annie checked his IV. They hadn't cleaned him up very well and there was dried blood on the side of his face where he had hit the sidewalk. He looked puffy and the room was ominously quiet except for the sounds of mechanical ventilation.

"Are you all right, Doc?" Annie asked. She was an older woman, close to retirement. She had seen it all. Today was just another day at the office.

"Yeah, thanks."

"You're a hero."

I looked at her. "So everyone keeps telling me. I just hope Tony feels that way when he wakes up paralyzed from the neck down."

She came over to me and placed a hand on my arm sympathetically. "Don't be so negative. You've been around a while so you know how bad things can look at first. He's young and healthy. He'll be fine. You'll see."

I smiled. "Thanks for the pep talk, Annie."

"You're welcome."

"Well, take good care of him, Annie. I've got to run."

"I will, Doc. Rest assured about that."

I left the ER and was headed for the elevator when I spotted Goldstein walking toward me.

"Cesari, I'm glad I ran into you. We need to talk. How's Tony?"

"He's stable, Arnie, but there are a lot of questions concerning his future right now."

"I'll bet. C'mon, let's get a cup of coffee."

Chapter 7

*D*own the block from the hospital we found a small authentic
coffee shop that ground their beans to order. We grabbed
a couple of espressos with biscotti and sat at a small wooden
table. The smell of freshly brewed coffee was intoxicating.

Arnie was sixty, clean shaven with thinning white hair that
made him look older. Gold-rimmed glasses didn't help either.
He kept himself in reasonably good shape, but the constant
meetings and business lunches were taking their toll on him. He
had developed a bit of a belly and a ruddy complexion. I had
seen him in consultation for elevated liver tests last year and told
him to lay off the noon-time martinis. He was a hematologist by
trade and had been elected by the rest of us as chief of staff
for a two-year stint. He took both his jobs very seriously. I
filled him in on what had happened with Tony as we sipped
our coffees.

He soaked it all in quietly and eventually let out a deep
breath. "Not good, Cesari. Not good at all."

"You don't have to tell me. I just left Tony in the ER."

He nodded and took a bite of his chocolate-covered biscotti.
"Does anybody else know what happened?"

I wasn't sure what he meant. "The whole world knows,
Arnie. It was on television."

"I meant the Konstandin stuff."

"Oh, I don't think so, but Tony said he left a note for you on your desk explaining everything and taking full responsibility."

"On my desk? And you left it there? Out in the open? Cesari, don't you have any common sense?"

"I was a little busy at the time, Arnie. I didn't even get to look at it. It's probably still there."

"Shit. I'd better go up there now and find it before it goes viral. Look, please don't give any interviews to the media. In fact, I'm begging you not to talk to anyone at all about this just yet. I know it looks bad but we have to get all the facts in and this is only part of the story. I want you to complete your investigation and file a report despite what just happened, okay? Have you spoken with Mrs. Konstandin yet?"

"She was next on my agenda but I'm not sure that I should. I can tell you right now she's going to be hostile. I forgot to mention it but Tony spoke to her early this morning to apologize and she tore him a new one."

Arnie's jaw dropped and for just the second time since I first met him used profanity. "Why the fuck would he do that? He shouldn't have called her. The woman just lost her husband. Of course, she was bent out of shape. For God's sake, she's grieving. Anger is a totally natural response, and he apologized? You never do that either to a potentially litigious patient. Apologizing is the same as admitting guilt. In a situation like this it's like pouring gasoline on a fire."

"I know, but what's done is done."

He let out a deep breath. "Well, I want you to talk to her anyway. We need to put closure on this thing in a formal way despite today's drama, okay? Go gently with her and let her vent. You're just there to reassure her that we care about her and her husband and that we are doing everything we can to answer any and all of her questions regarding his care. The message she should come away with is that we are all on the same side."

I nodded. "Sure."

Arnie finished his espresso with a gulp. He was frustrated. "This is just great. The timing couldn't be worse. You know, I just came from a conference about new guidelines that are coming down the pike for electronic documentation. It's not pretty and shit like this is the reason why. New York State is cracking down on sloppy recordkeeping and they plan on linking it to financial reimbursement but they don't have a clue as to what the real problem is. They don't understand that physicians are overwhelmed as it is and now in addition they are being turned into data collection specialists for the government. They don't seem to understand that the electronic records are actually making communication less effective between physicians, not more so, because every note now says the same thing only in triplicate. Plus, look how easy it is to make a filing mistake and not even be aware of it. This must happen thousands of times a day across the country without anyone knowing it, and the government's solution? Get this. Are you listening?"

I nodded again, finishing my coffee. He was on a roll.

"They're going to make it harder: more passwords, more security, more documentation, more time staring at laptops typing in useless data. Did you know what the biggest complaint was by patients who filed malpractice claims in the last five years?"

"Tell me."

"Their doctor didn't pay enough attention to them because he was staring at his computer. Can you believe that? And New York State wants to make us spend more time staring at our computers."

"Great, I can't wait."

He chuckled. "Well, let me go to my office and hopefully, my nosy secretary hasn't read Tony's note yet. Stay in touch, Cesari." He hesitated and then added. "One more thing …"

"Yes, Arnie?"

"How well did you know Tony?"

"We went out for drinks every now and then. I had dinner at his apartment once. We weren't that close. Why?"

"This wasn't his first time."

"What's that supposed to mean?"

"This is strictly confidential and I shouldn't even tell you but I feel you've earned the right. Tony attempted suicide at least once before and has been under treatment for depression."

I was very surprised to hear that. Tony never seemed depressed to me, just a little on the sarcastic side maybe. "I didn't know that."

"Most people don't but as chief of staff I have to be made aware of these things."

I dabbed my lips with a paper napkin. "Well that does help put things into perspective for me. If he was emotionally down, taking antidepressants, drinking alcohol, sleep-deprived, and feeling guilty about what happened…"

"Exactly. If he was already teetering on the edge, all he needed was a little push."

We left the coffee shop and headed back to the hospital. He went to his office and I went to the medical records department. On the way, I called Mrs. Konstandin to set up an appointment to interview her. She agreed to meet me in her apartment at eleven tomorrow morning. She had a thick accent and it was difficult to tell if she was pissed off or not. She didn't mention whether she had seen this morning's events on television and I didn't bring it up.

I entered the medical records department and handed one of the women there a slip of paper with Jetmir Konstandin's name and medical record number on it. "Could you get me this chart please?"

She returned a short time later with his file, filled with mostly redundant documentation, consent forms and disclaimers. I thanked her and walked into a nearby doctor's room to examine it. There was a series of laptops on small desks and I sat down at one, logging onto the hospital's electronic medical record, commonly called EMR. Despite going paperless, every hospital and medical office ironically still relied on paper—piles of paper.

Reviewing both the electronic and paper charts, I suddenly remembered the call from the lawyer Julie had told me about. I pulled the slip of paper with the number on it from my pocket and looked at it. It was a Boston area code. Three rings into the call a woman answered.

"Hello, may I speak to Esha Deshmukh? My name is Dr. John Cesari and I'm returning his call."

A very polite voice with an educated English accent said, "Hello, Dr. Cesari. This is Esha Deshmukh. Thank you for returning my call."

"Hello, I'm sorry. My secretary told me you were a man. What can I do for you, Ms. Deshmukh?"

"No worries, Dr. Cesari. She may have been confused because my secretary, Todd, called your office earlier on my behalf looking for you. Do you have a moment?"

"That's why I called. I have a moment."

Ms. Deshmukh said, "Yes, of course. Well, I am an attorney with Darby, Smith and Tasker. I don't know if you've heard of us. We primarily handle medical malpractice cases." She paused to let that sink in.

Shit.

"Go on. What did I do?"

She chuckled. "You didn't do anything, Doctor, and just for the record we are the good guys. We defend physicians and hospitals; we don't go after them."

"Well, then there's a chance we could be friends. So, how can I help you, Ms. Deshmukh?"

"You can call me Esha or Miss Deshmukh. I've never bought into that Ms. stuff and I was hoping I could discuss the particulars of a case with you."

"What case is that?"

"My firm has been retained by Saint Matt's to review a case to assess exposure in the unlikely event of a suit ever being brought. As you know, about a month ago a Mr. Konstandin committed suicide when he found out he had incurable colon cancer. I am just trying to gather as much information as I can and the hospital told me to talk to you. I was going to contact Dr. Macchiarone but I've been told he jumped out of a window this morning. I'm very sorry about that. I hope he'll be all right."

I sighed. At least she didn't call me a hero. That was already growing old. Damn, this thing was starting to spin out of control. "Thank you. We're keeping our fingers crossed. Right now he's stable. So, what can I tell you? I don't know a whole lot more than anyone else."

"Maybe we can start with anything Dr. Macchiarone may have told you about the case?"

"He didn't say much other than he felt bad that he might have missed a colon cancer during a routine colonoscopy. He was very upset over it. He did mention some irregularities in the medical records that didn't seem to make any sense to him and I was going to look into that aspect some more."

"Irregularities?"

"Just some discrepancies that were hard to understand. I was in the middle of reviewing the chart when I decided to take a break and call you."

"Have you found anything?"

"Not yet, but I plan on digging—very hard—and very deep. Dr. Macchiarone is my friend and he's a very conscientious physician. Something's just not adding up about what happened, but I'll let you know more if and when I find it."

"Yes, I see. What about Mrs. Konstandin? Has anyone from the hospital spoken to her? Officially, I mean."

"No, not yet. I'm meeting with her tomorrow morning at eleven in her apartment. The hospital wants me to interview her to find out her take on what happened and to show her our support and sympathy without throwing anyone under the bus."

"I see. May I give you some advice about a situation like that, Dr. Cesari?"

"Sure, go ahead."

"Say as little as possible and let her do all the talking."

"Yeah, that was pretty much my plan. She expressed an interest in speaking to a representative of the hospital so we thought it would be a good idea to let her vent. You know, blow off a little steam. We thought it might help calm her down if we showed her how sympathetic we were. Besides, rumor is that she's primarily pissed off at Unicare, the insurance company."

"Naturally. Would you please keep me apprised of the meeting's outcome if it's not too much trouble?"

"Sure, why not. I'll give you a call. Is that all?"

"Yes. Well, thank you, and have a fabulous day."

"You too and God Save the Queen."

She chuckled. "You're a bit of a wanker, aren't you?"

"A what?"

"You can look that up."

"I'll be sure to do that. By the way, what kind of name is that, Esha?"

"It's Indian but I was born and raised in London. I moved to the States three years ago when I took this job, and Cesari, would I be safe to assume that you're Italian?"

"I wouldn't assume anything about me, Esha, especially the idea that you might be safe."

Chapter 8

*I*t was after five by the time I finished reviewing Mr. Konstandin's hospital records and I was deeply confused. The colonoscopy report said it was a negative exam but Tony had coded the encounter as colon cancer for billing purposes which meant he believed the patient had cancer. Yet, except for Mrs. Konstandin's complaint, there was no hint of that in any of the records. There were no CT scans, biopsies or referrals for surgery. He had his colonoscopy and nearly a year later committed suicide. That's all there was. No ER visits, no labs, no nothing. How could that be? No one in this country dies without at least one CT scan.

Then I thought about the billing process. It was a conscious decision on the part of the physician to select a billing code, so it wasn't an accident that he had selected that diagnosis. The hospital also had submitted its portion of the bill under that same billing code so Tony must have told the nurses at the time of the colonoscopy which code to use. I could track down the nurses he had worked with, but would anyone remember something like that almost a year later? I doubted it. And how would it change anything anyway? There was something wrong about all of this. It just didn't feel right but I couldn't put my finger on it.

I left the hospital and hoofed it back to the loft. As I opened the door and entered, I was greeted by the sounds of Tchaikovsky. I saw Cocoa sitting at a baby grand piano with Cleo lying nearby, staring at her adoringly. I closed the door quietly behind me but Cleo heard anyway and jumped to attention, woofing and bounding over to me. Cocoa stopped playing and welcomed me.

I hugged them both and said, "Don't stop playing, Cocoa. It sounded great."

She smiled and continued the piece as I took a seat on the sofa. Cleo jumped on the couch next to me, trying desperately to lick my face while I pushed her away.

When she finished, Cocoa came over and sat on my other side. She said, "My turn, Cleo." She put her arms around me and kissed me. "So how's my hero?"

I chuckled. "I'm good, thanks. You look nice." She wore tight blue jeans, a pretty red top and dress shoes with modest heels.

"Thank you. How do you like the piano?"

It was a beautiful ebony baby grand Yamaha about six feet wide. I said, "It's bigger than I thought it would be. I was expecting an upright, not a baby grand."

"Well, you have plenty of room and the difference in quality of sound is light-years apart. Remember, I've been practicing on a full grand the last few months so this is actually a step down. I think it looks great in here and the acoustics with the high ceilings are outstanding."

"Did they have any trouble getting it up here?"

"None at all. This building used to be a warehouse and has an enormous service elevator. The door was a little tricky but these moving guys are pros. You should've seen them. A big fat guy sweating bullets and a little wiry guy made of solid muscle. The little guy did all the work."

That made me laugh. "Well, they did a good job. The piano looks and sounds great. Okay, let me go clean up and change into fresh clothes and we'll go eat. Has Cleo been out recently?"

"She's been fed and I walked her about an hour ago. We're all good there. How's your head?"

"It hurts."

As I walked by the bed into the bathroom, I noticed a small suitcase opened on the floor. On the sink I spotted cologne, hair brush, skin moisturizer, lady's antiperspirant, a second tooth brush and cosmetics. In the shower, there was shampoo, body gel, a lady's razor and conditioner. Hmm.

I showered in silence and considered my options. I did tell her this morning that she could stay as long as she liked, but that was a figure of speech. Most people would not have taken that as an invitation to move in, but this wasn't most people. This was Cocoa. Accepting my fate for the moment, I finished cleaning up and put on loafers, jeans and a white dress shirt while Cocoa played with Cleo. I walked up to them. "How do I look, girls?"

Cocoa sized me up. "Good enough to throw you over my shoulder and take you to bed."

I laughed. I weighed 220 lbs. and she was about half that dripping wet. "Thanks. Say, I saw your stuff in the bathroom."

"Yeah?"

"Just wondering."

"Relax. If I'm going to take care of *your* dog in the morning I'd like to be able to clean myself up once in a while."

Ouch.

"Of course."

"I'm glad we cleared the air on that. So, where are we going to eat?"

"I thought we'd walk over to Babbo's and see if they can squeeze us in. They're always packed but they usually have a table for two if you're polite. Having a twenty dollar bill handy always helps but one look at you and I'm sure that won't be necessary."

"Sounds like a plan. Are we dressed up enough?"

I looked at her perfectly curved bottom, drew a deep breath and said, "We're fine." She smiled and we said good-bye to Cleo.

The restaurant was not even a block away and we arrived there in five minutes. It was a beautiful evening with the temperature in the low seventies and almost zero percent humidity. It was Thursday night and the place was packed and loud. I never understood that about Italian restaurants, even the better ones were deafeningly noisy. You never got that in a French restaurant. They must be very polite eaters.

The maître d' was a haughty guy in a black suit and tie. He was very civil but a bit short on the warmth most people expected in Italian restaurants. We were informed that there were no tables available for President Jackson so I put the twenty away and considered my options. As I scanned the crowded dining room, a large hand grabbed me by the shoulder.

"Cesari, good to see you out, and Cocoa, this really is my lucky day."

We both turned to see an oversized man about six foot three, 260 lb. in a hand-tailored silk suit, crisp white shirt, tie, gold cuff links and alligator shoes. He had a full head of jet black hair slicked back with mousse and his piercing gray eyes reminded me of an Arctic wolf. There were two even bigger goons standing respectfully behind him.

Cocoa and I both said, "Hi, Vito."

"So where have you been, Cesari?" he asked in a low raspy voice, the result of years of smoking unfiltered cigarettes.

"Keeping a low profile. You know what I mean?"

"Yeah, I know. Don't worry, I ain't taking it personally and what about you, Cocoa? It's good to see you again. You look great."

87

She responded warmly, "Thank you, Vito. Same here. I hope all is well."

"It is Cocoa. It is. So, were you guys coming or going?"

"The maître d' just informed us that there was no room at the inn so we were just leaving."

"Who told you that?" As we spoke the maître d' spotted Vito and headed over to us.

I nodded at the guy and said, "He did."

"Don't go anywhere. I'll take care of it."

The maître d' addressed Vito. "Good evening, Mr. Gianelli. Your usual table is ready and I took the liberty of pouring a round of eighteen-year-old Macallan, neat, for you and your guests."

Vito placed a large arm around the maître d' and walked him a little bit away out of hearing range. They spoke quietly for a few moments and then returned, the maître d' with a fresh attitude.

He said to me and Cocoa, "Allow me to seat Mr. Gianelli and then I will prepare a table for you. Please accept my apologies for the misunderstanding."

Cocoa smiled and excused herself to go to the bathroom. The maître d' turned to give instructions to one of the wait staff about us and I asked Vito. "Let me guess. You own a piece of this place too?"

He lowered his voice. "Nah. It's too high profile for a shakedown like that. Believe me I tried, and I'm still working on it. Mario Batali and I have a truce. He knows not to fuck with me and in return I don't perform liposuction on him in the kitchen with one of his carving knives. I eat here once a week just to remind him whose town this is. As long he shows me the respect I'm due, I'll be nice. By the way, your meal's on the house."

"Thanks but you don't have to pay for us, Vito."

"Who said I'm paying for anybody? I said it's on the house."

I must have looked confused. "Get out of here. You can't be serious?"

"Hey, Cesari, do I look like I have a sense of humor?"

He was right about that. He was all business. "I don't know what to say."

"Then don't say anything. I'm not doing this for you. I'm doing it for me. I want Batali to understand that he needs to respect my friends too, not just me. If I eat for free then my friends eat for free. I'm sending a message to everyone here."

He was starting to work himself up so I shook my head and acquiesced. "Fine, thanks. Can I at least give the guy a tip?"

"Sure and don't be cheap either. You take, you gotta give, capeesh?"

I nodded. "Don't worry."

Changing the subject he said, "So what's with you and Cocoa? If memory serves me right I thought she was off limits as per Uncle Leo."

"She is."

"Care to explain? Because she don't look like she got the memo."

The maître d' approached Vito. I said, "It's complicated and we're working on the Uncle Leo problem."

He chuckled. "Fucking Cesari. I don't think I ever met a guy who had as many girl problems as you. You got to learn to keep it simple like I do."

"Not everybody likes to end their dates by leaving a couple of hundred dollar bills on the night table, Vito."

"It's a lot easier than what you're doing. Look, I got to go. My boys and I are hungry. Stay in touch all right? I kind of miss you. If you want back in just say the word. Tell Cocoa I said bye."

He walked off with the maître d' just as Cocoa emerged from the bathroom and joined me. A waiter soon approached and seated us at a table for two, handing us menus and a wine list.

She said, "How cool was that? A real live mobster got us a table at a fancy restaurant."

"Yeah, real cool. Why does everyone think gangsters are cool and romantic? They're really not. They're mostly just assholes."

"Is your friend Vito an asshole?"

I laughed. "Biggest one I ever met."

"Do you still work with him?"

"No, I told him we could be friends but that I wanted no part of that life anymore. I have a good job and I help people. I make plenty of money and I'm happy doing what I do."

She nodded. "But I bet it was exciting, wasn't it?"

I nodded as I looked over the menu. "Like having a heart attack. How about we order? I'm starving."

"Did he hear about what happened at the hospital?"

"He didn't say anything so I would assume not. He's not much of a TV guy. The only news he's interested in is what those two guys he's with whisper in his ear about what's going on with his business interests."

"Who are those guys anyway?"

"Bodyguards probably, looking at their size and demeanor. He's probably got at least one or two more outside keeping a lookout. I'm sure Mario Batali's thrilled at having him as a regular guest."

"Well, I think it's exciting."

"Like I said it's like having a heart attack only it never lets up."

We ordered a Tuscan red wine to go with our pasta entrées of homemade tagliatelle with wild boar ragu and shaved white truffle complemented by aged parmigiano reggiano. The food and wine were wonderful and as we indulged ourselves, I brought Cocoa up to speed on everything that had been going on at the hospital. She was pretty smart and I liked bouncing things off her.

I sipped my wine. "I miss this, Cocoa. I always enjoyed talking with you about things."

She smiled. "Thanks. You're not violating some sort of code of conduct by telling me about Tony?"

Laughing, I said. "Probably, but who cares. Besides, who's going to get worked up about an ex-gangster telling an ex-stripper anything?"

She could take a joke and kicked me playfully under the table, giggling. "That's dancer not stripper, wiseguy, and don't make me say it again."

Continuing, I said, "You know, the two of us have enough skeletons in our closet to fill a cemetery."

We raised our glasses and clinked them in a toast and she said, "Here's to secrets."

"Cheers."

"Hi, Dr. Cesari."

Cocoa and I turned to see Julie, my secretary, waving to me. She was with several other secretaries waiting to be seated. I waved back and she approached our table.

"Hi, Julie. It's nice to see you and the girls get out together. This is my friend, Cocoa. I mean Myrtle."

"Cocoa?" Julie asked as they sized each other up. I hated when women did that. They couldn't help themselves.

Cocoa said, "Hi, it's nice to meet you, Julie, and please call me Cocoa. It's a nickname I've had since childhood. I actually prefer it."

I said, "So, what's the occasion, Julie? Somebody's birthday?"

She finally took her eyes off of Cocoa. "No, Ronnie from Unicare takes the secretaries out every so often to show his appreciation."

I was puzzled. "Ronnie from Unicare? Who's he, and isn't that an insurance company?"

"Yes, it is. He takes us to all the best restaurants in the city but Babbo's my favorite."

"Well, that's nice. What exactly is he showing his appreciation for?" I knew the pharmaceutical reps were always sucking up to the secretaries to gain access to the docs but this was the first I'd ever heard of a health insurance company doing it. I was a bit jealous. I wouldn't object to a free meal every now and then.

Before she could answer, the other girls called over to her that their table was ready. She said, "Excuse me, Dr. Cesari. I have to go now. Ronnie's here. He's so gorgeous, and has the most adorable English accent. Well, it was nice meeting you, Cocoa."

"Same here." Cocoa replied.

"Have a good time, Julie." I watched as she rejoined her group and they were escorted to one of the tables accompanied by a tall, medium-build guy, with thick, black wavy hair. He was wearing an expensive, hand-tailored, pinstripe suit. His back was to me, so I couldn't say whether or not I agreed with Julie's assessment of his looks, but he certainly seemed buffed from my angle.

After she left, Cocoa asked suspiciously, "She's your secretary?"

"Yes."

"Is that all she is?"

"What kind of question is that?"

"Just routine. Get used to it. So, how's Kelly and the kids?"

I hesitated before responding. "Who?"

She grinned broadly. "Black girl, very pretty, married, twin baby girls, might be your kids? Remember?"

"Oh, that Kelly."

"Well?"

"I don't know exactly."

"Do you talk to her or go see the kids?"

"Not since the restraining order."

She laughed but then got serious. "No way. A restraining order? What did you do?"

"Do you mind if we don't talk about this?"

Chapter 9

The next morning, Cocoa and I sat across from each other in an old diner on First Avenue sipping black coffee served to us by a bored waitress in a mustard-colored uniform with her hair up in a bun. This wasn't the greatest neighborhood in the world but I'd seen and lived in much worse. The diner itself was maybe a half-step up from what you would probably call a dump, and part of it had been cordoned off for renovation. From the look of the subfloor it was long overdue. With the carpeting removed, much of the supporting wood appeared severely decayed. The thought crossed my mind that the entire restaurant might be in danger of collapsing. Water damage, I suspected, but only God knew when. It could've been last year or last century. Near the entrance was a construction worker on his knees with his pants falling down ripping up floor boards with a crowbar. I watched him with great curiosity. I wasn't sure which fascinated me more—his activities, or that I was supposed to eat breakfast staring at his exposed butt. Didn't anybody ever tell this guy to say no to crack? New York City, it was a helluva town.

Studying my plastic menu, I became lost in thought, thinking of how I was going to approach my meeting with Mrs. Konstandin, who lived across the street in a rent-controlled apartment. The way I saw it, I had only one reasonable option. That was to show great sympathy and to offer what little explanation I had to her with the assurance that we were doing all we could to make sure a situation like this didn't happen again. She was going to be upset for sure, probably angry but hopefully not too hostile. I was the whipping boy for the hospital and my job was to take it any which way she dished it out.

As I sat there thinking things through, the lump on the back of my head pounded fiercely and made it difficult to concentrate. As a physician, I had anticipated this and had taken a couple of ibuprofen both last night and again this morning but this was way worse than I had imagined. The pain was ferocious. I squeezed my eyes shut tightly and took a deep breath letting it out slowly. It was so bad I couldn't take my mind off it and was starting to think that maybe I should go to the emergency room. Just when I thought it couldn't get any worse it was suddenly— gone. I heard a voice from far away calling me.

"John, snap out of it. Are you okay?" Cocoa reached across the table and tapped on the back of my plastic menu snapping me out of my trance. Startled, I put the menu down and saw Cocoa and the middle-aged waitress staring at me. Cocoa asked again, "Are you okay?"

I nodded but wasn't sure. I felt confused. Not disoriented, but not quite right and the pain was gone, completely gone. I reached up to feel the lump and it too was gone. That was peculiar but when I woke this morning I hadn't checked to see if it was still there. I just assumed it would be.

Cocoa said, "Are you going to order? That was the third time I called your name. The waitress has been standing here for five minutes trying to get your attention."

I looked at my watch. It was 9:30 a.m. We had arrived at 9:00 sharp. That was odd. Almost a full half hour had passed and I barely knew how. Putting it behind me for the moment I finally spoke, "I'm sorry. I was distracted thinking about my meeting with Mrs. Konstandin." I turned to the waitress. "Um, I'll have the short stack with a side of sausage. Thank you, and please bring extra maple syrup." I loved to drown my pancakes in maple syrup.

She took our orders and walked away. Cocoa stared at me wondering if I was really okay. The thought crossed my mind that maybe I had a concussion. It was possible. I looked out the window down First Avenue and saw a shiny new Mercedes slowly approach Mrs. Konstandin's building and then turn into the alley next to it. It was overcast and I looked up at the dark, foreboding sky wondering if it would soon rain.

We ate our breakfasts leisurely and at 10:45, I kissed Cocoa goodbye. "This shouldn't take that long. Are you going to wait here?"

"If they'll let me. Call me if you think you're going to be delayed or if there's a problem. I'd rather not sit here all day without knowing what's going on."

"Okay, one way or the other you'll hear from me by noon at the latest. See you later."

I crossed the street and entered the old building. The elevator was broken so I climbed the three flights of ancient wooden steps to her apartment, primping myself when I arrived. I wore khakis, a dress shirt and a lightweight sport coat. It was summer but I wanted to look official so I even wore my hospital ID attached to my breast pocket, easily visible. Reviewing one more time in my head what I was going to say, I approached her door, bracing myself for the potential torrent of abuse that might be heading my way as a representative of the hospital.

At the entrance I paused, took a deep breath and swept my hand through my hair one last time. I was on time. I pressed the door buzzer and waited—and waited. I knocked gently on the door also with no result. I looked at my watch and thought it through. I hadn't made a mistake. She had said 11:00 a.m. and not to be late because she had errands to run. After ten minutes, I was toying with the idea of bailing out.

Something had obviously come up and she wasn't home but what if she just went out for some groceries and was on the way back?

As I stood there pondering the situation, a neighbor emerged from the apartment next door holding a plastic kitchen garbage bag. She eyed me suspiciously. She was in her sixties and heavy-set with gray hair wrapped in a red kerchief.

I said, "Good morning."

"You doctor, wait Irina?" she asked in a thick Albanian accent.

I nodded. "Yes, I was supposed to meet her at eleven but she's not answering."

"Irina inside. I speak on phone maybe one hour ago. She tell me you come. Then we go lunch. Probably in bedroom, no can hear. You go in. Door not locked. Irina never lock. Afraid of fire."

I was amused that she was more afraid of fire than of intruders. Looking around the old building with its peeling paint and graffiti-covered walls, I wasn't sure that I blamed her. When I hesitated, the neighbor stepped in front of me, opened the door and led the way in. "Sit couch. I get." I closed the door behind me and watched her march off to the adjacent bedroom calling out for her friend.

The apartment was dark, musty and poorly furnished but clean. It was hot and I sat on an old sofa, regretting wearing a sport coat because I was already perspiring. There was a weathered wooden coffee table in front of me and on it was an open manila folder with a short stack of papers which caught my attention. On top was an insurance form she had submitted to Unicare with a big red stamp across it saying *Claim Denied*. Out of curiosity, I lifted it and saw underneath a form letter from the company explaining to her that due to inadequate documentation her husband's medical care would not be covered. I didn't feel too bad nosing around because I assumed she planned on going over it with me.

Taking a deep breath, I relaxed back into the sofa, staring straight ahead, and waited patiently. It was going to be a long morning for sure. I heard the neighbor call out for her once more then there was silence. Lost in thought, I didn't notice the uncomfortableness of the silence as it started to drag out. Just as it dawned on me that there was something odd about it, I heard a sound and stood up expecting to meet Mrs. Konstandin. Instead, a tall man stood in the doorway of the bedroom. He wore black leather gloves and pointed a silenced handgun in my direction. He was vaguely familiar. Before I could say anything he fired a round into my abdomen. I grunted and stepped backward in sudden pain. Clutching the wound, I watched as blood stained my new white shirt.

I looked up at him and murmured in disbelief. "Why?"

He smirked and in an English accent said, "Sorry, mate, but that would be a HIPAA violation if I told you. I hope you'll understand."

I didn't have time to try to understand what that meant. The pain crescendoed in intensity and a wave of nausea and fear swept over me. He looked at me, aimed the gun a little higher and pulled the trigger again. The second bullet tore through my neck and trachea. My hands jerked from my abdomen to clutch the wound in my neck as the force of the shot propelled me backward onto the coffee table. Choking and gasping for air, I twitched and writhed in pain. Inhaled blood and flesh caused me to cough and gurgle as I suddenly felt very cold. The guy came over and looked down at me as I wheezed and suffered helplessly. I was suddenly very scared. I was dying and there was nothing I could do about it.

He sneered at me saying, "Why are you Yanks always so melodramatic?"

All I could think was, *Why?* Moments later, I closed my eyes and felt myself drifting off, realizing that I no longer felt pain nor even cared as my hands relaxed from my throat and slipped down toward my sides. Through the fog of my last remaining consciousness, I heard him say, "Sorry old man, but this is what you get for trusting a lawyer, even an English one."

What the hell did that mean?

****

Unconscious for an unknown length of time, I eventually woke to find myself lying on the floor in a dark room. I mean really dark, pitch black and quiet. I couldn't even see my hand in front of my face. Standing up, I realized I was naked but felt neither cold nor warm. I felt my neck and abdomen for the gunshot wounds but there were none. With great difficulty, I tried to orient myself but couldn't find any walls, doors or furniture. As far as I could tell the room was devoid of objects of any kind. I called out several times but heard nothing in response and so, not knowing what to do, I picked a direction and walked.

I walked for hours, maybe days, maybe weeks, feeling neither hunger, thirst nor the need to perform bodily functions. Losing track of time, I would occasionally lie down and close my eyes, forcing myself to sleep, hoping I would wake up from this endless dream but I never did. Was I dead? Was this hell or purgatory? Or was it neither? I spent days cursing the blackness and then days pitying myself. What had I done to deserve this? I wasn't perfect. I was the first one to admit that but I always tried to do the right thing. As a child I believed in God but as an adult I was skeptical and hadn't been to church in years. I looked upward and yelled. "What do you want from me?"

No answer came so I decided to sit on the floor in one spot and wait. No more walking. What was the point? I was being petulant and didn't care. Weeks, months, years, I don't know how much time passed and I began to despair. Could I really pass eternity like this? A prison without walls, light or stimulation of any kind other than my own thoughts? Could I kill myself if I was already dead? And how would I do such a thing in my condition? I supposed I could try banging my head on the floor but I would lose consciousness long before I succeeded. I tried anyway—for days without success.

Uncontrollably, I started to cry and tremble. I got on my knees and with hands clasped, prayed out loud. "Dear God, forgive me for I have sinned. I have done terrible things and I don't deserve your love or your pity but I'm asking for it anyway. Please Lord, have mercy on me. I can't go on like this. I just can't."

I fell flat to the floor with arms outstretched. "Our Father, who art in heaven. Hallowed be thy name. Thy kingdom come. Thy will be done. On earth as it is in Heaven. Give us this day our daily bread..." I hesitated unsure of the next line. I hadn't prayed out loud since the eighth grade. "Give us this day our daily bread and forgive us our trespasses as we forgive those who trespass against us. Lead us not into temptation but deliver us from evil."

I said it again and again and again, thousands upon thousands of times. With each word and verse I became more and more convinced that I wasn't alone. Maybe I took comfort in thinking that someone was listening. Maybe I had already lost my mind? Exhausted, I closed my eyes and when I next opened them I thought I saw something different. In the distance, maybe miles away, I thought I saw a pinpoint of light. I rose and stared in that direction, hoping beyond hope that I wasn't hallucinating. I slowly started to walk in the direction of the light and then faster and faster and soon, I was running. I wasn't crazy. I was overjoyed. The light was getting stronger and stronger.

At first, the light glowed like a candle, then a street lamp, then the brights of a car, then stadium lights and before long I had to cover my eyes because it was like looking into the sun. Even worse, I couldn't escape the harshness of it by closing my eyes or covering them with my hands. The light seemed to burn through my eyelids causing me terrible pain. I turned around and tried to go back but there was no escaping it. The light was everywhere, surrounding me and swallowing me up.

What new horror lay in wait for me now? I beat my hands against my chest. This was unfair. Instead of me catching up to the light, I realized too late that the light had been coming for me. It glowed brightly in every direction; so bright that I could no longer tell if my eyes were open or shut. If God was trying to prove to me who was the boss, he had succeeded.

Just as suddenly, the light went out and I was alone again in the darkness but only briefly. Seconds later, just a few feet away, I saw a softly illuminated park bench with a woman sitting on it. I walked toward her and gasped with recognition. Falling to my knees, I threw my head onto her lap and hugged her, crying like a baby.

"Mom, oh Mom! Please tell me it's you. Please …"

She placed her arms around my head and kissed me. "Giannuzzu, my Giannuzzu, of course it's me. Who else would it be? It's so good to see you."

Giannuzzu was Sicilian for Johnny. She and only she ever called me that. She looked so healthy as she smiled at me. The last time I had seen her she was in the late stages of cancer in a hospital bed, her body ravaged by metastases. I looked into her kind eyes and was overwhelmed. She had died when I was eighteen years old and not a single day had passed when I didn't think about how much I loved her. She was the best mother anyone could ever have wished for. Completely devoted to God and family, she showered love upon everyone she met but most of all on me.

101

She wiped the tears from my eyes. "My baby boy. I have missed you so much."

"And I have missed you too, Mom. Every single day I think about you."

She held me tightly and said, "There's someone else here, Giannuzzu."

Just then I noticed another person on the bench next to her. How I could not have noticed him I didn't know. It was my father who had died when I was seven. He looked the same as he did the last day I remember seeing him, young and robust. He was small, five foot eight and maybe 170 lb. I was giant in comparison: six feet, 220 lbs.

"Dad!" I threw my arms around him now and burst into tears again. "I've missed you so much."

He rubbed my hair and looked into my eyes. He was barely older than I was now. "My, how you have grown, John. So big and strong, but why are you crying?"

"I'm just so happy."

My mother smiled. "We can't stay long, Giannuzzu. Remember always how much we love you and how much He loves you. Do you remember what I used to tell you?"

I shook my head. "What's that, Mom?"

"Let Him into your heart son. Let Him into your heart."

The light suddenly flashed bright, blinding me and I instinctively drew back, covering my eyes. Then, just as suddenly darkness returned and my parents were gone.

"Mom—Dad—please don't go." I begged and pleaded but they didn't return.

In the distance, I saw another small glimmer but this time I hesitated. After a while, my curiosity got the best of me and I walked toward it. Hours later, as I approached, the light grew stronger and I heard familiar sounds. I felt as if I were leaving a dark jungle heading toward sunlight. I now recognized the sounds of birds chirping and waves rushing in toward a beach. I felt soft sand under my feet, and smelled the salty breeze of ocean air. I found myself on a vast shoreline of white sand with no end in sight in either direction. The ocean was in front of me, clear blue sky above and an ancient virgin forest behind. The trees were as tall as skyscrapers and flocks of seagulls swarmed overhead numbering in the tens of thousands.

As I looked at the pristine blue water, I became aware of a presence by my side and I turned, trying to understand. It was a man but not a man. He was black. No, white. No, Asian. No—. He had blue eyes, brown eyes and green eyes all at the same time. He was everything and all things, and I fell to my knees with arms outstretched, bowing my head in total submission. I dared not speak.

I heard a voice in my head, not my ears. It boomed so loudly I thought my head would explode. "Touch me." The voice commanded.

As I reached out, the figure grew larger and larger such that by the time my hand came within inches I was no longer looking at him, but rather, the side of his foot. His pinky toe was now the size of an elephant. Making contact with him felt like sticking my finger into a high voltage electrical socket, the surge making me shudder. Visions and images flew at my head at light-speed and I was soon overwhelmed and frightened.

We hovered in darkness as the sand, ocean and forest disappeared. There was nothingness all around us. "Watch," said the voice and I peered into the abyss.

There was a tiny popping sound and a miniscule flash of light, barely visible, in the distance. Soon particles of dust appeared far away spreading in every direction. I couldn't be sure what was happening, but in my mind he allowed me comprehension. I had just witnessed the Big Bang, the greatest, most important event in the history of the universe. An explosion hundreds of millions—no, billions, maybe trillions—of times greater than the combined explosive power of every nuclear device on the planet and to him it was nothing more than a firecracker on the Fourth of July. His pinky toe was growing larger every second and I now felt like I was at the bottom of Mount Everest.

Images blew by me now and I had a difficult time focusing. I saw the dawn of man, the Pyramids, the Temple Mount, the Taj Mahal, the Great Wall of China, Moses, Jesus, da Vinci, Gandhi, Einstein, Martin Luther King—mankind at his pinnacle. Then the mood changed abruptly: Genghis Khan, Ivan the Terrible, Stalin, Hitler, Nanking, Auschwitz, Hiroshima—Dick Cheney.

The last images caused me to tremble with fright. "Why do you allow such horrors?" I thought, without meaning for it to be a direct question.

"Man is my most prized creation and free will is the greatest of all gifts I have bestowed on him. Without free will, man is but a marionette. When you *choose* to do great things I am filled with joy and pride."

"But what about all those people who have suffered because of *poor choices*?"

"I love all of my children. Those who have suffered in their mortal lives are blessed and now sit with me at my table. Your earthly existence is but a fraction of eternity. Imagine a small blister on your finger that lasted but a day. Such is earthly suffering compared to eternal bliss."

I wanted to ask what happened to the bad guys but things were moving by me at a dizzying speed, and exhausted, I collapsed. When I opened my eyes again, I was back in the darkness where it all started, but I wasn't alone.

The voice in my head thundered, "Will you follow the light, John?"

"What light?" I looked around in all directions and saw nothing.

Even louder this time so that my head split and I quivered. "Will you follow the light always, John?"

I fell to my knees in obeisance. "Yes, oh Lord, my God, I will follow the light—always."

Chapter 10

There was a cacophony of sounds and I couldn't breathe or move. Something jammed tightly in my throat hurt like hell and I felt like there was an elephant stomping on my chest over and over. I was confused and felt differently than I had moments before. What was happening and why could I hear but not move? Pain—so much pain.

A faraway male voice said, "Okay, people, that's it. There's nothing more we can do here."

What did he mean by that? Suddenly, the elephant on my chest eased up and a woman said, "I can't believe he's gone. I just can't. Isn't there anything more we can do?"

Closer now the man said, "Amy, you've been an ICU nurse for ten years. You know there's nothing more we can do. He's gone. We've been coding him for over an hour. That's way longer than I would have done for anyone else. This is his third cardiac arrest in as many days. His EEG yesterday showed no brain activity whatsoever. He's my friend too, but at this point we're doing him a favor by ending this."

She sniffled. "I know, Dr. Jordan. I just can't believe it."

Another woman said, "What should we do? Did he have family?" The voices were right next to me now, but where was I?

The male voice said, "Amy, turn the ventilator off and I want you and Monica to clean him up. There's a woman out in the waiting room. Her name is Myrtle Rosenblatt. She's his girlfriend. I'll go talk to her and bring her in to see him. I don't know about any family. I know he was an only child and he never spoke about any aunts, uncles or cousins."

I felt someone stroke my head. "John, this is Amy. I'm so sorry. I'm going to miss you. I'm going to miss you a lot." She cried softly as she spoke.

The other woman said with great sympathy, "Amy, I'm sorry, but we have work to do and there are other patients we have to care for. Are you going to be okay or should I get someone else to help me?"

"I'll be fine, Monica. Thank you."

As they adjusted me and cleaned the bed, someone new entered the room. I sensed her emotional pain as she approached me. Her voice quivered and she was nearly hysterical, sobbing uncontrollably. She kissed me on the cheek and forehead. "John, it's Cocoa, I know you can hear me. John, I love you. With all my heart I love you. Remember me. Wherever you are, remember me."

Everyone in the room started sobbing and all of a sudden I felt something I hadn't felt before, something deep inside me. It was small but growing rapidly. It felt like a fuse had been lit and I was going to explode. I suddenly remembered what my mother had said.

"Let Him into your heart."

Then I remembered the thundering voice.

"Will you follow the light, John?"

I will—I will. Oh Lord, I will!

I felt an excruciatingly painful thump in my chest as my heart kick-started. My chest heaved off the bed from the force of it and I squeezed Cocoa's hand as I wheezed and sucked air in through and around the endotracheal tube taped to my face. Cocoa screamed as I lurched forward and my eyes popped open.

The monitors started screaming and beeping as signs of life returned. One of the nurses fainted and the other started yelling for help. Pandemonium ensued as the entire ICU sprang to life in shock, disbelief, and joy.

Soon, the room was packed and a doctor was staring into my face. He ordered Cocoa to leave and she refused, holding onto me for dear life. Someone hooked me back up to the ventilator and I waved at them to take the tube out. My body wanted to be free of all restraints. The doctor was paralyzed with indecision and who could blame him. I had been clinically dead for over an hour and had the burn marks from the electric shocks on my chest to prove it. He gently placed his hands on my shoulders and pushed me back down to a lying position.

He asked gently but firmly. "John, can you hear me?"

It had taken a while for my eyes to focus but I recognized him now. Terry Jordan, the intensivist, who managed the ICU at Saint Matt's. He was a good guy and an expert in critical care medicine. I nodded and gently squeezed his hand. I could see the strain in his face. He was in the middle of something he didn't understand and that his brain told him was impossible.

I looked at Cocoa, squeezed her hand too and then gave everyone in the room a thumbs-up. Word had spread like wildfire and people were spilling out into the hallway as staff from every floor in the hospital had come down to see for themselves. The neurologist, Medhat Saluum, and Arnie Goldstein fought their way to the front of the pack and Terry filled them in on recent events as they stared incredulously at me.

With time, normalcy slowly returned and I gradually started to feel almost as if I had awakened from a deep sleep and could use a cup of coffee. In fact, a cup of coffee would definitely hit the spot right now, but first I needed to convince them to take the tube out of my throat because that was really starting to annoy me. I let go of Cocoa's hand and signaled for a pen and paper which they gave me.

108

I wrote, *Take the damn tube out. I don't need it anymore.* I turned the pad for everyone to see but Jordan shook his head and said, "I don't think that's such a good idea just yet, John. You haven't breathed on your own for over two months. You might not be strong enough."

I was shocked and looked at Cocoa. I wrote on the pad. *How long have I been here?*

Arnie said, "John, you've been in a coma for eight weeks, ever since the shooting."

The shooting? What shooting? Eight weeks? Damn.

I wrote. *What shooting?*

Arnie said, "One thing at a time, all right. We'll talk about that later. We're in uncharted territory here and need to figure out what the right thing to do is."

I wrote again. *What shooting?*

He said, "Do you remember when you went to visit Mrs. Konstandin?"

I did vaguely. Not really. I wrote. *Not a hundred percent.*

"Someone shot you. We don't know why. You've been in a coma ever since."

I thought about that. *Fine, but I don't need the tube so take it out or I'll rip it out myself. It hurts.*

Terry jumped in to help Arnie. "Can we at least let Medhat do a quick neuro exam on you? I'll call respiratory therapy and we'll see how you do on a T-piece. If you can breathe fine on your own we'll yank the tube. I promise we'll move as fast as we safely can."

Okay, but hurry. I have to get out of here. I got a lot to do.

The room broke out into laughter when they saw what I had written. Apparently, no one was taking me seriously. Cocoa smiled broadly and gave me a hug. "I am so happy right now. You couldn't possibly imagine."

I smiled although I was starting to get frustrated. I understood where they were coming from. They didn't want to extubate me too quickly and then have me go into respiratory arrest an hour later. I had seen that happen many times myself. As I thought through how best to convince them I was all right, Medhat stepped forward to examine me. He was the neurologist who had declared me brain-dead yesterday. I waved at him and wrote *Hi Medhat* on my pad.

He smiled. "Hi, John. I see we're having a busy day."

I shrugged.

He nodded and proceeded to examine me. He flashed a light in my eyes, then had me look in a bunch of different directions, squeeze his hands, and raise my legs against resistance. After he tapped on all my joints with a small hammer to test my reflexes he turned to Arnie, Terry and the crowd and announced. "As incredible as this sounds, he's seems totally intact, nonfocal and without any signs of neurological impairment. From my point of view there's no reason to keep him intubated. I say we give him a chance and see what happens."

I wrote, *Thank you, Medhat,* and showed it to him.

Respiratory therapy put me on a T-piece and an hour later I was extubated and sitting up in bed. My throat was sore and my voice weak and hoarse but I had no trouble breathing. The nurses had cleared out and returned to their duties although I noticed the same faces walking by my room over and over to catch a peek. Cocoa sat by me staring in wonderment as a lab tech drew a blood sample from my arm.

She said, "This is nothing short of miraculous. I hope you realize that, John."

"I haven't thought it through yet. From my point of view, all I did was wake up." I whispered. "But I guess it is. How's Cleo?"

"She misses you and cries every night when she realizes you're not there. I took the liberty of moving in completely to take care of her. I hope you don't mind. I can move my stuff out when you're discharged."

I looked at her and smiled. "That won't be necessary and thank you. I really appreciate you doing that."

"So, what's the next step?"

"Dr. Jordan and Dr. Saluum want to run a few tests including a CT scan and they've called a psychiatrist and physical therapy to evaluate me. I haven't moved in months and everybody's worried that I'll be too weak to take care of myself but I feel fine."

"Why are they calling a psychiatrist?"

"Many reasons but most importantly they're concerned about post-traumatic stress and depression. It's not unreasonable. I'm not worried; the shrink they called is Mark Greenberg. He's a friend of mine. We've known each other for twenty years."

She nodded. "I've met Mark. He's been here many times to visit you. He's a very nice person. So, when do you think you'll be released?"

"Technically, I'm not a prisoner and can leave anytime I want as long as I'm strong enough but I'd rather not upset these guys. They're worried about me and I respect that. I'll let them do whatever it is they feel they need to do to satisfy themselves as long as it's within reason. Besides, Arnie says the police want to talk to me about what happened and he would like to have his own little debriefing as well."

"What did happen, John?"

I hesitated as I thought that over. "I'm not really sure. You probably know more than I do. I remember walking into the apartment building to talk to Mrs. Konstandin but not much after that."

"That's it? That's all you remember?"

111

"I'm trying hard but I'm not there yet. Just some vague things, like an old sofa, stuff like that. Why don't you tell me what you know?"

"Well, I only know what's been on the news. We went to breakfast at a small run-down diner on First Avenue across the street from Mrs. Konstandin's apartment building. After we ate, you went to interview her and I waited for you in the diner. An hour later, when you didn't return or answer your cell phone, I started to get concerned but didn't know what to do. I just thought that maybe the situation required a little more handholding than you had thought, but by early afternoon, when I didn't hear from you, I knew something was wrong. I hadn't seen you come out from the building so I went there myself to find you. Someone must have discovered the crime scene because as I crossed First Avenue, police cars and ambulances began swarming the place. By five o'clock you were the headline news on all the networks. It was terrible. There were three dead people found in the apartment, Mrs. Konstandin, her sister and you. Only you weren't quite dead—almost. The EMT guys managed to resuscitate you but you had lost so much blood and were unresponsive for so long no one thought you would ever regain consciousness."

As she spoke a hazy recollection returned. I said, "I remember something now. When I went to the apartment no one answered. There was a neighbor, a middle-aged woman with a thick accent. She let me into the apartment. I didn't know they were sisters. They're both dead?"

"Yes, Mrs. Konstandin was found drowned in her bath tub and her sister Katrina was shot in the head. The police think that you and her sister may have interrupted the murder in progress. It's possible that whoever it was may have been trying to set Mrs. Konstandin's death up as an accidental drowning like maybe she had a heart attack while bathing."

"And me? What happened to me?"

"Well, they think the sister surprised the murderer while you were in the living room, and he shot her. When he went to leave he found you there and that's all we know."

"Damn. I got to get out of here. Hey, how's Tony?"

"Your friend who jumped? I don't know. I've been sort of preoccupied. I haven't heard anything bad though, and why do you have to get out of here?"

I hesitated, not sure. "People have been murdered, Cocoa."

"That's not your problem, John. This is a police investigation not a Cesari investigation. Your job is to get better."

"I am better and anybody who thinks they can shoot me and get away with it is my problem."

She smiled and shook her head, exasperated.

I said, "Do me a favor. Would you mind going to the cafeteria and getting me two cheeseburgers and fries? I'll never get better if I don't eat and I'm starving. I'm going to pass out soon if I don't get some real food in me. This stuff they're pouring into the IV just isn't cutting it. And tell my nurse to come in here. I need this catheter taken out of my penis. It's killing me."

She laughed. "Well, I have to say. You really do sound as if you're back and in rare form too. I'll go get you some food but I better not get into any trouble with the nurses or doctors. They didn't want you to eat just yet."

The nurse had taken out the catheter by the time Cocoa returned with a tuna sandwich, chips and a coke. "Sorry, no cheeseburgers."

I wolfed down the sandwich and food never tasted better. As I finished and was wiping my face with a napkin Arnie came in with Terry Jordan.

Terry rolled his eyes when he saw me eating. "I thought I told you I didn't want you to eat anything yet?" He gave Cocoa a sideways glance and she looked away.

"Sorry, Terry. I just couldn't take it anymore. My body is screaming for food."

"Cesari, you should know better than anybody that after prolonged lack of use the intestines have to be gently reintroduced to normal food. Well, don't be shocked if you throw up later or have diarrhea."

"Relax, it was just a tuna sandwich."

"Fine."

"Look, guys. I feel great but I don't know how much longer I can sit still."

Arnie jumped in. "Okay, Cesari. I can see you're starting to be your old irritating self but cut us some slack here. We've been in mourning over you for two months and just a few hours ago you were pronounced dead. Now you're begging to run laps around the nursing station. Give us some time to adjust, all right? We've got a lot of unanswered questions here, not the least of which is whether you're going to suddenly collapse on us after you've exhausted your newfound wind."

I sighed. "You're right. I'm sorry. I'll be patient. It's just that I really feel fine."

"Okay, we got that part. Give us at least a day or two to sort things out. By the way, your friend Greenberg is coming by after his office hours today to do whatever it is shrinks do. Are you sure you feel all right?"

"I'm not lying. I feel like I could run a marathon right now and that truly is amazing."

"And why is that?"

"Because I never felt like I could run one before. I hate running. I've always been a weight room guy."

Arnie took a deep breath. "You better not drop dead tonight, Cesari." He said goodbye and left the room. Terry and Cocoa chuckled.

I said, "He doesn't seem too happy for me."

Jordan said, "Arnie's just being Arnie. He is actually ecstatic. He's been feeling terribly guilty about sending you to that apartment."

"He told you about that?"

"He told the whole world. He had to. The police were crawling all over the place trying to figure out why one of our doctors was slumming it with a couple of Albanian immigrants in a dilapidated, should-be-condemned, apartment building. He had to put the kibosh on the notion that maybe you were there for shall we say—*romantic purposes*."

Cocoa giggled and I said, "You're kidding!"

"I'm just saying."

I laughed. "Oh, brother." I looked at Cocoa who found this very amusing.

"Seriously now, Cesari. Do you really feel fine? Try to understand why this is so hard to accept. You've taken care of sick people. They don't just jump out of bed after two months of being in a coma and multiple cardiac arrests."

"Move your chair away, Terry, and let me show you how I feel."

He slid his chair away from the side of the bed and I quickly pulled my covers off and stood up in front of him in my hospital gown. By all rights, I should have at least been a little unsteady but I wasn't. Cocoa clapped and cried at the same time. Terry's jaw dropped and his eyes grew wide. I said jokingly, "Want me to do jumping jacks? How about push-ups?"

Before he could stop me I fell to the floor and cranked out twenty-five push-ups easily. I got back in the bed not in the least winded or fatigued. Indeed, I was feeling stronger with each passing second. He didn't say anything but looked like he was going to pass out. "Terry, are you okay? I didn't mean to startle you."

He took a deep breath and let it out. "Goddamn, I've never seen anything like this. I've never even heard of anything like this. It's just impossible."

"Look, Terry, I don't know what to say. Maybe my body just went dormant like in a simulated deep freeze and now I'm all defrosted and ready to go. Look at Lance Armstrong. He survived widely metastatic cancer and is totally cured. Everybody thought that would have been impossible at the time, let alone his going on to win the Tour de France several more times."

"Yeah, but he cheated."

"Indeed he did, as did everyone else he was racing against, so the playing field really was level. Besides, most experts agree that in all probability, he would have won even without the use of performance enhancers. He was that good."

He nodded. "Maybe. Look, Cesari, there's something I have to tell you..." He hesitated to finish.

"Go ahead, Terry. I'm pretty much convinced that nothing could surprise me at the moment."

"When you first came in, you were in shock, hemorrhaging badly. One bullet had lacerated your spleen, barely missing your aorta and the other went through your trachea. You went right to the OR with ENT, vascular, and general surgery working side by side. They removed your spleen and part of your small bowel. Twelve hours into it they were finally able to stop the bleeding and get you stabilized."

"Well, they all did a great job, apparently. I'll send them a basket of fruit, and maybe buy them dinner."

"The problem I have is that the surgeons couldn't remove the bullet from the abdomen. It was a 9 mm slug that concluded its journey by ramming through your spinal cord, effectively dissecting it and taking up permanent residence there. Neurosurgical and orthopedic consults were called and everyone agreed that the best course of action was to leave it there for the time being and maybe come back at a future date to try to remove it if you survived. Post-operatively, you went into septic shock, respiratory failure and acute renal failure from peritonitis. You've been on hemodialysis for weeks. Naturally, the bullet lodged in your spine became a back-burner issue since no one gave you much of a chance of making it out of here except in a body bag."

"Sounds bad."

"It was bad and gets worse. Neurologically, you were a mess and difficult to assess because of everything that was going on but everyone agreed on one thing."

"And what was that?"

"Stand up for me again, Cesari?"

I stood up. "Now what?"

"Walk to the door and back."

When I returned, I sat back down on the bed and looked at him. "So, what did everyone agree on?"

He said, "That if by some miracle you did live, you would most certainly never walk again. Cesari, don't you see how impossible this is? The bullet transected your spinal cord and it's still there. You were completely flaccid from the waist down for weeks. It is simply not possible that you are walking right now. It defies everything we know about neuroscience and anatomy."

"And yet here I am. Is that why we're getting the CT scan tomorrow? To see if the bullet has moved?"

"Yes."

I nodded. "Did my blood work from earlier today come back yet?"

"Yes."

"And?"

"You're not in renal failure anymore. Again, impossible." He shook his head slowly. He was simply at a loss for words and had no explanation.

There was a knock on the door and we both looked up. It was Mark Greenberg, my psychiatrist and friend. I no longer saw him professionally but we'd been through a lot together and I trusted him. "Hi Mark."

He was in his mid-fifties, with a deeply receding hairline, black-framed bifocals, maybe five foot six and 160 lbs. dripping wet. He nodded at Terry and said, "Hey there, Cesari. Welcome back. Hello, Cocoa."

Cocoa returned the greeting and Terry stood up, saying, "I'll be going now and let Mark do his thing but we'll talk more, okay?" Terry waved at Cocoa and Mark as he left the room.

"Sure thing, Terry. It's good to see you Mark. Grab a chair."

He sat next to me and took a yellow pad from his leather briefcase. Clicking on a pen, he crossed his legs and looked at me like he was studying an object in a museum. "I'm not here right now as your friend. You do realize that, don't you?"

I nodded. "Arnie told me that I have to undergo psychiatric evaluation before they can discharge me. They don't want me leaving here and throwing myself in front of the first bus I see."

He nodded. "Or walking into a crowded movie theater with an assault rifle because you think you've been to the other side and want everyone else to have the same joyous experience."

Boy, he got right to the point. "Got it."

"Do you think it might be better if Cocoa left the room?" he asked.

"Whatever you think is best, Mark, but as far as I'm concerned Cocoa has earned my trust and I don't have anything to hide from her."

He nodded. "Okay. I'm comfortable with that. Besides, we've gotten to know each other pretty well these last two

118

months. We'll talk about what a nice Jewish girl is doing with the likes of you at another session. Before we begin I just want to say one thing…"

"I'm getting a lot of that today."

He looked carefully at me and I could see his eyes water up. His voice cracked just a little. "I can't even begin to tell you how happy I am that you're alive." He took off his glasses and wiped his eyes. "I'm sorry."

I took his hand in mine. "Thank you, Mark, and I can't tell you how happy I am to be alive."

"Okay then. So much for my Freudian objectivity. Ready to begin?"

Chapter 11

Sitting at a small table in the bar of the SoHo Grand Hotel on West Broadway, Rutherford Cecil McCormick strummed his fingers and studied his son. He was furious. They spoke in hushed tones even though the place was empty except for the bartender watching a ballgame at the other end of the room. "Interesting turn of events, wouldn't you say, Duncan?" he asked, his voice dripping with sarcasm.

They had just learned of Cesari's full recovery and release from the hospital, which was on every news station. The younger man let out a deep sigh and nodded. "Agreed, Father. It seems impossible, if you ask me. I checked; he didn't even have a pulse when I left him."

"Apparently, he did. Tell me again why you felt all that mayhem was necessary?"

"Mrs. Konstandin repeatedly refused my offers of compensation for her husband's untimely demise. She was adamant about suing Unicare and was even threatening to go to the press. She forced my hand, really. It was almost like she wanted me to kill her. Then Esha found out this Cesari person had stumbled upon certain irregularities in the medical record and was performing a spirited investigation to clear his friend's good name. Even worse, was that she discovered that he was on his way to personally debrief Mrs. Konstandin so I decided I had to act decisively. I really think you should be patting me on the back for my quick-witted determination. If our ancestors had acted with similar resolve, we would be the world's sole remaining superpower and the colonials would still be buying our tea."

"Bollocks, lad! I've coddled you too much. Go on."

"Well, at any rate, for better or for worse, I decided the Konstandin woman needed to be silenced in a more permanent fashion. The idea was to have the police find Cesari in the apartment with the murdered Konstandin woman. The obvious suggestion being that he was either trying to silence her from defaming his friend or as an act of vengeance for causing him to jump out a window. The other woman, her sister, caught me by surprise in the bathroom as I was just getting ready to leave through the fire escape and call 911 to sic them on Cesari, anticipating his arrival there. With the sister dead too, the story wouldn't hold up, and I couldn't bloody well leave Cesari alive to piece things together. The rest you know."

Deeply frustrated, the older McCormick said, "Indeed I do. The rest is that you went on a murderous rampage. What is it about this damned country that makes people commit mass murder?"

"Technically, it wasn't mass murder, Father."

"The hell you say."

"The FBI defines mass murder as the murder of four or more people so technically it wasn't a mass murder. It's a fine line, I know."

Now thoroughly annoyed, the old man hissed, "Don't play word games with me. I'm not some silly harlot you've just bedded for the night and are trying to impress with your intellect."

"I'm sorry, Father, but remember, it was you who said make her an offer she couldn't refuse. Well, she refused and I didn't feel that I had many options especially with Cesari on the way to interview her. He would certainly have found out that I had been talking to her."

"When I said make her an offer she couldn't refuse I meant money, Duncan, and lots of it. Everyone has a price. For God's sake, drowning the woman in her own bathtub? Are you daft? If I didn't know better I'd think you had some type of learning disability." The senior McCormick took a deep breath and let it out. "Duncan, I have big plans for you—big plans. This isn't the seventeenth century anymore. People don't like world leaders to have blood on their hands." He paused to take a sip of whiskey from the glass in front of him. He savored the liquid before swallowing it. Calming down, he said. "Okay, water under the bridge. Could this Cesari person possibly identify you?"

"He did see me briefly, so maybe, but with everything he's been through I would think it highly unlikely."

"That's just grand, isn't it, the future Leader of the House of Lords, confidant to the queen herself, fresh from his financial conquest of America being identified as a suspect in a double homicide by some peasant immigrant physician in the states? That will give them something to chortle about in their sitting rooms as our family name goes down in flames once again. Don't you realize, Duncan, that our family was stripped of its titles and land years ago because of a similar scandal?"

Duncan nodded. "Yes, I am familiar with great-grandfather's salacious behavior."

His brow furrowed, Rutherford mused, "Can we discredit this Cesari chap? I have contacts in the news industry. Is he even here legally? We should look into that. That's a big thing these days."

The younger man reasoned through the problem at hand. "I don't know about that, Father. He's a bit of a hero right now. Trying to smear him might not go over well."

"Well, we can't bloody well have this doctor give your description to some New York City police sketch artist, can we? In less than six months, your name will be on the cover of every newspaper and magazine of note in the world as I hand over the reins of McCormick Enterprises to my heir. We are almost at the tipping point in Parliament as well. With any luck, the title of Earl of Wessex will be returned to me by year's end, and with our family name vindicated, I can live out my old age in peace. The only thing holding you back is your youth but a few years of running roughshod over the colonists ought to give you the credibility you need. No, the more I think about it, the clearer it becomes. This Yank, guinea, or whatever he chooses to identify as, is going to have to take one for the team as they say; team McCormick, that is. For better or worse, we have no choice but to go down the rabbit hole after him. Do you follow me lad? But you cannot be personally involved this time, Duncan. That was reckless of you."

"I understand, Father."

"Do you?"

"Whatever do you mean, Father?"

"I mean that I am well aware of how much you enjoy the *hands-on* approach. You are very much like your great-grandfather in that regard."

"He was never found guilty, I believe."

"And with any luck, neither will you, but we live in a different age now. Murdering chambermaids after they've been sexually assaulted is now frowned upon even by the upper crust of society."

"A shame."

"Yes, without doubt. I'll call Leo and tell him we have a problem."

"Leo? The lawyer from Philadelphia? But we have plenty of lawyers right here in New York."

"Leo Rosenblatt is much more than a lawyer. He'll know what to do."

Chapter 12

$\mathcal{I}$ sat in my apartment staring at Cleo lying on the floor in front of me. It had been just over two weeks since my discharge from the hospital and I was bored to tears. I felt great but Arnie had insisted I go to outpatient physical therapy as well as take at least a month off from work to clear my head and smell the roses. I didn't think I needed to, but he was adamant. He said if I wanted to attend academic conferences I could but generally he wanted me to relax, lay low and keep my stress to a minimum. Since I was working for the hospital at the time of the shooting, he convinced the board that this was a form of work-related injury so they kept me on the payroll the entire time I was out. That was nice and the electronic deposits kept my bank account solvent. Cocoa had been paying my rent and other bills for me and I needed to settle up with her post haste.

I needed something to do. Tony had survived his injury but was in long-term rehab recovering physically and receiving intensive psychiatric counseling for depression. There were rumors circulating that he was delusional. He declined any visitors, including me, which left one last bit of unfinished business—Kelly.

Cocoa told me that she had come to the hospital to visit me several times when I was in a coma. Apparently they were pals now. Kelly and I had a long and sordid history which had come to a climax when she dumped me and married Omar, the accountant. Shortly after the dumping, she found out she was pregnant with twin girls, Beatrice and Gwendolyn, who were now approaching a year old. She claimed they were Omar's kids and I was forced to accept that but I never did. I didn't like Omar and thought he was an asshole. I told him so on several occasions including that spirited yelling match months ago when he found me naked under Kelly's bed.

That incident led to Kelly obtaining a restraining order against me. The judge was black, Kelly and Omar were black and the children were black. I was the odd man out and the judge had no sympathy. In fact, I'm surprised I didn't get jail time. I was clearly the victim of racial discrimination but no one cared. It was nice that she had come to visit me. She even told Cocoa that if I survived, she might drop the restraining order but I wasn't holding my breath on that one.

I tried to clear my mind of the clutter and focus in on the matter at hand. Like what the hell happened that morning in the Konstandin apartment. My memory of events was sketchy and unclear at best. I felt like there was a giant puzzle in front of me. I was trying to fit one small piece in at a time and making little progress. Everyone keeps saying that it's a miracle I'm alive and I accept that but it has no meaning really. I feel the way I do and that's all I know. I don't feel particularly special or different. Well, that wasn't necessarily true. I felt like running and I didn't know why because I never liked to run. It was a very boring activity and I had flat feet so after a couple of miles I was always in pain.

The desire to run, however, was almost overwhelming. I decided to give in to the craving so I went into the bedroom and put on a cotton T-shirt, shorts and sneakers. Filling Cleo's water bowl, I said, "I'll be right back girl, okay?"

She lay on her bed and pouted. Outside I looked at my watch and took off at a slow jog up Fifth Avenue. I smiled inwardly knowing that Arnie would have a fit if he saw me. It was one in the afternoon and a beautiful early autumn day in the city. The leaves were changing and the air was damp. After ten minutes, I expected to be winded from deconditioning but I wasn't. After twenty minutes, I expected to be bored and sucking wind but I wasn't. In fact, I felt great. My feet didn't hurt, my lungs felt great, and the girls looked pretty. I was riding an endorphin rush the likes of which I had never experienced. I soon zoned out and got lost in thought.

The police had interviewed me the day after I left the hospital but I didn't have much to tell them. I hadn't met Mrs. Konstandin and had no idea who might want to kill her or her sister, let alone me too. Apparently robbery wasn't a motive as nothing was missing from the apartment, and for the record, neither woman was sexually assaulted. They asked if the murders could have had anything to do with why I was there in the first place. I couldn't even begin to see why and finally they wanted to know if I saw who shot me. This was the most difficult question to answer. From the wounds I received it was obvious that I had been facing my assailant, but for the life of me I could not remember anything other than in the vaguest way. In my mind, I saw a dark shadow and a flash of light but that was all. Call us if you remember anything, they said and then they left.

I asked Arnie about the Konstandin situation and he said that since she was dead, so was the threat of legal action against the hospital. As far as he was concerned, it was time to turn the page. There was no legitimate explanation for what had happened other than Tony had fucked up one way or the other, and since he was suffering enough already, might as well let sleeping dogs lie. The attorney representing the hospital, Gary Ippolito, had advised him to bury the whole thing.

Still, there was something that didn't sit well with my recollection of things, sketchy as they were. In my mind's eye, it was like looking at a portrait of a man and woman and suddenly realizing that one of the hands had six fingers. Tony jumps out a window because he has underlying depression and feels guilty over his mistake which led to a patient's death. The patient's wife requests to speak with someone from the hospital and when I go to her apartment we all wind up dead, but why? I must have been collateral damage because no one knew I was going to visit the wife other than Cocoa, but no, that wasn't quite true. Arnie knew I was going to talk to her but he didn't know when or where. What about that lawyer, Esha Deshmukh? I had told her about the meeting. Who was she anyway? It was coming back to me now.

Passing the Metropolitan Museum of Art and Mount Sinai Hospital, I reached the upper end of the east side of Central Park and turned left on 110th Street to jog back down to the Village from the west side. The neighborhood I passed had taken a decided turn for the worse as I passed the Lincoln Correctional Facility on the north end of Central Park so I instinctively picked up the pace and gleefully noted that I did so without the slightest bit of resentment from my heart, lungs and legs. Rounding the corner down Columbus Avenue, I was now running briskly and barely concerned about fatigue. It was midday, and I had to occasionally dodge traffic and pedestrians which simply served to make my activity all the more fun, soon becoming a game for me.

Most New Yorkers ignored me but those who watched did so with great curiosity, probably wondering how long I could keep up my pace. I wondered the same thing but put it out of my mind as I passed Broadway and realized I was at the entrance to Juilliard. I stopped and took my pulse. It was barely over sixty beats per minute and although I was fatigued, I should have been lying on the floor panting, waiting for an ambulance. Looking at my watch, I was surprised to see that it was just after two. I had been running for over an hour and had covered close to ten miles. Damn, that was unbelievable. I had never run that far in my entire life and at just over six minutes a mile, maybe closer to six and a half minutes. Not bad at all. In fact, rather incredible.

Spotting Cocoa walking toward me with her briefcase jammed to overflowing with sheet music, I waved to get her attention. She saw me and smiled. As she came closer she grew concerned. "What are you doing up here and why are you dressed like that? Yuck, you're soaking wet. Is that sweat? Are you okay? What have you been doing?"

"I was feeling good so I went for a run."

She rolled her eyes. "You can't be serious? John, you just got out of the hospital. What are you trying to do? Get re-admitted?"

"I couldn't help it. I needed to move. I can't explain it any other way."

"C'mon, let's go back to the loft. You're all gross. C'mon, the subway is only two blocks away."

"You sure you don't want to run with me?" I asked smiling.

"Very sure. How's Cleo?"

"Upset that I left her alone."

We chatted as we entered the Lincoln Center subway station, bought our tickets and went through the gate. Our train was right there so we boarded and took seats.

"I don't blame her. Running around Manhattan in midday. That's more dangerous than getting shot. So what'd you do, take the train up here and run in the park?"

"No, I ran up Fifth Avenue from the loft."

She studied me carefully to see if I was joking. "You're fibbing."

I looked at her deadpanned. "No, I ran down Waverly Place, made a left on Fifth Avenue, ran up the east side of the park to

110th Street, made a left and came down Columbus Avenue to Lincoln Center where I found you."

Cocoa was astonished. "How far is that?"

"Not sure but my internal odometer is reading it at about ten miles."

"Your internal odometer?"

"Yeah, I can't explain that either. It's just that as I was running, there was something about my speed and the length of my stride that just kind of did a rough calculation of distance for me."

"And how do you feel?"

"Great."

"Aren't you thirsty or tired?"

"Yeah, a little."

"A little...?"

She stopped talking, staring at me or more specifically, my neck, and I asked. "What's the matter?"

"Pick up your T-shirt. I want to see something."

"What?"

"Just pick up your shirt. Will you?"

I lifted my T-shirt so she could see my abdomen. Several people in our car watched but most politely ignored our antics. Staring at strangers on the subway was a sure way of getting into trouble.

"John, the surgical scars are gone from your abdomen and neck. Didn't you notice?"

Until now, I hadn't. I tried to remember if I had seen them when I woke this morning but couldn't. Certainly, when I left the hospital they were there. "No, I didn't. Not until just now." I pulled my shirt back down.

Cocoa was very concerned as the train pulled into our stop and we got off. The loft was a block away.

She asked, "What does this mean?"

"I'm a fast healer?"

She wasn't amused. "I want you to call Arnie and tell him about all this, including your little half-marathon."

"Sure, I was going to call him anyway. Bits and pieces of things are starting to come back to me and I wanted to ask him something."

In the loft, I showered and looked at myself in the mirror as I dressed. Not a trace of residual scars anywhere. I rubbed my throat to see if I could feel some irregularity but couldn't. This was very strange and yet didn't bother me in the slightest. The medical literature was rife with anecdotal stories of people who had survived worse scenarios than me and the fact that I was a fast healer—big deal. So I had good genes.

I lay on the bed and called Arnie as the sound of the television drifted in from the living room. "Hey, Arnie, this is Cesari."

"Hi John, how are you feeling?"

"Very well, thank you."

"I was just thinking about calling you, Cesari. I have the results of your last CT scan in front of me."

"The scan from two weeks ago?"

"Yeah well, at the time they didn't see the bullet that was supposed to have been lodged in your spine and we just assumed that it had migrated to some other place and wasn't showing up for some reason. Unlikely, yes, but it could happen. The point is we were focused too hard on that and missed something else equally extraordinary."

He paused and I said, "I'm listening?"

"Your spleen is back. I was reviewing your scans again with radiology today. We were going to use them at a teaching conference with the medical students and house staff. When you came in you underwent an emergency splenectomy because the bullet had passed through it, but there it is completely intact like nothing happened."

Now I took a deep breath. "Are you sure you have the right scan up, Arnie?"

"I have the right scan up, John. I've been looking at it over and over for the last hour. It's you all right. I have no idea what this means. This is beyond impossible."

"Okay, Arnie, don't lose it on me, all right. There has to be some logical explanation. I mean, spleens can regenerate, can't they? And hospitals screw up and mislabel reports all the time. That's probably what happened. My guess is they put the wrong name on the scan."

Arnie was quiet as he thought it over. "Spleens do regenerate but not in that short a period of time, and I guess a mislabeled report is a possibility. Okay, I'll check all the scans done that day to see if I can find one with a bullet and no spleen. It'll take some time though. We must do a couple of hundred CT scans every day."

"Well, I'm glad we solved that. Now, I need to ask you a few questions. You told me the lawyer representing the hospital with the Konstandin case was a guy named Gary Ippolito, right?"

"Yeah, and …?"

"Well, the day before I went to the Konstandin apartment, a British woman named Esha Deshmukh, called me and identified herself as the lawyer representing the hospital. She told me that the hospital had referred her to me. She sounded legit so I spoke with her. You had told me that there were going to be two parallel investigations into the Konstandin case and I assumed that's who she was."

"What did you tell her?"

"That's not the point. Have you ever heard of her?"

"No, and that is definitely the point. What did you tell her?"

"Nothing really because I didn't know anything and still don't but the cops asked an interesting question that got me thinking. They asked me if I thought the shooting at the apartment had anything to do with the reason I was visiting her. I told them that I had no idea but couldn't see why it would. Well, that made me start thinking about who knew I would be visiting her and I definitely remember telling this Esha woman I was going there and what time I would be there."

"I see your point, but that would imply that you were targeted for assassination and not simply a victim of random violence. That's a whole different can of very paranoid worms."

"Yes, it is."

"Look, before you start dwelling on morbid things like that, can you answer the simple question of why anyone would want you dead?"

I laughed at that and thought about all my ex-girlfriends, not the least of whom was Kelly. Before I could respond however, he continued. "Besides, what could possibly justify a triple homicide like that? I mean, you were just going there to let the woman use you as a scratching post. If somebody wanted you dead, they could have waited for you to leave the apartment."

"I don't know, Arnie. I'm just grasping at straws, trying to connect whatever dots I can."

"Well, look, I never heard of this woman, Esha, but that doesn't mean she tried to kill you. Maybe she works with Gary. I'll look into it. Don't jump to conclusions just yet."

"I won't. By the way, she said she works for a law firm called Darby, Smith and Tasker. Is that Gary's law firm?"

"Yes, it is, see? Gary probably asked her to make contact with you. I'll call him later and check into it, but it's probably no big deal. Okay, look, I've got to go. You've just given me God knows how much work between reviewing those CT scans and tracking down Gary. Say hello to Myrtle."

I hung up, went into the living room and sat on the sofa next to Cocoa.

"How's Dr. Goldstein?" she asked.

"He's good. He said hi."

"What did he say about the wounds?"

"I forgot to mention it."

She looked at me sternly. "Forgot or neglected to mention it?"

"Be nice to me. I just got out of the hospital."

She pushed me playfully. "If you want sympathy, you can't be running marathons."

I nodded. "Good point. Are you up for an adventure?"

"Like what?"

"Let's go back to Mrs. Konstandin's apartment and have a look around. I was thinking that it might jog my memory a little and who knows, maybe the cops missed something."

"You can't be serious? John, you need to drop the whole thing. It's over. She's dead, no one's suing anybody, and you need to rest."

I looked at her very seriously. "I really want to know who shot me. Besides, rest? Really? I've been sleeping for two months."

She got quiet and shook her head in disapproval. I said, "Please."

"Don't whine."

Chapter 13

As we entered the apartment building and walked up the stairs, I was suddenly filled with great trepidation. I barely remembered being here and although everyone had told me what had happened, it didn't carry any personal significance because my recollection of events was so cloudy. It was different now, being here in person, smelling the damp, humid air and feeling the old worn, wooden bannister. When we arrived at the third floor apartment, I was relieved to see the yellow police tape still crisscrossed over the entrance which meant no one had rented it yet. That made sense. Who would rent an apartment so soon after such a horrendous tragedy?

I pulled the tape away and checked the door knob to see if it was locked. It was. Looking at Cocoa, I mulled over what to do. It was 7:00 p.m. and I was in a low- rent apartment building on the east side of Manhattan. There were five other apartments on this floor and I knew that the one next door was in deep mourning. Mrs. Konstandin's sister had been married and who knew what kind of condition her husband was in. Most likely the I-could-care-less-if-I-heard-someone-break-into-my-dead-sister-in-law's-apartment condition. The other apartments were at the far end of the hallway so any sounds we made wouldn't be heard as well there.

I grabbed the handle, looked around one last time, took a deep breath, and lunged my shoulder forcefully into the wooden door. It flung open and I practically tumbled into the apartment off balance. The door hadn't been locked, just jammed tightly because of the humidity causing the wood to expand. Cocoa grabbed the back of my shirt to help me stay upright. We closed the door behind us and turned on a light.

Cocoa looked around and whispered, "Not a very big place, is it?"

"No, and I'm having trouble believing that I let myself get ambushed here."

"Just be thankful you're alive and talking about it."

"I am, Cocoa. Believe me, I am. All right, let's look around."

The kitchen was small. All the food had been taken out of the refrigerator and the plug had been pulled. The cabinets as well were empty. The living room revealed a blood-stained carpet in front of the sofa, which I presumed was where I had gone down. I looked at Cocoa and she nodded apprehensively. I had asked the police to go over in great detail with me their reconstruction of events and now I tried to imagine it in my mind. I had been sitting on the sofa; that much I remembered. I stood, turning toward the bedroom as I heard someone approach and then was shot twice, once in the abdomen and again in the neck. From the position I was found in, it appeared that I had been taken completely by surprise by the shooter. I lost consciousness shortly thereafter. The bullets found in Mrs. Konstandin's sister's head and the one in my neck were both 9 mm rounds and were fired at close range from the same gun. No one in the other apartments had heard anything, so the weapon had either been silenced or New Yorkers were so damned numb to violence they didn't notice or care.

"Are you okay?" Cocoa asked watching me stare at the carpet.

I nodded. "Just trying to bring it back but not doing too well. Let's go into the bedroom."

The Konstandin sleeping quarters were efficient with a full-sized bed, a small night table on either side and a wooden bureau at the foot. The bathroom was on the opposite side of the room from the entrance and with both the bathroom and bedroom doors closed it could explain why I might not have heard a weapon discharge when he killed her sister. Even silenced weapons made some noise. It was a great misconception promoted by Hollywood that silenced handguns were totally silent. I was more than a little preoccupied with how I got bushwhacked mainly because I had spent most of my life developing instincts for such situations. Plus, I wanted to learn from the experience—just in case.

The bathroom was small and had been wiped clean. There was an old-fashioned porcelain tub and shower combo to the right as we entered the room, along with the toilet and a small, empty linen closet. The door opened inward and I guessed the assailant had hidden behind it when the sister entered. He probably closed the door quickly behind her and before she could even register surprise or fear she was lying on the floor dead. She was found face down by the side of the tub with a bullet hole in the back of her head and the theory was that she entered the room, saw her sister dead in the tub, became transfixed by the sight, and didn't notice what was going on behind her. While she stared at her sister frozen in horror, he placed the gun up to the back of her head. She never had a chance. I thought about that. Not a great way to die but not the worst way either. No pain, no fear. Well, a little fear.

Cocoa said, "C'mon, John, this place is giving me the creeps. There's nothing here."

"Hang on, Cocoa. I need to think things through."

Back in the bedroom, I searched through the night tables and bureau but they were empty and the bed had been stripped down. I searched underneath the bed but found nothing. There was a small window which led out to a metal fire escape and I looked down into a small alley between this and the neighboring apartment building. The alley was narrow but wide enough for a car to fit in. It dead ended on one side and fed into First Avenue on the other. The fire escape was made of rusted wrought iron and looked rickety. The window was unlocked and I suddenly remembered that the sister had told me Mrs. Konstandin was afraid of being trapped in her apartment in the event of a fire so she never locked her door. I wondered if she never locked her window for the same reason. If she never locked her window, had the assassin come into the apartment that way? Why would he go through that trouble if the door was unlocked? Maybe he didn't know that or maybe he didn't want to take a chance on one of the neighbors seeing him. So what did he gain by killing a poor, grieving immigrant woman? The cops said nothing was stolen. Not from the apartment or from my person. I had a wallet full of credit cards and cash, and not a penny was missing.

I sighed deeply in frustration. No repressed memories flooding to the surface of my consciousness as I had hoped; just pieces of a puzzle circling about aimlessly. "Cocoa, I want to try an experiment. I'm going to sit on the sofa like I did when I first came here that morning. I want you to stay here in the bedroom with the door closed for about five minutes to give me time to try to recreate events in my mind as best I can. Then I want you to enter the living room, okay?"

"You want me to stay in here alone? Are you kidding? I'm already freaking out just being here."

"C'mon, it's just five minutes and I'm right on the other side of the door. What could happen?"

She rolled her eyes. "I knew I shouldn't have come here."

"You'll be fine, but please don't make any sounds while you're waiting and don't announce yourself when you come in. Just open the door and enter, okay? Remember, give me five minutes."

"Fine."

I closed the door to the bedroom and took a seat on the sofa, looking down at the blood-stained carpet again. What a mess this must have been when they found me. I felt bad for the first responders. What a job. They were always coming across scenes like this and worse.

I closed my eyes and willed myself to remember. I thought about what had happened. Tony had missed a cancer or erroneously documented the chart causing a distraught Mr. Konstandin to shoot himself rather than be a financial burden on his family because Unicare wouldn't pay for his medical expenses. Unicare wouldn't cover his claim because of what Tony had written in the chart. Mrs. Konstandin was upset with Tony, naturally, but was even more upset with Unicare. Unicare, Unicare, Unicare. I came to talk to Mrs. Konstandin to show support and let her vent. Her sister let me into the apartment and I sat on the sofa just like I was. Just like I was— it was coming back to me, in dribs and drabs but definitely coming back.

I remembered. The sister had gone into the bedroom as I waited. I heard a sound and thought it was either Mrs. Konstandin or her sister returning. I stood and turned. There was a man, a flash of light and a muffled explosion. I felt pain and surprise. Why? Another flash of light, more pain. I couldn't breathe. The neck wound. I fell backwards onto the coffee table, gasping for air, terrible pain in my abdomen and throat—then nothing.

Something was wrong.

I opened my eyes but couldn't see anything. The room had gone dark. I called out to Cocoa frantically but she didn't respond. I stood up frightened looking for a light switch and realized I couldn't even find a wall let alone a switch. I was alone in the black silence.

A voice in my head boomed. "Follow the light."

Suddenly in the distance, I saw a small glimmering light which grew with each step I took toward it. Soon the light overwhelmed me and I closed my eyes, falling to my knees, overwhelmed by its brightness. It penetrated my eyelids and entered my brain. I felt a pain in my head from which I couldn't escape.

"What are you trying to show me?" I shouted. "What do you want from me?"

Suddenly, the light went out and I was sitting in darkness again. In front of me a movie started to play as if I were in a large theater, only it was me on the screen. I was watching a replay of the night Cocoa and I had been to dinner at Babbo and we ran into Julie, my secretary. I had just finished introducing Cocoa to her.

I said, "So, what's the occasion, Julie? Somebody's birthday?"

"No, Ronnie from Unicare takes all the secretaries out every so often to show his appreciation."

What the hell did this mean? The movie abruptly ended and the pain in my head returned. Throbbing, intense—I felt like my brain was on fire. I started sobbing uncontrollably. Where was Cocoa? Why had she abandoned me?

"Cocoa? Cocoa? I need you!"

The ground beneath me started to tremble and then gave way like an earthquake. I was shaking all over and felt myself starting to fall when I heard a voice from far away. "John, I'm here. It's Cocoa! John, can you hear me?"

The voice was getting closer and soon was right next to me. "John, snap out of it!" Cocoa shook me roughly, and I opened my eyes, reassured to find myself still sitting on the sofa in the Konstandin apartment. My heart raced, I could barely breathe, and I was sweating profusely. Cocoa sat next to me, with an arm around my shoulder.

140

She was upset, "What happened? The door was barely shut before it all started. You were moaning and groaning terribly. I got frightened for you and tried to come in quickly but the bedroom door jammed and I couldn't open it. I practically had to break it down to get back in here. I've been trying to wake you up for at least ten minutes. I was about to call for help."

I was trembling and Cocoa had to help me to my feet. Short of breath and a little unsteady, I said, "I don't know what happened." I walked over to the bedroom door and looked at it. It seemed fine. I closed and opened easily. I thought maybe the humidity had caused it to jam like the entrance door but that wasn't the case. I didn't like this at all.

I turned to her. "Let's just get out of here. I have a massive headache."

Chapter 14

*B*ack in the loft, I lay on the bed with a cool, wet towel on my forehead, waiting for the ibuprofen I had taken to kick in. Cleopatra watched me sympathetically, sitting on the floor with her huge head resting on the edge of the bed. In a moment of weakness, I had confided in Cocoa what had happened and now she was in the next room talking quietly to Goldstein. After a few minutes, she came into the bedroom and handed me the phone.

"Dr. Goldstein wants to talk to you."

Covering the phone I said, "I told you not to call him, Cocoa. Now he's going to get wild."

She didn't care. "Tell him what happened."

"Hi, Arnie."

"Don't 'hi' me, Cesari. I heard what you just said."

"I'm sorry. I'm a little cranky right now and I have a headache."

"So I heard. Didn't I tell you to drop the Konstandin thing? This is a police matter now, and I don't care that you feel fine. You're obviously not. You've been through a lot and you need to rest. Whatever possessed you to go to that woman's apartment?" He paused to take a breath and I looked at Cocoa, shaking my head in admonishment.

"I know. I just thought it might jog my memory of events that night."

He seemed to calm down a bit. "Well, did it?"

"A little, but no game changer."

"Tell me about this headache."

"Bad, Arnie. Real bad. Worst headache I've ever had in my entire life, but the ibuprofen is starting to take effect. It's like a hand grenade went off right in the center of my brain."

"Any other symptoms? Sudden blindness, nausea, vomiting—you know what I mean."

"No, not really."

"Myrtle told me she found you in a trance and had a hard time rousing you."

"Oh she did, did she?"

"Cut the attitude all right?"

"I guess. I don't really know what happened."

"Give it an hour. If you're not feeling better I'll meet you in the ER and we'll get you a CT of the head. Am I clear? Maybe you've got a brain aneurysm."

"Thanks, Arnie." I said sarcastically.

"Hey look, Cesari, what do you want me to say? Everything's okay? Because it's not. One more thing. I tracked down Gary Ippolito and he said he never heard of anyone named Esha Deshmukh and that there is no one by that name working at Darby, Smith and Tasker. I went one step further and did a search. I can't find any lawyer in New York by that name."

"Great. Well, this is getting clearer all the time. So who the hell is she?"

"I don't know and I don't care so just forget about her, okay? Right now I can't even be sure that you didn't just dream the whole thing up. Now that I think about it, even if you're all better by morning I want to see you anyway. I'm also going to call the neurologist and tell him what happened. That trance you were in might represent some type of seizure activity. You know what, change of plans. Meet me in the ER right now."

"C'mon Arnie, it's almost ten p.m."

"Put Myrtle on."

"I'll be there. You don't need to talk to my mother."

"Bye."

I put the phone down, held the towel on my head with the other hand and sighed deeply. "Cocoa, why…?"

She was sitting at the foot of the bed listening. "It was for your own good. Where are we going?"

"The ER. He's going to meet us there. He wants me to have a CT scan."

Less than an hour later, I was lying inside the CT scanner at Saint Matt's hoping I didn't have a stroke or tumor. My headache had pretty much resolved and I was feeling much better. I looked over at Arnie, Cocoa, and the radiology technologist, all three of whom stood behind a specially designed window to protect them from the x-rays. It was over in five minutes and the technologist helped me off the table.

"So, how'd I do?"

The tech responded. "Looked fine to me but I'll forward the images to the radiologist on call. We should have a definitive answer in about fifteen minutes."

"Thanks."

We walked back to my room in the ER and Arnie said, "Neuro should be here soon."

"Is this really necessary, Arnie? I mean I feel better and the scan's probably normal."

"I'll feel better when I get the official report from the radiologist and neurology tells me it's safe to send you home. If you didn't have a stroke and neurology doesn't think you're

144

having seizures, then I want you to call your shrink friend first thing in the morning and tell him what happened. Who knows, maybe you experienced some sort of flashback phenomenon. Besides, even before all of this happened I was thinking you should be in some type of therapy."

Cocoa chuckled and I snorted. "Thanks, Arnie."

"Just think about it."

Maybe he was right. A flashback made sense but also implied that I was suffering from post-traumatic stress, and I probably was. I had been through a great deal of physical and emotional trauma after all. On the other hand, what I experienced wasn't really a flashback as much as a vision. Maybe I should call Mark tomorrow, or better yet, go see him.

I said, "You know, Arnie, that sounds like a pretty good idea."

He looked at me suspiciously. "Since when did you start being reasonable?"

Cocoa said, "I'll make sure he follows through, Arnie."

"Thanks, Myrtle."

The neurologist showed up twenty minutes later, read the CT scan, told me it was normal, and performed a neurologic evaluation. He declared me fit but wanted me to undergo an EEG to look for occult seizure activity. He felt there was no reason this couldn't be performed as an outpatient and said I could go home. As an aside, he also recommended I follow up with psychiatry. By the time the paper work was finished, Cocoa and I left the ER just before midnight and decided to walk home. Saint Matt's was on Third Avenue by Ninth Street so we strolled down to Waverly Place by the north end of Washington Square Park. It was a fifteen-minute walk to the loft and we were enjoying the night air. There was a half-moon in the sky and the city was thoroughly alive like no other in the world.

By her body language, I could tell Cocoa was worried, so I said, "I'm fine."

She nodded. "I'm sure you think you are."

I chuckled. "That was very diplomatic."

"Thank you. I want you to call Mark first thing in the morning, and then we'll schedule that EEG as soon as possible, okay?"

"Fine, anything else, Doctor Cocoa?"

"Are you in the mood to talk?"

"Sure."

"There's been something on my mind for a quite a while now, John."

"I'm listening."

"Tell me about the pictures I found underneath your bed."

"Pictures? What pictures? Nothing hardcore I hope."

She squeezed my arm. "You know exactly what I'm talking about."

I didn't say anything.

"Well, are you going to tell me?"

"What were you doing under my bed?"

"I've been living in that apartment for the last two months. I was cleaning under the bed and found the pictures. I also found a gun in the night table drawer which I removed and put in a safe place."

I had forgotten all about the gun. I kept a loaded .38 nearby at all times. I'd been a little fuzzy since my discharge from the hospital and hadn't noticed it missing. I said, "Where is it?"

"It's secured and in a safe place, and when you're fully recovered I'll return it to you. Right now you shouldn't have access to guns. So are you going to tell me about the pictures or not?"

I let out a deep breath. "Obviously, they were pictures of a certain ex-girlfriend and her children."

She nodded. "Hmm. Some of them seemed to have been taken from quite a distance and I noticed that in none of the pictures did she appear to be posing. That's interesting."

I let out a deep breath. "Okay, what do you want me to say? It was the only way I could get to see Kelly and the kids since she had the restraining order placed on me."

"John, stalking is illegal. It's a form of harassment. Plus, it's really creepy."

"Take it easy with the stalking accusation. It's more like I'm her personal paparazzo is all."

"Well, it's not healthy for you and I doubt the judge who issued the restraining order would find this so amusing."

"Well, you said Kelly might be inclined to have the restraining order lifted if I made it and I made it. Besides, I haven't stalked her since I got shot."

She was exasperated. "No more stalking Kelly, okay?"

"Okay already. No more stalking ex-girlfriends. Geez, a guy gets sick and when he wakes up, there are all sorts of new rules."

Chapter 15

Rutherford Cecil McCormick sipped his Old-Fashioned sitting in a corner booth of a fairly noisy and blatantly pedestrian bar in midtown, his brow furrowed deeply in thought. He turned to his son and said, "Remember, Duncan, let me do all the talking. You never want to say more than is necessary to any lawyer even the ones working for you."

Duncan nodded. "As you say, Father, but why are we slumming it in this place?"

"Not sure, but you know how these Americans love drama. They all think they're Humphrey Bogart in Casablanca and I'm sure Leo is no different than the rest of the lot."

"So what is the deal with this Leo person?"

"Leo is a very good lawyer and has furthered my interests on multiple occasions in the past. He has been known to skirt around the edges of the law to seal the deal if you know what I mean. There have been rumors about his underworld connections for years, which is why I eventually had to distance myself from him. Abbeline and Sons now handle most of my legal work. They're the big dogs here in Manhattan and lend a certain legitimacy to our brand, but I still like to throw Leo a bone once in a while for old times' sake. A situation like this is right up his alley. He'll know what to do. The key to handling chaps like this is to never say anything you don't wish to have regurgitated back at you in court. Here he is now."

Both men stood to greet the newcomer. Extending his hand, Rutherford Cecil McCormick said, "Thank you for coming, Leo. I trust you had a good journey from Philadelphia."

Leo Rosenblatt was a robust man several inches over six feet, sixty years old, tanned with silver, perfectly coiffed hair. He wore a silk hand-tailored suit and sported a diamond Rolex wristwatch. At heart he was a tough street lawyer from South Philly who had grown up the hard way, mixing it up with ne'er-do-wells his entire life. Now the senior partner in the law firm he first started thirty years ago, he was a straight talking take-no-prisoners kind of guy. Making money was what he did and like most lawyers he didn't particularly care how he did it. He knew bullshit when he saw it and these two were covered in it, but they were also two of the wealthiest men in Manhattan.

"Always a pleasure to see you, Rutherford, and may I assume this is your son, whom I've heard so much about?" He turned toward Duncan and offered his hand.

"Assume away, Leo. Meet Duncan Ronald McCormick, heir apparent to McCormick Enterprises."

"That's a helluva name you got there, Duncan."

"Quite," replied the younger man.

Rutherford said, "Duncan was named after his great-grandfather, who flew a spitfire during the Battle of Britain in 1940. Shot down thirteen Me 109s and fought with Montgomery in North Africa without a scratch only to get run over by a bus in Trafalgar Square the minute the war ended. Proof positive there is no justice in this world. Why don't we get you a drink, Leo? You must be parched."

"That I am." Leo ordered a scotch and soda and they resumed their seats.

"I greatly appreciate your coming all the way here to assist us in this delicate matter, Leo."

"No problem, Rutherford. I read in between the lines when I got your message the other day and figured this was the kind of thing we should talk about in person."

"You're right, of course. We wouldn't want to have any misunderstandings, would we?"

"Definitely not, and we wouldn't want anybody listening in on the lines either. Hence, I asked to meet you here. So, what's the problem if you don't mind my asking?"

"Well, Leo, I'm a little embarrassed to say, so I might as well just blurt it out. There's a man who has the potential to rain on our parade and we were hoping you could persuade him otherwise."

"I see, and the reason this can't be done through ordinary channels is …?"

"Not at liberty to say, I'm afraid."

"I see, and what if this individual can't be persuaded to see things your way?"

Rutherford shrugged. "That would be—disappointing."

Leo looked at Duncan, who was staring into his cocktail, and then back at his father. "Maybe we ought to take this from the top, fellas?"

"Whatever do you mean?"

Leo sat back, took a sip of his drink and smirked. "Cut the crap, Rutherford. You have a thorn in your side and you want it removed. If you want it done properly then I need to know why and exactly what's at stake. You didn't make me come all the way from Philadelphia to fix a parking ticket so start talking and remember, I've spent my whole life figuring out who's lying and who's not. Everything you tell me is protected under attorney client privilege so go for it. Nothing you say could possibly shock me. I've seen it all, I've heard it all, and I don't give a shit as long you brought your checkbook."

"Hmm. You are very direct, aren't you?"

"It's why I've prospered."

"Well, I was hoping this might help us get past the unpleasantness of a full disclosure." He took out a pen from his jacket and wrote down on a napkin a number with five zeroes after it and passed it to Leo. Leo smiled as he read it and said, "Rutherford, Rutherford, Rutherford, you cheap bastard." He then took out his own pen, added two more zeroes and passed the note back saying, "This is my fee for handling personality problems, but you're still going to tell me everything or I walk now so make up your mind."

Rutherford Cecil McCormick looked at the napkin, raised his eyebrows and chuckled. "When did you become the Merchant of Venice, Leo? Well, all right then. Here it is."

Leo interrupted him. "No, I want to hear it straight from sonny's mouth. I've been helping rich dads bail out their kids from their mistakes for thirty years. It's pretty obvious that's what's going on here. So what did you do, Duncan? Get caught with your hand in some little girl's knickers and the family won't be bought off?"

Duncan smiled. "Nothing nearly so much fun as that."

Chapter 16

"Well, I'm glad you're feeling better, John."

"Thanks, Kelly. I appreciate your calling and I appreciate the fact that you came to visit me in the hospital. Cocoa told me all about it. That was very nice of you."

"John, believe it or not, I do care about what happens to you, despite everything."

I sighed into the phone. This was very hard for me. "I know, Kel, and I'm sorry about getting you in trouble with Omar."

She chuckled. "Well, it wasn't exactly *all* your fault."

"Sure it was. I came there that day for the strict purpose of seducing you."

"Thanks for accepting full responsibility but if I didn't want to be seduced in the first place it wouldn't have happened. It takes two to tango as they say. Well, it's water under the bridge now and Omar's over it—mostly."

"You're very understanding."

Kelly hesitated and I heard noise in the background. One of the girls was crying. "John, I have to go now. Gwendolyn's crying and Beatrice needs a diaper change for sure. I really am very happy that you pulled through. It was so awful seeing you like that. We'll talk some more, okay? Maybe it's time we reassessed the situation, if you know what I mean?"

"Thank you, Kel. I appreciate that. Go take care of the kids and give them hugs for me."

"I will. Bye."

I put the phone down and stared off into space. Cocoa had taken Cleopatra for a walk in Washington Square Park while I had taken care of my doctors' appointments. Damn. I felt like an old retired guy, bouncing around from doctor to doctor and test to test with a few ER visits in between. The EEG was scheduled for Monday of next week and Mark was going to meet me later for lunch. Kelly had called to say hi and now that was all I could think about. How on earth did things go so wrong with that relationship? I was the father of those two little girls and everyone knew it. Kelly was in love with me and everyone knew that too. Yet, she was married to another man and had a restraining order placed on me. Oh well, I forced myself to put it out of my mind. I had too much to do.

I looked at my watch. It was 10:00 a.m. I wanted to go to the office to see my secretary, Julie, before I met with Mark, so I figured I'd walk to Saint Matt's by way of the park and hope to catch up with Cocoa there. It was Thursday, cool and overcast with no precipitation predicted, but Mother Nature looked like she was going to make fools of the weather guys again.

At the entrance to the park, I became aware of a commotion between two groups near the central fountain. One group of six older men appeared to be retired military. Some wore VFW hats and a few wore shirts with military insignia. One was in a wheelchair and several used canes for support. They were almost completely encircled by a much larger group of younger, college-age kids, mostly males wearing T-shirts and jeans. Both sides were hurling insults fast and furiously at each other. The college kids were holding an assortment of anti-American, anti-war, anti-the-rich, anti-capitalism, anti-police, anti-religion signs. There were maybe twenty of them in all. I chuckled to myself. The fucking sixties just wouldn't go away.

I politely stepped in between two young men in their twenties and approached the vets. The noise died down with my approach as everyone sized me up, and I asked the more senior of the group, "Hey, what's going on?"

A man in his seventies, with a metal cane and a baseball cap with the insignia of the 101st Airborne, studied me. He said, "These ungrateful sons of whores want to tear down everything that's good about this country and I'm sick and tired of it."

"Fuck you, grandpa!" A voice called out from behind me.

The old man turned scarlet and replied. "Any time you want a piece of me just step up to the plate, sonny."

I said loudly for all to hear, "Hey, how about we all calm down, all right?" Turning back to the old vet I asked, "What's your name, soldier?"

"Alvin C. Hooper. Sergeant, retired. United States Army, 101st Airborne. Two tours in 'Nam, Purple Heart and the Bronze Star and I'll be damned if I'm going to take shit from any spoiled brat here."

I nodded. "Thank you for your service, Alvin. I'm John Cesari. So where'd you get wounded?"

"Hamburger Hill '69. Lost my right eye and a lot of good friends. You didn't even notice, did you?"

I looked at him more carefully, and now that he mentioned it, it was pretty obvious. I saluted him, then extended my hand and he shook it vigorously.

The crowd behind me booed their disapproval and somebody yelled. "He's one of them! He's a fucking Wall Street suit."

I turned to face them better. "Take it easy, cowboys. You know, at one point, we were all your age, and believe it or not, we understand your frustrations and concerns. There's no need to be disrespectful to people who have done you no harm and who have sacrificed so much so that you can have the right to express yourselves so freely. We're all on the same side here."

"That's bullshit. The old geezer's a fucking baby-killer and you're a fucking one-percenter, raping and pillaging wherever you go." His friends cheered their approval at his insightful assessment of me.

I said very calmly, "Hold on. If we treat each other with civility and mutual respect, stop the name calling and harsh judgments, we will all be able to get our points across much more effectively, don't you think? There's no reason for us to be at cross purposes. We should discuss our differences calmly like intelligent people rather than drowning our opponents with insults and hate."

"You want to drown in something? Here, drown in this you prick!" Someone from the back of the group tossed a cup of coffee at me. I raised my hand but it was too late and it hit me in the chest, splashing coffee all over my white shirt. The crowd roared in laughter. Fortunately, it was only warm and not hot. Alvin said, "Nice try, son, but you're wasting your breath. They're real assholes."

I grunted and brushed myself off. I was angry but not out of control. Not yet. It was just then that I noticed several other coffee cups on the ground nearby with spilled coffee. I said, "I gather that wasn't the first missile today?"

"Nope. That's why we're so pissed. All we did was try to explain to them that just because they're upset about the way certain things are, there's no need to piss on peoples' beliefs and traditions. Before you know it coffee cups were flying in our direction, but nobody's hurt."

An arm reached out and touched me, and I turned to find Cocoa standing next to me. She said, "I think we should leave, tiger. Dr. Goldstein said no more stress."

"Where's Cleo?"

She nodded over at one of the park benches about twenty-five yards away. She was lying down peacefully observing the proceedings with her leash tied to the metal leg of the bench. Thankfully, she had her muzzle on.

I nodded.

Alvin said, "Go on, young fella. We'll be all right. I spent over a year up to my eyeballs in the mud and blood in a Vietnam jungle. I'm not worried about this crew."

I didn't want to leave them but I was starting to think that things might escalate if I stuck around so I saluted the group of vets and took Cocoa by the hand. As we turned to leave the guy nearest us smirked and said, "That's right. Take your whore and hit the road."

He was maybe a little older than the others, with long unkempt hair and beard, and I couldn't help thinking he was either a professional student or professional agitator. He just had that look to him. There was something cynical, sarcastic, even sinister about the way he lobbed that verbal bomb at me. He was deliberately trying to provoke me—and he had succeeded. I felt a blood vessel in my right temple begin to throb. My whole body tensed and Cocoa grabbed me tightly whispering, "Keep moving. I've been called worse—by much worse than him."

No doubt about that. She had led a risky lifestyle at one time as a pole dancer, but I'd be damned if I would let any woman be subjected to that kind of abuse while I still had a pulse, let alone a woman I cared about.

My heart rate quickened and my senses snapped to attention as I shifted into battle mode. Time seemed to slow down as I scanned the crowd, my eyes focusing in on the guy like an eagle tracking his prey. He had turned to his buddies who were now all laughing and chanting "whore" at Cocoa. Cleo had risen to her feet and was growling as she strained against the leash, instinctively sensing something was wrong. Alvin also sensed things were about to take a turn for the worse and cautioned me. "Easy, Colonel, he's not worth going to prison over."

I looked at Cocoa and then back at Alvin. "Maybe he isn't, but she is."

He liked that and nodded in approval, "Some things really are worth fighting for, aren't they? That's all I wanted these kids to know."

Cocoa clutched me even more tightly. "John, don't—I won't let you."

I pushed her arm away gently. "Go take care of Cleo. If she breaks free there's going to be chaos here even with a muzzle on her."

"John, no. Please don't. I assure you I'm not worth it."

Hmm. I placed my hands gently on her shoulders and looked into her eyes. "I beg to differ, Miss Rosenblatt. I think you are definitely worth it. In fact, the more I get to know you the more I realize just how special you are. Now please calm Cleo down before she hurts herself or someone else. I promise not to do anything rash." I smiled confidently to reassure her. She hesitated and finally nodded in acquiescence. I turned and walked up to the troublemaker who was still chuckling as I entered his personal space. He was about my height, overweight and smelled of cigarettes and pot. He looked me in the eye, and I could tell that he had no intention of backing down an inch, but the crowd grew quiet behind him with my approach. He had found my buttons and was enjoying pushing them.

"What do you think you're going to do, tough guy?" he asked, swaggering for effect. "There's twenty of us and one of you unless you want to include the six escapees from the nursing home on your side."

Without blinking I said, "I want you to politely apologize to my girlfriend and then to these men. I guarantee you that you will feel better when you do."

There was dead silence as he searched my face to see if I was joking. Behind me I heard Alvin say, "Uh-oh."

Suddenly, the agitator started laughing uncontrollably as did the entire gang behind him. He slapped his thigh and put his hands on his hips. "Jesus, dude. What asylum did you come from? Man, you just made my day. I'll tell you what. Why don't you take the old man's cane and shove it up your ass? Now, how's that for an idea? You know what? Why don't you shove the cane up your girlfriend's ass too while you're at it?"

Before he could start laughing again, I punched him hard in his big mouth, causing him to fall backward onto the pavement with a split lip. Blood oozed from the wound and he cursed in pain. He was stunned and pissed, not having expected me to attack him in front of so many witnesses and potential defenders. I should have warned him that I never worried about whether I might win a fight before I started one. I was now pretty damned angry and that wasn't good for him or anyone else who got in my way. I had a thing about guys who picked on girls. He didn't know that but too bad. He lay on the ground propped up on his elbows and I stepped over to him.

Commanding him in a voice that left no room for doubt in anyone's mind, I said, "Get up, asshole. You're going to apologize to my lady friend or you're going to the emergency room."

He hesitated and I reached down, grabbing him by the front of his shirt roughly with both hands. With a great heaving effort, I lifted him off the ground, jutting his chin up in the air, my fists pushing in tightly on his windpipe. He dangled on tip-toes, and reflexively clutched my wrists in a futile attempt to break free from my vise-like grip. Not a chance of that. None of his friends tried to intervene as utter silence descended on the park. His face was an inch from mine and I could smell the blood dripping down his chin. I flexed my muscles tightly, and he gasped for oxygen, wiggling and squirming frantically as panic set in.

I looked into his hate-filled eyes and—saw something I hadn't anticipated. Instead of giving him the thrashing he deserved I studied him carefully. What was that? I looked and looked, and finally saw it. Deep in his eyes, behind the sockets, I saw a light which transfixed me. Suddenly, I was somewhere else watching a dreadful scene unfold before me, causing me to shudder.

A man in uniform. An angry man in a military uniform. A woman on the floor in front of him and a bottle of liquor in his hand. He was drunk, very drunk and very angry. I couldn't hear him but I knew he was calling her a whore. She didn't respond. She didn't move at all and appeared to be unconscious. Then I saw something else which made me cringe even more. There was a small boy in the corner of the room, whimpering in fear as he watched. He had a black eye and other bruises. The man put the liquor bottle down on the table and slowly took his belt off. The boy screamed, "No, Dad, please don't." The boy had witnessed this scene many times before.

The scene changed and I now saw the same boy, only now he was a teenager. He had just come home from school and was looking for his mother. He called out several times and searched the house. Room to room he searched until he found her in the bedroom, face up, glassy-eyed with a needle sticking out of her arm. Dad was long since gone. The boy was all alone. He didn't cry. He was way past that. He simply lit up a joint and left her there.

I felt Cocoa tugging urgently on my arm. "John, John, put him down." I looked at her and then at him. I had been holding him airborne and he had stopped struggling, almost unconscious from my chokehold. I gently put him down and he slumped to the ground coughing and wheezing. I looked at him and he glared back. He knew and I knew. I don't know how but he had seen the same thing I had. He started to tremble, shake, and then to cry.

I touched his shoulder sympathetically and asked, "Are you all right?"

He pushed me away, sobbing. "Leave me alone. Just leave me alone."

"I'm sorry."

"Yeah, I bet."

I knelt down next to him and spoke consolingly. "I meant about your mom and about your life. No child should have to go through the things you did, but these men here behind me are not your father just because they wore uniforms like he did. They are brave men who have sacrificed greatly on our behalf. We are all on the same side, and you would find that out if only you would give them half a chance."

He sat there looking at me, confused and conflicted. I said, "Your mother didn't abandon you. She suffered and escaped from her pain the only way she knew how. Try to understand her agony and forgive her, and don't be so hard on women."

His eyes watered up even more and he started to bawl like a baby. Cocoa said gently, "John, let's go. This is getting out of control." For the first time, I noticed that the crowd around us had swelled into the hundreds, maybe more, and no one made a sound as I spoke to the guy. I stood to leave with Cocoa and ran into a burly police officer wading through the crowd. Spotting the guy on the ground with blood on his face he demanded, "What happened here?"

Raised voices and shouts from both sides suddenly filled the air with confusion. Not wanting to make things worse than they already were I said, "I assaulted this young man, Officer, and I'm very sorry. It was all my fault."

He bent down to check on the guy and once he determined that he would live returned to me. His name tag read *Kisatsky*. He looked around and spotted the anti-military and "Cops are Fascists" signs.

He said to me gruffly, "Turn around and put your hands behind your back."

He cuffed me none too gently and I turned to Cocoa. "I'll be okay. Take Cleo home, and I'll call as soon as I can."

"Oh, John!" She was very upset.

Turning back to the crowd Officer Kisatsky ordered. "Everyone stay here. I'm going to need to ask some questions."

I looked at Alvin and said, "Some things are worth fighting for."

He nodded and then saluted me.

Officer Kisatsky said, "Come with me." He grabbed my arm roughly and we walked to his cruiser parked outside the portico by Fifth Avenue. We reached the squad car and he helped me into the back as curious onlookers watched. He whispered, "Turn your wrists in my direction."

Discreetly, as if he was adjusting something he unlocked the cuffs and let them fall onto the seat of the car. He whispered into my ear. "Wait until I'm out of sight, and then get the hell out of here. I never saw you and you never saw me."

I was bewildered. "Why?"

"I'm an ex-marine. Spent eight years servicing F-14s, including six months in Gulf War I with Stormin' Norman. Those punks are in the park every week screaming shit about cops and the military. It's about time somebody stood up to them. Everybody hates cops until they need one. Now sit back and I'm going to pretend to lock the door." He walked back into the park, and once he was out of sight, I calmly exited the vehicle and hustled away. Those who noticed barely raised an eyebrow. This was New York City, after all.

Chapter 17

I called Cocoa to let her know what had happened, and she was shocked. "He let you go, just like that?"

"Turns out he was an ex-marine and didn't appreciate some of the sentiments being expressed by the well-intentioned youths we encountered."

"Wow. You got lucky. Where are you now?"

"I'm on Third Avenue approaching the hospital. I wanted to stop in and talk to my secretary and then I was going to have lunch with Mark. I'll catch up with you after that, all right?"

"Okay, I'll hang out in the apartment and practice piano. How do you feel?"

"Feel? You mean about what happened?"

"Of course that's what I mean."

"I'm sorry. I know I should have just walked away but he really pissed me off."

"Just how strong are you anyway?"

"What do you mean?"

"You lifted him off the ground like he was a feather and just held him there. You didn't even look like you were trying very hard."

"I don't have an answer for that. He didn't feel very heavy."

"Well he looked pretty heavy, and what did you say to him that made him start crying?"

I hesitated. I wasn't sure if I wanted to go into that with her because I wasn't sure how many marbles I still had upstairs. What happened the other night at the Konstandin apartment was bad enough. "I can't really remember. Something about treating others the way you want to be treated."

"Whatever it was, it seemed to do the trick."

"Yeah, well, he was under a fair amount of stress at that point. Okay, I'm entering the hospital now. I'll call you later."

"Bye."

I pocketed my cell phone and walked through the main lobby toward the elevators. Making my way to the GI department, I found Julie sitting at her desk. Her eyes went wide when she saw me and I thought she might start crying. She jumped up and came around from her desk, throwing her arms around me. She started to cry.

"I can't believe it. I am so happy to see you. We've all been wondering when you were going to come back to work."

"Thank you, Julie. It truly is amazing that I walked out of the hospital in one piece. I'd like to thank you and everyone else for your support. The get well cards were greatly appreciated. I'm sorry I haven't called or come by sooner. I've been kind of preoccupied."

She beamed at me. "I'll bet. Please, don't worry about stuff like that. The important thing is that you're getting better and we're all so happy for you." She looked at my coffee-stained shirt. "What happened?"

"Oh, that. I got jostled by accident on my way here and spilled my coffee."

Her phone rang and she let go of me, returning to her seat to answer it. I waited patiently while she spoke, glancing around the office to see if anything had changed in my absence. When she hung up I asked, "Julie, do you remember that night we met in Babbo's? I was having dinner with a girl named Cocoa."

"Sure I do. She was gorgeous. How could I forget? Oh my, I just remembered. That was the night before—you know, the shooting, wasn't it?"

"Yes, it was. There was a guy there you said was taking you and the other secretaries out. Remember?"

"Oh, sure. Ronnie, the Unicare rep. He takes all the secretaries out, sometimes once, sometimes twice a month. Talk about gorgeous. In fact, we're going out tonight."

"Really, where to?"

"We have reservations for seven at the Café del Rio in midtown. It's a new French place, supposed to be very avant-garde. Have you heard of it? It's on West 43rd Street, just off of Seventh Avenue."

"It sounds great. I'll have to try it sometime. One more thing, Julie. That night, you said that he takes you guys out to show his appreciation but you never said what he was showing his appreciation for."

"Nothing much really, he does all the work and it's so nice to have someone cut through the red tape for us."

I looked at her without saying anything. From the look on my face it was obvious I didn't know what she was talking about so she continued. "Well, he represents Unicare, right, and they insure at least fifty percent of our patients so we have to deal with them a lot, and I mean a lot. Phone calls, pre-authorizations for x-rays, cat scans, prescriptions, consults, etc. The fax machine runs constantly with the paperwork. Real pain in the rear if you know what I mean. Well about a year ago, I think it was about a year ago, I can't be sure, Unicare started this program to help us get through the bureaucracy. They send reps to various hospitals to work with the secretaries to make sure that the sickest patients get the care they need, especially the ones with terminal diseases like cancer. Ronnie's the rep they sent to Saint Matt's. He helps us with minimal effort on our part and to thank us for our support he takes us out once in a while."

She paused to take a breath while I digested this bit of corporate humanitarianism. I said, "And just how does he cut through the red tape for you? I'm curious."

"That's easy. The minute we hear from one of the docs that he has a patient with cancer or some other diagnosis that's going to require a lot of work, we give Ronnie a call with all the particulars and whatever tests, x-rays or consults the physician has requested. He takes it from there and makes sure everything gets taken care of with the patient. Saves us hours on the phone scheduling things and fighting with the insurance company. He does everything from soup to nuts. I personally haven't had any problems scheduling Unicare patients for CT scans or MRIs since Ronnie started coming around."

I was speechless. "He does the scheduling for all of our patients?"

"No, not all. Like I said, just the ones with cancer or who are severely ill. He makes sure everybody gets their pre-authorizations done promptly and without any hassles and then calls the patient up personally with all their appointments."

"And you haven't had any problems or complaints from patients? You know, like who's this strange guy from the insurance company calling me?"

"No, I let them know ahead of time that Ronnie's going to be getting in touch with them concerning the necessary tests they need, and in fact if they agree to the process then Ronnie waives any co-pays they might incur as a courtesy. The whole program is really a godsend for everyone."

"This really does sound like a great program. I'm glad it's working out but I am a little surprised I haven't heard anything about it."

"Ronnie said that's because you docs are so busy Unicare didn't want to bother you, and since it benefits your patients they couldn't see why anyone would object. Kind of made sense. Did I do something wrong by not telling you?" She suddenly seemed apprehensive.

"No, not at all, Julie. I was just surprised that I hadn't heard, but we really are so busy and there are so many of us it doesn't shock me that I didn't notice. So, he's basically acting as a secretary to you secretaries but only with the sickest of the sickest patients."

She smiled. "Exactly. They're the ones that take up most of our time."

"I have to say, this Ronnie sure sounds like a great guy. Do you have his business card or phone number? I think I would like to reach out to him about this program. You know, if the doctors participated, maybe we could help even more patients, not just the ones with terminal diagnoses."

She reached into her desk and gave me a business card which I read to myself.

Ronald Duncan
Unicare Field Representative
617-789-6502

I looked at the card. It was a Boston area code. "One more thing, if you don't mind, Julie. How does this guy, Ronnie, schedule appointments for patients and coordinate care so that we are all on the same page?"

She seemed to hesitate ever so slightly and I wondered if she was thinking about leaving something out. She said, "He does most of it from Unicare where they have all of the patient's pertinent information on file."

I nodded, thinking that over. "Thank you, Julie. Well, you have a great day. I'm going to take care of a few things in my office before I meet a friend for lunch."

"You're welcome. You're going to like, Ronnie. I guarantee it. He'll charm the pants right off you."

I laughed. "Well, just make sure he doesn't charm the pants off of you."

She smiled as her eyes darted furtively back and forth.

Hmm. What did that mean? I got the feeling I was already too late with that warning. Maybe I stepped over a line with that one. Besides, I had no right to judge her. "Well, I hope you and the girls have fun at dinner tonight."

"We will and I really am so glad that you're all right, Dr. Cesari."

"Thank you, Julie. Hey, by the way. How's your fiancée, Thurman? Did he win that sharpshooting contest you told me about?"

"Oh yeah, that. I can't believe you remembered. Of course he did. He always wins."

Clearly, all was not well on the domestic front. "Is everything all right with you and Thurman, Julie?"

"Yeah, I guess. It's just that he's so jealous and possessive I feel like I can't breathe sometimes, and he's always so angry too." She rolled her eyes as she spoke.

I nodded. "Well, that's too bad. I'm sorry. I know how difficult that can be."

"We're working on it but thanks for asking."

Her phone rang and she answered it. I waved goodbye, went into my office and sat behind my desk in my high-back leather chair. It felt good to be back in the control room. Everything was right where I had left it. They had simply locked the door and waited to see if I would survive. That was nice of them. I booted up my laptop and studied Ronald Duncan's business card. Boston, that was interesting. That woman, Esha, also had a Boston area code phone number. What did that mean? Who the hell was she anyway and why did she pretend to represent the hospital? She knew I was going to the apartment. Did she set me up? Why? Arnie and everyone else wanted me to drop it but I couldn't do that. I had one friend in psychiatric lock-up on the verge of getting electroshock therapy and two dead women on my hands, and I couldn't shake the feeling that they were related.

I googled Unicare out of curiosity and learned that its corporate headquarters were in the Prudential Tower on Boylston Street in Boston. It was the third largest health insurer in the United States and was rapidly growing through its aggressive marketing campaign and use of social media. From an investor's point of view, Unicare was a dream come true, yielding a ten percent rate of return every year for the last five years despite a bear market. It was projected that this coming year was going to be its best ever with eighteen percent growth. The estimated worth of the company was in the billions. Hell, I needed to call a stock broker soon and get in on this. Unicare was a subsidiary of McCormick Enterprises, a global investment corporation with multiple and varied interests including, CryoLabs Inc., a leading computer software company which regularly contracted with the Pentagon.

Well, that didn't tell me too much, although the thought of how wealthy these insurance companies were made me want to vomit. It was disgraceful that so many poor people who couldn't afford private health insurance were being shoveled into government health plans which were little better than Medicaid. In medical school we were taught that Medicaid meant no-aid, and they were right. It was both a joke and an embarrassment that a country as prosperous as ours threw crumbs at the least well-off of our citizens. I sighed deeply, finished reading and powered off the laptop. It was almost noon and I was supposed to meet Mark for lunch in a bistro across the street from the hospital.

Chapter 18

I had known Mark Greenberg since I was fourteen years old when I had a variety of behavioral and maladaptive personality issues stemming from the loss of my father to gangland violence. I was an angry kid and enjoyed pummeling people to blow off steam and frustration. Drugs and alcohol didn't do much to help my bad attitude but Mark had hung in there and eventually convinced me that I didn't want to end up just another street statistic or somebody's girlfriend in one of the state's correctional facilities, so I turned it around.

We had remained friends throughout my college and medical school years, and even though we lost touch from time to time we had bonded permanently for reasons that were not clear to either one of us. I wasn't the psychiatrist here but I suspected he represented the father figure that was missing in my life and I the son that was missing in his. He and his wife Sarah lived on the Upper West Side. They had one daughter and a grandchild in Westchester. Mark was contemplating retirement within the next few years.

"Hi Mark, thanks for meeting me on such short notice." We sat as far back in the restaurant as we could. We were near the kitchen and out of earshot from the other patrons. I ordered a Caesar salad with grilled chicken and Mark a prosciutto and provolone panini. They offered French roast coffee in a press.

"No need to thank me, Cesari. I always enjoy our little conversations and it's totally understandable that you might have a few things you want to talk about after the ordeal you've been through. That perfunctory exam I did in the ICU to get you released just barely scratched the surface of what must be going on in your head. What happened to your shirt?"

"Just my usual clumsy self. I spilled my coffee on it."

"So, please tell me what is ailing you."

Where did I begin? I looked past him at the counter and through the glass window out onto the avenue. He saw I was having difficulty and said, "Just say it as if you were dictating a lab report. Don't try to analyze it. That's my job."

I nodded. "Mark, there's some crazy stuff happening and I'm starting to wonder if I've suffered some type of anoxic brain damage during my hospitalization and cardiac arrest."

He raised his eyebrows at that as he depressed the filter of the coffee press and then filled our cups. The aroma was hypnotic and the first sip gave me yet another reason to be glad I was alive. He said, "Okay, but I'm afraid a statement like that is going to require a few details."

So I told him everything that had happened since my discharge, pausing only to let the waitress serve us our lunches. He interrupted me briefly on one or two occasions for clarification, but for the most part listened without any overt signs of passing judgment. We finished our meals in silence and he wiped his face with a napkin as he sat back in the booth.

"Okay, I agree, some of this sounds a little off the beaten path, but I don't think any of it falls under the category of anoxic brain damage unless you suspect that you're experiencing complex motor seizures. That should be easy enough to figure out with the EEG you're scheduled for next week. I'm more concerned that these visions and voices in your head are suggesting that you could be on the verge of a psychotic break."

I sighed. I knew he was going to say that. "But Mark, I feel fine, otherwise."

"Take it easy, Cesari. There's no need to get all defensive. I'm just trying to help sort things out and you called me, remember? Okay, you said these visions have only happened twice but both episodes occurred when you were under a fair amount of stress, right?"

"Yes, the first time was yesterday when I was in the apartment where the shooting occurred and the second time was just a few hours ago in Washington Square Park. Some guy was provoking the crap out of me and I got angry."

"Hmm, even if you were experiencing auditory and visual hallucinations that wouldn't explain the physical phenomena you told me about although the rapid wound healing may not be that big a deal. After all, you were in the ICU for two months so the healing wasn't *that* fast if your surgeries took place on day one, but you're saying the scars are completely gone without any residual and I'm guessing that would be unusual."

"Exactly, and I don't know if there are any studies that have specifically addressed the issue of complete healing vs. *can't even tell if there was surgery in the first place*. Once you're out of the hospital and doing well, no one really cares what you think of the scar."

"Okay, let's shelve that for a moment. Then, there's the issue of the missing bullet and the spleen regeneration. Where do we stand with that?"

"Arnie is reviewing all of the CT scans from that day to see if there was some mistake in the labeling. If he finds a CT scan with a bullet lodged in the spine and no spleen then we'll know what happened. If he doesn't then we have another mystery."

"Hmm. I remember enough basic medicine to know that a spleen can regenerate but where would the bullet be? Could the body digest it? Help me out, Cesari. I'm just a shrink."

"Digest it? No, but it could have migrated out of the spine and down into the pelvis. The scan might not have been carried out to the lowest part of the pelvis for some reason. That happens all the time. It all depends on the proficiency of the technologist doing the scan."

"Hmm."

"You keep saying that."

"Hmm. So, does everything else seem to be all right? You know, your appetite, energy level, bodily functions, etc.?"

"Yeah, I think so."

"Hmm."

"Okay, Mark, what's that supposed to mean?"

"Are you sleeping okay?"

"Yeah, I think so."

"What about sex?"

"What about it?"

"Cocoa tells me you've been missing in action."

I snorted. "Oh please, give me a break. I've only been out of the hospital a couple of weeks and why are you talking to Cocoa about my sex life? Hasn't either one of you ever heard about patient confidentiality?"

"She called me this morning because she was afraid you might not tell me everything. She's concerned about you."

"I'm fine."

"Look Cesari. This is a highly peculiar situation you're in so I'm going to reserve passing judgment on what's going on but when a guy tells me that he's seeing and hearing things and his girlfriend tells me he's not acting himself then I tend to be a little worried about him."

I nodded. "I get it and that's why I called you. So where do we go from here?"

"We keep talking. I want to see you once a week until we've got a better handle on this situation, and I want you to call me with any and all recurrences of these episodes. Secondly, I agree with Arnie. You have got to drop this Konstandin thing. It's over. You're not going to make Tony better by driving yourself nuts, okay? I think maybe you and Cocoa ought to consider going away for the weekend and stop playing junior detective. Who knows? Maybe a weekend away will light that fire again, if you get my drift?"

"Yeah, I get it, but it's hard to just drop it. There's something very strange about the whole thing. Tony was a very meticulous guy. For him to have erroneously documented a patient record like that seems very odd to me, and then for the patient's wife to get herself murdered the same day I'm coming over to interview her about her husband's care. Boy, that seems like quite a coincidence."

He took off his glasses and cleaned them with a napkin as the waitress cleared the table and asked us if we wanted more coffee. "Sure, I'll grant you that, but so what? This is New York and strange shit happens all the time. Look, I don't know much about solving murder mysteries, Cesari, but I watch a fair amount of TV. Whenever a crime is committed, the detective or whoever always asks the question, *who benefits*? If you can answer that then you'll be well on your way to solving the crime. In this situation, there doesn't seem to be an answer. Trust me, the whole city was speculating about it for the entire two months you were in a coma including Sarah and me."

"Mark, bear with me on this for a minute, will you?"

"Fine, but I don't want to encourage you to keep focusing on this. The police are doing all they can."

"I understand. So let's just say that I was collateral damage. You know, I just happened to be in the wrong place at the wrong time, which is what the police think. Who then benefits from Mrs. Konstandin's death? The only person I can think of is

Tony because she was clearly heading toward a malpractice suit against him, and possibly a civil suit as well, but he was already in the hospital when the shooting happened which clears him. After that, the hospital itself would also have been named as a secondary defendant, but they had little to worry about. If things had gone bad for Tony in court they would have simply thrown him under the bus and terminated his contract. No, to the hospital this would have been just a tiny hiccup. Arnie told me she was pretty mad at her health insurer, Unicare, but I can't imagine they would have given a rat's ass about a pissed off Albanian immigrant whose husband died as a result of the doctor's incompetence. Even if she had successfully brought suit against them, it would have washed off them like rain. Unicare is a financial juggernaut worth billions. I've been reading about them."

"You answered your own question then, Cesari. The only person who might conceivably have benefited was Tony and he was already under observation in the ICU so the crime was either random or had some personal motive that we'll never find out."

I thought about that. "There's still the question of who that Esha person is and why she was asking me all those questions about Mrs. Konstandin."

Mark sat back and rubbed his chin. "Is it possible she was a reporter on a fishing expedition? It would have made a great human interest story by anybody's standards, and even more so now, actually."

I took a sip of coffee and thought over his logic. "Maybe, but how would a reporter know about a case that hadn't even been filed yet? No, that doesn't make sense."

"Can you be sure that Mrs. Konstandin didn't make contact with the press?"

"No."

"Look, Cesari, I know this isn't easy for you, and I would love to help you get resolution for what happened but life is not always that convenient. Part of your road to wellness is going to be your ability to accept what happened and be at peace with it."

The bill came and I tossed my credit card on the table. "I know, Mark, and I'm sure I'll be able to do that. It's just that I'm not quite there yet. Lunch is on me, okay?"

"Of course it is, but just for the record this doesn't count towards my fee."

Chapter 19

*B*ack in the loft, Cocoa and I sat on the sofa discussing plans
for the weekend. I said, "Mark thinks it might be a good
idea to get away for a couple of days. You know, to clear the
cobwebs from my head and stop thinking about what happened.
Tomorrow's Friday, would it be a big deal for you to take a day
off from school?"

She flipped through a magazine while Cleo nuzzled her leg
for attention. "No, I don't think so. Where'd you have in mind?"

I looked at Ronald Duncan's business card. "How about
Boston?"

"Sure, why not? I've never been."

"Really?"

"Really."

"I thought your parents took you everywhere when you
were a kid?"

"Everywhere worth going. I guess Boston wasn't on the
list."

Very seriously, I asked, "Did you have to tell him?"

"Tell who, what?"

"Mark, about you know what?"

"Oh, please. What are we going to do with this puppy dog
here for the weekend?" Having deftly changed the subject,
she put the magazine down and wrestled with Cleo's head

affectionately. Women always did stuff like that: ignore the question, change the subject, and then move on as if nothing had happened.

I sighed and let it go. "I guess we'll have to put her in a kennel although I don't like the idea. Sorry girl."

"How about asking that college girl to apartment-sit for the weekend? Cleo already knows her and I'm sure she could use the money."

I scratched my head. "What college girl?"

"That girl Bridget. She was dog-walking for you when I came on the scene. She seemed nice enough and told me she'd be happy to help out if we ever needed. I have her number."

"Oh, yeah, I almost forgot about her. That's a great idea. Would you mind giving her a call? Tell her to be here at eight sharp tomorrow morning. I'd like to get up there for lunch. You call her and I'll take care of the hotel arrangements in Boston."

"I'll call her right now. See how much we love you, Cleo?" She stroked Cleo's giant head lovingly.

I wandered off into the bedroom for privacy and looked at my watch. It was almost 5:00. This day had flown by. I lay on the bed and made reservations for the weekend at the Mandarin Oriental on Boylston Street. The price was steep but I liked the location. I then looked long and hard at Ronald Duncan's business card deciding what to do—if anything. Everybody wanted me to drop it but I knew that wasn't going to happen. Unicare, Unicare, Unicare. Ronald Duncan. Ronnie. Why were you in my vision? I let out a deep breath and dialed the number on the card. Three rings and he answered.

"Hello, Ronnie here."

Interesting, a cultivated English accent just like Esha Deshmukh. "Hello, Ronnie. I'm Dr. Frank Tortone. I'm a gastroenterologist at Montefiore Medical Center in the Bronx. We've never met, but I've heard a great deal about you and the program Unicare is spearheading to help physicians' offices cut through the red tape when scheduling patients for tests and x-rays. I hope you don't mind my reaching out like this?"

There was slight hesitation, I thought. He said, "No, not at all, Doctor, but do tell me. How did you get my number and how is it that I might assist you?"

"Pure coincidence. I was at a dinner party in the city last weekend. Just a social gathering and met some of the secretarial staff from one of the hospitals there. I think it may have been Mount Sinai or Saint Matt's, I'm not sure. Well, at any rate, she was going on and on about what a great guy you are and what a godsend your program has been for the patients. Long story short, my department would love to get in on the action. She gave me your number and said you probably wouldn't mind if I called. Is that all right?"

Hesitation for sure this time. No doubt about it. "Of course, it's all right. In fact, I'm thrilled to make your acquaintance, Dr. Tortone. I can certainly pass this information along to my superiors. We at Unicare are always eager to do whatever is necessary to help our customers and providers."

There was something about his voice that was oddly familiar. "Do you think that maybe we could meet in person, sometime? I discussed it with the other members of my department and they are extremely eager to find out more about your program. The paperwork is burying us all. You know how it is, I'm sure."

"That sounds like a jolly good idea. I think I would really like that. I have been telling my supervisors for some time that it would benefit everyone to get physician input. When would you like to meet?"

That sealed it. I wasn't sure what this guy was up to but he was full of shit. *I've been telling my supervisors for some time now ...* yeah, I bet. My office is less than twenty feet from

Julie's desk and you've been coming by for a year and yet I never saw you except for the back of your head at Babbo that night? How is that possible?

"How about dinner tonight, my treat?" I asked congenially.

"I'm afraid tonight would be out of the question. As we speak, I am waiting to board a plane for Chicago on business. So sorry."

"Oh, that's too bad. Some other time then?"

"Absolutely, doctor. How about I give you a ring sometime next week? I'll use this number. Would that be all right?"

"That would be great. Well, nice talking to you. Bye."

"Cheerio."

You lying sack of …. Cocoa came in from the other room and sat next to me on the bed with Cleo close behind. She said, "We're all set with Bridget. She'll come by at eight tomorrow morning and will stay the weekend. I told her fifty bucks per day plus a food allowance, say two hundred and fifty dollars total for the weekend. She jumped at it. I know it sounds steep but this was last minute and she had other plans she has to cancel."

"Doesn't sound steep at all. You have no idea what Manhattan kennels cost for a dog that size for the weekend. Easily that much. In fact, I think I'm getting a bargain."

She nudged me playfully. "So now what? Want to go down to the park and pick another fight?"

"No, I don't want to go down to the park and pick another fight. I can pick one right here, thank you." I sat up suddenly, grabbed her by the shoulders and pushed her down onto the bed, pinning her under me. Cleo woofed in protest. Trapped under my weight and out of breath from the assault, Cocoa stared helplessly into my eyes waiting for my next move. I studied her features carefully and gently caressed her auburn hair as I brought my lips close to hers, kissing her long and passionately. She wrapped her arms around me and held me tight.

I whispered, "Don't even think about resisting."

She smiled, "If I do you'll have no choice but to spank me."

I nodded in agreement and saw a tear form in one of her eyes.

"What's the matter?" I asked.

She shook her head. "I'm just happy. That's all."

I said, "Want to go to a nice restaurant for dinner?"

"Sure."

"Okay, go get ready. I'm hungry."

"Now?"

"Sure."

"But I thought—you know. You seemed kind of frisky." She wiggled her hand down between us and grabbed me rudely, smiling. I flinched and laughed.

"Oh, is that what you thought?" I reached down and put my hand between her legs and grabbed her just as impolitely and we both started laughing.

"Yeah, that's what I thought."

"With the dog watching?" I asked.

"She can get her own guy."

"Let's not rush into this. It might set me back medically."

"I'm not rushing into anything. I've been very patient."

"Good, we'll talk about it some more over dinner."

"Fine."

We stared into each other's eyes some more and she said, "If you get off me I can go change for dinner."

I rolled off her and she scampered away to the bathroom. I got on my hands and knees and reached under the bed, retrieving a black duffel bag. Inside was a Canon Rebel digital camera with a 70-300 mm zoom lens and a cardboard shoebox filled with photos of Kelly and the twins.

I pushed the shoebox back under the bed and zipped up the duffel bag.

Thirty minutes later, Cocoa came out of the bathroom and twirled around for my approval. "How do I look?"

"As always, you look great." She wore jeans and modest heels with a very attractive burnt orange top. Hoop earrings and a gold necklace finished off the ensemble. Casual but gorgeous. Very nice. I put on a sport coat and grabbed the duffel bag.

She asked, "Is that the duffel bag I found under the bed? The one with the pictures."

"Yes, but it only has the camera in it now."

"And why are you taking a camera to the restaurant? Is Kelly going to be there?"

I laughed. "No, it's supposed to be a nice place. I thought I'd take a few pictures and maybe have the waiter take a few of us too."

"And what's wrong with taking pictures with our smart phones?"

"Nothing really. It's just that the quality will be much better with this baby." I raised the bag for her to see as if somehow that proved my point.

She remained suspicious and I withered under her gaze so I decided I'd better come clean during the cab ride to the restaurant. I filled her in on who Ronald Duncan was and my recent phone call with him. She shook her head but decided it would be better to humor me.

The driver made a left down Greenwich Avenue and Cocoa, looking concerned asked him, "Hey where are you going?"

In a thick, Middle Eastern accent he responded. "Pretty lady say Café del Rio? I take Café del Rio."

I whispered, "What's the matter?"

"I don't understand why he got off Sixth Avenue. It would have taken us straight to 43rd Street."

"Just let the guy drive, all right? He does this for a living."

"He may do it for a living or he may be taking the scenic route. Trust me. I have an infallible sense of direction."

I chuckled. "Oh, please. Refresh me on something. Weren't your people lost in the desert for forty years looking for the only mountain in a piece of land smaller than the state of Rhode Island?"

She smiled. "I see being in a coma hasn't put a dent in your sense of humor. Well, if we're going to compare history lessons, wasn't it one of your people who announced to the world he had found the East Indies when in fact he was hopelessly lost? Oh, yeah, that was Columbus. An entire continent got in his way and he didn't even know it."

Touché.

I thought about correcting her. Columbus was Italian and my people were Sicilian. Non-Italians tended to lump us all together in a racist potpourri. A Sicilian never would have made a blunder like Columbus did but why get bogged down in technicalities with a girl who had such a great ass. Yep, let it ride. I watched her gloat and simply smiled in return.

We arrived just before seven and noted that midtown was mobbed with theater goers and tourists creating a carnival-like atmosphere as we fought our way into the entrance of the Café del Rio.

A well-dressed woman greeted us. "Do you have reservations?"

I said, "No, do you think you might be able to squeeze us in? It's just the two of us. We'll sit anywhere."

The girl perused her floor map carefully searching for a table while Cocoa and I scanned the large, crowded dining room. The atmosphere was noisy, chaotic and vibrant. It reminded one of—

well, New York. There was a large semicircular bar in the center of the room and dozens of tables all around. Wait staff sporting white aprons bustled busily back and forth serving customers. I spotted two empty chairs at one end of the bar and said, "Can we sit there? Those two seats would be fine with us."

She looked up from her papers, relieved at not having to turn us away, and smiled. "Certainly, please follow me." She escorted us to the seats and wished us bon appetit. The high-back swivel stools were made of good quality wood and leather and were quite comfortable. We ordered a couple of gin martinis with two olives each and sat back enjoying the atmosphere while I casually took out my camera, placing it on the counter in front of me.

Sipping our drinks, I studied my menu while Cocoa checked out the other women and their attire. Out of the corner of my eye, I saw Julie enter with a tall, strikingly handsome, well-dressed man in his early thirties. He had a shock of long wavy black hair and a fair complexion. He carried himself with an air of importance. He was thin but athletic-looking and I suspected that although he didn't spend much time in the gym pushing iron around he probably was very physically active in some other way. Tennis, maybe. He didn't look familiar—or did he?

The hostess escorted them to their table at the far end of the room from where we were and I breathed a sigh of relief when Julie sat with her back to me. I wasn't ready to have a confrontation yet with this guy and certainly didn't wish to do so in front of Julie. I just wanted to confirm in my mind what a liar he really was. He didn't look to me like he was on his way to Chicago.

I ordered the NY strip steak au poivre, medium rare with shoestring fries and asparagus. Cocoa had the sole almondine with green lentils. While we waited for our food, I asked the bartender if he would mind me snapping a few photos of him at work for our memories. He had no problem with that and

I aimed the camera in his direction but zoomed past him at Julie and Ronnie, quickly firing off a series of photos of them chatting. I returned the camera to the duffel bag.

The food came and we started eating, ordering another round of martinis. Cocoa asked, "Not to marginalize your concerns, but what exactly do you hope to accomplish by spying on them? So he lied about what he was doing tonight? He didn't know who you were and didn't want you to know where you could find him. That doesn't really sound so unreasonable to me. Besides, he's out with a woman who's engaged to be married. Maybe he didn't want that broadcast across the country?"

She was right, of course, on all counts but especially the out with an engaged woman, especially one who had a very jealous, very large New York City cop as a fiancée. I noticed that none of the other secretaries had shown up like Julie had told me they would and that she appeared to be just a little too cozy with my new friend Ronnie. I thought about that. Was she having an affair with this guy? Why not? She had a fling with me and had wanted more. Ronnie was a pretty good-looking guy too. Okay, Cocoa made a valid point. Maybe when I called the guy he was a bit reserved because when I told him I met a secretary from one of the hospitals he couldn't be sure exactly what they told me about him, such as the fact he was doing Julie. Maybe that was also why he kept such a low profile at my office too? Possibly. I was going to have to take it easy. I didn't want to ruin Julie's life barking up the wrong tree like this. Still, there was something not quite right here. Since when did insurance companies give a crap about making life easier for the providers, their staff, and the patients?

Since never, that's when.

Chapter 20

At 3:00 a.m., my cell phone buzzed on the night table. It was Vito. I rubbed my eyes and answered it. "Vito, what do you want? It's three in the morning." I tried not to talk too loudly but Cocoa woke anyway.

"John, who is it?"

"I'm sorry, Cocoa. Go back to sleep."

Vito said, "I'm outside your apartment. Let me in."

"Outside my apartment? Why?" I whispered, sitting up.

"Let me in and I'll explain."

Cocoa said, "Who's outside the apartment?"

"It's Vito."

"He's here? Now?"

"Yes, he's here, now. Vito, give me a second. Cocoa, I'm going to see what this is all about." I got out of bed and walked to the front door as Cleopatra opened her eyes and watched with curiosity. I unbolted the door and let him in— or should I say them. Vito was accompanied by two of the largest men I had ever seen: gorillas wearing two-piece suits with pistols in shoulder holsters bulging out from under their sport coats.

"Cesari, meet Herbie and Sebastiano." Sebastiano had thick, curly black hair and a mustache. Herbie's head was shaved and he wore a gold earring. Not a small one, mind you but a big hoop like a pirate. They grunted in my direction and bolted the door closed behind them.

I grunted back. "Vito what's going on?"

"This is a hit, Cesari, and you're the target."

My heart skipped a beat and all I could think about was how I could get Cocoa out of this safely. Fighting my way out wasn't an option with these guys. Sebastiano and Herb were probably 275 lbs. each and Vito alone had to be at least 260 lbs. They were armed and I was in my drawers still half asleep. Shit.

Without showing alarm I said, "Vito, can we talk about this?"

He laughed. "Relax, Cesari, don't piss on the floor all right? I just got these clothes back from the dry cleaners."

I let out a deep breath. "That's your idea of a joke? So what do you want or did you come here to give me a heart attack?"

"I came here to save your ass—once again. Make a pot of coffee and I'll explain, and for God's sake put some pants on. I hope you don't think we're queer."

They all grabbed seats and I put on a pair of jeans. I was in the kitchen preparing coffee when Cocoa entered wearing a short silk robe and fuzzy pink slippers. Every eye in the place suddenly became glued to her shapely form. Her hair flopped in front of her sleepy eyes which made her look even sexier. "What's going on out here? Hi, Vito."

"Hi, Cocoa, I'm sorry about the intrusion but I had urgent business with your boyfriend and it couldn't wait."

She asked, "What kind of business is so urgent that it couldn't wait till morning?" Cleo had followed her into the room and was busy sniffing the new guys, who were sitting on the couch. They were apparently dog friendly and rubbed her head which she loved.

Cocoa, Vito and I sat around the kitchen table looking at each other and I finally said to Vito, "Well...?"

186

"I wasn't joking about the hit. Somebody really is gunning for you."

"What are you talking about? I've been in a coma for the last two months. Who would want to put a hit out on me?"

"That's kind of a dumb question, don't you think? Maybe it's the same people who put you in a coma in the first place. Welcome back by the way. You look great. I came to see you in the hospital. I don't know if you know that. Several times in fact."

"I didn't know. Thanks for caring, but everyone seems to think that it was a random shooting so what do you know that caused you to come here in the middle of the night?"

"Well, a couple of hours ago I caught wind of the fact that an attack against you was imminent. I only waited long enough for my sources to confirm it before coming over here as fast as I could. Whoever it is, is rolling in it. I heard the contract is for five hundred grand. Some low-life called Sammy Beans was trying to make himself seem important and bragged to one of the girls in the whore houses that he knew about a hit going down. She recognized your name and remembered that you and I were pals. She told the madam and here I am. By the time I found out, Sammy Beans had disappeared back into the wood work but I'll find him. He won't get far. I made a couple of quick calls and confirmed it with my contacts. There's no doubt about it."

"That's all you can tell me? Who's Sammy Beans?"

"Don't worry about who he is. I know who he is and that's all that matters, and no, that's not all I can tell you. I heard the contract is coming from Philadelphia, but I have no idea who or why. Apparently, somebody from Philly put out feelers to see if I would get upset if they did the hit in my backyard without permission. Sammy Beans was present when the call came in.

Since nobody knew who you were they figured I wouldn't care. Real geniuses I work with, huh?"

I got up and poured everybody a round of coffee. "This is just great."

"Relax, Cesari, the cavalry got here in the nick of time."

Cocoa sipped coffee from her mug and although concern was etched in her features, curiosity got the better of her. "Why do they need your permission?"

"Because, if it's in my territory, I need to approve the hit and they need to pay me a commission, which in this case would have been ten percent. Which means, I just lost out on the easiest fifty thousand dollars ever. You owe me Cesari."

I said, "Well, thanks, I appreciate your sacrifice on my behalf. So what happens now?"

"I'm going to finish my coffee while you two go pack your bags. Since I don't know who got the contract I can't stop him so you ain't safe here anymore. Five hundred grand makes people do crazy things. I may not be able to stop whoever it is anyway."

Cocoa looked upset and depressed. She spoke dejectedly almost as if to no one in particular. "But John and I were going to Boston tomorrow for the weekend."

Vito nodded, "Leaving town for a while is probably not a bad idea once we're sure no one is following you. Until then you should lay low and let my guys keep an eye on you. Honestly, from what I heard I was only half expecting to see you breathing when I came here."

"So where are we going?" I asked.

He said, "Well, I have five bedrooms and the entire second floor above the Café Napoli on Mulberry Street. You're welcome to stay at as long as you like but I'm thinking a few days at the least ought to give me time to get to the bottom of things."

I knew the apartment well. It was Vito's home base for operations as he managed his criminal empire in lower

Manhattan. It was like an armed fortress. I looked at Cocoa. "Why don't you go pack a bag with some clothes for a couple of days? If you don't mind, I want you to stay at Vito's apartment where you'll be safe. Unfortunately, I still need to go to Boston. There's something there I have to do."

Cocoa objected vehemently. "Well, I do mind. That's not even close to being fair. Why do I have to hide in Vito's apartment if you're the one they're trying to kill? And what do you have to do in Boston anyway? You didn't tell me anything about that. I thought we were going on a mini-vacation?"

Vito chuckled at our nonmarital discord. I said, "It was going to be a mini-vacation but there was something I needed to look into while I was there. Now, in case you weren't listening, there's a contract out on my life. If they get lucky enough to find me, they will not hesitate to kill whoever is with me, i.e., you. Even worse is that if they know about you, they might use you as leverage to get to me so you're probably in as much danger as I am. You and I need to separate for a while and you need protection until we sort it out and that's that."

She shook her head in frustration. "I don't believe this."

"I'm sorry."

Vito added, "He's right, Cocoa. Anybody standing next to him is probably going to take a bullet in the head as well."

I said, "Which is unfortunate for you, Vito, because I need you to come with me to Boston instead of Cocoa."

"The hell I will."

Cocoa said sarcastically, "Oh, that's just great."

"Listen Vito, there's been a lot going on that hasn't made any sense to me and everyone's been trying hard to convince me it's all a coincidence, but now it's obvious that is not the case. I need to go to Boston to do some sniffing around and I need someone to watch my back."

Cocoa pouted. "And I can't do that?"

"It's not that you can't. I don't want to place you in harm's way like that. Plus, it would be a massive distraction for me worrying about you. If Vito gets killed it won't bother me as much."

Vito said, "Shit."

Cocoa finally surrendered and came over to me to give me a hug. "Fine, I guess. What about Cleo? Can I take her with me at least?"

I looked at Vito. He said, "Fine."

I added, "Cocoa, call Bridget and cancel her. I don't want her coming here at eight in the morning and running into a hit squad."

She nodded and went to the bedroom to pack her stuff.

Outside the loft, we split into two groups. Cocoa and Cleo went with Sebastiano and Herb to Vito's apartment in Little Italy and I got into Vito's black Lincoln Towncar. We took off up the West Side Drive to catch 87N to the Massachusetts Turnpike. I filled Vito in on the pertinent details as we drove minus the supernatural stuff. He was the most dangerous guy I ever knew but couldn't watch the Exorcist without covering his eyes with a pillow and every light in the house on.

"So you think Unicare is up to some shenanigans?" he asked.

"I've never heard of an insurance company that gave a rat's ass about anything but its own profits, and will you take it easy? There's no need to do a hundred miles an hour."

"Relax, Cesari. That's true what you said about insurance companies. They're bloodsuckers for sure but murder? That's a whole different level of asshole. I don't know if that makes sense. I just don't see the point. If they're going to murder everyone that files a complaint or lawsuit they're going to be pretty busy for sure." He lit a cigarette, filling the car with smoke, so we both cracked our windows a bit and the car got really noisy.

Gagging I said, "Do you really have to do that? It's the unhealthiest habit ever invented. You'd be better off shooting heroin. And I didn't say they murdered anyone, but they're up to no good and I don't like it."

He ignored my admonition about smoking. "Let me get this straight. You don't think they're the ones who killed the old lady and you don't have any proof that they were involved but we're going to pay them a visit—why?"

"Somebody called me pretending they were a lawyer representing the hospital. In retrospect, she was on a fishing expedition to see what I knew. I told them I was going to see Konstandin's wife and the next thing I know I'm in a coma in the ICU. Who else would care about what I knew about that particular case? I can't think of anyone other than Unicare because they were potentially going to be named in the lawsuit, and there's this guy Ronnie from Unicare I told you about. He's crawling around my hospital wining and dining secretaries. I don't like it. I don't like any of it."

Vito digested that as we pulled onto the Massachusetts Turnpike. "Might as well close your eyes, Cesari. We'll be there in a couple of hours. No point in both of us being up all night."

191

Chapter 21

*W*e got lucky and were able to check in early at the Mandarin where we crashed for a couple of hours, exhausted from the trip. I had decided to keep the reservation I had made for Cocoa and me but had cancelled the couple's massage in the spa. By noon, we woke hungry and feeling refreshed so we cleaned up and had lunch in the hotel restaurant, The Drunken Goat. The Mandarin was an elegant hotel, four stars bordering on five, with spacious rooms, plush carpeting, crystal chandeliers and attentive, crisply dressed staff.

Vito sipped hot coffee and shoveled forkfuls of shepherd's pie into his mouth while I thought over what to do. I had brought the memory card from my digital camera and needed to find a place to print out a few pictures of Ronnie. After that, the plan was completely up in the air. I mean, realistically, this was most likely a dead end but I felt I should at least try to see what's going on.

Vito looked up and said, "So what's the plan, Cesari?"

"Not a hundred percent sure, but I want to check out Unicare's headquarters in the Prudential Tower. You know, your basic sniffing around, trying to get a feel for things. I doubt that anything will turn up but you never know and it's worth a try. I'll need to find someplace to print out those pictures first."

He dabbed his lips with his napkin. "You're just going to walk in, show his picture to people and ask if they know him?"

I shrugged. "Sure, why not? It's not against the law."

"They're either going to think you're a cop or a private dick. I hope you realize that."

"What do I care what they think? Like I said, I'm not breaking any laws."

He thought about that. "How big is this company?"

"Really big. Third largest insurer in the United States and growing. Maybe the second largest by the end of next year. They occupy the top ten floors of the Prudential Tower."

"Suppose they ask us to leave?"

"Then we'll leave."

He nodded. "Just like that?"

"Just like that."

He snickered. "Yeah, right."

"C'mon, let's pay the bill and get those pictures developed. Then we'll mosey on over to Unicare."

"Relax, Cesari, we got the whole day, and I'm still waking up."

I rolled my eyes. Vito and I had known each other our whole lives, and at this point were more like brothers than friends. And just like brothers, there were times we wanted to kill each other and had even tried. I said, "Take your time, Vito. It's not like there's a hit out on me or anything."

He chuckled. "Fine, let's go."

We stopped quickly at a nearby Walgreens, printed out a few photos and drove to the Prudential Tower, parking in the underground lot.

"Unicare occupies the 41st through the 50th floor where the observation deck is," I said.

"Do you think we should have worn ties?"

"Not a bad thought but too late now. I think we look all right for what we want to do."

He wore the same dress slacks, white shirt, and black sport coat he had last night because I hadn't wanted to waste time stopping at his apartment to pack. He looked fine. I wore khaki pants, a blue button-down dress shirt, and a lightweight navy blazer. Standard doctor apparel. You could walk into almost any medical office in the country and at least half the male physicians would be dressed like I was. The elevators were modern, clean and fast and I felt the blood rush to my head as we zipped up to the 41st floor.

The doors opened into a spacious vestibule and fifty feet in front of us was a set of huge glass doors manned by a security guard sitting at a desk. Above the doors in large bold letters read a sign: *Unicare Because We Really Do Care.*

Right.

I stepped up to the guard and said, "Hello, I'm Dr. John Cesari. I'm a gastroenterologist from Saint Matt's in New York City and this is Mr. Vito Gianelli, my office manager." I showed him my Saint Matt's ID which he studied with measured indifference.

Finally, he looked up at me. "Hello, Doctor, what may I do for you?"

"Well, I was in Boston for the weekend and was hoping to get a quick tour. Unicare is one of the biggest insurers covering my hospital and patients. It seems like they're all you hear about these days."

The guard was not impressed but buzzed someone inside the glass doors and passed along my request. A minute or two later, an attractive brunette in high heels and a tight skirt sauntered out to greet us. The guard made the introductions as she sized us up through her designer glasses before finally offering me her hand.

"My name is Sarah Osborne, Doctor, and I'm the section manager for Unicare. It's a pleasure to meet you and Mr. Gianelli.

It's not every day we get requests for tours but as we have a long and valued relationship with Saint Matt's, I'm certain we can spend a few minutes showing you around. Was there anything in particular you wanted to see or know about?"

"No, not really. We were just curious about Unicare because the name comes up so frequently at work, literally every day. Besides, I've never actually seen how a real insurance company operates."

"Well, I trust your experience with our company has been an entirely pleasant one. Please follow me and I'll give you a quick run-through." She turned and slinked back through the glass doors.

As we followed, Vito nudged me, nodding at her rear end and raising his eyebrows. I gave him a stern "knock it off" look and we entered a very large and busy office filled with many if not hundreds of cubicles, workers, computers, fax machines and printers.

She said, "The first eight floors of Unicare, forty-one through forty-eight, are similar to this one: the nuts and bolts of any insurance business. This is where all the claims are filed, processed, and adjudicated. Unicare employs ten thousand people world-wide, twenty-five hundred here in Boston alone, the hub of our operations. We insure over twenty-five million people in the United States and expect that number to double within the next five to seven years."

We walked through the floor casually observing the hordes of worker bees at what must surely be very tedious and monotonous labor. I actually felt bad for them. Being a doctor could be a pain in the ass at times but it was almost never boring. You were always meeting new people and dealing with fresh problems so you were always being stimulated mentally.

After thirty minutes of listening to her describe the mundane operations of the health insurance industry, I thought I would pass out from boredom. I was thankful as we eventually looped around the office heading back to the elevators. Vito was thankful that Sarah managed to stay one or two steps ahead of us at all times providing him with a great view.

Reaching the elevators Sarah turned to us. "If you come with me, we'll go to the corporate offices on the 50th floor where management resides." Once inside, she took out a key, slid it into an electronic keypad, and turned it. Then she punched in a four-digit access code and the elevator promptly took us to our destination.

I commented, "That was a neat trick with the key. I don't think I've ever seen that before."

"Well, we're not huge on security but we do take some basic precautions. For instance, from the lobby you can only get to level forty-one without a key and access code. The typical workers only have access to get to level forty-eight, and the programmers to level forty-nine. The executives, of course, and certain others such as myself have full security clearance. Then there are the security cameras." She pointed at the mirrored glass all around us.

Vito and I nodded. Concealed cameras. Very interesting.

"So, what is on the 49th floor, you didn't say?" I asked.

"An army of computer geeks and software gurus live there. Nothing you would be interested in," she responded in a tone suggesting she thought I was too much of a rube to bother going into any greater detail.

The elevator brought us to the 50th floor and she began her impromptu tour, showing us luxurious offices with Persian carpets, large potted palm trees, and tall ceilings. Every now and then a sharp-dressed man or woman would come out of one of the offices, say hello to Sarah, look at us curiously and go about their business. She explained, "There are fifty junior executives, ten VPs, two executive VPs, and the CEO. The 50th floor opens onto the world-famous Prudential Skywalk, which offers a spectacular 360 degree view of the Boston skyline and although the executives here can access it any time through a private door, members of the public can gain entrance for a small fee using a separate elevator down in the lobby."

We walked down the long hallway as she pointed out things of interest and educated us on minor points of the health insurance industry, some of which I knew and some I was surprised by. Toward the end of the hall, some twenty feet from the entrance to the Skywalk, we found ourselves staring at two large wooden doors at least ten feet tall with highly polished brass doorknobs. She pushed them open and we entered a large room at least a hundred feet long and fifty feet wide. Its highlight was a magnificent lacquered oblong table in the center, surrounded by numerous high-back leather chairs. Each position at the table had a name plate, laptop and phone.

She said, "This is the Unicare boardroom, gentlemen. The executive staff meet here weekly to discuss day-to-day operations, and once a month the entire board of trustees convenes to discuss the wellbeing of the business. This is the end of the tour, so please look around."

Vito and I meandered the length of the room to the far end, truly in awe. The walls were lined with oil paintings, and there were several busts of famous historical figures sitting on marble pedestals scattered around the perimeter. Behind the CEO's chair was a ten-foot-tall portrait of a man, his wife and, I presumed, his son. The man appeared to be in his late sixties or early seventies as was the woman and the younger man in his mid-to-late twenties. They were all dressed formally; the men in suits and ties, and the woman in black velvet with lots of bling.

I stood in front of the portrait, flabbergasted and mesmerized. Sarah noticed me staring and came up behind me. "Impressive, isn't it?"

197

"I'll say. So who are these people?"

"That's Rutherford Cecil McCormick, his deceased wife Lady Jane, and his son, Duncan Ronald McCormick. The portrait was commissioned just before her death in a motor vehicle accident ten years ago. Rutherford is the founder and president of McCormick Enterprises, which is the parent company to Unicare. He is very active in the management of Unicare and both he and his son regularly attend our weekly staff meetings. In fact, they should be here for tonight's meeting."

"The son is actively involved in the business?"

"Duncan is the business. Dad is the wheeler-dealer and very good at money things but Duncan is the future of the company. He is Oxford-educated and holds a Masters in programming from MIT. He is one of the most brilliant software developers of our time and has practically single-handedly brought Unicare online and into the twenty-first century. The 49th floor we spoke of earlier is his baby and those techies down there are like his private little army. Well, that concludes the tour, gentlemen. I hope that I was informative and able to satisfy your needs. Unicare thanks you for your support."

Vito who had been subdued during most of the tour now sprung to life. He said, "That was perfect, Sarah. Thank you. Say, I was wondering if you knew any good restaurants that you could recommend to a hungry and adventurous traveler. I was dining alone tonight and thought I might splurge a little. Money's no object." As he finished, he flashed her a huge smile showing all his teeth. He was about as subtle as a bull elephant in musth.

She reflexively looked in my direction as if to say, *"What's he doing?"*

Vito noticed her glance and answered, "Dr. Cesari is meeting his wife later to take the kids to the aquarium."

He caught me off-guard and I raised my eyebrows. I remained quiet however, mostly because I was stunned that he would have the balls to chat her up knowing we were on a mission. This was unbelievable, and just when I thought it couldn't get worse, she smiled and went for the bait. "Well, I've always been fond of the North End restaurants. Maybe not as upscale as some but the food and atmosphere are wonderful. It's a shame you have no one to share the experience with …"

She hesitated and sized Vito up. He was a man's man, for sure: Six foot three, 250 lbs. of pure muscle with dramatic dark southern Italian features. Having made up her mind, she jumped in and said, "Prezza is my favorite restaurant there. It's on Fleet Street just off of Hanover, but you know, Mr. Gianelli, the streets in the North End are narrow and dark. It may be difficult to find—on your own." She flashed her teeth at him in an equally big smile.

Jesus!

He smiled back at her. "Please call me Vito, Sarah."

While they brazenly flirted, I pulled one of the photos out from my coat pocket. I stared at it and then stared again at the portrait on the wall. There was no question about it. Except for the golden blonde hair in the portrait, Ronald Duncan, aka Ronnie, and Duncan Ronald McCormick were one and same person. What did that mean?

I said, "Well, we've taken up enough of your time, Sarah. This was very enjoyable. Thank you."

"You're welcome, Doctor," she said, as she continued to stare at Vito.

Oh, brother, she was falling for the charming guinea routine.

I couldn't take it anymore. "Well, I guess we'll be going now. C'mon, Vito."

She said, "I'll see you to the elevators."

"That would be nice," Vito said. "Say, Sarah, I hate to impose, but is there any way I could reach you if I get lost? For directions, I mean."

"I could give you my number I suppose." She said coyly. "Why don't I do that? Do you have your phone on you?" Vito took out his cell phone and she gave him her number to plug in.

"Where are you staying?" she asked.

Vito replied, "The Mandarin, not too far away."

"Really? I have an apartment on Boylston Street in the Back Bay. I can practically see the Mandarin from my window. You know, Mr. Gianelli, I mean Vito, rather than take the chance of you getting lost perhaps I could show you the way. That's if you don't mind sharing a taxi with me."

"Why would I mind that?" If she batted her eyes one more time I was sure I would puke.

She added, "Great, I'll meet you in the lobby of the Mandarin at seven."

The elevator opened on the 41st floor and Sarah got off. I put my hand against the edge of the door to prevent it from closing. "Sarah, before you go. I had one more question, if you don't mind?'

"Sure." From the way she was smiling at Vito, I could've asked about a thousand more questions.

"A while back, one of my patients had a problem getting coverage for his medications and I called Unicare and spoke with a representative who was extremely helpful. I know there are a lot of employees here and you probably don't know all of them personally but I was wondering if you could thank the person on my behalf if you run across them."

"I would be happy to, Dr. Cesari. What is the person's name? I'm sure they will be thrilled to hear such positive feedback."

"I think her name was Esha—Esha Deshmukh. Yes, that was it."

She laughed politely. "Esha Deshmukh? Are you certain?"

"Yes, why?"

"Esha Deshmukh is the President and CEO of Unicare. I think it very unlikely she took a service call like you just described."

I was surprised, to say the least. "She said she was a lawyer and she had an educated British accent."

"True and true. Esha Deshmukh graduated in the top ten of her class at the University of Cambridge Law School and she is undoubtedly one of the most cultured human beings I have ever met, but it simply doesn't make sense that she would do that. I'll look into it to see if there is another person by that name employed here. If there is, I'll let Vito know over dinner tonight."

"Thank you, Sarah."

Chapter 22

Vito was in the bathroom humming and singing "Strangers in the Night" to himself as he prepared for his date with Sarah. After we left Unicare he had gone shopping and bought himself some new clothes. I had just finished talking to Cocoa. She and Cleo were doing fine in Vito's apartment. Vito came out from the bathroom and looked in exceedingly good humor.

"Sorry about leaving you alone, Cesari, but when nature calls, nature calls." Apparently, he thought that was real funny because he started to chuckle as he sat on the edge of his bed to put his shoes on.

"No problem, Vito. You have a good time. Did I mention that someone is trying to kill me?"

"You'll be fine, just stay in the hotel room and don't answer the door for anyone but me. If you want, go down to the parking lot and get the .45 I have in the trunk."

"Why'd you leave it there?"

"I didn't want to take a chance on someone in the hotel spotting it and raising a ruckus. Massachusetts has strict gun laws and not only don't I have a permit but I didn't exactly purchase it from a licensed gun store."

"Well, thanks for the tips on self-preservation, but I thought I brought you here to watch my back, not to get laid by the first girl that smiles at you. Is this some new technique in the world of personal security? Someone takes a shot at me and

I text my bodyguard who's in another part of the city getting his rocks off?"

Nothing I could do or say was going to ruin his mood. He just chuckled at my rebuke. "Hey Cesari, no offense but did you get a look at the melons on that girl? You can't expect me to sit around a hotel room all night watching the golf channel with you when I got a chance at those love-apples. I mean, I hope nothing happens to you while I'm gone but you have to admit that it's a small price to pay."

I had to laugh. "Sure, I understand perfectly and I want you to enjoy yourself. I really do. Please don't misunderstand me either. I sincerely hope that she doesn't have AIDS."

He tossed his car keys at me. "In case you want the gun. Okay, it's almost time to go. Sarah will be downstairs in a few minutes and then we got to get a cab."

"Out of curiosity, why don't you just drive down to the North End instead of taking a cab?"

"Are you kidding? On a Friday night? Traffic is impossible down there let alone parking, especially by Prezza's."

"You've been there before? It didn't sound like it."

"I've been there many times. It's one of my favorite joints in the North End. As a matter of fact, I've been there so many times that I already called the maître d' and warned him to pretend he doesn't know me."

I was confused. "I don't understand? Why did you act like you never heard of it?"

As if he were lecturing a small child he said, "What's wrong with you, Cesari? What don't you get about the female of our species? Nothing turns them on more than when they feel like they're in charge. You act a little helpless and their nurturing instinct kicks into high gear."

"Oh really, is that how it's done? Then maybe I should have mentioned to her that I was shot?"

He laughed. "Worst thing you could have done. Helpless isn't the same thing as hopeless to a chick. Let me give you an example. Let's say a woman comes home exhausted from work, right? She can barely stand she's so tired. You're lying on the couch sucking down a cold one and watching the ball game because you're unemployed and she's making plenty for both of you. She asks you to help her clean the apartment, like say, vacuum or something. Your justifiable instinct is to say fuck off, but you know deep down that wouldn't be smart so you say sure. You get the vacuum cleaner out of the closet while she's watching. After ten minutes of unsuccessfully attaching the hose or something she offers to help. You smile and say, no sweetheart, you rest, I got it under control. Now you plug it in and start banging it around into the walls and her furniture. Maybe you knock a glass off the table or accidentally suck up the cat. Then you spot something on the ceiling and start vacuuming up there. After a while like that damaging the house, what do you think she says?"

"You're an asshole?"

"No, she says go sit down and she'll take care of it. Thanks for trying."

"Seriously?"

"Hell, yeah. Getting shot, on the other hand, is like wearing a sign telling a girl that you're an evolutionary dead end, the last of your species. Girls are always sizing guys up whether consciously or not to see if they'll be there for them and their children. Almost getting killed is a sign that your genetic makeup is suspicious, that maybe you can't cut the mustard. Just remember, Cesari, an eagle would never go on a date with a dodo bird and you, my friend, are the dodo bird."

Thankfully, just when I thought I couldn't take it anymore, he changed the subject. "Okay, Cesari, I'm wasting time. How do I look?"

He wore black pants, a crisp white dress shirt, gold cufflinks, a solid red tie and the same black sport coat that he had brought with him from New York. He was an awkward size because of his massive, muscular chest and shoulders. He simply did not look right in an off-the-rack jacket without extensive tailoring. He looked good for a guy who had his nose broken more than once in his life without the benefit of proper medical care.

I said, "You look great. So, what's the plan if you get lucky? I have no intention of sleeping in the lobby."

"You worry too much, Cesari. If things go my way, and I know they will, then we'll either go to her apartment or I'll just get another room. See you in the morning."

"Have fun."

He left and I thought about what I had learned tonight from our trip to Unicare. I was more confused than ever. Why would the son of one of the more important and wealthy people on the planet dye his hair and go around helping secretaries at a busy New York City hospital? And why would Esha Deshmukh, the CEO of the company, care personally about what I knew about the Konstandin case? She must have an entire legal department at her disposal to handle such matters. This was beyond nuts, unless there was something uniquely different about this case. The kind of something that kept you up at night worrying that someone else might find out.

Hmm. So what could that something possibly be? I had already reviewed the case and spoken to Tony before he jumped out the window. The only discrepancy was that he had dictated the colonoscopy report as normal but had submitted the bill as colon cancer. So, he had either dictated the report wrong or submitted the bill wrong, and since the guy really had colon cancer, clearly the report was in error. Tony was supposed to request the file from Unicare to review it himself but never got around to it and since I wasn't involved personally with the case,

Unicare was under no obligation to let me look at it. I looked at my watch. It was almost 8:00. The skywalk observatory was open to the public until 10:00. It was time to kick it into high gear and find out what was going on at Unicare. More specifically, I wanted to know what Duncan Ronald McCormick was doing on the 49th floor there with his army of techies.

It was a balmy autumn night. I drove Vito's Lincoln over to the Prudential Building and parked in practically the same spot as earlier in the day. In the trunk, I found a black duffel bag with a loaded .45 caliber Springfield which I shoved into the back of my pants, hidden from view by my blazer. I walked up the stairs to the lobby and found the elevators to the 50th floor observation deck, paid for my ticket, and boarded. Just before 9:00, I was truly enjoying a breathtaking view of Boston through massive floor-to-ceiling windows. There was quite a crowd of tourists milling about and I blended in, trying to get my bearings as I cruised around. The circular enclosed walkway was lined with displays highlighting the historical development of the city together with an excellent and informative history of immigration into Boston's neighborhoods. Outside the enclosed observation deck was an outer walkway with a metal safety railing. This could be accessed through another set of doors but was not open to the public tonight.

As I walked around, I noted two emergency exits in addition to the elevators that I had come up on. There was one maintenance door near the bathrooms and concession stands and then off by itself there was a door with a decorative frame and brass placard that read *Private*. There was no outward indication as to where this door led but it had a highly polished brass latch handle rather than a door knob. Whoever built this door was trying to please the people who were going to use it. Casually passing by, I tested the handle which of course was locked. This had to be it. The executives would want easy access to and from the observatory for lunch and leisurely strolls to relieve the stress. It was hard work making money hand over fist while people were dying.

I passed the time reading posters and walking in circles until 9:45 when an overhead announcement informed visitors that it was almost closing time and we should start thinking about boarding the elevators. A few minutes later, I discreetly ducked into the bathroom to take up position in one of the stalls. I was sure that by 10:15 or 10:30 at the latest an exhausted minimum wage employee would check the bathroom for stragglers. This would consist of a quick sweep around the room and a perfunctory glance for feet under the stalls. No one there, then lights out. I waited patiently and at 10:00, I stood on top of the toilet seat and crouched so my head wouldn't stick out above. I was uncomfortable and hoped I didn't have to wait long.

After ten minutes like that, I noticed that the noise outside the bathroom had died down considerably. Within another five minutes the bathroom door opened and a voice called out to see if anyone was there. No response forthcoming, the lights went out and the door closed. I waited a few more minutes in the dark for the last remaining employees to leave and then cautiously came out of the bathroom. The observatory had gone dark and quiet. Ambient light filtered in through the large windows from the moon and city lights allowing me reasonable visibility once my eyes adjusted.

I found the door with the shiny brass handle and tested it again just to make sure. It was locked and I studied it. It wasn't particularly high tech and why would it be? They weren't expecting anybody to break in from the observatory deck. What would they be after anyway? You couldn't even use the elevators without a key and an access code. My greatest concern was about any security features that might be triggered when the door opened. If that happened, I might have to spend the night in the bathroom or under the boardroom table. I was praying that, like in most big corporations, egos and arrogance soared high with profits and with those came a certain amount of complacency.

My immediate problem, however, was that the door and frame were metal so I wasn't going to be able to kick the door in. It also looked like high quality craftsmanship and I doubted that I'd be able to wiggle my credit card into the mechanism, an old but reliable trick. Thinking it over, I walked to the concession stand and searched behind the counter for anything useful, using my cell phone as a light. I found a small screwdriver but didn't think that would help. As I walked back to the door, resigning myself to blowing out the lock with the .45, I heard a sound and stepped back quickly into the shadows, leaning against the wall.

The door opened and two people emerged onto the observation deck. There was almost no light accompanying them which meant they were also trying to keep a low profile. It was a man and a woman and they giggled as they proceeded toward the windowed walkway. They held a bottle of something, maybe wine, and a blanket. As they got closer to the window overlooking the city, I could see them better in the moon light. It was Duncan McCormick, aka Ronnie, and he was with a very beautiful dark-skinned woman whom I had no doubt was Esha Deshmukh. They wrapped their arms around each other and kissed passionately. Hmm, a little tryst to unwind following the board meeting?

So that was that. Hugging, they moved along the observatory deck to find a more suitable location for their liaison and were soon out of my field of vision. I tried to listen but really couldn't hear anything well from where I was. Taking advantage of the opportunity, I inched over to the door which they had left partially open and silently crept through. Once inside, I thought about jamming the lock mechanism so they would be trapped outside but decided it was unnecessary and might give away my presence.

Looking around, I found myself in the same hallway through which Sarah had taken me and Vito on our tour earlier, only the elevators were on the opposite end, maybe half a football field's length away. The entrance to the board room was maybe twenty feet down the hall on my right and there was a bathroom just a few feet away on my left. The corridor was dark except for low-level floor lighting and fire alarm safety lights blinking on the walls. Moving quickly down the corridor toward the wide-open doors of the elevator, I remembered the security cameras Sarah had told us about and gave it a wide berth. Next to the elevator was an emergency stairwell and I went to it, hesitating in front of the door. What if the alarm rang when I opened it? Could I possibly explain my presence here? I laughed inwardly at that. Once again, the thought entered my mind that I might be spending the night up here hiding in a closet.

I took a deep breath and pushed the door open and nothing happened. That was good to know because now at least I had a way out of the building. I walked down to the 49th floor, the technological nerve center of Unicare, where Duncan kept his minions hard at work saving the world.

There was a panel on the wall near me with a series of light switches controlling various sections of the large room. Turning them on I found myself in a gigantic space that had almost none of the amenities that would define a modern office. It had the warehouse-like atmosphere that we have all become used to at places like Costco and BJ's. The multitude of inexpensive desks and furniture were not even separated by cubicle walls and there were no potted plants, plush carpeting or drop ceilings with soft lighting. People in this room came to work and nothing else. Each desk had a laptop on it and massive servers rimmed the entire room. There were hundreds of laptops on hundreds of small metal desks. Miles of electrical wires crisscrossed the room connecting the laptops and their peripheral devices. For a second I thought I was in NASA. My mind boggled at the maintenance required for this place as I thought about my one little laptop which crashed or froze on me at least two or three times every day.

I walked around the room taking it all in and wondering where to begin. The room seemed rather insecure, but that might have been my perception because of how I had gained access. Surveillance cameras aside, one could not get physically past the 41st floor without a key and security code and one could probably not use the elevators coming down from the 50th floor for the same reason unless you took the emergency stairwell like I did. So, it begged the rather obvious question: Why was there no alarm system in the emergency stairwell? Good question.

Did Ronnie disable the alarm so he and Esha didn't accidentally trigger it while they wandered around after hours in their amorous fervor? Possibly. He was a computer genius after all and may have designed the whole thing himself. If anybody would know how to disarm the alarm system he would. That definitely made sense. It seemed that I may have gotten lucky that Ronnie needed to satisfy his more visceral side tonight. Or maybe it was Esha who needed to be satisfied. Was Ronnie her plaything or the other way around? You never knew with women anymore. They were all out of control.

Walking around the room quickly, I scanned several desks for anything of interest. The vast array of laptops was daunting and the sheer number made it improbable that just randomly swiping one would be of any benefit. I needed to hone in better.

There was only one private office on this floor and the door to it was unlocked. I entered an unassuming, sparsely furnished room that was approximately twenty feet square with industrial carpeting, a six-foot-long faux wood desk and imitation leather chair, both of which could have been obtained at Staples. On one of the walls there was a portrait of a man in later life. A small brass placard at the bottom read *Konrad Zuse,* whoever he was. I made a mental note to look him up. Even more interesting were the red Valentino pocketbook on the desk and the black thong lying on the floor by the chair. I smiled. I was on to something. This was Ronnie's office and she was his girlfriend. Fair enough. At least I was in the right place.

On the desk was a closed laptop, which I immediately decided was the prize I was hoping to find. First, however, I opened the Valentino handbag and found her wallet confirming her ID with her driver's license. *You're a bad girl Esha, but I'll deal with you later.* I sat at the desk and looked around the room. There were no file cabinets and the desk drawers were empty. I looked at his laptop and opened it. It was after 11:00 and I couldn't afford to waste too much time. They were both young and healthy, but how long could they go at it up there? I thought about myself and guessed a long time depending on the mood I was in, at least before the shooting that was.

I figured that I would need a while to examine the computer thoroughly so I took a big risk. Closing the laptop, I decided to take it with me and examine it at my leisure. The problem was that now Ronnie and Esha would know that somebody had been here and maybe knew about them and whatever scam they were running. I used the word scam hypothetically because I still had no idea what was going on but I was getting warmer. I felt it deep inside.

Heading toward the door, I hesitated, glancing once more at the picture of Konrad Zuse. I went back to the desk and took a pencil from a cup holder and picked the thong off the floor with it. Studying it briefly, I carried it over to the portrait and jabbed the pencil through the canvas, suspending the thong in midair. That should give them something to think about.

I went to the stairwell and walked quickly the whole way down to the garage. By the time I made it there my legs were wobbly and my shins were killing me. Before entering the Lincoln, I turned around to look at the building.

What the fuck was going on here?

Chapter 23

It was just before midnight by the time I got back to the Mandarin, thoroughly satisfied with myself. I boarded one of the elevators, swiped my room key and pressed the button for the seventeenth floor. Lost in thought, I barely noticed the motion upward. Before reaching my destination, the elevator stopped with a jolt and I momentarily lost balance almost dropping the laptop. The lights went out suddenly and the doors didn't open. Shit. I thought I might be stuck in between floors. After perhaps a minute in total darkness, the lights came back on and the elevator resumed its ascent safely reaching my floor. I breathed a sigh of relief.

The doors opened and I exited the elevator turning to the right to find my room. I fumbled for the room key and held it up against the receiver. The light went from red to green and I heard the lock open. The room was dark and I thought I smelled the odor of a cigarette. Vito smoked but he wouldn't be here unless things had gone very badly with his date. For some reason, I thought that was funny.

I turned on the room light and no Vito. Too bad, I would have loved to bust his chops about Sarah. I put the laptop down and sat on the edge of the bed. Something was wrong. I looked around the room and noticed the bathroom door was closed. I called out, "Vito, are you in there?"

I stood up, suddenly feeling the hair on the back of my neck jump to attention. It was then that I noticed a hand sticking out from under one of the beds. It was a small hand, a delicate hand—a woman's hand. Curious, I bent down to see better and realized it belonged to one of the housekeepers. My mind raced, trying to digest what was happening. Suddenly, I heard the bathroom door swing open. I jumped to attention and spun around quickly, trying to reach the .45 in the small of my back but I was too late. He fired the shotgun directly into my chest and the explosion was deafening. I was in total darkness again.

When the lights came on, the elevator doors opened onto the seventeenth floor. I was perspiring, my heart raced and I could barely breathe. What the hell had just happened? I poked and prodded myself to see if I was awake. I was losing my mind for sure. No doubt about it, but I was still alive. I stepped out of the elevator, turning to my room, only this time I placed the laptop safely on the floor by the entrance. I wasn't taking any chances. I reached for the .45 and made sure a round was chambered. Opening the door slowly, I saw the closed bathroom door and detected the scent of tobacco. Don't overreact, I told myself. The sound of unnecessary gunfire would bring a whole lot of attention that I didn't want.

Barely breathing, I turned on the light, and walked slowly into the room never taking my eyes off the bathroom door. When I saw the hand sticking out from under the bed, I knew I wasn't dreaming. According to the time frame in my head, I had about ten seconds before he charged out of the bathroom looking for me, gun in hand.

I moved quickly back to the room's entrance and scrunched up to the side of the bathroom door so that when he emerged, I would be behind him. As an added measure, I turned off the lights and waited in the darkness. *Five, four, three, two, one.* The bathroom door burst open and he charged into the center of the room surprised to find the lights out. He cursed and I made out his silhouette, bringing the butt of the .45 crashing down on the back of his head.

He fell limply to the ground unconscious and I turned the lights on. He was white, with brown hair, about six feet, 200 lbs. I dragged him further into the room, restraining his hands behind his back with his belt. I shoved a washcloth from the bathroom into his mouth in case he woke up and positioned him face down on the floor next to the housekeeper he had strangled just so he could borrow her room key. Asshole. I searched through the guy's wallet to see who he was but didn't recognize his name. His driver's license indicated he lived in Philadelphia.

I called Vito. "What's up, Cesari?"

"I need you here—now."

"Are you out of your mind? Sarah and I are just getting started."

"I'm serious. I got a dead housekeeper here in the room and some hit man I never heard of unconscious on the floor next to her."

"You're kidding? What happened?"

"Just get over here."

"Okay, God damn it. You owe me, Cesari. This girl is totally wild when she gets going."

"Will you shut up and hurry? This guy could wake at any minute and I don't know if he has any backup."

"All right, all right, I'm on the way."

The guy on the floor hadn't woken up and I was wondering whether I should voluntarily check myself in for psychiatric evaluation when Vito barged into the room disheveled and flushed less than thirty minutes later.

"Sorry about ruining your date, Vito." He didn't answer me as he inspected the dead housekeeper first and then the hit man next to her. He rummaged through the guy's pockets like I had and then his wallet, staring at his driver's license.

"How'd you get the drop on him if he was waiting for you?" he asked.

"I got lucky."

Vito nodded looking at the sawed-off shotgun. "I'll say. Well, we've got to be creative here, Cesari. It's after one in the morning. We can't have the Mandarin waking up to a double homicide in our room tomorrow."

"I know that. The room's on my credit card, and it's only a single homicide."

Vito said very seriously, "If he even makes one sound, it's going to be a double homicide, understand?"

I nodded. "Yeah, I understand. Thank God he strangled her. At least there are no blood stains to clean up."

He was deep in thought. "All right, where's the room key he used to get in here?"

"It's still on her, connected to her waist by a retractable string device."

Vito searched her and yanked the card off. "C'mon, let's find out if there are any available rooms on this floor."

He took out his cell phone and dialed the Mandarin's main lobby. "Hi, I know it's late but my wife and I are at Logan Airport. There was a major delay of our flight from Chicago due to mechanical problems and we just arrived. We had reservations at the Omni Parker downtown but missed check-in and they have no rooms available now. Well, my wife just reminded me that we stayed at the Mandarin five years ago on our honeymoon and I was wondering if we could stay in the same room that we did then. We would both be very grateful. We stayed in room 1721 but I'm sure anything on the seventeenth floor would make her happy."

"Give me a moment, sir, and I'll check."

"I'm sorry, sir, room 1721 is not available but there are two other rooms on that floor which are, 1735 and 1709. Would one of them be to your satisfaction?"

"Either one will be fine, thank you. We'll be there in an hour. The name is Smith."

"Do you want to give me your credit card information now or when you arrive?"

"Our taxi just pulled up and it's raining out here. How about we take care of business when we arrive?"

"That would be perfect. Safe travels and we look forward to your stay with us."

He hung up and looked at me. "Okay, let's get cracking and make sure this key works."

I picked room 1709 because it was marginally closer and tested the key, which worked without a problem. Then I went back to Vito and we carried the guy quickly to his new home, throwing him on the bed. Breathing heavily and perspiring, we rested briefly. He wasn't that heavy but our adrenaline was in hyperdrive. The activity must have stimulated the guy because his eyes started to flutter and he coughed. Vito had retaken possession of his .45 and now took it out of his pocket and smashed the guy in the head with it. His eyes stopped fluttering. We went back and carried the housekeeper down the hall in the same fashion. I was more worried about what would happen if somebody saw us with her. The other guy we could always say was a drunk friend. Her uniform would raise suspicions but we were lucky and didn't run into anyone. She was considerably lighter than the guy and we were able to move faster.

We looked at them lying side by side on the queen bed and were about to go back to our room when Vito snapped his fingers. "You know, Cesari, if we just leave them here like this he might get off scot-free. It looks like he might be a victim too."

I thought about that and said, "We could just kill him, but that would be way below my standards."

He snapped his fingers. "I got an idea. Let's position him on top of her, take the belt off his wrists and wrap it around her neck. Get the picture? It will look like he strangled her during an attempted sexual assault and maybe he passed out from whatever."

I thought about that, but he had two lumps on the back of his head which might suggest to a bright investigator that this was a setup. "That might work but we'll have to dress it up a bit better than that. Let's unzip his pants and pull them down to his knees before we put him on top of her."

After we positioned them, we studied our handiwork. Vito said, "Not bad, Cesari."

"Yeah, but not perfect." I took the woman's left hand and dragged her finger nails forcefully down his right cheek creating long scratch marks. I said, "Now that's perfect. Let's see him explain how his DNA got under her fingernails."

"What about the lumps on his head?"

I took a bottle of wine out of the minibar and put it into her right hand and swung it hard against the back of his head smashing it. The smell of white wine filled the room.

"Damn, Cesari. Remind me never to piss you off."

"He deserves it. Let's get our stuff and check out."

On the way out to the parking lot, I dialed 911. "Hello, I'm a guest at the Mandarin hotel on Boylston and just saw a man drag a housekeeper by the hair into one of the rooms against her will. It was room 1709. Please hurry. She was crying and I think he is going to hurt her." I hung up quickly and then made the same call to the Mandarin main lobby as we got into the Lincoln.

Speeding off, Vito chuckled, "I hope that guy's got a good lawyer."

"Too late for that. I don't see any way of his getting out of this."

"Well, I hope he spends his time in prison learning how to make himself a better person."

I chuckled at Vito's sarcasm. "He'll be better off learning how to make a shiv."

Chapter 24

The next morning, Vito and I were sitting in the living room of his apartment above the Café Napoli on Mulberry Street in Little Italy, sipping espressos and nibbling on pistachio biscotti. The apartment was large, with only one way in and out, guarded day and night by Vito's men. The windows were bricked up and the only way out besides the front entrance was a trap door Vito had installed in his bedroom, which led down into the kitchen of the restaurant below. No one knew about this except for the carpenter who had installed it in the middle of the night and now no one knew the carpenter's whereabouts. The trap door was covered by a throw rug and an exercise bike Vito never used. He had told me about it just in case something happened and I needed a quick exit.

I asked, "So what happened to the carpenter? Please tell me you didn't …?"

"I didn't do anything. I paid him a fortune and one day he just disappeared. Rumor has it that he's living on some island in the Caribbean building Tiki bars."

"Not a bad plan B for me if things don't work out in healthcare."

"How are you doing for scratch, by the way? You've been out of work for a while now."

"I'm fine for the moment. Cocoa took care of the rent and maintenance while I was hospitalized and I'll reimburse her for that. The hospital kept me on the payroll for the two months I was out and my disability will kick in if I don't return to work soon, but I should be back within a week or two. In the meanwhile I have plenty in the bank to cover me for now."

"Well, if you need anything you know where to come."

"Sure and with only thirty percent interest compounded daily."

He chuckled. "Thirty percent is the family discount, Cesari."

Cocoa joined us, taking a seat beside me on the sofa. "Hi, guys. Vito, I have to tell you I am impressed with this apartment."

"Thank you, Cocoa. I hope your room is comfortable?"

"It is. I especially like the loaded handgun I found under the sink in the bathroom."

He chuckled. "Sorry about that. There's one in every room as a precaution. I'll take it out later if it bothers you."

"It doesn't bother me at all. So, that was quite a night you guys had up there in Boston." I had filled her in when we arrived minus my premonition. I would save that for Mark later.

I said, "Yeah, I'll say, but at least the dots are starting to connect. I'm going to spend the day deciphering the laptop and doing background research on Unicare. Vito's going to try to figure out who it is that wants me dead and hopefully call them off."

Cocoa asked, "So we still have no idea why or who it is?"

I thought about that. "No, not really, and I don't know anyone in Philadelphia let alone someone who would go to such trouble for me."

Vito took a sip of coffee and said, "Cesari, just because the contract's from Philly, it doesn't mean that's where the money's from. It could be someone right here in the city that's simply covering his trail, and God knows, you've offended plenty of people here over the years. Maybe they just felt it was the right time to strike."

I nodded. You never knew with these things. "Great, so somebody from my past just decided to even the score the minute I got released from the hospital? That's quite a coincidence but I guess it's possible."

He said, "It's more than just possible. It happens all the time. I'll know more this afternoon anyway. I have my guys working on it. Now that we know who it is that came after you last night, we can start spreading cash around the street. Somebody will talk. They always do, and my boys think they know where Sammy Beans is, so with any luck we'll have him too before the day's over."

Cocoa seemed very distracted. I asked, "Is everything okay?"

She looked at me. "Yeah, but you two sound awfully busy today."

"I'm sorry, but we have a lot to do. Do you want to go uptown to Juilliard to practice? My apartment's probably not such a smart idea right now. Who knows who's watching it."

"I think maybe I'm going to take the train to Morristown and visit my parents. I haven't seen them in a while and they have a piano I can practice on there. It's not the greatest but it'll be fine."

There was something in her tone that didn't seem right to me, but I wasn't sure. I hadn't thought about her parents or her Uncle Leo in quite a while. I wondered if she had told anyone about her reconnection with me. That would have been natural when I was sick in the hospital. Oh well, nothing I could do about that now.

I said, "Well, I'm going to get cracking on the laptop. Vito, I'll talk to you later, okay?"

He said, "I'm going to take a nap first before I do anything else. Cocoa, you know your way around, right? If you need anything just holler. I can have one of my guys drive you to

Penn Station or the PATH hub at the World Trade Center when you're ready."

"Thanks, Vito, but I'll be fine. I'm just going to make myself a cup of coffee and then I'll get going."

I went into the bedroom that Cocoa had set up in and sat at the desk there. I was about to open the laptop when I suddenly realized how tired I was. Two all-night drives to Boston and back in as many days had taken their toll and I yawned. The bed was looking pretty tempting so I lay down thinking that maybe an hour nap would do me a world of good. Within minutes, I was out cold and didn't even hear Cocoa enter the room to get her stuff.

When I woke two hours later, there was a note on the desk next to the laptop from her, apologizing for not waking me to say goodbye and that she would call me later. Even the note sounded like there was something wrong. Well, whatever it was, I was sure she would get around to telling me. She was young and spirited. Maybe it was time for her to move on. She had done her duty and seen me through an exceptionally difficult time and now maybe things were starting to look different. We hadn't had sex since I had come out of the hospital. Maybe that was it? We had tried a few times but I just wasn't ready. Maybe I needed to try harder?

I opened the laptop and booted it up. As I did, I wondered what Ronnie and Esha's reaction had been when they returned from their tryst to find the laptop missing and her underwear dangling from the wall painting. That must have been priceless.

After a few minutes, the boot screen appeared requiring a password. I anticipated that and tried several combinations of Duncan's name and then his father and mother's names without success. Then I tried Esha's name and Unicare also unsuccessfully. Guessing someone's password was generally a frustrating and unrewarding experience and I was thinking I might need professional help to hack into this laptop.

On my own laptop I googled Duncan's birthday and other important facts about Unicare and tried them to no avail. I sat there for over an hour becoming increasingly discouraged. We choose passwords we can remember easily or with minimal prompting or else what would be the point? I had looked around his office and hadn't noticed any notebooks he might have kept a list of passwords in. That was also a foolish thing to do but people did it anyway—all the time.

Then I remembered the portrait on the wall of Konrad Zuse, who now had a thong hanging from a pencil jammed into his face. I plugged in his name and nothing happened. Who was he anyway? I googled him up. He was a German civil engineer born in Berlin in 1910 and was credited with having invented the first programmable computer called the Z1. He died in 1995. So, he was probably a hero of sorts to this computer whiz kid, Duncan Ronald McCormick. I read on about him. Konrad Zuse wasn't a Nazi per se but he collaborated with them extensively and much of his work went unnoticed in the west because of the war. And then I saw it. He initially called his computer the V1 but it was changed to Z1 so that it wouldn't be confused with the V1 rockets that had devastated London. V1 in turn was an abbreviation for VersuchsModell 1 which was German for Experimental Model 1. I typed in VersuchsModell 1, hit the enter key and watched as the laptop completed its boot process. I chuckled to myself. Ronnie went to Oxford and MIT and he wasn't even Cesari-smart.

After two hours of reading through mostly mundane reports and records, I came across an unlabeled folder and opened it. It was a list of physicians in various departments of Saint Matt's, patients, and diagnoses. At the end of each line was a simple yes or no. I saw Tony's name next to Mr. Konstandin and the word yes. In all, there were twelve physicians' names and patients. Ten said yes; only two, no. What on earth was this all about? I breathed a sigh of relief that my name wasn't on the list.

I scrolled through his list of programs and folders and came across an executable file called simply Z1.exe so I clicked on it and an error message popped up stating that I was not connected to the network. Hmm. I checked the wireless connection and it seemed to be working just fine. What network was it referring to?

I turned to my laptop and logged onto the electronic medical records system at Saint Matt's. One by one, I plugged in the names of the twelve patients that I found listed on Ronnie's laptop. Now that was interesting. Eleven of the twelve patients were deceased, but I couldn't tell what they had died from. According to the records I was looking at, the last doctors' notes indicated that they were under routine care for routine medical problems. No less than half had undergone negative screening colonoscopies. Two had undergone negative chest x-rays and the last four had negative screening mammograms. I logged out of the electronic records and sat there deep in thought. The only living patient of the twelve was a sixty-year-old woman named Chow Liu, who lived deep in the heart of Chinatown in a second story apartment on Mott Street. It also said that she only spoke Mandarin and required an interpreter. I wrote down her phone number and address.

I called up Helen Ho, the hot orthopedic surgeon. I knew she had grown up in Chinatown and spoke fluent Mandarin. "Cesari, it's so good to hear from you. The entire hospital has been buzzing about your amazing recovery. Will you be coming back to work soon? I've missed you."

That was a pretty warm reception from a girl who had turned me down for a date no less than six, maybe ten times. I guess nearly dying had changed her perception of my repulsiveness, and she did send me a get well card. Well, actually she had signed a card with about fifty other hospital staff. Still—maybe Vito was wrong about girls thinking I was an evolutionary dead end. "Thank you, Helen. It's good to be back but Goldstein won't let me work for a couple of more weeks or until he's convinced that I don't have any brain damage."

She laughed. "Do you?"

"It's hard to tell, sometimes. Look, Helen, I was calling to see if you'd like to get some Peking duck with me over on Mott Street? I'd like to see you and catch up."

She hesitated. "When were you thinking?"

"How about in an hour?"

"An hour would be fine." Then she chuckled. "Is this a date, Cesari? I mean I feel bad for you and all that …"

"Not that bad, huh?" I laughed this time. "Just friends, Helen. I like to look at you."

Then she said something in a very different tone than I was used to hearing from her. Quietly, with emotion, almost a whisper. "And I like it when you look at me."

I thought to myself that she was just being nice because of what had happened to me. I said, "I'm glad we found common ground. I'll meet you at the Peking Duck House on Mott Street. Do you know it?"

"Of course I know it. I grew up around the corner."

Glancing at my watch I said, "Then I'll see you at six."

I quickly showered, shaved and splashed on some Old Spice. It couldn't hurt to smell nice. The restaurant was just a couple of blocks from Vito's apartment and I arrived with two minutes to spare and just as she turned the corner from Bayard Street, waving at me.

We entered the Peking Duck House and sat in the corner by the window. "It's really so unbelievable, Cesari. I mean the whole thing. First getting shot, then being in a coma, and then just waking up and walking out of there." She spoke in an excited voice and her cheeks were flushed.

"You don't have to tell me. Every morning I wake up and pinch myself. It's really good to see you, Helen. You look great." Tall and slender, she had an adorable face with shoulder-length black hair kept in a bob. She liked to run and was building her way up to an Iron Man event. She was sexy like Cocoa, but in a different way. The scent of her perfume drifted across the table at me and I noticed that she wore makeup and lipstick. The thought crossed my mind that maybe she had a date later.

"Thank you, Cesari. So, talk to me. Tell me everything and don't leave anything out."

"You go first, Helen. I've been a coma and don't have much to tell that you don't already know from the news."

The waiter came over and we ordered a pot of tea and the Peking duck for two. I liked restaurants like this. There wasn't much stress involved since ninety percent of the patrons ordered the same thing. You could get other stuff but why would you?

After he left, I finished my thought. "What have I missed in the last two and a half months? I mean I know what Arnie has told me but what's the word from the rank and file?"

She smiled. Every hospital now used a form of doublespeak that was made famous in George Orwell's *1984*, and everybody knew it. *Everything's fine* meant uh oh, *it's under control* meant it isn't, *we're working on it* meant don't hold your breath, and *tell me what you think* meant only if you don't need this job.

She said, "Well, let's start with my department. The new orthopedic guy they hired last year is about to get fired but he doesn't know it. He's all thumbs and the patients hate him. I feel kind of bad because he's married and has a kid. They just bought a condo in Brooklyn too. The cardiologist, Breamer, I don't know how familiar you are with him, but his wife was having an affair with his junior partner, Olaf, the guy from Sweden. They got into a fistfight over it right in the emergency room and both got suspended. That's it for the fun stuff. Arnie's been on the war path about documentation because we got cited by the state for deficiencies after several patients filed complaints."

I chuckled about the cardiologists. "I remembered Arnie talking about documentation problems. What are patients complaining about exactly?"

"That the doctors are either poorly documenting their care or completely falsifying the record for God only knows what purpose since no one benefits in the slightest from any of it."

That's what Mrs. Konstandin had complained about. "And that's got Arnie's panties in a bunch?"

"I'll say. That's about all the gossip I got, Cesari. Otherwise, things have been more or less quiet except for you, that is. You're the really big news, all day, every day."

I smiled at that. As a guy who generally liked to keep a low profile I wasn't doing too well at the moment. While we chatted, the chef wheeled the cart over with our duck and started slicing it in front of us as another waiter placed the pancakes, scallions and accompanying sauce on the table. I poured us some more tea and we started eating.

I swallowed my first mouthful and savored it for a moment. Delicious. "Well, Helen, the reason I called you is that I've been catching up on some unfinished medical business from before the shooting and I need to interview a patient who lives upstairs from here and she only speaks Mandarin. I knew you did as well so …"

She stopped chewing and sat back in her chair with a hurt look on her face. "You've got to be kidding? You brought me out on a Saturday night to act as an interpreter?"

The obvious answer was yes but from the tone in her voice and the look on her face I knew better than to say it out loud. I studied her appearance. She wore gold hoop earrings and a silk blouse that was open just a tiny bit too much at the top. Helen wasn't one to doll up for no reason.

Oh shit! I just stepped in it. She thought this was a date.

I opened my mouth to begin damage control but she snorted. "And here I was thinking you were going to finally act like a man and make your move instead of beating around the bush like you always do. Do you have any idea how sad I have been over what happened to you? I think a part of me may have died that day when I saw you in the ICU. All I could think about was all the time we wasted flirting when we could have been making passionate love. When you called earlier, I was ecstatic. I wasn't sure if you even remembered who I was, let alone still had feelings for me."

Christ almighty, how was I supposed to handle this? "Helen, I'm sorry. I thought you didn't—you know—like me in that way."

"You're awfully thickheaded, Cesari. You were dishing it out and I was giving back to you. I thought you understood that."

I blushed and stammered. "But you asked me if this was a date …"

"I was just teasing you. Why else would you call a girl up on a Saturday night to have dinner? Look, Cesari, guys like the chase because it turns them on. It's the male instinct. Something about prey running away drives them forward. The same is true for women only in reverse. We like to be chased. The harder we get chased the more it turns us on, but at some point the chase has to end and we have to get caught. That's what I thought this was about, that maybe your near death experience had given you the gumption to step up to the plate."

Between Vito and Helen, I was learning a lot about women this weekend. I let out a slow breath and, deeply contrite, said, "Well, I'm sorry I didn't pick up on the body language. I actually thought you found me sort of—repugnant."

"Repugnant? If I found you repugnant, would I dream of riding horses with you on a warm summer day in the countryside ending with you taking me passionately in the stable like some farm animal? When you called me tonight, I almost jumped out of my skin with sexual excitement."

Geez. I needed to head this off at the pass. "Helen, I don't know what to say. I do find you very attractive and really did mean it all those times I asked you out. I would have given anything to be with you but right now I'm kind of involved with …"

She interrupted. "I know, Cocoa, a very nice girl. I met her at the hospital and I really don't care. I'm a big girl and so is she. All's fair in love and war."

Oh, brother. We sat there quietly for a moment, staring at our food. I said stupidly, "So you thought this was a date?"

"Maybe you do have brain damage."

What could I say?

She shook her head in frustration.

At a loss for words and how to proceed, I remained silent. Suddenly, she stood up to leave and I said, "Helen, please, don't go. Can't we at least finish the meal?"

"I don't know about you, Cesari, but I'm feeling pretty embarrassed right now. So I think maybe you should find yourself another interpreter."

I stood up, crossed over to her side of the table and wrapped my arms around her. She resisted—a little—and I saw tears in the corners of her eyes. She said, "I feel so stupid."

"Please don't feel like that, Helen. I'm the stupid one. I had no idea you felt this way." People were starting to stare. "Please stay and talk to me. I didn't mean to hurt your feelings. Besides, you're not missing out on anything. The plumbing hasn't been working quite right since I got out of the hospital."

She looked at me curiously and then finally understood what I was getting at. That made her chuckle and she sat back down collecting herself. "Oh, yeah? I didn't know you were shot down there."

"I wasn't. I think it's psychological."

She snickered. "The great Dr. Cesari can't get it up. Now, that really is funny, and oddly, it does kind of make me feel better."

"Thanks. It's also quite personal so I hope you'll keep it to yourself."

"Maybe—I'll think about it. So what's going on that you need an interpreter?"

I gave her the short version while we finished our dinner and paid the bill. I told her that I was following up on a case that I had started reviewing before I was shot and wanted to see how the lady was doing.

She didn't buy it. "On a Saturday night? Really? You expect me to believe that?"

I started to say something but she held up her hand to cut me off. "It doesn't matter. Let's get this over with so I can go somewhere and lick my wounds. Give me her number and I'll call her to let her know we're on the way up."

Chapter 25

*C*how Liu lived in a small one bedroom apartment above the Peking Duck House. She was sixty, short with graying hair, and wore a dirty apron. A very old man sat on the sofa watching Chinese television. He nodded politely in our direction as Helen introduced us in perfect Mandarin.

Helen turned to me. "She said to have a seat at the kitchen table with her and would you like some tea? I already thanked her and accepted her offer."

We sat around the small table and Chow Liu smiled at me. She had very poor dentition. I asked, "Who's the guy on the sofa?"

"That's her father."

"Is there a Mr. Liu?"

Helen spoke a few words and said, "No, he died last year from a heart attack. The doctors said he ate too much duck. Very fatty."

"Okay, ask her how she is feeling."

"That's it? Just a general question?"

"Yeah, to start."

Helen turned to Mrs. Liu and asked. It took a minute for the full answer but it clearly wasn't, *I feel great*.

I asked, "What did she say?"

Helen looked puzzled. "She said that she is not feeling too poorly but lately has been feeling more and more rundown, and that the pain in her chest is getting worse."

I looked at Chow Liu carefully and determined that she did seem a little pale. "Ask her about the pain in her chest. What's it like?"

"She said it's sore and hurts every day now. She can't wear bras anymore because the chafing makes it bleed."

Helen and I looked at each other. I said, "Ask her what is bleeding?"

"She says there is some kind of growth in her chest."

I thought it over. "Look, Helen, I know this is highly irregular but ask her if I can examine her."

Helen wasn't too happy about that. "Right here, in her kitchen? Do you have any idea how many codes of conduct we'll be violating? She's not even your patient."

I sighed. She was right. Technically, this was highly inappropriate and unprofessional. "Helen, it's important. There's something going on that's not right. I promise to fill you in on everything."

She turned to Chow Liu and asked. "She says it's fine."

"Okay, not a full exam. I just want to see the area that's bothering her."

Helen expressed my wishes to her and she took the apron off and unbuttoned her top, partially exposing her right breast. I observed a small perhaps two inch wide, circular sore with raised margins and an angry-looking, red, inflamed center.

Helen instinctively gasped and I stood up to get a better look. Walking over to her side of the table, I told Helen to ask her if I could examine it with my hands.

"She said yes, but be gentle because it's tender."

Gently placing my fingers on the outside of the lesion I probed slowly and carefully until the look on her face told me I was hurting her. It was indurated and encompassed a much larger area beneath the surface of the skin. It was oozing a small amount of mostly clear, slightly bloody fluid.

"Helen, ask her to raise her arm."

When she did, I palpated multiple lymph nodes along the length of her arm leading up to her armpit. I even saw a lump the size of an apricot bulging out from the back of her neck. I sighed deeply and looked at Helen.

"I can't be sure, Helen but my guess is the cancer is already widely metastatic. Ask her if she is being treated."

Helen posed the question, and Chow Liu shook her head no. She then proceeded to explain why as she buttoned her blouse.

When she finished, Helen translated, "She says that she told her doctor several months ago, maybe longer, that she felt a lump in her breast and that he sent her for a test which sounds like a mammogram. Later somebody called her and said the test was negative and that with time the lump should go away. He gave her a number to call for further problems and when the lump didn't go away, she called and was given an appointment with a "specialist" who told her she had cancer and that there was nothing anyone could do because it had already spread."

"How long ago was that?"

"The visit with the specialist was four months ago."

"Ask her if she still has the phone number and address of the specialist."

Chow Liu rummaged through a kitchen drawer until she found a piece of paper with a phone number and address on it. She handed it to me and I had Helen ask her if it was okay for me to keep it. She nodded yes.

"Ask her if the old man in there is all right to leave alone."

"She says he's fine. She leaves him alone all the time. Why?"

"We're taking her to the emergency room at Saint Matt's right now to have something done about that. Hopefully we aren't too late."

Helen spoke to the woman at length and seemed frustrated. She turned to me. "She won't go. The specialist she saw told her that her insurance won't cover any more treatments or tests and she can't afford it out-of-pocket."

"Tell her not to worry and that I'll make sure she doesn't get billed for anything her insurance won't cover."

After several minutes of bickering the woman finally acquiesced, put on a light weight coat and explained everything to the old man who nodded, smiled and I think passed gas.

In the ER, I explained everything to the physician there in an attempt to facilitate Chow Liu's care. A CT scan of the chest and abdomen was ordered, and I personally called the surgeon and oncologist, apologized for bothering them on a Saturday night, but insisted that they come in as a personal favor to me. I made it clear that I would not allow this woman to go home under any circumstance until she was fully plugged into the system and a clear plan of action outlined in plain language to her. Helen had graciously agreed to stay nearby to act as an interpreter.

"Thank you for staying with her, Helen. I think that's really nice of you."

She smiled. "No need to thank me. I think you're the one who's being extraordinary here. How did you know she was sick?"

"I can't go into it right now. To say the least, it's complicated. Let's just say that I had a hunch."

"The next time you have a hunch like that remind me to buy a lottery ticket."

"I will. Look, I'm going to grab a quick cup of coffee from the doctor's lounge before I go. Would you like me to bring you one?"

234

"I'll come with you. Mrs. Liu will be fine." She told her she would be right back and Chow Liu smiled and nodded.

The doctors' lounge was off to one side of the mammoth emergency room and required a four-digit access code to enter. It was really an efficient apartment with a small kitchen, a living room area with a TV and sofa, and one small bedroom with a set of bunk beds for the ER physicians to rest in case there was a break in the action, which there never was. We brewed ourselves a couple of cups of coffee from a Keurig machine in the kitchen and sat on the sofa.

"I hope you don't mind, Helen, but I can't stay much longer. I have to take care of a few things."

"That's fine with me. I'll call you if there are any hiccups here."

I sipped my coffee and she touched my shoulder lightly. "John…"

She never called me John. I turned toward her and waited. She continued, "I—I'm sorry for—you know, overreacting."

"It's okay, Helen. Please forget about it. In fact, I owe you an apology. I didn't realize all the mixed messages I had been sending in your direction." They weren't really mixed messages. I just wasn't interpreting the return signals correctly.

Without saying anything, she put her cup down on the coffee table and then reached over and took my cup from me, also placing it on the table. She then got on her knees on the sofa next to me and wrapping her arms around my neck, kissed me gently once and then more passionately the second time. We looked into each other's eyes and I saw a longing there that wasn't going to be denied. She delicately turned and sat on my lap, pulling me down to her face. I cradled her head in my arms and we locked lips for what seemed like an eternity. Her breathing came in short, rapid bursts, and I felt all sorts of things happening everywhere in my body. I thought about the ER and how long it might be before someone barged into the room and I became the talk of the town—again. Not caring, I ran my hand over her breasts, rubbed her nipples through her blouse and then slid my hand down across her abdomen below her waist as she arched backward in pleasure.

God, I wanted her right now more than anything. "Helen, maybe we should go into the bedroom. At least there's a lock on the door."

Her eyes were glazed and she wasn't thinking too straight. She whispered in a throaty purr, "The bathroom might be safer. There's somebody's stuff in the bedroom. I checked when we came in. They might come back for it."

"You checked when we came in?"

She smiled. "We're wasting time, Cesari."

"All right, the bathroom it is."

We went in and I locked the door, turned and threw her against the wall, holding her arms over her head. I pressed my chest into her, making her breathless as I kissed her and she ground her hips into me like a cat in heat. Moments later, we frantically unbuttoned each other's jeans yanking them down. I thought we were both going to pass out from excitement. Neither of us could speak. We were that out of breath. She looked down at me and smiled with satisfaction. Apparently, I had been cured. I brought her roughly over to the sink, spun her around and bent her over it as she moaned with desire. I had two and a half months to catch up on and let her have it as she hung on to the porcelain for dear life.

Twenty minutes later, we came out of the doctors' lounge, flushed, panting, and reeking of guilty pleasure. She had a big smile on her face as she said, "Well, I feel better."

I was still breathless. "Me too. Well, I gotta go. I'll call you later to see how things went with Mrs. Liu." I turned to leave, hesitated and turned back. I leaned down, kissed her on the lips and whispered into her ear.

"Oh, my God, Helen, that was unbelievable."

She laughed. "And obviously therapeutic as well. Just remember, there's more where that came from."

I didn't know what to say.

There was no one in our immediate vicinity so she hugged me, beaming all over, and said, "There's nothing like dirty sex, is there?"

"I guess not. I feel like I should have thrown a twenty dollar bill at you as a tip or something."

Giggling, she said, "Now that's what I'm talking about, and I should have given you a couple of fortune cookies."

She was too funny. I laughed this time and gave her another quick kiss. She said, "Get out of here, Cesari. You know where you can find me if things don't work out with Cocoa—or even if they do." With that she walked away. I stood there winded, weak and dazed.

Chapter 26

O utside the hospital, I shook it off and pulled out the slip of paper with the name and address of the specialist that Chow Liu had been referred to.

John Burgoyne MD
304 E. Fifth Street Suite 7F
212-453-9072

The name seemed vaguely familiar for some reason, and since the address was only a few blocks from Saint Matt's I decided to take a walk over there to check it out. I didn't see any point in calling ahead. It was Saturday night, and no legitimate office would be open at this time anyway. I reached the address in less than fifteen minutes and found a sharp-looking office building, which of course was closed. There was a directory of occupants on the wall outside. Lawyers, doctors, dentists, accountants and financial advisors, and there on the seventh floor was John Burgoyne MD. Using my phone, I googled his name in the New York State physician registry and could not find it. Interesting. What did that mean? You couldn't practice medicine in New York State without being registered. I made a mental note to return during working hours and meet this guy.

Back in Vito's apartment, I found him in his living room in consultation with several of his lieutenants, five of them to be exact.

Vito looked up and said, "Hey, Cesari, are you stupid or what?"

I stopped in my tracks as all eyes turned on me. "What did I do?"

"Do you think whoever it is stopped trying to kill you just because you neutralized one guy in Boston? From now on, you don't go anywhere without one of my guys, understood? Sebastiano, don't let him out of your sight."

Sebastiano said, "Got it, Vito."

I said, "Fine, I just had dinner with another doctor from the hospital a few blocks from here."

"Great, now we need to talk. The rest of you guys fan out. Sebastiano, grab a coffee in the kitchen while I talk to the doc."

I sat down on his black leather sofa while he poured us two fingers of eighteen- year-old limited edition single malt Oban into crystal glasses. He handed one to me and sat in an armchair while I swirled mine, sniffed it, and took a sip, savoring the moment. Good stuff.

"So what's up, Vito?"

"Nothing good. That's what. Let's start with the guy in Boston. He's nobody, a bit player who got lucky. He heard about the contract and decided to muscle in fast and furious to make a name for himself. We're not sure how he found you but it's possible he had your apartment staked out and followed us all the way to Boston. It don't matter, he's in police custody and from what I heard he isn't going to see the light of day for many years to come."

I said, "I don't get it. He heard about the hit? He wasn't hired to kill me?"

"No, not specifically. He heard about the contract on the street and figured if he knocked you off, not only would he make a name for himself but that he would be rewarded with the fee or at least part of it. In other words, even though there's a contract out for you and a specific person hired, anybody else who wants in can treat it as a bounty. You got a price on your head like in the Old West."

"So, if this guy knew about the hit then there might be any number of people out there who might conceivably take a pot shot at me."

"Unfortunately, that's the way it looks."

"So, who's behind it all?"

He crossed his legs and sipped his scotch. "They're bringing Sammy Beans in as we speak, so we'll see what he knows, and I got guys crawling all over Philly sniffing around for me. It's just a matter of time before something breaks our way."

I sat there staring into space, numb from the news. "Is there anything else?"

"No, I'll keep you posted though." His phone rang and he answered as I walked to my bedroom, placing my scotch glass down on the desk next to Ronnie's laptop. I looked at the time. It was almost 10:00. I reclined on the bed and dialed Cocoa. I pushed Helen out of my head, at least for the moment.

"Hi, John."

"Hey there. Where are you?"

"I'm still at my parents' house. I'm going to spend the night here. Dad's a little under the weather and Mom needed some help around the house. Hope you don't mind?"

"Why would I mind? Tell your mom and dad I said hello. Oh, wait a minute. Do they know about us?"

"Yes, they do. When you got shot I was very upset and told them everything. I'm sorry but I needed somebody to talk to. My dad was furious with Uncle Leo but promised not to say anything to him and I don't think he has."

"You told your parents about the gun?"

"I told them everything. I couldn't help it."

I sighed deeply. "Okay, that's all right and perfectly understandable."

"Have you found out anything new about what's going on?"

"Yes, but I'm still trying to hammer out the particulars. I'll tell you all about it when I see you. Okay, so then I'll see you tomorrow?"

"Yes, I'll probably be back in the late afternoon sometime."

"Sounds good. See you then. Bye."

I lay there a few minutes staring at the ceiling thinking things through. What was the significance of those twelve patient names on Ronnie's laptop? Was Ronnie, or should I say Duncan, tracking misdiagnoses at Saint Matt's for Unicare and didn't want anybody to know? Was this some potential scheme by Unicare to curtail hospital payments or cut their losses in case of litigation? And who was John Burgoyne MD? Was he working for Ronnie?

I was curious about Ronnie's laptop and tried to access the Saint Matt's EMR from it but was unable to without a VPN or virtual private network. A VPN allows one to securely access remote private networks from a public network. Basically, a VPN is an encrypted secure tunnel between the computer you were logged onto and the remote one you wanted to access. It was easy enough to set up a VPN if you were the administrator of both computers but in this case I wasn't.

My laptop, on the other hand, already had a VPN set up on it for me by the Saint Matt's IT department. I accessed my records and reviewed those charts again, looking for any similarities. Other than the fact they all had pristine records and negative screening procedures within the last year I couldn't see any real connection. Were they all misdiagnosed? Was this some type of new breed of incompetence? I pulled up the report of Mrs. Liu's mammogram and reviewed it. Totally normal even though she said she felt a lump. Unfortunately, that wasn't too uncommon.

Women and their doctors felt things all the time that weren't necessarily cancer.

I looked at Ronnie's laptop and spotted the Z1.exe file and tried to open it again but couldn't without being on the network. Then I thought about the list of patients from Saint Matt's and how he might have acquired it. His company would undoubtedly keep track of those things, but why was it on his secure laptop and not in risk management? Maybe he was doing his own recordkeeping, or maybe he was the only one who knew about this seeming epidemic of medical ineptitude at Saint Matt's. The Z1 file bothered me and I didn't know why. It just seemed too cute and convenient. I used his laptop to send myself the Z1 file as an email attachment. I was curious about something.

I then opened the email on my laptop and downloaded the file. I decided to delete the email because I didn't trust the security of free email accounts like Hotmail and Yahoo. I had been hacked on more than one occasion and didn't want to take the chance of anyone seeing what I was doing. Maybe I was being overly paranoid or maybe it was brain damage. Besides I now had two copies of the Z1, one on my laptop and one on Ronnie's. I made sure my VPN to Saint Matt's was still open and then clicked on the Z1.exe file now on my desktop. The screen went suddenly blue and a white rectangular box appeared in the center prompting me for a password. Interesting. The network it was searching for was Saint Matt's medical records but it couldn't access the network remotely. I punched in all the permutations of passwords I tried before on Ronnie's laptop, including VersuchsModell 1, without success.

Sitting there for a while, I pondered what password I might use if I were a pompous British asshole pulling a fast one on a bunch of American rubes. Then I silently laughed to myself and typed in "Yankee Doodle" and watched as the screen opened up to the Saint Matt's EMR. The interface was slightly different than the one I normally used but other than that I seemed to have full access. Now this was starting to get really fascinating. He had created a program to piggyback into the EMR as long as it was already logged on to the VPN. Why didn't he create his own VPN? Maybe he couldn't. Maybe that would leave too much of an electronic trail. Maybe that was why he needed to be physically at Saint Matt's where physicians and secretaries were always logged in. Was that why he was wining and dining the secretaries? Maybe he was monkeying with the medical records using the secretaries' computers. They were always logged on and if they thought he was trying to help them they might have let him have access. On the other hand, if he was romancing Julie she might even have given him her passwords so he could log onto the EMR anytime he wanted, like after hours when no one was around. No wonder she seemed evasive when I asked her about how he performed his little miracles.

Hmm. I still didn't quite get what he was doing though. He had created a program with a parallel interface that only seemed to be functional when someone was already logged on. I didn't think anyone could access secure networks just like that, but I wasn't particularly skilled at computers, nor did I fully understand the encryption process other than in a most rudimentary way. If Ronnie were half the computer genius Sarah had said he was, then this might have been child's play for him. Teenagers routinely hacked into the Pentagon for crying out loud, and that was about as secure as you could get. Hospital EMRs were nothing compared to that.

I sat back in my chair thinking about the possibilities. So, I had just hacked into my own medical records using Ronnie's Z1 program. Well, no, I hadn't really hacked in. Technically, I was already in. This was more like having someone in the passenger seat of your car while you were driving. The question was, did he have his own steering wheel and set of controls? It was time to find out. I pulled up one of my notes from six months ago on a patient that I had seen with ulcerative colitis. It was a relatively short note. The patient was well and his colitis in remission. He had come in for a routine checkup and medication renewal.

I copied the original note and saved it in a folder I created. I then clicked the edit button and began rewriting the note from the Z1 interface. When I finished it I saved it to the medical record, rebooted the laptop and logged onto the record again. I found the new note and examined it carefully. The changes persisted but what was even more disturbing was that I could not find any hint that any changes had been made at all. All electronic records are required by law to document in plain sight on the record itself any changes made to the original note. In other words, somewhere easily visible on the page should have been an indication that the note had been edited with the date and time automatically recorded. This had none. It looked like the original in every way, shape and form including the date and time from six months ago when the note was first written. It even had my electronic signature on it at the bottom.

That son-of-a-bitch! So that was the game. Change the notes, and tell the patients they don't need any tests. Then you have the patients call a Unicare representative directly so the doctor and his staff never catch on that there's a problem. You even have some bullshit doctor, if he even is a doctor, available to send patients to. He tells them there's nothing more that can be done and that if they insist they will be stuck with the cost. They die and Unicare saves a fortune. Nobody can tell from the charts what happened.

If anybody complains, the doctor gets thrown under the bus for either a misdiagnosis or poor documentation. Either way, he takes it up the exhaust pipe, not the insurance company, except Mrs. Konstandin wasn't buying it. She started making noise and lots of it.

I thought about things for a minute. What if Tony had taken biopsies of Konstandin's colon cancer and it simply wasn't reflected in the altered chart? There must be a record of that somewhere, right? Ronnie could simply have deleted the result from the record but the pathology department itself should still have the physical slides. I wasn't sure how long they kept things like that. There was only a finite amount of storage space in the hospital but there were probably laws and governmental guidelines for stuff like that. If there was tissue pathology, it would certainly prove that Tony didn't miss the cancer but it wouldn't save him from the accusation of incorrect documentation, which in this day and age was only a marginally better offense.

There had to be some place in cyberspace where the original record was stored. Every electronic medical record system had automatic backups. The question was, could those be altered or replaced with the new notes? I didn't have an answer to that but would soon find out. It would be my high priority in the morning to call the company that manages Saint Matt's EMR to ask them about their backup procedure and how to retrieve stored records. In the meanwhile, a trip to the pathology department to look for stored tissue samples was also in order. But what if Ronnie had infiltrated the pathology department like he had my office? Who knew how many secretaries he was banging, and I didn't want anybody raising the alarm that I was onto him.

I picked up the phone and dialed Arnie.

"Cesari, what's going on?"

"I need a favor, Arnie?"

"At eleven o'clock on a Saturday night?"

"Yeah."

"Okay, so what is it?"

"I need you to meet me in the basement of the hospital and let me into the pathology department. I need to review a slide."

"Are you out of your mind? Why can't it wait until Monday morning, and why are you reviewing pathology slides anyway? I told you to rest, remember? Besides, there are no slides in the basement of the hospital at least not if they are more than two weeks old. Anything older gets sent to an outside storage facility. The hospital ran out of physical space years ago. So, what are you up to?"

"I didn't know that about the path. I was just trying to keep myself busy and was catching up on some cases that I had left open-ended before the shooting."

"On Saturday night? Do you think I'm that stupid? Go to sleep."

I persisted. "So, if I wanted to see the slides, how would I contact this storage facility?"

"You're a pain in the ass, Cesari. Did I mention that? The company is called Medi-Save, get it? They own a warehouse in Brooklyn just over the bridge. Call my office Monday for the number."

"Hey Arnie, as long as I got you on the line, who would I contact to retrieve a backup note if I lost or deleted the original by accident?"

"The same company. We try to keep things as streamlined as possible. All of your backups are stored on servers in the same warehouse. If you're missing a note just call them with the medical record number and they'll upload it to your laptop."

"Thanks, Arnie. Sorry for bothering you."

"Yeah, I bet." He hung up.

I turned my laptop on and googled Medi-Save. It was a medical storage and security company with offices and facilities all along the East Coast. It was Medicare certified and was considered one of the premier data protection firms in the country. At the very end of the Wikipedia description it stated that Medi-Save was a subsidiary of Allentown Medical Inc., an international and well-established health services company headquartered in London. Allentown Medical was in turn owned by a much larger corporation—McCormick

Enterprises. Well, how about that. Then I googled the name of that quack physician, John Burgoyne, that Chow Liu had seen. He wasn't listed as a licensed doctor in New York State so I performed a general query and watched as the page loaded its results.

Now that was interesting…

****

Rutherford Cecil McCormick ran a bony hand through his silver hair in frustration while his son Duncan Ronald sat impassively waiting for the storm to pass.

"Let me see if I have this right, Duncan. You decided to have a rendezvous with Esha up in the Skywalk observatory and so you turned off the security system temporarily so as not to have the tryst recorded or accidentally trigger the alarm yourself. Am I correct so far?"

"Yes, Father."

"Hmm, and when you returned to your office on the 49th floor you discovered your laptop was missing, but we have no way of knowing who took it because the security cameras were turned off."

Looking down Duncan replied, "That sums it up."

"Was there anything on the laptop besides the Z1?"

"No, nothing incriminating, and it may not be as significant a breach as it appears. First off, the laptop and Z1 file are password protected but let's assume that whoever snatched it has the ability to get past that. When I finish hacking into the records, I always upload the data to our secure servers and then delete any local files. There's little if anything of use on the hard drive and I have multiple copies of the Z1 so this won't slow us down at all."

"Who do you think would have the audacity to do such a thing?"

"That's hard to say, Father. My best guess is one of the other insurance companies doesn't like the fees we've set for our services and would prefer to go into business for themselves, but without understanding how to use the program it will be useless to them. In addition, I've programmed the Z1 to auto-delete if not shut down properly. In other words, the program is written in such a way that you can shut down by simply clicking on the x in the upper right corner like any other Windows-based program or you can pull up a password prompt by pressing Ctrl-P. If you don't use the password method the file immediately and permanently deletes itself. I figured most people would not anticipate that. It was a safety feature I thought of in case the file was ever stolen or copied without my authorization. Furthermore, each copy of the Z1 is site-specific and coded to log onto only one electronic medical records system. The copy that was on that laptop can only log onto the records at Saint Matt's. So, unless whoever took the laptop knows that, he will have the most frustrating time of his life before watching the file miraculously disappear right before his eyes.

The old man nodded and sipped tea from a fine china cup. "Good thinking, Duncan. I'm glad the hundreds of thousands of pounds I've spent on your education didn't go completely to waste."

"It gets even better than that, Father. If I don't change the password to the laptop itself every forty-eight hours the entire hard drive auto-erases, a complete scrub of all data."

"You don't say. Well, you certainly are a paranoid bugger, aren't you? Is there a chance that they've gotten to one of your programmers? What do the colonials like to say—could there be a mole in the operation?"

248

"Unlikely, as they are all handpicked mates of mine from Oxford and MIT, but nonetheless I intend to rigorously explore that possibility."

"And what about this Cesari fellow? Has there been any progress on that front?"

"Our friend Leo says that the wheels are in motion and we need to be patient."

"Did he now? Patience is not my strong suit, Duncan. I don't like the idea of some foreigner running around who might at any time suddenly remember that you are the one who shot him."

"He's not a foreigner, Father. He's Italian-American and was born here in New York City."

"I thought you told me he was from the Bronx?"

"I did, Father."

"Well, that's not New York. Being from the Bronx is like being Scottish or even worse, Irish. At any rate, let's not quibble about his lineage. Suffice it to say, his people came here long after ours did all the hard work. Probably grew up on welfare and other handouts."

"You're right of course, Father."

"All right then. Let's get back to the business of making money, and Duncan …"

"Yes, Father."

"The next time you get a burning in your loins for your stepsister would you kindly get a hotel room? For God's sake, we own at least three in Boston itself."

"Yes, Father."

Chapter 27

*W*aking up early Sunday morning, I showered and took Cleo for a walk down Canal Street. I looked for Sebastiano to ask him if he wanted to come but was told he was in a meeting with Vito. Not being a child or a prisoner, I went anyway. Besides, I wasn't going that far. Cleopatra was happy and seemed to be handling her new home pretty well and Vito's guys really liked her. Vito had given her one of his empty bedrooms to frolic in and his men took turns minding her. There was already a plethora of doggy toys strewn about the apartment.

When I returned, I found Vito in his living room with Sebastiano and several others, including a new guy sandwiched between two behemoths on the sofa. He was a clean-shaven, slender guy, maybe 170 lbs., which made him a shrimp in this room. He looked frightened and I guessed this was the now-famous Sammy Beans in the middle of his debriefing.

Vito greeted me with exasperation. "Cesari, which part of 'don't go anywhere by yourself' didn't you understand?"

"I wasn't by myself. I was with Cleo. Nobody's going to bother me with her around."

He snorted his disapproval and returned to the matter at hand. "Say hello to Sammy Beans. Sammy, this is Dr. Cesari."

I nodded at the guy but didn't offer him my hand. He wasn't my friend so there was no point in pretending. I said, "Good morning, guys."

Several grunts returned in my direction. Vito continued, "Sammy was just telling us an interesting story. Weren't you Sammy?"

Sammy Beans stammered, forehead dripping with sweat. "I didn't know he was your friend, Vito. I swear it. I didn't know."

Vito snarled. "Is that supposed to be an excuse?"

"Please, Vito. I'll do anything. It won't happen again. I swear."

"Trust me, Sammy. I know it won't. As long as the doc is here, why don't you tell us again what you know?"

He looked at Vito and then back at me. "I have a cousin in Philly. He's a laborer on a construction crew but does odd jobs now and again to pick up some extra dough. He called me last week to let me know something was going down and I needed to stay clear of Washington Square Park on the Sixth Avenue side for a couple of days. He didn't want to tell me at first but I pushed him pretty hard and he eventually told me your name and that guys were coming for you."

"What's your cousin's name and what was his role?" I asked.

Sammy Beans sighed, "His name is Dominick Lampone and all he was supposed to do was hang out on Sixth Avenue and act as a lookout when they went up to your apartment. He's not a trigger guy."

"So who is the trigger guy then?"

"I don't know. He wouldn't say. That was going over the line for him, but I know he's done jobs like this in the past for a guy called Mickey Two Fingers."

I looked at Vito, who nodded. "I believe him, and I already got guys looking for his cousin. He's not answering his phone at the moment."

Sammy Beans asked, "You're not going to hurt him, are you?"

Vito looked hard at Sammy Beans. "The only person you better worry about getting hurt right now is you."

Sammy Beans nodded and Vito turned to one of his guys. "Take this slug into one of the spare rooms and lock him in. Take his phone away and remove the gun from the bathroom. From now on he's your responsibility. He can eat but that's all. I don't want to hear a sound out of him. Every time he utters even one syllable, I want you to break a bone. Take one of the softball bats with you so you don't accidentally hurt your hands on him."

Turning back to Sammy Beans, who was now trembling, he said, "I hope you caught all that. You're staying here until we find your cousin and you better pray he tells me what I want to know. Now get out of my sight."

After they left the room I asked, "Do you know this Mickey Two Fingers guy?"

"Yeah, I know him. If it's him, then I don't get it. I wouldn't trust him with a five hundred grand contract. He's a lowlife, and small time. They say he's into drugs both selling and using. I wouldn't rely on him to knock off a candy store let alone pull off a hit. We'll find him. Guys like that aren't usually very good at keeping a low profile."

"Okay, Vito, thanks. Keep me posted. I'm going to my apartment to check my mail and grab a few personal items."

Sebastiano snapped to attention at that, putting his sport coat on. I looked at his gigantic frame and wondered how much a guy had to eat to get that big. He was six foot four inches tall and roughly 280 lbs. of pure pasta and meatballs. His neck was roughly the size of my thigh. I said, "C'mon. Let me put Cleo in her room and then we'll go."

Vito said, "You don't have to do that. Just leave her out here with us. She'll be fine. I bought a truckload of doggy treats for her."

I couldn't help smiling. Vito a dog lover. Who would've guessed?

Sebastiano and I grabbed a bunch of cannolis and coffee at the Café Napoli downstairs and headed over to Saint Matt's, eating as we walked. I had one cannoli and Sebastiano had four.

As we meandered down Mulberry Street toward my apartment, we heard church bells and got caught up in a stream of people entering Saint Patrick's Old Cathedral by Prince Street. It was almost time for mass and we stopped to watch. Saint Patrick's in Little Italy was one of the oldest Catholic churches in America and had been constructed over two hundred years ago. It was the place where the famous baptism scene of *The Godfather* was filmed. I hadn't been to church in years, and maybe I was just curious because I had never been inside, but I suddenly felt compelled to join the congregation.

"Sebastiano, I'm going inside. You can wait out here, okay?"

"Seriously?"

I nodded and he hesitated. He had strict orders not to let me out of his sight and I saw the confusion in his eyes. The lifestyle he led often brought him into conflict with church doctrine. However, being in conflict with the church might be better than being in conflict with Vito, so he threw his last half-eaten cannoli into a nearby trash can and followed me into the basilica where we took up seats in the back row.

The organ music began and Sebastiano looked furtively at me. "You gotta be kidding, Doc?"

"Relax, no one's going to bite you."

The church was very beautiful inside built in the tradition of the cathedrals of medieval Europe. Two long rows of wooden pews and two long rows of tall stone colonnades led up to a massive altar, presided over by beautiful stained glass in the background. Behind the marble altar, the stained glass illuminated the heart of it all, a massive wooden crucifix suspended from the ceiling high above a semicircular conclave of statues of saints.

Within minutes, the Mass began with the choir singing the entrance hymn and we watched as the priest and altar servers walked past us from the rear of the church toward the altar. Once they were in position the service began in earnest and I handed Sebastiano a mass book in case he wanted to follow along. He shrugged politely and took it, but didn't open it. As a kid, I went faithfully with my mother every Sunday, Holy Days and of course the high holidays of Palm Sunday, Easter and Christmas and it struck me how easy and relaxed it felt to follow the Mass right now. It was like that saying about riding a bike. You just never forgot certain things after they'd been ingrained in you. For years after I had stopped attending Mass on a regular basis, I continued to attend Good Friday services. I always felt a pang of something as the clock struck three, the time it is said that Jesus breathed his last as his spirit ascended into Heaven.

There was something about Good Friday that gripped me deep inside and to this day wouldn't let go. The fact that a man voluntarily went to a most unpleasant death to prove a point to the rest of us really shook me up when I thought about it. If he wasn't the son of God why would he do that? Was he insane, misguided, delusional? None of what we know about him suggested anything other than complete rationality. Whether you believed that Jesus was divine or not, you had to admit, that at the very least, he was a good man who led a good life. He left us with a philosophy of life, which if we all tried to live by it, would undoubtedly make our world a better place. Be nice to everyone, forgive those who offend, and accept those who are different. Man, it was hard to argue with that, and yet, somehow, thousands of years later we were still slaughtering each other in his name. How on earth did we get from there to here?

Lost in thought, I looked up just as the procession for communion began up the center aisle. Technically, I hadn't received communion in such a long time, it would be baldfaced hypocrisy for me to do so now but I stood up anyway, hesitated and stepped into the aisle, the last one to join the long line of faithful. Out of the corner of my eye, I saw Sebastiano shake his head and I could tell he was drawing the line at this activity. I shuffled slowly forward, hands clasped, listening to the choir. I looked around admiring the architecture and design of the church. In due time, I neared the altar. The priest was an elderly man assisted in his duties by a male deacon off to his right and several altar servers, both male and female. The choir was made up of five women and one man.

There was one person ahead of me now and as she received the host, I looked beyond the priest transfixed by the image of Jesus on the crucifix behind the altar. The light shining through the stained glass was dazzlingly beautiful. It lit up the cross in a way that was not readily apparent from where I was sitting in the way back. I heard the woman ahead of me say, *Amen,* and let her move to the side before advancing.

As I stepped forward, time seemed to slow down. I saw the priest's lips move but didn't hear any sound. I stood there listening to my heart thump loudly in my chest. I felt blood rush from my left ventricle up into my aorta to my brain and other vital organs. I could feel each corpuscle arrive at its destination, unload its oxygen, and hop the return train back to pick up another load. The priest must have said something again because I saw his lips move. I suddenly felt weak and fell to my knees in front of him with arms outstretched. He looked like he was going into shock and called to someone for help but I didn't need any. I never felt so good. I looked at the statues lined up behind the altar and to my amazement they were all moving their lips in prayer. I looked up at the crucifix and it was gone, replaced by a bright, white light which blinded me. I closed my eyes and when I opened them I heard the priest say, "The body of Christ."

I was sweating profusely and breathing rapidly as I looked around. No one seemed to have noticed. I said, "Amen" and he placed the wafer on my tongue, blessing me as if nothing had happened.

Back in the pew Sebastiano whispered, "Are you okay, Doc? You look sick."

Trembling and scared, I said, "I'll be okay. Let's get out of here."

Outside, I leaned against a parked car to catch my breath and let my racing pulse slow down. I asked Sebastiano if he noticed anything unusual when I went to receive communion. He shrugged his shoulders. "No, not really. You were pretty shaky when you came back though. I just figured it was kind of on the warm side in there. As a matter of fact you don't look too shiny right now."

"I'm fine. I just need a minute." I let out a deep breath and forced myself to relax. The church was letting out and people were starting to approach the street where we stood. I said, "Let's go."

We arrived at the loft uneventfully, and I put on a pot of coffee while Sebastiano made himself comfortable on the sofa, watching TV. I went through my mail and spotted a formal-looking letter from the law firm representing Kelly telling me that the restraining order had been lifted, effective immediately. That was nice to hear, except now I couldn't go near her or the kids without placing them in danger. There were assorted utility bills and several throwaway magazines that all doctors received, not quite junk mail but close. Ostensibly, they were educational in nature but in reality they were paid advertisements by various pharmaceutical and health insurance companies. Most of us scanned the covers and tossed them into the trash.

I went into the bedroom, closed the door and called Mark. He answered on the second ring. "What's up, Cesari?"

"I'm in trouble, Mark."

"What happened?"

"I've had several more episodes, visions, seizures or whatever. I don't know what to call them anymore. I'm starting to doubt my sanity."

"I'm sorry to hear that. Where are you?"

"I'm in my apartment. Remember it? It's on the corner of Sixth Avenue and Waverly Place. You were here once."

"Yeah, I remember it. How are you right now?"

I realized that my hand quivered and my voice cracked. "I'm okay, just a little shaken. I'm lying down trying to relax."

"Okay, look, I'll come right over. Stay put, all right? Have a glass of wine or something. Give me thirty minutes."

"Thanks."

I hung up and went into the living room, poured Sebastiano a cup of coffee and said, "I'm going to lie down and close my eyes for a few minutes. A doctor friend of mine is coming over. Would you mind letting him in if I don't hear the door?"

He took a sip from his cup. "Sure thing, Doc."

I went back into the bedroom, leaving the door open a crack so I could listen for Mark. After turning the lamp off, I lay on the bed staring at the ceiling. There were no windows in the loft's bedroom so it was quite dark, which helped me relax. My mind drifted, wondering if I was going to have to be medicated or institutionalized. Medicated at a minimum, I thought. Closing my eyes, I practiced some deep breathing exercises a yoga instructor patient of mine had taught me. It actually did help and I gradually began to calm down and eventually dozed off.

I don't know how long I was out but a loud explosion jolted me back to reality and I jumped out of the bed, running to the door. Peering through the crack, I saw Sebastiano sprawled on his back missing half his face and most of his brains splattered on the floor. A large black guy, easily as big as my now-dead bodyguard, stood in the doorway holding a short-barreled pump action shotgun with smoke wafting gently from its barrel.

My mind raced as the guy entered the living room, locking the door behind him and scanning for something, probably me. I had a .38 special that I kept in my night table and quickly ran over to it opening the drawer. No gun!

Shit. I remembered Cocoa telling me she had removed the gun for my own good. I had to think quickly. The loft was big with plenty of hiding spaces but he'd have to be an idiot not to focus in on the bedroom in a hurry. I went into the bathroom where I kept a junk drawer filled with odds and ends: crazy glue, tape, twisties, AA batteries, a couple of loose screws, a penlight and an eight-inch-long flat head screw driver with a plastic handle. I took the screwdriver and ran back into the bedroom hiding behind the door. I slowed my breathing and prayed that this was just another vision like in Boston, that I would snap out of it and be okay. Until I did, however, I was going to have to ride it out as best I could.

The door opened slowly in my direction and soon the tip of the shotgun poked its head in, leading the way. He fumbled for the light switch but couldn't find it because there wasn't any. The room was illuminated primarily by a floor lamp and two smaller lamps on matching night tables.

I could sense his frustration as he resigned himself and took another slow, deliberate step into the room. He was a big guy. I wasn't going to pretend that I could take him on in hand-to-hand combat, assuming I got past the shotgun, but the room was dark and I had the element of surprise on my side. For all he knew, I was creeping up behind him right now.

He stood in the shadow of the doorway staring at the bed and said in a low throaty voice, "Come out, come out, wherever you are …"

I could hear his breathing now, and light from the living room illuminated his massive forearms holding the weapon out in front of him. He was huge and outweighed me by about a hundred pounds. Not a good matchup. And judging by what just happened to Sebastiano, I assumed that surrender was not an option.

I dismissed trying to disarm him because that would leave me in an unequal wrestling match. Stabbing him in the chest would place me in front of the gun and his dense pecs might protect his heart. Wounding him in any place but a vital organ would be a fatal mistake. No, I only had one reasonable choice and that was to immediately go for the kill.

His next step brought his full bulk into view as he peered around the room with squinting eyes. He was perspiring and I sensed his anxiety. Hunting other human beings for a living was stressful. I knew that because at one point in my life I had been on the other end of that shotgun. I raised the screwdriver high above my head and held my breath. All I needed was for him to take one more step and just as he did, there was a loud knock on the front door.

It was Mark.

The big guy jumped and accidentally discharged the weapon. The flash lit up the room and the report was deafening at close range. The smell of burnt gunpowder filled the room. I must have gasped because he became aware of me and turned, suddenly spotting me in the shadow behind the door. Surprised by the sight and trying to comprehend what he was looking at, he failed to ratchet another shell into the chamber. His eyes grew wide as he saw the screwdriver raised over my head and just as the danger dawned on him I struck with savage ferocity, driving the steel tip into his right eye, piercing the back socket and plowing through his gray matter. Blood bubbled from the wound and although he wanted to scream he found that he couldn't. He dropped the shotgun and I let go of the screwdriver as I watched him stagger backward and collapse silently to the floor, twitching uncontrollably. At the sound of the blast, Mark began banging loudly and frantically on the door and shouting through it. I ran to let him in before he attracted attention.

I opened the door and pulled him in quickly. He saw Sebastiano's corpse and his jaw dropped as he demanded, "What the hell is going on here, Cesari?"

At this point, I had given up on the idea that this was just a dream. "It's complicated, Mark. This guy was my bodyguard."

"Bodyguard? He's not a particularly good one. Why do you need a bodyguard and why is he dead? What happened here?"

"It's a long story and I don't want to make you feel bad but I think he's dead because of you. I told him you were coming over and I think he must have let his guard down. When he answered the door, an assassin looking for me killed him."

Mark looked alarmed. "An assassin? Here? Now? Where?"

"He's in my bedroom."

"The killer is in your bedroom? Doing what? Taking a nap?"

"Hopefully a permanent one."

He was horrified. "You're kidding me, right? There are two dead guys here? Who killed the assassin?"

I didn't answer him right away and he said even more excitedly, "You?!"

"Unless I'm having one of those visions I've been telling you about, then yes. I honestly don't know what's real and what's not anymore. I'm fully expecting to wake up any minute and find out this never happened."

"We'll talk about that later. Let me see this other guy. I want to confirm the facts first."

260

"It's not pretty, Mark."

He looked at Sebastiano, who was missing much of his face. "And this is?"

In the bedroom Mark gasped at the sight of the screwdriver buried up to its hilt in the guy's eye socket. He had stopped twitching, thankfully, because I had no intention of calling an ambulance. Mark said, "God almighty. I can't believe this. We should call the police, Cesari."

"Mark, you're a straight shooter and I'll accept whatever you want to do, but hear me out first. Calling the police isn't going to bring these guys back and will only make my life that much more complicated. I have a friend who can take care of this in a more—delicate fashion."

"Delicate fashion? You can't be serious? You're going to try to bury this?"

"Not bury it so much as move it to a different location."

"Jesus Christ, Cesari."

"Take a deep breath, Mark."

He looked pale and I thought he might throw up but he kept a lid on it as he paced back and forth around the room. I was sure the smell of gunsmoke, blood, and exposed human tissue was stressing him out to the max. He was an uptown shrink with soft, delicate hands. This wasn't his gig. He sighed deeply, "I already know too much, don't I?"

I felt bad for dragging him into this. "Probably. Look, I know this isn't going to make you happy, Mark, but you need to do exactly as I say until the danger has passed."

"Great. The crazy guy is giving orders to the shrink."

I called Vito and told him what happened. Needless to say he was pissed but sent a team of guys with hacksaws, plastic garbage bags and large suitcases to collect the bodies and clean the place up. He ordered Mark and me to stay put but I decided that it wasn't in our best interests to act as sitting ducks in case the dead guy's friends came looking for him. I searched Sebastiano and relieved him of his pistol, tucking it in the back of my pants. Mark knew me from way back and although he was upset, he wasn't quite as shocked by what was happening as he might have been with another patient. He knew that years ago I had walked on the wild side.

Seeing me take the gun he asked, "Are we going to shoot our way out of here?"

"Only if we have to. C'mon."

We took the stairs down to street level and peeked out the door, searching for anything out of the ordinary. There was a guy with a baseball cap across the street, sitting on a bench smoking a cigarette and reading a magazine. I noticed that he kept glancing back and forth up and down the avenue and then back at my building. He was unshaven, wore sunglasses, and looked like he was in decent shape. I looked up at the cloud-covered sky and wondered why he wore sunglasses. As I watched him he rested the magazine on his lap to reach into his pocket. He wore a green Philadelphia Eagles sweatshirt. What a pair of balls this guy had.

I turned to Mark who waited patiently behind me. "Mark, wait here. I need to talk to that guy across the street, the one with the Eagles sweatshirt. I think he's the lookout man for our friend upstairs. I don't want him to relay to anyone the bad news about me still being alive."

"Are you going to kill him?"

I was offended. "Is that what you think of me? I'm a board-certified gastroenterologist, a man of healing."

He repeated, "Are you going to kill him?"

"I don't know yet, but here, to show you my intentions are good, hang on to this and it will reduce the chances of a fatal outcome slightly." I handed him Sebastiano's 9 mm.

Stepping out onto the sidewalk, I slipped in and out of the current of people walking back and forth along the avenue, gradually wading my way through to the curb. The light changed to green, and I took a deep breath as I marched across the street directly at him. At first, he was unconcerned but as I neared, apprehension registered on his features. He stood up, unsure of himself, and when I reached the twenty-foot mark he took off at a dead run down Waverly Place with me in hot pursuit. He was young and healthy and had a head start. At the end of the block he cut over into Washington Square Park and lost himself in the throngs of people there. The place was jammed. Apparently, I had just entered the annual Pagan Pride festival. Booths selling and promoting Wiccan philosophy, clothes, and other paraphernalia filled the center of the park by the fountain and most people were dressed as witches or warlocks. I wasn't sure what pot had to do with being a witch, but I noticed there sure was a lot of it in use as I hunted for the guy. In any other city you might have thought there was a big Halloween party going on. Annoyed that I had let him get away so easily, I stood on a bench and scanned around.

I was unhappy as I pushed my way through the crowd in frustration, searching behind the vendors selling trinkets and recruiting new members. A witch blessed me by blowing a cloud of marijuana smoke in my face from a massive reefer. There were multiple entrances in and out of the park and I was just starting to think that I had lost him when I noticed a bit of a ruckus at one of the booths not too far away. Some guy dressed as a witch, complete with long cape and tall, pointed black hat, with his back to me, was rummaging through his pockets looking for cash while a woman in street clothes reprimanded him. Then I got it. He was trying to buy her outfit as a disguise and realized he didn't have enough cash on him. I presumed she didn't accept credit cards and was getting pissed. What an asshole. She was a witch not a Marxist. I chuckled as I approached him from behind. Everyone was a socialist until it came time to give away their own stuff.

I tapped him on the shoulder. He turned around and I quickly yanked the cape off of him revealing the Eagles sweatshirt. Before he could react or say anything, I kneed him hard in the nuts and he lurched forward into my arms, gasping in pain. I took the hat off him and tossed it at the woman. "He won't need this now."

I put an arm around him and helped him hobble to one of the nearby benches while the woman and several others watched with curiosity. I put my arm around him so that everyone could see the hostilities were over and there was no need to call the authorities. No one did, either. It was a beautiful day in the park. Why spoil it with the police? When he had started to collect himself I said, "Yes or no, asshole. Do you have a weapon of any kind on you? Please don't lie. I'm already upset."

He was a little pale and ashen from the knee. "No."

"Good. Now give me your wallet and your cell phone."

Still grimacing, he handed me his wallet. I looked at his driver's license and said, "So you're Sammy Beans' cousin, Dom, from Philly?"

He nodded, surprised. "Yeah, but how do you know Sammy Beans?"

I smiled and whacked him hard in the back of the head. "I ask the questions, all right? So, what did I ever do to you?"

He hesitated. No point in admitting anything he didn't have to, so I leaned real close to his face and whispered, "Don't insult my intelligence, Dom. I could shoot you just for wearing an Eagles sweatshirt in broad daylight here and everyone in this park would cheer."

"It was just a job, man. I get a thousand bucks to sit outside and watch your apartment for an hour. Anybody shows up don't look right, I call Tyrone."

"Who hired you?"

He gulped nervously. "Tyrone did. What happened to him?"

"The usual thing that happens when you try to kill someone who's twice as dangerous as you are. So, I'm going to ask you one more time and I want you to think it over carefully before you lie to me again. Who hired you?"

Sensing real and imminent danger he said, "Mickey Two Fingers."

"That's better, but now I need you to tell me something I didn't know like who hired Mickey Two Fingers."

"I have no idea. Mickey Two Fingers calls us up one day and says I have a job. We don't ask questions like that."

Fair enough. "So what was the plan after you finished me off?"

"We were supposed to call Mickey and tell him how it went down and tomorrow he drops off our cash at O'Neal's Pub on Third Street in Philly."

"Does he care who makes the call?"

"He's expecting Tyrone. If I call, he'll know something's wrong."

"How'd you get here, Dom?"

"I have a car. An old Buick parked on Sixth Avenue."

"Okay, Dom, empty your pockets onto the bench."

"Why?"

"Because I said so."

He emptied his pockets as he was told. There was a five dollar bill, car keys, some loose change and a Bic pen. I picked up the pen and showed it to him. Then I slapped him hard in the back of the head again and he winced. "I thought you said you didn't have any weapons?"

"C'mon, it's just a pen."

"Dom, do you have any idea how much I could hurt you with a pen?"

He didn't say anything as he thought over that proposition. I continued, "Okay, unlike you I am armed, extremely dangerous and really pissed off. There's blood and shit all over my apartment that needs to be cleaned up. So here's what's going to happen. We get up and walk out of here with my arm around you like we're more than just pals. Look happy and try to blend in. A friend of mine is waiting for me back at the apartment. We're going to use your car to drive down to Little Italy where we got your cousin Sammy Beans under wraps."

"You got Sammy?"

"Once we're out of here, you're going to call Mickey Two Fingers and tell him you got me but I had a gun and took out Tyrone and that you'd like to pick up your payment as planned, understood?"

He nodded. "Understood."

I looked at him carefully, making him very uncomfortable. He asked, "What is it? I told you all I know."

"Tell me one more thing."

"What?"

"That you're not going to force me to kill you."

Safely in Dom's Buick, with Mark in the back and Dom driving I asked, "So why do they call him Mickey Two Fingers?"

He looked at me as he turned the car onto Houston Street. "When he interrogates people he likes to cut them with a knife and then jam two fingers into the wound to cause them even more pain."

I turned around to look at Mark. "Nice guy, huh?"

His rolled his eyes. "Any chance of dropping me off in a place called normal?"

Chapter 28

*B*ack in Vito's apartment, we locked Dom in the room with his cousin Sammy Beans. Both guys were being cooperative so we ordered them a pepperoni pizza. Vito and I sat at the kitchen table while Mark splashed cold water on his face in one of the bathrooms. This had been an unusually taxing day for him, to say the least.

Vito asked, "You set up a meeting with Mickey Two Fingers at O'Neal's Pub in Philly tonight?"

"Yeah, I got too much going on. I can't keep dodging bullets like this. It's better if we meet the threat head on. Don't you think?"

He nodded as he strummed his fingers on the table. "Yeah, I guess. What about these guys?"

"I don't know what to do with them. Neither one of them did any actual harm to anybody."

"Neither of them did any harm, my ass. Tell that to Sebastiano."

I sighed deeply. I was trying to advocate for a more moderate position but that was going to be a tough sell now that blood had been spilled. "True, but Dom didn't actually pull the trigger. Sit on it for a day. They're not bothering anybody for the moment and if they cooperate then maybe we can consider some sort of penance for them."

He nodded. "Maybe. I'll think about it. What time are you supposed to meet Mickey?"

"He's expecting Dom to meet him at nine p.m. in the back of the bar in a corner booth. I don't know what Mickey looks like so I'll get there an hour or so early and hang back somewhere in another part of the bar until Dom IDs him for me."

"What if Dom blows your cover?"

"Then he not only signs his own death warrant but his cousin's as well, who we'll keep here on ice."

"I guess that might work. Fine, I'll go with you. What about your doctor friend, Mark?"

"Me and him have to talk a little about what happened. He's not used to all of this and is a bit shaken up but he'll be all right. Look, let's synchronize our watches. It's almost three. We need to leave here no later than six so have your car ready downstairs."

I left him there to make a few phone calls and went to find Mark, who was reading a magazine in the living room. "Dr. Greenberg, I presume."

"Dr. Cesari."

Smiling, I took a seat on the sofa opposite him. He looked much better and was sipping Remy Martin from one of Vito's snifters. "I suppose I have a lot of explaining?"

"I'm pretty sure I don't want to know every detail."

"And I won't tell them all to you but just so you know, there's a significant chance that whoever shot me the first time may be trying to finish the job."

"I thought we decided that was a random shooting?"

"I'm sure that's what they want everyone to believe, but there's a lot I've learned about the events leading up to that day that are very suspicious. It seems my presence in that woman's apartment may not have been as much of a coincidence as we all thought."

268

I stretched out on the leather couch and looked at the copper ceiling's ornate design. Over the course of the next thirty minutes, I filled him in on everything I had learned about Unicare and Duncan Ronald McCormick's manipulation of Saint Matt's medical records with his Z1 program. He interrupted me briefly from time to time to fill in the gaps. I told him about the latest visions as well.

"So you think that this guy Ronnie manipulates the records and then controls what happens afterward, allowing patients with fatal diseases to simply die without treatment to save his insurance company money and that when Mrs. Konstandin started to make waves he decided to silence her rather than just pay her off?"

"For all I know, he tried to pay her off but she refused to be bought. She was pretty outraged about the whole thing and then I started investigating and tripped upon some irregularities in the records. He may have decided that it was time for me to go, too. And Mark, don't look at it as a single case that might save Unicare thousands of dollars but think of the big picture of thousands, maybe millions of patients not receiving the care they need. The savings to the insurance company would be in the hundreds of millions, maybe even billions of dollars."

"That's quite a whopper of a story, Cesari. I hope you realize that."

"I have the proof on Ronnie's laptop in the other room. I'll show you the Z1 program and how it works. It's quite clever."

"I think I'd like to see that."

I poured myself some Remy Martin and we went into the bedroom, fired up my laptop, and logged onto the EMR at Saint Matt's. "The beauty of this program, Mark, is that it simply piggybacks onto my VPN to access the records so there is no trace of a separate login and then once he's in he has carte blanche to do whatever he wants."

269

"Yes, but you said that you could only get the program to work if it was physically on your laptop. Wouldn't that be a bit inconvenient?"

"Sure, but the program is quite small and what I think he was doing was simply using my secretary's PC under the guise of helping her schedule patients for their exams. She has access to all the doctors' medical records. All he would have to do is plug in a USB stick with the file on it and he would be home free to do whatever he wanted."

He nodded trying to digest it all. "Wouldn't she realize that she could get in trouble for doing that?"

"Maybe, maybe not. She's young and naïve plus there's a possibility they may be romantically involved. Women do crazy things when they think they're in love."

He chuckled. "A bit cynical, don't you think, Cesari?"

"No, it's just that I've been around the block a few times."

After signing onto the VPN, I searched for the Z1.exe file on my desktop but couldn't find it. I did a Windows search of the hard drive and still couldn't find it. Puzzled, I went through my laptop folder by folder while Mark stood patiently waiting. Finally, I said, "Something's wrong. The file is missing."

"Hmm, are you sure?"

I turned on Ronnie's laptop and waited patiently for it to boot but it didn't. In fact, it didn't do anything. It did the usual pre-start assessment but then went to a black screen and made a shrill beep. I tried turning it off and on again with the same result.

"Shit. I don't get this."

Mark asked, "That's Ronnie's laptop? The one you took from his office in Unicare?"

"Yes."

I scratched my head in frustration. What the hell was going on?

270

"Is everything all right, John?"

"No, somebody's been tampering with these laptops. I'm going to ask Vito who's been in here while I was out." I was starting to get pissed off.

"Take it easy, Cesari. Let's not make accusations to large men with guns. Walk me through what you think happened to these laptops, all right?"

I told him about the Z1.exe file and how I transferred it to my laptop and figured out the password. He said, "There it is. You sent it as an email attachment. Just open up your email and re-download the file."

I groaned. "I deleted the email because I don't trust the security of my Yahoo account and I instinctively knew this file was important. Since I thought I had two copies I didn't think I needed a third."

He was suddenly very serious. "John, I'm going to ask you something and I don't want you to take it the wrong way."

"What?"

"Is it possible that you imagined the whole thing like one of those visions you told me about? Certainly, you see what this looks like from my point of view. Some super villain creates some evil software to hurt you and your patients. You've discovered his secret but now all traces of factual evidence have mysteriously and conveniently disappeared. Do you see my point?"

I nodded sullenly. Great, a board-certified psychiatrist whose care I'm under thinks I'm nuts. "You're suggesting this could all be some type of complex delusion."

He shrugged and took a sip of his cognac. "You're the one seeing and hearing things."

I sat back in my chair. I was starting to get really confused. Could I have imagined it or dreamt it? But then where did the laptop come from? I picked it up and examined its exterior.

There were no identifiable markings on it. Did I buy it myself and just can't remember? Wait a minute. I said, "How do you explain the dead guys in my apartment?"

"I didn't say you imagined that but maybe you're just filling in the gaps or …"

"Or what?"

"Forget it."

"Or what, Mark?"

"How can I be sure that you didn't murder those two guys before I arrived and just can't remember exactly what happened so you dreamed up some wild story of deranged hit men trying to kill you?"

"I already admitted I killed one of those guys but only after he blew Sebastiano's head off and was trying to kill me."

"When is your EEG?"

"Tomorrow morning at nine."

"Good. Why don't we get a head start and do a little therapy here and now?"

I looked at my watch. "Sure, why not? You've got an hour and then I have to go, crazy or not."

"Lie down on the bed."

"Really?"

"Just do it and try to relax."

He closed the door, dimmed the lights and then sat on a chair next to me. "Close your eyes."

"You're kidding? You're going to try to hypnotize me."

"Breathe in deeply and let it out."

I did.

"Do it again. Nice and easy. Let yourself go."

I looked at him. "I don't think I'm capable of being hypnotized, Mark. Just warning you. I'm too intelligent."

Ignoring me he said in a soothing voice, "Close your eyes, Cesari, and think peaceful thoughts. I'm going to count backwards from ten. With each descending number I want you to become more and more relaxed. I want you to imagine yourself gently floating in a pool of calm water. You are now in a world of total tranquility. Ten."

I tried to do as he said, but it was a little hard to relax at the moment.

"Nine, you are even more relaxed. Absolutely stress-free."

Okay, I thought, what's the worst that could happen? Go with the flow, Cesari.

"Eight."

I actually felt calmer.

"Seven, Six…"

It wasn't working.

"Five. Breathe in, breathe out. That's it. You're floating gently, rocking back and forth, back and forth. So peaceful, so safe. Breathe in, breathe out."

I breathed in and I breathed out.

"Four, you are so comfortable. Not a care in the world. We are almost there, John."

Almost where?

"Three, two…"

I woke with a start. Vito had come crashing into the room yelling. "What the fuck's going on in here?"

Startled and confused, I jumped up and looked at him and then back to where Mark should have been. His chair had fallen backward onto the floor and he lay sprawled unconscious on his back. Vito and I carried him to the bed. He had a strong pulse and was breathing comfortably. I checked him for any obvious injuries and found none. He seemed fine so I gently tried to rouse him.

Vito demanded. "Cesari, what happened?"

"I don't know, Vito. He must have fallen backward. You saw what I saw."

"What was he screaming about? I thought you were murdering him."

"Screaming?"

"Yeah, screaming bloody murder at the top of his lungs, like he saw a ghost. I never heard anything like it."

I stammered. "I—I honestly don't know. I didn't hear anything. I laid down for a minute and must have fallen asleep. The next thing I know you came bursting into the room."

"A minute? Cesari, it's almost six o'clock. You've been locked up in here with him since before five."

I looked at my watch. Shit.

Mark made a sound and I shook him little. "Hey Mark, are you okay?"

He murmured. "Where am I?"

"We're in Little Italy. In my friend Vito's apartment, remember?"

He nodded and opened his eyes. He looked very confused. I asked, "How do you feel, pal?"

"Tired and goofy. Where are my glasses?"

I looked around. They had fallen off and either Mark or one of us had stepped on them in the confusion because the lens on one side had shattered and the frame was bent at an extremely awkward angle. I handed the broken spectacles to him. "I'm sorry, Mark. They're not in great shape."

He frowned as he eyed them. "Too bad. I'm blind as a bat without them, but no biggie, I'll get a new pair."

"Are you having any pain? Like in your chest or your head?"

"No, no pain. Just exhausted. Like I could sleep for a month. What happened, Cesari?"

"I think your chair tipped over and you may have hit your head. I'm not sure."

He instinctively felt his head. "Well, I don't feel any lumps and I feel fine now."

Vito said, "Look, Cesari, I don't mean to be a ball breaker but we've got to go. I'll have my guys look after him. This Mickey Two Fingers guy isn't going to hang around all night waiting for us."

After a minute or two Mark really did look okay as he sat up and swung his legs around to the side of the bed. He let out a deep breath. "Do you have any coffee in this place?"

Vito chuckled. "American or espresso?"

"Either one will be fine."

"I'll have one of my guys make you a cappuccino."

I asked, "Do you remember anything about what happened, Mark?"

"Nope. The last thing I remember was you and I talking about Saint Matt's EMR and the next thing I know I'm lying in this bed."

I looked at him and then at Vito. "We'll talk about it some more tomorrow, okay? When you're feeling up to it, one of Vito's men will drive you to your apartment but in the meanwhile you should call your wife and let her know where you are and that you're all right."

He nodded. "Where are you going?"

"The city of brotherly love."

Chapter 29

Vito parked the car in front of O'Neal's Bar and Lounge in case we needed to beat a hasty retreat. It was an old saloon in a rundown part of Philly with beat-up wood floors, booths and counter top—a neighborhood joint where everyone knew each other and more importantly, minded their own business. Inside, Dom sat toward the far end of the dark room in a high-backed booth. Vito and I sipped draft beers sitting on bar stools near the door, facing him. We were maybe thirty feet away and had a clear view of his table. We were armed with 9 mm Glocks under our windbreakers. It was almost 9:00 p.m. Sunday and the room wasn't very crowded, just a few hardcore alcoholics getting plastered at the bar. A jukebox played a mellow country tune. The idea tonight was to move fast, instill terror, and disappear from whence we came. If Dom played nice, he'd live to see the sun come up. Looking around, I was relieved that I couldn't spot any surveillance cameras.

At 9:00 sharp, Vito elbowed me as the door opened and a burly six-foot guy with a full beard, knit hat, and serious look on his face entered. He casually checked out the room, nodded at the bartender, and made a beeline for Dom's table. His hands were huge—the size of small hams—and he wore jeans and work boots. He wasn't quite what I expected. From Vito's description of him I half expected to see an emaciated crackhead, not a longshoreman from the one of the wharves.

I threw a twenty on the counter to pay for the beers and said, "Stay here and keep an eye on the door."

I got up and followed Mickey to Dom's table. As he slid into the booth I pulled the 9 mm out and slid in next to him, pressing the muzzle into his side so that my intention was unmistakable. He grunted, looked at Dom and then at me and asked gruffly, not the least bit concerned, "Who the fuck are you?"

I looked at Dom. "Beat it."

Dom took off like a jackrabbit without saying a word. I looked at Mickey closely. He was forty, rough and wind-burned like he spent a lot of time outdoors.

"Put your hands on the table where I can see them and try to remember that I'm the one holding the gun."

He put his hands on the table in front of him and I quickly frisked him, finding a five inch switch blade and snub-nosed, hammerless .38 in his coat pockets.

"So what do you want?" he asked, in a low rumbling voice like a man who was used to having his questions answered.

Vito slid into the booth opposite us and collected Mickey's weapons. I said, "I thought you were watching the door?"

He replied, "I can see it fine from here."

Mickey said, "Somebody going to tell me what's going on?"

Vito stood up and without warning cold-cocked him hard in the jaw. Mickey's head flipped backward, smashing into the hard wood of the booth. He was dazed but alert, and now had a swollen lip. He got the message.

Vito said, "That was for Sebastiano."

"Who?"

I said, "Shut up and listen. There's a Lincoln Towncar parked out front. We're going to walk out nice and calmly and get in. We need to talk to you in a private setting. One sound out of you and you're gone. Nod your head if you understand." I pressed the gun extra hard into his side as I finished speaking.

He nodded his head.

We placed plastic wrist restraints on him and walked out of the bar together with him in between. In the Towncar, they sat in the back while I drove. I turned on the radio when I got tired of listening to Vito use Mickey as a punching bag. He was pretty pissed off about Sebastiano and wasn't holding anything back.

I looked in the mirror and when I thought things were getting a little out of control said, "Take it easy back there. I need to ask him a few questions too."

Traffic was light and it took just over two hours to drive back to Manhattan. By the time we pulled in front of the Café Napoli it was after midnight. Vito was exhausted and his hands were bruised. Mickey's face was swollen and bloodied and he couldn't see out of one eye. I was very upset by what I had learned during the ride but the facts were undeniable. Vito and I got out of the car assisted by two of Vito's men, who were waiting for us on the street.

He told one of them. "Take him to the garage I own on First Avenue. Keep him alive but don't let him out of your sight. We need him around for a while."

In the apartment, I was surprised to see Cocoa on the sofa sipping tea. It had been an extraordinarily busy day for me, and when she hadn't returned in the afternoon like she had said she would, I just assumed she had decided to spend an extra day with her parents for some reason. Vito waved hello and went off to his bedroom to clean up. She put down her cup and ran over to me, throwing her arms around my waist. "I'm so sorry. One of the guys told me about what happened earlier today."

"Thanks. I'm sorry for not calling you about that but I didn't want to get you upset. When did you get in?"

"I got in late, maybe twenty minutes ago. I barely had time to say hello to Cleo when you arrived."

"So, how's everything in Jersey?"

She hesitated. "John, I don't want to lie to you. I didn't go to New Jersey to visit my parents. Well, that's not entirely true either. I did stop in to say hi, but I didn't stay there long ..."

She hesitated and I waited patiently, curious. "I'm listening, Cocoa."

"I went to Philadelphia to talk to my Uncle Leo."

Now I was really intrigued. "Well, when I heard that whoever was trying to kill you was from Philadelphia, I went there to ask him if he knew who might be involved but he didn't."

"Why would he know anything about that?"

"Because he's a street lawyer who worked his way up from the bottom. He's defended mobsters, murderers, gangsters, bikers, you name it. If they're bad and live in Philadelphia then he or his partners know them."

Okay, that made some sense. "Why didn't you just tell me where you were going? Why all the secrecy?"

"Because, I had to tell him about us—you know—being back together."

I nodded. "Oh, I see now, and how did he take that?"

"Not well, but I also told him that I knew about how he had blackmailed you into breaking up with me. I actually got pretty steamed up and gave him a piece of my mind."

"Oh, boy."

"I knew you weren't going to be happy about that but I felt it had to be done and now it's all out in the open. Uncle Leo apologized to me and even agreed to put feelers out on the street to his contacts to see if he can find out anything for us."

"That was nice of him."

"I actually feel much better knowing he's on our side."

"Yeah, me too."

"Well, it's almost one in the morning. How about we go to bed? I feel like snuggling. Do you think you're starting to come around in that department?"

I tried not to think about Helen but that was impossible. "We won't know until we try. I'll meet you in the bedroom. I just want to talk to Vito for a minute. We were in the middle of something when we came in."

I found Vito in his bedroom reclining back on top of the covers watching TV with his right hand in a bucket of ice. I said, "Dude, we have a problem."

He muted the TV. "How many does that make now? Did you say anything to Cocoa?"

"No, but she said a lot to me."

"Like what?"

"Like she went to see her uncle and asked him flat out if he knew anything about what's going on."

Vito sat up, suddenly concerned. "You've got to be kidding?"

"No, I'm not. She thought he might know something because of his contacts in the Philadelphia underworld. Get this, he even offered to help find out who it might be that's trying to kill me."

"Man, he's got balls, doesn't he?"

"Unless Mickey fingered the wrong guy."

He furrowed his brow thinking about that. "C'mon, what are the odds of that? He's getting his brains bashed in and suddenly blurts out the name of a high-priced lawyer in Philadelphia who just happens to be Cocoa's uncle? That doesn't even make sense. Besides, he knows we're going to check it out."

"I know."

Vito shook his head. "Nah, Uncle Leo's lying through his teeth. Cocoa caught him with his pants down. What else could he do? He ordered the hit because he probably found out about you dating Cocoa again, got pissed off and decided jail wasn't good enough for you so he bailed out on the gun charges and went for a more permanent solution. It's not unheard of. For all we know he may have been behind the first shooting as well and Mrs. Konstandin may have been the collateral damage."

"Well, that's certainly an interesting spin on the Konstandin murder, but Cocoa said that when she told him about us he seemed genuinely surprised."

"Bullshit. So, he's a great actor? Aren't all lawyers? If he didn't know, then why would he be trying to kill you? I thought that was the whole reason."

I hesitated. If Uncle Leo was trying to kill me because I was back with Cocoa then he would have placed her life at risk. I found it hard to believe that he would do such a thing, but if that wasn't the reason, then why? He wasn't a nice guy, that was for sure, and I knew he was as mobbed up as they came, but would he place his own niece in danger like that? I chuckled to myself as I thought about that old saying about the apple not falling far from the tree. Cocoa didn't look dangerous but most women didn't until they got mad. So, what made women mad? Cheating on them with Chinese orthopedic surgeons for starters.

I nodded. "Well look, Vito, keep this to yourself, all right? Cocoa's feeling pretty good about her uncle right now and I'd rather not burst her bubble if I don't have to."

"I won't say anything but this is going to be hard to contain if you know what I mean."

"Just try, okay? What about Sammy Beans?"

"Already let him go and told him I'd better not hear a peep out of him or his cousin."

"I doubt that we'll ever hear from those two again. Say Vito, could you do me a favor? I know you have contacts in downtown real estate."

He smiled. "You could say that."

"There's an office building on East Fifth Street, number 304. I need to know who signed the lease for suite 7F. The lobby's directory said the occupant is a Dr. John Burgoyne but I think that's a cover. I'm sure I'll get nowhere with the landlord."

"No problem. I never met a landlord yet who wanted his trash pickup delayed by weeks or months. Besides, I think I know the building you're talking about. I'll have the name for you by tomorrow afternoon. Now, can I go to sleep?"

"Yeah, see you in the morning."

I went to my bedroom and found Cocoa lying under the covers holding a book. "What're you reading?"

She laughed. "It's just a romance novel. Guy meets girl, they fall in love and right before the wedding he becomes gender-confused."

I chuckled. "Welcome to the twenty-first century."

She put the book down and turned off the lamp on her night table. "Why don't you come to bed and we'll see how your recovery is coming along."

A half hour later, we lay there and it was obvious my recovery wasn't coming along as well as we had hoped. I said, "I'm sorry."

"What do you think it is?"

"I don't know. I feel perfectly fine otherwise."

"Is it me?"

"I doubt it. You are one seriously sexy woman, Cocoa." A night light shone in from the bathroom and I looked at her near perfect shape and beautiful face. Any man would consider himself lucky to be with her. I needed to get my act together.

"Maybe you can try Viagra?"

"Viagra? I don't know Cocoa. Those drugs scare me. Have you ever seen those commercials where they say consult your physician for an erection lasting more than four hours? They never say what happens after that."

She laughed. "Oh, brother."

I was starting to feel guilty because I knew that it wasn't a physical problem holding me back. Maybe it *was* her for some reason. I looked at the bathroom door and then back at Cocoa. I said, "I have an idea." Standing up, I grabbed her hand, gently tugging her to come with me.

"Where are we going?"

I said, "The bathroom."

"The bathroom?"

"Yeah, and bring your pillow. You're going to need it." I looked down and realized I was starting to feel better already.

She noticed too and giggled, "Oh boy, will you look at that. C'mon, let's get going while we got the wind at our backs."

I laughed and slapped her bottom as she eagerly walked past, now pulling me instead of the other way around.

Afterward, we lay on the bed staring at the ceiling, exhausted and breathless. She said, "Oh, my God. That was great."

"Yeah, it was. You know, Cocoa, we haven't talked about it, but I want to thank you for being so patient with me. Between my hospitalization and now, it's been a long time for a young healthy woman to go without sex."

She was very quiet and didn't say anything in response.

"What's the matter?"

"John, I have sort of a confession to make."

"A confession?"

"Yeah …"

"And …?"

"I haven't really gone quite that long …"

I reached over and turned on the lamp, sitting up in the bed. "What's that supposed to mean?"

283

She took a deep breath, avoided making eye contact, and spoke very softly, "John, you know I hate to lie. I was with someone while you were in a coma."

She hesitated and I said, "Go on."

"It was about a month into your hospitalization. After your second or third cardiac arrest, the doctors told me you had a zero percent chance of recovering. I was very upset and sad and lonely … things just kind of happened. I didn't mean for it to happen. It just did. I'm sorry. Maybe I shouldn't have said anything."

I sighed as I thought about it. I had no right to be upset but I was. We had made no promises to each other and I shouldn't have expected her to be celibate. We weren't married. Besides, after what had just happened with Helen, I had no right to sit in judgment on anyone. I said soothingly, "It's okay. I understand. I honestly do so put it behind you. There's no need to feel guilty. Let's move on, all right?" I turned the light off and put my arm around her.

She snuggled close and rested her face on my chest. "It's been bothering me and I needed to get it off my mind. Thank you for being so understanding. I know Vito feels just horrible about it too."

There was an uncomfortable silence and I turned the light back on. "What was that?"

"What?"

"You said Vito feels horrible about it too."

Sensing my agitation, she hugged me tightly. "I thought you said that everything was okay between us and that you understood."

"You didn't tell me it was Vito."

"I didn't think it mattered."

I gently pushed her away. "Of course it matters. He's my friend."

She pulled me back, hugging me even more tightly. "What difference does it make? He feels awful about it too."

"What difference does it make? It's a huge difference and I don't care how he feels." I tried pushing her away again but she was hanging on with all her might and I didn't want to hurt her.

"Well, I'm sorry and so is he. We haven't even been able to look each other in the eye for months."

"I don't believe this."

"Turn the light off. You must be exhausted. Let's sleep on it, okay? Things always seem worse when you're tired."

She was right. I was tired. I let out a deep breath and turned the light off. Without uttering another word we drifted off to sleep.

But make no mistake, I was seriously pissed off. I knew I was being a bit hypocritical but I couldn't help it. Vito and Helen weren't moral equivalents in my mind.

Chapter 30

I slept fitfully and woke at 5:00, dressing in the dark so as not to wake Cocoa. The rest of the apartment was also deep in slumber and I left a note on the kitchen table that I had things to do. Outside, dawn hadn't yet broken as I hoofed it over to my apartment on Sixth Avenue. Vito and Cocoa. Unbelievable. I was irritated. Cocoa was going to be upset when she woke up and found me gone but I needed to be alone so I could calm down and the last thing I needed right now was to run into Vito.

In the loft, I showered, shaved, and put on a pot of coffee while I thought things through. Vito's boys had cleaned up the apartment pretty well. They had removed the carpet and wiped down the hardwood floors with ammonia. Even in the bedroom, I could hardly tell what had happened. I didn't know where they had taken the bodies and I didn't want to.

My EEG was scheduled for 9:00 at Saint Matt's. Arnie and the neurologist were going to meet me there. Arnie was going to be pissed when I didn't show but I had too much to do. I was also a little scared anyway at what they might find but knew I was going to have to face the music sooner or later. My choices were limited. I was either having complex motor seizures brought on by anoxic brain damage or I was a raving lunatic and was going to be on a lot of unpleasant medications. Given those choices, I was hoping for the seizures, but either way I had work to do.

I retrieved my black duffel bag from under the bed and took the pictures of Kelly and the kids out, placing them in the night table drawer. The camera I tossed on the bed. I still had the Glock with an eight-round clip that Vito had given me last night and I placed that in the duffel bag. It was almost 6:00 a.m. when my cell phone rang. It was Cocoa and I let it go to voice mail. Five minutes later, she called again and I let it go to voice mail again. I didn't want to talk to her. My ego had been bruised and needed time to heal. Even an exotic dancer should know that.

I took the duffel bag and walked over to the Seventh Avenue parking garage where I kept my Toyota Camry. I paid fairly exorbitant monthly rates but that was the price of owning a car in the city. I popped the trunk and rummaged around until I found my crowbar. Six pounds of blackened steel: it was my preferred weapon in almost every situation I could think of except an all-out gunfight. I placed it too in the duffel bag. I would pick up duct tape and a small flashlight at the nearest convenience store. I wasn't exactly sure what I was going to do but it was always a good idea to have a few essential items.

Pulling out of the garage, I called Mark to see how he was doing. It was early but I took a chance.

"Good morning, Dr. Cesari. You're up early." He was cheery.

"You too, Dr. Greenberg. How are you feeling this fine day?"

"Never been better."

"Good to hear. No headache or anything?"

"No, no headache or anything like what?"

"Anything like maybe—a bad dream?"

"Not sure what you're getting at, but no, nothing bothering me at all."

I stopped at a red light on Canal Street while we talked. "Well, that's good. By the way, I'm sorry about your glasses. I think I was the one who stepped on them."

"Funny thing about that, Cesari. When I got home last night I couldn't find my spare set and I had a bunch of papers to read. Well, you've known me a long time and you know I'm useless without my glasses, right? But I needed to read those papers so, I figured I'd give it a shot anyway. Guess what?"

"I don't know. What?"

"I didn't need them."

The light turned green and I pressed on the accelerator. "Would you care to expand on that, Mark?"

"I didn't need my glasses and can read just fine without them all of a sudden. I have no idea how that could be. I've been wearing eyeglasses since the first grade, but I just don't need them anymore. Is that crazy or what? You probably think I need my own psychiatrist."

"Or maybe a new ophthalmologist. Well, look, I'm glad you're feeling okay and that's good news about the glasses, I think."

"So what happened last night, Cesari? I'm a little fuzzy on details. I remember going to your friend's apartment, talking with you, having a glass of cognac and not much else."

"That's about it. We shot the bull for a while is all. I got to go now, Mark. I'm driving but I'll stay in touch."

"All right, Cesari. I know when you don't want to talk. Keep me posted and I'll see you soon."

I clicked off. Doesn't need his glasses anymore. What did that mean?

Morning traffic was light as I crossed the Brooklyn Bridge, found the Medi-Save warehouse on Water Street, and parked discreetly about a block away. Arnie had told me this was where Saint Matt's stored its records and other important data such as pathology slides. Medi-Save was a subsidiary of McCormick Enterprises and that tidbit alone made me very suspicious. The neighborhood was deserted and rundown. I wasn't getting a good vibe as I approached the warehouse, which was a three-story old brick structure that looked like it had been abandoned years ago. I double-checked the address I had googled and confirmed I was in the right place. There was even a sign over the front door that said Medi-Save on it. I looked in the duffel bag one last time and put the gun inside my windbreaker pocket.

I cut the engine, exited the car, and headed for the back of the building. Scanning around, I didn't notice any security cameras or guards. Seriously? What kind of security company was this?

There was a rusted old metal door in the back of the building and using the crowbar, in full view of the East River just beneath the Brooklyn Bridge, I pried it open and entered. It was dark and I couldn't find any working light switches so I turned on my flashlight. There was lots of dust, rusted machinery and a few ancient wood crates. This warehouse hadn't been used in years let alone been the site of a high-tech security storage facility. What the hell was going on here?

Continuing my search, I found a large furnace at one end of the room with stacks of freshly-cut wood next to it, suggesting that it might still be in use. I went over to examine it and opened the metal door, sniffing the smoky residue. The ashes inside looked relatively fresh and certainly not more than a few days old. I poked around with the crowbar and saw fragments of glass amidst the cold cinders. Actually there were lots of fragments of glass. At the front edge of the furnace, there was a three-inch-long by one-inch-wide rectangular piece of intact glass that had escaped its fiery fate. It was easily recognizable to anyone in the medical profession or to anyone with a television as a pathology slide. I picked it up and saw that it had a Saint Matt's identification marker and a patient's name on it.

I thought it over for a minute. The only conclusion possible was that they were destroying the pathology slides so no one could ever prove the records were falsified. But this was kind of clumsy, wasn't it? I mean sooner or later someone's going to want to know where the slides were, right? I put that thought on the back burner while I searched the rest of the warehouse. The place was very large and I wasn't sure if I should waste too much time rummaging around when something else caught my eye. There was a long row of large wood crates to one side and at the very end I noted one that was relatively cleaner than the others, as if it had been dusted off recently. The floor around it looked as if the crate had recently been slid into its current position. Upon closer inspection, I also saw several sets of footprints in the dust on the surrounding floor.

The top of the crate was nailed shut so I used the crowbar to wedge it open. I removed the top and then looked in with my flashlight. I gasped in horror as I saw Julie, my secretary, staring back at me with lifeless eyes. Her head was twisted at an unnatural angle and I suspected her neck had been broken. She was stuffed into the box without any dignity whatsoever and her skirt must have caught on something because it had been dragged up to her chest. She couldn't have been dead for very long because I just saw her out at dinner a few nights ago with that scumbag Ronnie.

Fuck. What had happened?

I drew in a long deep breath and let it out slowly. Did Ronnie do this? Who's kidding who? Of course he did, but why? I was shocked and upset. Julie was one of those people you just hated to see bad things happen to. She didn't stick her nose in other people's business and was perpetually nice to everyone. All she really wanted was for someone to care about her. Certainly, she was harmless and didn't deserve this. I was getting angrier with each passing second.

Okay, Duncan or Ronnie, I've had just about enough of you. It's time we sat down and had a chat. Maybe it was a good idea if I were crazy. I could always use that as my defense in court when the shit hit the fan, as I was sure it would. As long as I could stay alive that is. Then it dawned on me. If Ronnie was such an asshole that he was capable of murdering Julie, then maybe he was capable of murdering Mrs. Konstandin and by extension me as well. But what would that, if anything, have to do with Uncle Leo? Did he have a relationship with Ronnie or McCormick Enterprises I didn't know about? A lot of good questions.

I looked down at Julie. She was such a sweet person. The gold locket with pictures of her parents dangled loosely around her neck and I reached down and took it, snapping the gold chain. It was in the shape of a heart and I opened it to view the photos of her mom and dad again. How do you tell this to a mother and father? I let out a deep breath and put the cover back on the crate. I would call the police anonymously when I had the chance. I don't know why I did but I decided to hang on to the locket.

My cell phone buzzed. It was Cocoa. I answered it this time. "Hi."

"John, why did you leave without saying anything? Are you okay? Please tell me you're not upset."

I hesitated. Finding Julie's body had taken the edge off of my temper. Life was too short for petty tantrums. "I'm sorry. I was a bit off when I woke up, but I'm okay now. How are you?"

"Worried sick that you were never going to talk to me again."

"Well, you can stop worrying. How's Cleo?"

"She's fine. I walked her and we've been playing with a chew toy. I'm going to school today but the guys here really like her a lot. They'll take good care of her."

"Yeah, I noticed that they've taken to her."

"When will I see you?"

"I'm not sure. I have a lot going on, but I want you to stay away from my apartment right now. I'm still not sure how safe it is."

"You want me to stay away because it's not safe or because you just want me to stay away?"

"It's not safe, Cocoa, and I'm going to stay away from it as much as I can too. I'll come back to Vito's place later, I just can't say when."

"All right. I'll call you later then, okay?"

"Yes, we'll talk later. Have a great day and stop worrying. I'm fine."

"Thanks, I'm glad. Talk to you later."

I hung up and poked my head out the back door of the warehouse to see if anybody was around, then hurried back to the Toyota, calling Vito as I pulled out and headed back to Manhattan.

"Cesari, where are you?"

"Checking some things out. Do me a favor. Look into Uncle Leo's law firm and see if there's any connection with McCormick Enterprises."

"Sure, when will I see you?"

"I'm coming to pick you up in fifteen minutes. We're going back to Philadelphia to say hello to Uncle Leo."

"Are you out of your mind? You can't just waltz in there and muscle the guy, and if you do you can kiss Cocoa goodbye, guaranteed. That's her uncle, like it or not, and blood is thicker than water."

"You'd probably like that, wouldn't you?" I didn't feel as kindly towards him as I did towards Cocoa.

"What the fuck is that supposed to mean?"

"You know exactly what that's supposed to mean, Judas. Some friend you are and don't insult me by pretending you don't know what I'm talking about."

He hesitated and then turned conciliatory. "Hey look, Cesari. It was a mistake, all right? We were both very upset. We thought you were dead. I can't tell you how much I regret it ever happening and she does too. I don't know what to say. I'm sorry."

"Yeah, well, we'll talk about it more later so be ready. I just crossed the Brooklyn Bridge and I'll be there soon. Have that information for me."

"Give me a break. I'll need more than fifteen minutes?"

"Not if you stop yapping and get to work. You got computers, right? Start googling things and do me a favor. Call his office to make sure that he's in today."

Stuck in rush-hour traffic, I picked Vito up nearly thirty minutes later as he held a hot cup of coffee and a half-eaten blueberry muffin. I said, "Buckle up, asshole."

I lurched the car forward deliberately trying to spill his coffee on him but he was ready for that and smirked. "Nice try, Cesari, now cool off."

"That's easy for you to say. I'm in a coma and you're banging my girlfriend. What kind of an asshole does that?"

"I can't believe she told you."

"She felt guilty, but personally, I wish she hadn't."

"Are you going to be okay, Cesari?"

"Maybe, I don't know. I'm kind of pissed off."

"I understand."

"So what can you tell me?"

"Well first of all, thanks for giving me so much time. This is what I got. Yes, Uncle Leo has represented McCormick Enterprises in the past. Officially, the last time was five years

293

ago when he was part of the legal team that brokered the deal securing Unicare as part of McCormick Enterprise's growing empire. You're going to like this. It's classic. The former head of Unicare was a guy named Jonathan Leibowitz. He grew the company from nothing and was on record as having been strongly against the acquisition initially. Okay, are you ready for this?"

He paused for effect and I got annoyed. "Oh for God's sake, will you just tell me what you know?"

"Well, negotiations between McCormick Enterprises and Unicare had been dragging on for almost a year and apparently were not going so well when this guy Leibowitz decides to take a weeklong vacation with his wife in Napa Valley. He says goodbye to everyone and gets on a plane never to be seen or heard from again. A month later, our boy Rutherford McCormick shows up at a Unicare board meeting waving a letter of intent predated before his disappearance and signed by Leibowitz in front of a notary that he had changed his mind about the acquisition and that he was now all in favor of it and that he thought McCormick was a great guy etc. etc. With him gone, the head of the board of trustees and majority shareholder, Marvin Trolley, happily signed over the company to McCormick Enterprises and then went into early retirement. He died in a DUI-related car accident six months later."

"Holy shit."

"Yeah, these guys ain't fucking around, that's for sure. Hey, where are you going?" I had just made the turn toward the Holland Tunnel heading for New Jersey, planning to pick up I-78 and eventually I-95 to Philadelphia.

"To see Uncle Leo in Philadelphia like I told you."

"Well, he's not there. He's on his way to Boston. You told me to find out if he's in the office today so I called down there on a fishing expedition and told them that I represented McCormick

Enterprises. I just wanted to see their reaction. His secretary sounded surprised because Leo had told her he was going to Boston today to meet with Mr. McCormick at Unicare."

"Well, that settles who knows who, and how convenient to have all the rats in one place. This should be fun."

"It gets even better. I told the secretary that Mr. McCormick wanted to surprise Uncle Leo with a bottle of champagne waiting for him in his room but he wasn't sure where he was staying."

"You're kidding?"

"Guess."

I thought about it. "The Mandarin?"

"Yup. Room 2023."

I smiled. "Good work, Vito. I still hate you but good work."

"Hey look, Cesari, if it's any consolation, I felt so guilty about what I was doing with Cocoa I could barely enjoy myself."

"Will you shut the fuck up? Now call the Mandarin and see if you can get us a room."

"One step ahead of you. One of my guys was on the phone with the Mandarin when you pulled up. He'll text me with the information. I also have my guys doing more research on this Leibowitz thing. I just told you what Wikipedia and the headlines said. I didn't have time to go into details. There's got to be a whole lot more to it I'm sure. You don't just board a plane and disappear."

I asked, "You're packing heat right?"

"Of course, a 9 mm in my shoulder holster, a .32 strapped to my ankle, and a six- inch switchblade. What about you?"

"I've got the Glock you gave me when we went to Philly, and a crowbar."

"Great, now if we only had a change of underwear, we'd be all set."

I pulled onto the West Side Highway and soon was speeding up I-87N. Just as I crossed over into Massachusetts for the second time in the last several days my cell phone rang and I answered it on speaker phone.

"Yeah, Arnie. Look, before you begin. I'm sorry I missed my appointment for the EEG this morning."

"Forget that, Cesari. We got much bigger problems right now." I could hear the strain in his voice.

"What happened?"

"Tony's dead."

I didn't say anything as I absorbed the news and looked at Vito. He didn't know Tony personally but knew he was my friend and everything that had occurred. "Keep talking, Arnie."

"We're not sure what happened. He was in the psychiatric unit and his door was locked from the outside. The staff there said he'd been responding slowly to therapy although he still had to be heavily sedated every night. Everyone was of the opinion that with time he was going to turn it around. This morning he was found lying in bed cold and blue. We'll need to perform an autopsy, of course, but it looks as if he may have been strangled while he slept. There was trauma around his neck. There were no signs of forced entry and the door was completely intact and locked. There was a small window with metal bars maybe a foot and a half square which opened onto the hospital's central courtyard, but his room was fifteen floors up and the window was still locked from the inside. Can you believe this? There is absolute pandemonium right now down here."

"I don't even know what to say. I'm stunned." I slowed the car to a stop, pulling over onto the shoulder."

"Yeah, you and me, and then there's Julie, your secretary."

"Julie?" Did someone find the body already? I hadn't called the police yet.

"Yeah, she came to work last Thursday and no one's seen her since. Her boyfriend called the hospital today to let everyone know she's missing. No note, no nothing. The poor guy's a basket case. The police came by to interview everyone she worked with, and I've got the worst case of heartburn I've ever had. I've already been on the phone twice with the state about Tony and it's not even noon."

I couldn't say anything about finding Julie's body without digging myself into a hole. I said meekly. "Well, hopefully Julie will turn up safe and sound."

With a sudden change in tone Arnie said, "Between me and you, Cesari, you're the one who better hope that she shows up safe and sound. There's an ugly rumor circulating around that you and she had something going on before you got shot. I'm not going to ask you if it's true or not because I don't want to know. I'm just letting you know that one of the other secretaries may have told that to the police. They asked me if I could confirm it. Of course I said I couldn't but they will be looking to have a word with you for sure. So as a friend, I would advise you not to tell the police about those visions you've been having. To them, that would make this an open-and-shut case if you get my drift."

"I get your drift. If I had an affair with her and she's missing and I'm crazy, I must be guilty as sin. Thanks for the heads-up, Arnie."

"One more thing, Cesari, and I'm not trying to make you worried, but I think you ought to know. If you were having an affair with Julie, and like I said I don't want to know, you should also be aware that her fiancée is a New York City cop and apparently from what I've been told is the size of a male silverback gorilla. You know how fast rumors of this nature spread so keep that in mind as well."

"I will. Thanks again, Arnie."

"Talk to you soon, Cesari."

"Yeah, bye."

I looked at Vito and said, "Shit."

"I'm sorry about your friend Tony. What do you think happened?"

"I don't know."

"Can you strangle yourself?"

"I don't know that either. Without any help like from a rope or a belt? I doubt it. I've never heard of a case of it but I'm hardly an expert. I suppose if you were motivated and psychotic enough you could really do some serious harm to yourself but they said he was starting to get better. Damn."

"So—are you or aren't you …?"

"What?"

"Banging your secretary, Julie, a married woman?"

I groaned. "Past tense and she's not married. She's engaged. We did it once at a party, maybe a couple of months before the shooting. We were alone in my office and we'd been drinking and well, you know the drill. Things got carried away."

"That's it? One time? That doesn't sound like you."

I shook my head dejectedly. "There was another time too. A week later, we started reminiscing about the first time and before you know it we were going at it again, but that was it."

He chuckled. "You got some balls, Cesari. You're banging your secretary, who's engaged to marry a cop, and you get mad at me about Cocoa."

"Shut up, Vito. It's not the same thing and you know it. Besides, Julie's dead. We are way past the amusing part."

"She is? Really? How do you know that?"

I told him about my trip to the warehouse this morning.

"Damn."

"I know."

He thought about it and solemnly assessed the situation for me. "You are in deep shit now, Cesari. When this cop boyfriend of hers finds out, there isn't anybody going to be able to save you. Not me, not anybody."

I sighed deeply. "I know, especially with all the secretaries shooting their mouths off."

"Okay, enough with that. So are you going to tell me or not?"

"Tell you what?"

"Your pal, Goldstein, mentioned something about visions. Are you going to tell me what that's all about?"

"Only if you promise not to jump out of the car."

Chapter 31

We checked in again at the Mandarin shortly after noon and Vito threw himself on the bed, covering his face with a pillow. He wasn't happy with all that I had told him. This was a guy that I'd seen start fights unarmed with men twice his size simply because he detected a slight twinge of disrespect in their voice. This was a guy I'd seen interrogate guys with cattle prods because he was mildly curious as to what they might know. Now he lay there groaning.

"Okay, Vito, are you going to make it?"

"Fuck you, Cesari. You know I hate this kind of mumbo jumbo stuff. I can't even watch *The Omen* because I get so scared."

"I know it's weird but it's probably because I suffered brain damage. Most likely, it's some type of seizure disorder and nothing supernatural so take it easy."

"Great, I'm about to barge into a meeting with homicidal maniacs and my backup is a guy with brain damage. I can't tell you how much better that makes me feel. Besides, I thought seizures made you twitch and salivate and things like that?"

"There are many types of seizures and yes, some do that, but others are more complicated involving areas of the brain medical science doesn't really understand that well. They're called complex motor seizures and can sometimes be confused with psychosis."

"Are you telling me you might be psychotic too?"

"I didn't say that."

"You didn't deny it either. Shit."

I was in danger of losing my wingman. "Listen. You need to calm down. We have a job to do and I have a bunch of doctors waiting for me in New York to figure out what's really wrong with me. What I do know for sure is that there's going to be a grand meeting of assholes tonight at Unicare, and in addition to hurting a lot of innocent people they probably killed Julie and Mrs. Konstandin and are probably trying to kill me as well. Who knows, maybe they even killed Tony. What's even more important is that they're planning on hurting a lot more people through manipulation of their healthcare records with that Z1 program I told you about."

"Fine, and you know I'm okay with all this O.K. Corral stuff, but is there a reason why you just can't alert the proper authorities as to what's going on before we risk getting arrested or worse?"

"What am I going to tell them? That I'm having hallucinations since I woke up from a coma, and uncovered a conspiracy by one of the pre-eminent healthcare companies in the country to fraudulently alter the medical records of sick people allowing them to die without proper treatment using a fantastical program that I can't prove exists? Oh, and by the way, they murdered my secretary, who I was having an affair with, and now they are trying to kill me."

Vito cleared his throat and sighed. "I see your point."

"Well, I am so glad about that."

"Take it easy, Cesari. You don't have to be so grouchy."

"I get that way around guys who sleep with my girlfriends. You're such an asshole."

"Are you going to go on forever about that?"

301

"No. Now can I have some quiet while I call Unicare?" I dialed the number to the main office. Vito's cell phone rang at the same time and he walked into the bathroom to answer it.

Someone from Unicare greeted me. I said, "Hello, this is Michael Bennett. I'm Leo Rosenblatt's personal assistant and I'm calling to confirm the time and place of Mr. Rosenblatt's meeting with Mr. McCormick this evening."

I waited while she checked.

She spoke for a few seconds and I said, "Yes, 8:00 p.m. in the boardroom, thank you, and one more thing. Mr. Rosenblatt asked me to find out if Mr. McCormick's son Duncan would be there as well. He brought a present for him. He will? Perfect. Thank you and have a great day."

Vito returned from the bathroom. He said, "That was one of my guys. He got a hold of the landlord to that apartment building you asked about and apparently suite 7F is being leased to McCormick Enterprises."

I nodded. "Well, that settles that. Now help me figure out a way to get up to the boardroom. Uncle Leo's meeting the McCormicks there at eight tonight."

"Want to just grab Leo as he comes out of his room and stick a gun to his head?"

"No, too much could happen between here and there. Besides, Leo's not a shrinking violet. He wouldn't go down without a fight. Trust me. He's almost as big an asshole as you."

"For crying out loud. Will you drop it?"

"I'll drop it as soon as I sleep with *your* girlfriend."

He started chuckling and then laughing. "Don't hold your breath waiting for me to get one."

Ignoring him, I said, "I suppose we could wait by the elevators at Unicare for him to get on and grab him there, but that will only get us to the 41st floor. We'd have to recruit someone else with access to escort us to the boardroom on the 50th floor. Not a good idea. Too risky and too many variables."

"What about from the skywalk observatory like you got in before?"

"I thought about that. Problem is that it's open until ten tonight and the meeting is at eight. There will be people all over the place and we'd have to break in using the crowbar or the gun. I can't count on getting lucky like I did the first time."

I sat on the edge of the bed thinking it over. Then suddenly it hit me and I snapped my fingers. I practically shouted. "Sarah!"

"Who?"

"The girl from Unicare you took out the last time we were here."

"I'm not going to kidnap Sarah for her key and access code, Cesari."

"I didn't say kidnap her. How did you leave off with her?"

"Not great, if you ask me. She was blindfolded and handcuffed to the headboard about to get the full Vito experience when you called in a panic. How do you think we left off?"

"That's not what I meant."

"Well, she wasn't thrilled at being left at the edge of the cliff like that but I think she understood I had a needy friend who required immediate attention. You know, Cesari, it's never a good idea to leave a woman at the precipice, but all in all, I think she'd consider giving me a second chance if I promised to deliver the goods without interruption. What are you thinking?"

I looked at my watch. "Call her. Tell her you're in town and would like to see her again to finish what you started. Suggest taking her up to the skywalk observatory for a drink and then dinner afterward. Meet her at the Unicare main entrance on the 41st floor so it will seem natural for her to take you up there through the executive offices rather than go all the way back down to the lobby. When you get there, just make sure she doesn't lock the door behind her. I'll be waiting up there for you and I'll just sneak in after you come out. I'll hide somewhere until the meeting. If I recall correctly, there was a bathroom not too far from the door to the observatory."

"What if she insists on locking the door?"

"Use your charm to distract her and when that inevitably fails, tell her something clever like you're paranoid about locked doors stemming from a childhood incident when your parents locked you in an abandoned car and tried to drown you in a lake. Women love it when big guys act scared. Isn't that what you told me?"

He snorted and said defensively, "My parents would never try to drown me. They loved me."

I continued. "Just call her. Tell her you'll be there at five. I'll go directly up to the skywalk and hang out while you're meeting her. Okay, go ahead and make the call and let's keep our fingers crossed that one, she's at work today and two, she doesn't hate your guts for leaving her high and dry."

"Sounds like a decent plan, Cesari, except for one thing."

"What?"

"If I'm with Sarah, I'm not going to be able to back you up, and if I ditch her I won't be able to get back up to the 50th floor."

I thought about that. He could always go back to the lobby and come up to the observatory by way of the visitor elevators. Since, I was already on the inside I could unlock the door. On the other hand, I would have to come out of whatever hiding place I was in to do that and thus take the chance of revealing myself. Plus, Vito wasn't exactly the smoothest covert operative I had ever worked with. He was about as stealthy as a bull in a china shop.

I said, "Have a good time with Sarah."

"Seriously? You think you can handle them on your own?"

I snickered. "Two Englishmen and a lawyer? I'm not even sure I'll need a gun."

Chapter 32

Things went smoothly with Vito and Sarah, and I gained access to the 50th floor as planned. At 7:30, I came out from my hiding place in the executive bathroom located near the door leading out to the observatory. Just as before, the hallway was quite dark except for low level floor lighting. I remembered well where the boardroom was and made a bee line for it. The door wasn't locked and I let myself in using my flashlight as a guide. The room was large and dominated by the massive oval table in its center and the oversized portrait of the McCormick family at the far end of the room. The table was easily forty feet long by ten feet wide, and I ducked under its surface just as I heard elevator doors open in the hallway. I turned off the flashlight and put it in the duffel bag, creeping stealthily on hands and knees toward the center of the table. Soon, the door opened and the lights flicked on, as I lay silently in position.

Two men walked past me toward the far end of the table with the McCormick family portrait. Both wore dark navy pants and highly polished wingtip dress shoes. "Shall I pour you a bourbon, Father?"

"Yes, thank you, Duncan. Make it neat."

He poured their drinks and took a seat next to his father. Rutherford said, "First order of business, Duncan. I want this Medi-Save thing wrapped up. I don't like it. I never did. It's a weak link in the whole process. We can't keep telling people their pathology slides are missing or accidentally destroyed."

"Yes, Father, I know. It was a miscalculation on my part. I just assumed that people would accept the falsified records on face value. Oh well, it's all part of the learning curve, I guess. Fortunately, no one's made much of a fuss. At any rate, I plan to burn down the warehouse in Brooklyn to account for the missing pathology should anyone inquire and I have our people in London divesting us from Allentown Medical, the parent company of Medi-Save. We are sufficiently removed that we have plenty of plausible deniability should anyone raise a flag. Just to be safe, I'm going to have the president of Medi-Save canned and leak to the press that he's a scam artist."

"Bollocks, boy. You are a savage, aren't you? And what about the pathology?"

"Already taken care of. McCormick Enterprises funds research at Tufts Medical Center, and as a result of the numerous projects going on, many normal biopsy specimens are obtained. In return for our generous financial support, we have requested that a few normal specimens be turned over to us for teaching and reference purposes at our pharmaceutical divisions where we do our own research. Tufts doesn't need the slides and they would be destroyed eventually anyway. Because of the large amount of money involved and the fact that they can't see any harm in it, they agreed. I've set up a brand new medical storage facility in Medford that should withstand any scrutiny. We will store the normal slides there and when a physician or hospital requests one for review we simply substitute the name of the sick patient onto the normal slide and send it out. When they're done with it, they send it back to be recycled endlessly. Much simpler and cleaner. Now when a record says the biopsy was negative we'll have tissue to back it up."

"Excellent, and the real slides?"

"They go into Boston Harbor in wooden crates marked East India Tea Company."

The older McCormick chortled. "A tea party? You do have a remarkable sense of humor, Duncan."

"Karma."

"Quite."

"So, what do you think this is all about, Father? I mean with Leo. I thought we made it clear to him that we shouldn't meet in person anymore."

"Indeed. We made it very clear, so I can only assume that an urgent matter came up that Leo felt required a breach of security. Well, we will find out soon enough. Esha will bring him up in a few minutes."

As they chitchatted, I slowly and quietly pulled the crowbar out from the duffel bag. The Glock was harnessed under my windbreaker in a shoulder holster I had borrowed from Vito. I barely breathed.

In a few minutes, the door opened again. I saw a pair of sexy, stockinged legs in high heels followed by gray silk pants and another set of black dress shoes—Leo.

Let the games begin. I inched closer to that side of the table to hear better. Esha said, "Hello Father, Duncan. Mr. Rosenblatt is here."

Father?

I was surprised to hear that. So Duncan and Esha were brother and sister? They didn't seem like that the other night. Father and son stood and greeted Leo as he and Esha approached. They all shook hands, and Duncan poured Leo a bourbon. Esha declined a drink and sat next to Duncan, across from Leo and the senior McCormick, which I could tell from the position of their legs. I was within a few feet of them now and settled in.

Leo began, "Look, Rutherford, I'm sorry about breaking protocol, but what I have to do needed to be done in person."

"What happened, Leo?"

"An unexpected complication and I'm going to have to bail out on our deal. I came to apologize in person and to refund your money. Here's a cashier's check plus interest. If you prefer, I can wire the money to whatever account you choose."

Rutherford looked at the check and said, "Two million dollars, Leo? That's quite a bit of interest, don't you think? That's double what I paid you."

I watched as Esha slid off one of her shoes and began running her stockinged foot up and down Duncan's leg. He discreetly placed one hand on her thigh, massaging it.

Leo explained, "This is the first time I've had to let a client down and I want you to know how serious I take this. Also, I was hoping that maybe I could convince you to perhaps use other methods of persuasion on Cesari rather than lethal force."

"Interesting. Does this newfound concern for Cesari's well-being have anything to do with your niece being—involved with him?"

There was an uncomfortable silence, which I assumed meant that this caught Leo by surprise. He recovered quickly, cleared his throat and said, "When I agreed to take the job I was unaware of her relationship with him and just learned of it recently. It doesn't matter. The answer is yes, that is the reason I can't be involved anymore. She's already asking too many questions, and I don't want her to get caught in the crossfire. I do have an idea however, how we can neutralize Cesari without killing him or placing my niece in danger."

"Pray tell, Leo. I'm all ears."

Esha had slid her hand onto Duncan's crotch and was rubbing it back and forth.

"My niece told me that since Cesari left the hospital, he's been acting really weird, seeing things and hearing things. He even attacked some guy in Washington Square Park last week. He's seeing a shrink and a neurologist at Saint Matt's."

"That is interesting. What are you suggesting?"

"I'm suggesting that you have Junior fix his medical records so that he appears to be a raving lunatic. Say that he's delusional and paranoid and probably a danger to himself and others. It won't be too far from the truth anyway. This way, on the outside chance that he does remember something from the night of the shooting, no one will take him seriously. With any luck, we can have him committed before the shit hits the fan. Then he'll be a sitting duck like his friend was and there'll be no chance of my niece getting in the way of a stray bullet."

"Hmm, I must say, Leo. This is rather creative and less primitive. I like it—a lot. So, you don't object to us destroying him one way or the other?"

"As long as my niece doesn't get hurt, you can do whatever you want with him. The world isn't going to cry because there's one less guinea. By the way, just how did you know about my niece and him?"

"One of our sources inside Saint Matt's just recently alerted us to the fact that he was dating a girl named Myrtle Rosenblatt. It wasn't too hard to figure out from there. We were just starting to wonder if you were aware of the relationship also or accepted the project because of it. I know I wouldn't want an Italian in my home for the holidays—unless they were doing the cooking." He chuckled and slapped his knee in amusement.

Duncan snickered, "Good one, Father."

Leo wasn't as amused and remained serious. "I have other reasons to dislike him so, to each his own. Well, I'm glad that we were able to come to a mutually agreeable understanding concerning this guy. I hope you aren't too disappointed with the change of plans, but I honestly think this is a cleaner way of handling the Cesari problem."

310

Rutherford agreed. "I have to admit, it does have a certain kind of irony that appeals to me.

"I guess I'll be on my way then."

"Why don't you join us for dinner on the observatory, Leo? We're having fresh lobster and Dom Perignon once the tourists clear out. There's a full moon and we have a string quartet playing chamber music. Boston's upper crust should be arriving shortly and we'd love to have you join in the celebration. We're expecting the mayor, the chief of police, and the president of Harvard, just to mention a few. It will be a regular Who's Who of Northeast elite." I looked over at Esha. She had unzipped Duncan's pants and wiggled her hand inside.

Jesus!

"What are you celebrating?" Leo asked.

"Duncan here will be taking over the reins of McCormick Enterprises starting in the New Year. So we thought we would kick it off with a little bash and of course a million dollar donation to Harvard."

Leo stood up. "Thanks, Rutherford, and congratulations, Duncan. I would love to stay but I'm beat. I'm going to turn in and leave early in the morning. It's been a long day."

I watched Duncan hurriedly and discreetly zip his pants up as Esha put her shoe back on.

Rutherford said, "Of course. I'll have someone drive you to your hotel."

"That won't be necessary. I rented a car, but thanks anyway."

"Have a good night then. Esha will escort you downstairs. Good to see you, Leo."

They all stood and shook hands goodbye. After they left, Rutherford and Duncan resumed their seats. I could hear the older man strum the table, deep in thought.

I thought about what I should do but tonight's conversation made me hesitate. I had initially planned to confront them—and

311

perhaps beat at least one of their brains in with the crowbar—but decided that might not be a good idea with the mayor of Boston and the chief of police about to arrive imminently so I lay quietly, listening.

"So what do you think, Father?" asked Duncan.

"I think Leo's getting too sentimental for my taste but I do like this new tack. I love the idea of sending this Cesari character to the looney bin for a while before we terminate him. Do you think you can pull that off, Duncan?"

"Child's play, Father. Now that the Z2 is operational I don't even have to be in the same city, let alone the same room, with whomever it is I'm hacking. I'll just have to find out who his psychiatrist is and which EMR system he is using. Just for fun, I'll throw in an addendum that Cesari's a compulsive masturbator and shouldn't be allowed near children."

They both chortled and the older man said, "Duncan, I must say I am glad we are on the same side. By the way, your man did outstanding work with that other doctor. Exactly, how did he pull that one off?"

"Easy peasy, Father. He paid off the night nurse to allow him to make an unauthorized late night visit to this Dr. Macchiarone fellow. He sold her the story that he was a relative who just arrived from out of the country and that's why the late hour. She was very sympathetic and felt bad for him. Although not so bad as to turn down a significant monetary gift, mind you. According to my man, the doctor was so heavily sedated, he barely knew what was happening."

"It's disgusting what people will do for money."

"Quite."

"Where is this nurse now?"

"Sadly, she was in a fatal hit-and-run car accident crossing Third Avenue on the way home from work this morning. New York can be such a dangerous city. The good news for her is that her shift ended an hour before anyone discovered the body so she died with a clean conscience."

"Excellent, although I do have a bone to pick with you, Duncan. There was no reason to kill that secretary from Saint Matt's. I must object when you behave gratuitously."

"I beg to differ, Father. She practically begged for me to end her life. First off, she told Cesari about me and then she had the insane notion that I might be in love with her. Can you fathom that? When I told her I couldn't see her anymore she started making a public scene, crying and everything. You'd never know she was already engaged to be married. I had to do something." He took a deep breath and let it out as if he was deeply frustrated. "Why are these Yanks always so melodramatic?"

As he said that, I felt a hot pincer shoot through my brain and I clutched my head and bit my tongue to remain quiet. I felt the room going dark. Oh no, I couldn't let this happen. Not here, not now. I willed myself to stay in the present. There was something about what he had just said. Those words. They were dragging me to another place, another time but I couldn't let that happen. I was drifting …

"Well, Duncan, I'm not thrilled at how messy this thing has been so far, but all's well that ends well. All great nations and businesses have their growing pains, I suppose. Everything is falling into place just as I had hoped. The other insurers, the pharmaceuticals, the hospitals, hell, even the federal government is on board and has reached out to us to cut a deal. Your program is like rolling loaded dice at the high-end craps table in Vegas. People pay for insurance and we get to decide what we're going to cover after the fact and if it's too expensive, we simply change the diagnosis to one we like. We control outcome and that means money. These Yankee bureaucrats are so desperate to control healthcare costs that they are willing to sacrifice thousands of lives to do it rather than simply be honest and tell everyone they can't pay for all the things they've promised."

Duncan chuckled. "Politicians be honest? Really, Father, you can be too funny sometimes."

"All right then, one more bit of business before we greet our guests."

Struggling to remain conscious, I writhed in silence beneath the table. I could barely see the legs of the table and chairs. I felt like I was floating and rapidly losing control.

"Yes, Father?"

"Leo— it's time we ended our relationship with him."

"Seriously, Father?"

"Yes, I've been toying with this for a while but this little act of impertinence has proven to me that it is time for us to move on. Does he seriously think he is our equal that he can call meetings with us on our home turf any time he wants? Think about the audacity of changing our plan simply because his niece might be in danger, and what did he mean that she was asking too many questions? What kind of questions? I don't like this at all, Duncan."

"What shall we do?"

Rutherford paused to take a sip of whiskey. "Esha found out Leo's staying at the Mandarin, Room 2023. Make sure he doesn't check out tomorrow or ever. First thing in the morning, work on Cesari's medical records and be creative. Document that he demonstrated signs of psychosis with tendencies towards violent and suicidal behavior. Say that he was having difficulty with reality and was quite paranoid during the encounters, and that he was encouraged to admit himself for therapy but refused."

"If that's all, I'll need to start making phone calls."

"There's one more thing. To seal the deal as they say, collect Cesari's girlfriend, this Cocoa person, Leo's niece, and dispatch her as well. I don't know what kinds of questions she's been asking but they can't be good ones. Who knows what he's confided in

314

her? Where and how you dispose of her is unimportant, just make sure the body ends up in Cesari's apartment. Then call the police. At the same time, we'll accidentally leak his new psychiatric records to the press. I want this threat neutralized once and for all, Duncan, and I mean with the greatest urgency. Well, that's quite a night's work. Shall we greet our guests?"

Chapter 33

*D*arkness surrounded me and I walked in circles for hours until finally I saw a light in the distance and jogged toward it. I jogged, then ran, then sprinted and suddenly fell off a cliff as I ran out of ground in front of me. My arms and legs flailing in all directions, I landed unhurt in the middle of a bedroom I had never been in before. A man in his thirties sat on the edge of a bed sobbing uncontrollably with his face in his hands. He'd been drinking heavily and there, on the bed beside him, lay an empty bottle of gin. He looked unkempt, like he hadn't shaved or showered in a couple of days. This was a man in the grip of despair but why? I was very curious and called out to him but he didn't respond. He appeared inconsolable.

He stood slowly and walked over to the night table with his back to me. Opening the drawer, he pulled out a handgun, and I watched as he checked to make sure it was loaded. Slowly, he raised the weapon to his temple. Powerless to intervene, I closed my eyes just as he pulled the trigger. Blood and brains sprayed onto the clean white sheets and he slumped face forward onto the bed. I stepped closer to study the scene better though there was nothing I could do. Depressed people killed themselves all the time. It was a sad but unalterable fact of life. I looked around the room for a clue as to what had just happened and noted on the night table a picture that had been turned face down so I picked it up. It was Cocoa. She looked so beautiful and so full of life. Her beautiful auburn hair flowed around her face down to her shoulders. Even in a picture her smile was contagious. On the night table was a newspaper clipping of her death. Some random act of violence. I shook with anger—and fear.

I sat down next to the dead guy, my legs weak, tears welling up in my eyes. I heaved, shuddered and started bawling. Oh, God, please tell me this isn't real. I'd rather be crazy than to go on like this. I'll do anything, Lord, anything. Please don't let them hurt her. Standing up, distraught and frustrated, I looked down at the guy on the bed and watched blood ooze out of his skull. Who are you? I grabbed his shoulder, spun him around onto his back and gasped in horror as I looked at myself. I staggered backward awkwardly, tripped and fell, striking my head against the floor.

When I opened my eyes, I was back under the boardroom table in the dark, perspiring and breathing in rapid shallow bursts. My pulse raced and I forced myself to calm down. Rutherford and Duncan had left. They must be outside at their dinner party with the mayor. I took out my cell phone. It was 10:30; almost two hours had passed.

Shit.

There were two missed calls from Vito so I hit redial. He answered quickly. "Cesari, how'd it go? I was starting to get worried. Where are you?"

"I'm okay. Where are you?"

"I'm with Sarah, of course. She's wearing a French maid outfit and was just telling me how naughty she is."

"Well, you're going to have to skip the crème brûlée because I've got something urgent for you to do."

"Not again. You've got to be kidding me."

"I'm serious. You need to go to Uncle Leo's hotel room immediately and get him out of there. The McCormicks are going to try to kill him tonight. They may have already got to him. Go now and bring him to our room."

"Uncle Leo? I thought he was one of the bad guys? Who gives a shit if he buys it?"

"He's Cocoa's uncle so just do it."

"What do I tell him? He's not going to believe me. He doesn't even know me."

"Tell him Cocoa's in danger and that I don't care what happens to me but that he needs to get her to someplace safe until this blows over."

"Holy shit. Cocoa too?"

"Now Vito. Now."

"I'm on it. What are you going to do?"

"I have no idea."

I hung up and dialed Cocoa. "Hi, John. I was worried. Where are you?"

"I can't talk long. Please listen. Both you and your uncle are in danger. Stay in Vito's apartment until Vito or your Uncle Leo come for you and then I want you to go with them. I don't have time to explain right now. Just promise me you'll do what I say."

Sensing the urgency in my voice she agreed. "John, you're scaring me. Are you okay?"

"I'm fine but I want you to call Mark Greenberg right now and tell him to make paper copies of all of my psychiatric encounters with him. Every single thought he ever put on paper or typed into his medical records about me and he needs to do it now, not tomorrow morning. It will be too late by then."

"Too late? John, what's happening? This sounds so crazy. Please tell me where you are."

"Cocoa, do what I said, and please, go wherever your uncle takes you. I will find you."

"I don't want to leave you—I love you."

I hesitated. I didn't love Cocoa. I liked Cocoa—a lot. I loved Kelly, and she knew it, but how could I deny her what she needed to hear right now? Besides, wasn't love just an extreme form of like? So maybe I did love her a little. It was time to go. "I love you too, Cocoa. Now promise me you'll do what I said."

"I promise."

I powered off the phone, got out from under the table and took a deep breath. My clothes were drenched and I took my windbreaker off to cool down. I knew what I had to do. There wasn't really much of an option. The assholes had all the cards. I chambered a round in the 9 mm and grasped the crowbar with my free hand.

Opening the door a crack, I peered up and down the hallway, spotting a uniformed officer leaning backward in a chair. He was not more than twenty feet from where I stood, and was blocking the door leading to the observatory. He was young, confident, and relaxed, reading the swimsuit issue of *Sports Illustrated*. Of course there would be some basic security. After all, there was supposed to be a bunch of big shots here tonight but I bet most of the security would be downstairs in the main lobby because you couldn't even get up here if you didn't have a key and electronic code for the elevators.

Would there be more security outside on the deck itself? Possibly. On the other hand, a lobster and champagne party with Boston's elite wouldn't exactly be the same with a lot of big guys patrolling around with guns. No, the more I thought about it, I doubted there would be more than one—two, tops—armed men outside, if that. Life was full of educated guesses like this.

I stepped into the hallway, walking quickly and with determination toward the uniformed cop, hands at my side, smiling. I had covered half the distance before he even looked up, and when he did finally notice me he was caught off-guard and hesitated. Studying me with great curiosity from over the top of his magazine, he failed to act decisively and lost his window of opportunity. This was supposed to be a lightweight gig, a couple of hours of overtime watching the door in case one of the guests got drunk and couldn't find his way to the bathroom kind of gig. He wasn't expecting any trouble. My friendly demeanor added to his confusion but he soon spotted the weapons and his eyes went wide, alarm registering in his features.

Raising the Glock, I suddenly sprinted the remaining distance shouting. "Don't fucking move."

He didn't listen and dropped the *Sports Illustrated*, fumbling for his gun, and now panic-stricken, fell over sideways because of the awkward position he was in, leaning backward against the wall. I reached him in a hurry, and not nearly as hard as I could have, smacked him in the head with the crowbar. He dropped forward, unconscious, and I used his cuffs to restrain his hands behind his back. Besides a lump on his head the size of a lemon, a bad headache, and an embarrassing report, he would be okay. Maybe handing out parking tickets for the next twenty years, but still, that was better than dead. I felt kind of bad. I didn't like hurting cops. Some were bad but most were good. They had difficult, stressful jobs and guys like me were the reason.

Before stepping outside onto the skywalk, I stopped in front of the door to collect myself. I didn't know how many people were out there or who might be armed. There might be undercover security as well. This could get pretty ugly.

Opening the door slowly, I was bathed in moonlight shining through the large windows as the sound of a four-piece string quartet played peacefully in the background. The observatory lights were kept low to enhance the patrons' view of the city and to ensure a romantic experience. This was good for me because no one seemed to notice my presence, enraptured as they were with the entertainment and their cocktails. A quick head count revealed about forty guests in black tie, divided fairly equally between tuxedoed men, and women in their sequined gowns and diamond necklaces.

As I walked steadily forward, I scanned the room for uniformed officers and guys wearing suits standing around without champagne flutes looking overly serious. I saw none and breathed a sigh of relief. This didn't really bother me at all. I mean, why would anybody here be worried about anything except maybe a bad hangover in the morning? I passed a full bar busy serving thirsty guests and then the quartet, now fervently into some Beethoven piece.

It was a beautiful warm night and the doors to the outside walkway had been opened. Quite a few of the guests were taking advantage of the view from there. Many things crossed my mind as I meandered through the dark room, hands at my sides. I thought of my parents and how much I missed them. I thought of the many friends and lovers that I had had over the years. I thought about right and wrong and how mixed up things got some times, but most of all I thought about Cocoa. She loved me and I had to admit that made me feel great. I didn't love her back. I had said so because it would have been wrong to do otherwise in that circumstance. I hoped that was the right thing to do. It certainly seemed like it. That meant a lot to women—to be loved. Not so much for men. Why? I smiled. Because men were assholes, that's why. Regardless, she loved me and that meant something. It was nice to hear that from someone, and that's why I knew what I had to do because when someone loves you, you have to protect them even if you don't love them back.

It was the cello player who first noticed something was wrong. He stared at me. I wasn't dressed for the party or to qualify as wait-staff. Then he spotted the gun and then the crowbar. Abruptly, he stopped playing and soon the others followed suit. A woman in a long black evening dress turned to see what had happened, saw me and gasped, dropping her champagne flute which shattered on the floor. Gradually, others turned toward me, confusion slowly turning to fear. A young man full of bravado and vodka approached with his right hand raised as if to halt me.

He said, "I don't know who you are but you've gone far enough."

I cracked him over the head with the crowbar and he went down like a brick. The crowd gasped and everyone froze. I found Rutherford and Duncan entertaining a group of well-dressed men and women in the center of the room. They stared at me speechless as people all around started to beat a hasty retreat to the elevators or back into the boardroom as they realized they weren't being held hostage. The braver ones used their cell phones to dial 911.

I pointed the pistol at Duncan's group, waved it at a round table nearby and said, "Sit."

After I quickly frisked the men, the six of them sat, and I pulled up a chair, scrunching myself in between two older women who I felt would be unlikely to try and overwhelm me. I told everybody to keep their hands on the table in front of them. Opposite me were Duncan and his father and to either side of them sat middle-aged men I didn't know, but we soon began the introductions. One of the men was the chief of the Boston police, named Earl. He was fifty, bald, ruddy-faced and muscular with old-fashioned mutton chop sideburns. To my immediate right was an eighty-year-old woman with white hair and a gentle, kind face. I knew immediately I could never hurt her. That could be a liability for me if things didn't go right. She smelled of old money and traced her ancestry back to the Mayflower. The Kennedys were minor players in Boston compared to her, and most of the Massachusetts General Hospital had been funded by her family's philanthropic efforts over the last several generations. No self-respecting fundraiser in the Northeast would even consider not reserving a seat in the front row for her. She told me her name was Madeline Sinclair. To my left was the current president of Harvard University, a sixty-seven-year-old, woman with gray hair, glasses and sharp inquisitive eyes. Before I got to meet the last guy, the chief of police decided to take charge.

He demanded, "Who are you and what do you want?"

I glared at him and said, "First of all, Earl, let's get some ground rules straight if you don't want anybody to get hurt. One, nobody speaks unless I tell them to. Everybody nod if you understand."

I looked around as they all nodded. The rest of the room had completely cleared out by this time and we were all that was left. A gentle breeze of warm night air filtered in from the outer deck through the open doors. Except for the gun and crowbar, we might have been playing bridge on somebody's back porch.

"Rule number two. If I ask you a direct question, I expect a direct answer. No bullshit. Understood? Chief, use your cell phone and call downstairs. Tell everybody to stay where they are. First person I see come through that door, I shoot everybody at close range with 9-mm hollow points and I'll start with you. You know exactly what that will do, and no helicopters please. I'm allergic to snipers. Nod if you understand."

He nodded and pulled out his cell phone to make the call. While he did that, I took a forkful of lobster that someone had left on a plate in front of me, dipped it in clarified butter and washed it down with champagne. Yum.

When the chief hung up, I asked Duncan. "Where's your sister?"

He looked surprised. "I'm not sure. The bathroom, maybe."

"Call her and tell her we need her here."

He made the call as I listened to the sound of approaching sirens in the distance. Soon, Esha showed up, walking slowly, gracefully, with great apprehension. Extremely beautiful with dark skin and great elegance, she could easily have been a model. She pulled a chair up next to Duncan. Gradually, Rutherford regained his composure. This was his party after all. "So, who are you exactly and what do you want?"

"I think you know very well who I am but for the sake of the others, my name is John Cesari and I'm a physician, a gastroenterologist to be specific. I want to tell you nice people a story about greed and power and what it does to some who just can't seem to get enough of it."

Rutherford flinched and Duncan gulped. Esha turned eight shades of pale and looked like she might throw up. The others glanced back and forth furtively not knowing what to expect.

Madeline asked, "What do you mean, Doctor? Please explain."

"You're going to have to brace yourself for what I have to say, Madeline, because it isn't pretty and sometimes wealthy people like yourself aren't always willing to look in the mirror. They are generally afraid of what they might see."

Rutherford gasped. "How dare you speak to Mrs. Sinclair in that tone? Her family practically built Boston brick by brick and stone by stone. Her grandfather laid the foundation for this very building and almost every other in this neighborhood. She personally has devoted her entire life to helping the needy and supporting the arts."

The chief thought it was time to flex his muscles again. "Mr. McCormick's right. Mrs. Sinclair has done you no harm. Why don't you at least let her go?"

I slammed the crowbar down on the table hard like an angry judge in an unruly courtroom. A glass of champagne tipped over and the woman from Harvard flinched. "Don't forget rule number one, gentlemen." I lowered my voice and spoke gently to Madeline. "I'm sorry if I frightened you but no one's a prisoner here but these three." I waved the gun at the McCormicks. "Everybody else can leave anytime they want but I would prefer it if you heard me out first."

Even though I made the offer, no one tried to leave. The other guy on Duncan's right was sixtyish with a bad hairpiece. He looked like he was about to rise but thought better of it as he saw he had no company. I didn't like his face. It was pasty and he had a sneaky look to him. A politician, no doubt. I was interrupted before I got to find out who he was.

Mrs. Sinclair said, "Please tell us what's bothering you, Doctor. Maybe we can help." She spoke with sincerity and without an ounce of fear. I liked that.

So I told them all about the McCormicks and their plan to subvert the healthcare system with the Z1 and now Z2 program. I told them the whole story beginning with Tony's 2:00 a.m. phone call to me when he first noted a discrepancy in his records, Mrs. Konstandin's death and finally, this morning's discovery of Julie's body and the plot to kill Uncle Leo and Cocoa to cover their trail. When I was done everyone at the table was speechless, to say the least. Mrs. Sinclair covered her mouth in horror.

She asked, "Can you prove any of this?"

I shook my head and let out a deep breath. "Unfortunately no, I can't, and to be totally truthful, I am under the care of a psychiatrist, so I don't think anyone would take anything I say seriously."

Rutherford snorted contemptuously. "There you've heard it straight from the horse's mouth. The bugger's on the verge of a nervous breakdown and he's taking it out on my family. Doctor, I beg you, let us call you an ambulance and get you proper care."

I smiled. "Nice try, Rutherford, but the verdict's already in. The 49th floor of this building is where they keep their servers. I'm sure there are multiple copies of the Z1 and Z2 kept somewhere down there. I'm not smart enough to understand how it all works and I doubt that these guys are planning on confessing any time soon. It's going to take good people like you …" I turned to Mrs. Sinclair. "People who care, and I mean really care about other people, to turn the pressure up on this place to find out the truth. The evidence is there. You just have to want to see it."

Duncan finally had enough. Angrily, he said, "Why are we even talking to him? He's obviously insane."

I stood up and glared at him. If there was one person at this gathering I wasn't going to take any shit from, he was the one. "Bad move, Ronnie. I'd be very quiet if I were you." Reaching into my pocket, I retrieved Julie's locket and handed it to Mrs. Sinclair. I liked and instinctively trusted her.

"What's this?" she asked.

"It's my secretary's locket. Her name was Julie. I took it from her dead body this morning when I found her stuffed in a wooden crate in an empty warehouse owned by McCormick Enterprises. Please open it."

She opened it and showed it to the woman from Harvard. I said, "It's Julie's parents. They gave her the locket on her eighteenth birthday. If I don't make it out of here, would you please return it to them and tell them how sorry I am?"

I watched as Duncan's eyes went wide. Madeline nodded quietly and I thought I saw a tear forming in her eye. "I will."

"Now I want everyone to leave one at a time. Everyone but the McCormicks, that is."

Mrs. Sinclair said in a soothing voice, "Doctor Cesari, I know you feel strongly that great wrongs have been done and I don't disagree, but don't you think there's been enough violence? Isn't it time to let the law handle this? I promise you that a full investigation will be performed. I personally will not rest until the truth is uncovered."

I looked into her kind and gentle eyes and knew she spoke the truth. The president of Harvard also voiced her agreement. I knew they meant it from the bottom of their hearts but they didn't understand what they were dealing with here. They weren't used to dancing in the slime the way I was. If I let the McCormicks go they would probably be on a plane out of the country before the night was over, or on the phone with hit men arranging for the entire room to be in fatal car accidents. God only knew how much more chaos they could cause before the slow hands of justice finally got hold of them.

"I trust you, Mrs. Sinclair, but I'm afraid that I've already placed this whole room in great danger by revealing to you what has happened. These guys won't let any of you do any investigating of anything."

Rutherford feigned outrage. "This is patently absurd. This man is a raving lunatic. Investigate whatever you want for however long you want. We have nothing to hide."

Finally, the guy with the bad hairpiece spoke. "Hey slick, how about we make a deal?"

Slick?

I hadn't heard a thick New York City accent like that in a while and I lived in Manhattan. I said, "You know, I don't think we were properly introduced."

"My name isn't important, slick. What matters is that everybody's got something somebody else wants. We make a deal, you get what you want and the other guy gets what he wants. So how about it?"

Make a deal?

This guy was funny. You know, like I'm going to punch you in the face if you keep talking, funny. "Okay, you want to know what I want? I want those three dead, and if you don't stop talking I'm going to include you as well. So, here's the deal. Be quiet or you're going to get hurt."

I suddenly realized why the guy looked familiar. I didn't watch much TV and didn't follow politics, but I'd be damned if he wasn't that billionaire who owned most of Manhattan's

Upper West Side. Fuck! You'd think with all that money, he wouldn't be walking around with a dead squirrel on his head. The fact that he was cavorting with the McCormicks didn't surprise me at all. What was that saying? *Assholes of a feather flock together.* Yeah, that was it.

Mrs. Sinclair touched my arm gently. In any other hostage situation that would have been a fatal move. "Doctor Cesari, please don't pay any attention to him. If he had any more hot air in him, he'd float away, but I do wish to give you my personal pledge that justice will be carried out. Do you believe me?"

I looked at her and I knew she was sincere. "I believe that you believe that."

She continued. "Young man, I own the *Boston Globe* and am on the board of the Harvard Law School. Mrs. Smithover, sitting on your other side, is not only the president of Harvard but is married to the executive producer at CNN. I guarantee you the phones will be burning all night to the proper authorities about these accusations. Everyone at this table wants to know the truth. I don't know how much more I can reassure you." She thought it over for a few seconds and then offered, "Would it help if the McCormicks voluntarily surrendered control of their company to an oversight committee comprised of people from this table pending the outcome of the investigation?"

Rutherford gasped. "Madeline, this is preposterous. A maniac barges into a dinner party and you hand him control of my company? I won't stand for it."

Sagely she replied, "I'm trying to keep you alive, Rutherford."

Duncan stood up and leaned across the table at me, his eyes filled with hate. He hissed through clenched teeth. "Why are you Yanks always so damned melodramatic?"

Those words again! There was something about them. I felt like a truck had just hit me and I staggered backward.

328

I couldn't fight it this time and the room suddenly went dark. I was back in Mrs. Konstandin's apartment sitting on the sofa. There was a sound and the door to her bedroom opened. I stood and turned to see who it was—it was Duncan, tall and handsome wearing black leather gloves, holding a pistol. He smiled and shot me in the abdomen. I staggered back and whispered why. He shot me again in the throat and I fell backward onto the coffee table gasping and wheezing holding the wound in my neck. The last thing I remembered was staring into his face as he snickered about how melodramatic I was being.

I don't know how long I was out, but when I returned there was a heavy weight on my chest and I was having trouble breathing. I heard Mrs. Sinclair say, "There's no need to hurt him, chief. He's unarmed now."

Opening my eyes, I looked up at the chief who was sitting on me. I was surrounded by uniformed officers and SWAT team members. The chief said, "Thank you Mrs. Sinclair, but this is a police matter now, so please let us do our jobs. I would like everybody to leave now. Everybody but the McCormicks, that is, we have a lot to talk about."

Mrs. Sinclair came close and looked me in the eye. "Dr. Cesari, everything is going to be all right. I know that you are a good person."

I couldn't answer because of the chief's bulk pressing on my chest, but looking into her eyes I was bathed by her sincerity and goodness.

The police escorted everyone but Rutherford, Duncan, and Esha downstairs. I lay on the floor with my hands cuffed so tightly behind my back I couldn't feel my fingers. Two uniformed officers stood guard and the chief conferred with the McCormick family. I looked at Duncan with venom pouring out of my eyes. "It was you that day. You bastard."

He looked at me contemptuously and whispered something to the chief who nodded. He turned to his two men. "Get him up."

They dragged me roughly off the floor and plopped me unceremoniously into a chair. The chief came over and said to his men, "Good work, guys. You can leave him with me now. I'd like to have a private moment with him. Wait for us downstairs."

The two young cops looked at each other puzzled but without question did as they were told. As soon as they were out of sight, the chief punched me as hard as he could in the face. My head spun around and my left eye started to swell immediately.

He smiled, "You can't imagine how good that felt. Okay, Rutherford, what are we going to do with him?"

"Good question, Earl. I'd love to just throw him over the side of the building. A fifty-story plunge in the night air would give him plenty of time to think about what a nuisance he's been."

My gun, cell phone and crowbar were sitting on the table five feet away. The chief now held a .357 Magnum trained on me and I was starting to get a real bad vibe about his relationship with the McCormicks.

I said, "You can't possibly think you're going to get away with this?"

He answered my question by smacking me in the face with the three-pound steel Magnum. My face stung, I felt woozy, and spit out a bloody tooth. The blow caused me to bite my tongue and it hurt like hell. I didn't like where this was going and could barely see out of one eye now because of the swelling.

Rutherford put his arm around the chief's shoulder. "Good work, Earl. We obviously can't let him leave here alive but how do we pull off such a thing with an army of police and reporters waiting down below?"

The chief scratched his head for a moment as I looked at Esha. "Are you really part of this?" I asked.

She snickered. "Why not? Because I'm a girl? You really are a wanker, aren't you?"

Duncan chuckled. "Is she part of this? How extraordinarily quaint. He can't seem to fathom a woman being one of the bad guys. Well, here's a news flash for you, old chap, I may have created the Z1 program but it was my beautiful sister's idea."

The chief of police suddenly snapped his fingers. "I got it. We could say that he had another seizure and I undid his handcuffs because I was worried he might hurt himself flopping around. He broke free, ran out the door babbling and threw himself over the side before anyone could stop him. Of course, the old lady will be suspicious and will probably want to investigate Unicare anyway, but you could suspend operations until she was satisfied or …"

Duncan asked, "Or what?"

"She is pretty old after all, and old people die all the time, don't they? Maybe she could overdose on pain meds no one knew she was on. Just change her records and make it look like she was secretly an addict."

Rutherford chortled, "That just might work. Chief, you're worth every penny we pay you."

"After tonight, you're going to be paying me a lot more than pennies. Okay, so how are we going to set this up? We'll have to make it look like he hit me because no one will believe that he got by me without a fight."

Duncan offered, "Maybe when you uncuffed him, there was a struggle and he somehow got a hold of your gun or the crowbar there and struck you with it, temporarily stunning you. Father and I stepped in, and realizing all was lost he ran for the door and jumped over the side."

Rutherford said, "Excellent, Duncan, but don't we have to actually hit the chief to make it look real?"

The chief said, "Yeah, somebody's going to have to take a swing at me. I'm going to need a bruise to make it look real. Duncan, give me a shot in the kisser and make it a good one. Don't be afraid, I've been knocked around plenty in my life."

Duncan hesitated. "I don't know if I can do this, Earl. I get squeamish when it comes to physical violence. Besides, couldn't this hurt my hand as much as your face?"

The chief turned toward the older McCormick. "What about you, Rutherford? Want to take a shot at the chief of police?"

Rutherford replied, "I doubt that I have what it takes."

Finally, the chief looked at Esha who shook her head. "I'm out."

He was exasperated. "For God's sake, you guys. I can't face my men without some sort of injury. No one on earth is going to believe it. Look Duncan, just take my gun and slap me across the face with it. Like I just did to the doc. It won't hurt your hand and should give me a bad enough bruise that everyone will accept the story. Then I'll take his cuffs off and we'll throw him overboard."

He put the .357 in Duncan's hand and stood there in front of him. Duncan felt the heavy weapon in his hand and asked, "Is the safety on, I hope?"

"It's a revolver, Duncan. There is no safety. Just don't pull the trigger."

Duncan took a deep breath. "Okay, close your eyes, chief. I can't look at you while I do this."

The chief closed his eyes and Duncan, without any hesitation, pointed the gun at his head and fired. The explosion was deafening and gun smoke filled the room. The back of the chief's skull flew off and he dropped down to the ground dead.

The room reverberated from the sound and I cringed from the unexpected sight. Duncan said, "Oops."

The older McCormick chuckled, "Well played, Duncan. I was wondering where you were going with all that stuff about being squeamish."

Esha looked horrified. "What a mess."

"Sorry Esha, but we really couldn't have Earl hanging over our heads like that. Now we'll get rid of Cesari here and we'll have solved the GI problem once and for all." He leaned down and searched the chief for the handcuff key. Finding it, he turned to me. "Be a good fellow and stand up."

I did as I was told and he added, "Thank you. Now let's go outside together. There's no need to make a fuss. One has to recognize when one has lost and be at peace with it, and remember who has the gun."

As we walked toward the door leading outside Duncan picked up a cloth napkin and my crowbar from the table. Esha and Rutherford followed close behind as we stepped into the night air. There was a slight breeze and I looked up at the moon and said, "You're right, Duncan, you've won and I've lost. With me gone, you're all safe."

"Exactly. I'm thrilled you're being cooperative."

Outside, we approached the four- foot-high metal railing protecting visitors from accidentally falling off the walkway. I said, "So, there's no need to kill Leo and his niece."

"Hmm, I hadn't thought that far ahead yet. Leo definitely has to go and you're right, we don't necessarily need to kill his niece, but you know what, anybody with a name as crass as Cocoa really ought to be killed. So, I think I will anyway, sort of as a service to society; my contribution to American culture if you will. Okay, now lean forward against the railing. That's a good chap. Father, Esha will you lend me a hand and hold his ankles tightly? Then lift him up but please don't let go of him just yet. I need to get the cuffs off him first. If they find him on the ground still handcuffed we'll have a heck of a time explaining how he shot the chief. Let the railing do all the work."

I leaned forward at an angle, my abdomen pressing against the metal railing and they grabbed my ankles lifting me off the ground. I looked down into the darkness and knew the odds of my surviving the night were looking dimmer and dimmer. Out of the corner of my one good eye, I watched Duncan wipe the gun clean of his prints with the cloth napkin and felt him press the weapon into my right hand to get my prints on it. He then rested the gun on the floor and reached into his pocket for the handcuff key.

I wondered what it was going to feel like when I hit the cement or if I would pass out first. It would certainly be a quick death. Too bad these assholes were going to get off scot-free, and then there was Cocoa. I couldn't believe he was going to kill her just for the hell of it. I had a new reason to dislike the English. I did have one chance left though. When he undid the handcuffs I could quickly grab onto the railing, but my arms and hands were numb from the cuffs and the awkward position they were in.

As if reading my mind, Rutherford said, "Be careful, Duncan. Once you release the cuffs he may make a move for it."

"One step ahead of you, Father."

He lifted the crowbar high above his head and brought it down hard onto my right elbow. It made an ugly sound as the bone shattered. I moaned with pain and realized beyond a shadow of a doubt that all was lost.

He said, "That should contain him, and what's one more broken bone compared to what's going to happen to him when he lands on the pavement. Lift him higher please."

I was pointing downward now supported by the railing and my legs held firmly by Rutherford and Esha. Blood rushed to my head and I felt myself slipping slowly forward as Duncan played with the cuffs, trying to unlock them. I didn't really care anymore. The pain in my elbow was excruciating and supplanted all other thoughts. Soon, whether the cuffs came off or not, I would fall into the abyss. Rutherford and Esha, I sensed, were not strong enough to hang on to me for long and were rapidly losing control of the situation.

As he unlocked one cuff Esha said, "Hurry up Duncan, he's heavy."

"Almost there love. Remember, I don't do this for a living."

Turning my head backward I saw him fumbling with the other wrist, trying to unlock the second cuff while my wounded arm dangled helplessly. Duncan looked good in his bowtie and ruffled white tuxedo shirt. I was able to collect myself for one last taunt and whispered through the pain. "Relax, asshole, how hard could it be?"

I had slipped further over the side and now my thighs just above the knees were resting on the railing. Seconds later, I heard and felt the other cuff unlock.

Duncan said, "Now, heave him over."

Darkness.

Chapter 34

"John, snap out of it. The waitress is waiting for your order." Cocoa tapped on the back of my plastic menu snapping me out of my trance. Startled, I put the menu down and saw Cocoa and the middle-aged waitress in the mustard-colored uniform staring at me. Cocoa continued, "Are you okay? That was the third time I called your name. She's been standing here trying to get your attention."

The lump on the back of my head throbbed and I reached up to rub it. I looked at Cocoa and then at the waitress. Behind her on his hands and knees was a construction worker ripping up water damaged floorboards with a crowbar. His ass was hanging out of his pants. We were sitting in an old diner on First Avenue and I felt very, very strange.

I asked, "Where are we?"

Cocoa gaped at me. "Are you all right?"

The waitress said to Cocoa, "Do you want me to call a doctor?"

"Just give us a moment. Thank you."

The waitress walked away and Cocoa said, "What just happened? It's like you were hypnotized or something."

"Cocoa, what are we doing? I mean, right here, right now. I'm serious. Please bear with me."

She paused a moment and said, "We're about to have breakfast and in an hour you're going to meet Mrs. Konstandin in her apartment across the street to interview her for the hospital."

I nodded and looked out the window at the apartment building across the street. "So—she's not dead? Mrs. Konstandin, I mean."

Cocoa's raised her eyebrows. "Of course not. It's her husband who's dead. John, you're scaring me. Are you sure you feel okay?"

A gleam of light reflected off a car snaking up First Avenue, slowly, almost methodically, catching my eye. It was a brand-new silver Mercedes sedan and it was searching for something. I couldn't make out the driver from where I was but a beam of bright sunlight tracked the vehicle's movement, which was odd because it was an overcast day. The light on the car stood out like a beacon. I looked up at the sky. That was interesting. It was almost as if there were a hole in the dark clouds over just that one car. I looked at my watch. It was 9:45. I was supposed to meet Mrs. Konstandin at 11:00. I looked back at the Mercedes.

"John, what are you staring at?" Cocoa asked.

"Do you see the light over there shining on that Mercedes? It's pretty cool."

She looked out the window and said, "I don't see anything but a car."

"Really? It's like the light is following the car. I don't think I've ever seen anything like that."

She repeated, "I don't see what you're talking about."

Follow the Light!

Like a jolt of electricity, it all came to me—everything. I don't know how and I didn't care. The hairs on the back of my neck stood up. The Mercedes turned slowly into the alley between the Konstandin apartment and the neighboring building. That son of a bitch. He's going up the fire escape. I stood up suddenly, profoundly alarmed at my sudden cognizance. My pulse raced and my adrenaline surged.

Cocoa stood up as well, concern etched all over her face. "What is it?"

"I don't have time to explain. Do me a favor, stay here and wait for me to call." I turned to leave, hesitated and turned back to her. I put my arms around her and kissed her. "Cocoa—Cocoa …"

Breathless, she asked, "What, John?"

I stared into her eyes. "Cocoa— I love you."

She was speechless and I let go of her and ran over to butt-man. "Hey, buddy, how much for the crowbar?"

"What?"

"I'll give you a hundred dollars for the crowbar."

He looked at the old piece of metal barely worth eighteen dollars brand new. "Sure."

I grabbed the crowbar and sprinted across First Avenue, crashing through the main entrance and bounding up the stairs three steps at a time. Apartment 3B. There it was. I kicked the door open. It was unlocked but had been wedged shut tightly by the humidity. Jumping over the sofa, I made a beeline toward the bathroom. The bedroom window was wide open and the curtain fluttered in the gentle breeze. The bathroom door was closed and I rushed at it like a mad bull. At a full throttle, shoulder first, I slammed through it, hurtling into Duncan Ronald McCormick as he leaned over trying to drown the struggling but still living Mrs. Konstandin in her own bathtub. We both went sprawling into the far wall together but Ronnie got the worst of it by far, hitting his head hard against it. He now sat on the floor dazed and confused with me on top.

I stood up, looked briefly at Mrs. Konstandin and determined that she would be okay. She was leaning over the side of the tub coughing and gasping for air. When I looked back, Ronnie was reaching clumsily for something on the floor behind him—his pistol. I raised the crowbar and brought it crashing down on the arm searching for the weapon. The bone cracked loudly and he howled with pain.

Mrs. Konstandin yelled in Albanian, *"Vrases! Vrases!"* (Murderer! Murderer!)

Ronnie looked up at me, stunned and in pain. "You! But how?"

For my answer, I raised the crowbar and broke his other arm, and he lay there slumped and whimpering. I found his weapon, placed it in my pocket and helped Mrs. Konstandin out of the tub and into the bedroom. She was shivering from fear and excitement. I found her a towel and a bathrobe in one of the closets and handed them to her, introducing myself. By this time, her sister and brother-in-law next door had heard the commotion from the hallway and came to investigate. They were in a state of advanced Albanian agitation made worse by the sight of the crowbar.

Mrs. Konstandin, still coughing and breathless, signaled that I was a good guy and after eyeing me suspiciously for a moment, the brother-in-law asked in broken English, "What happen here?"

I started to answer as best I could and Mrs. Konstandin, starting to collect herself, responded in much greater detail in her native tongue, frequently pointing and gesturing at me. The two sisters started hugging and crying. The man came over to me, extending his hand. I took it and he turned it into a bear hug.

Mrs. Konstandin stood up, still shaking, and also threw her arms around me, sobbing. "You are angel." Soon the sister followed suit and I was in danger of falling onto the bed under their combined weight.

The brother-in-law asked, "I call police?"

I said, "No, I'll take care of him, if you don't mind. I'll make sure he never hurts anyone again."

He nodded. He knew exactly what I meant by that. Immigrants were frequently old-school with things like this. It didn't take long for them to figure out that the American criminal justice system weighed heavily in favor of the bad guys, especially wealthy bad guys. I went into the bathroom and grabbed Duncan by the scruff of the neck, dragging him to his feet and hissing into his ear. "You're alive right now because I still need you, but don't think for a moment that you're indispensable."

I relieved him of all the contents of his pockets—wallet, keys, and cell phone—and then marched him out of the apartment as the Konstandin family watched with sheer disgust written all over their faces. The brother-in-law spit on him as we passed.

Outside, in the hallway, I perused the contents of his wallet. Along with the usual driver's license, credit cards and cash he had three formal business cards. One had his real name and title, Vice President of McCormick Enterprises. Another was the one I had already seen, Ronald Duncan, Unicare Field Representative, but the third was the one that really irritated me—John Burgoyne MD. The specialist who told Chow Liu she should just go home and die. John Burgoyne was a pompous British General during the American Revolution who had hoped to bring the colonies into submission with a grandiose plan of invasion launched from Canada. He got his ass kicked at the Battle of Saratoga in 1778 and was sent home with his tail between his legs. The irony here did not fail to escape me.

We reached the top of the stairwell and I said, "Duncan, did you know it's a felony to impersonate a physician?"

He was in too much pain and still a little fuzzy from hitting his head on the wall in the bathroom. Plus, he had no way of knowing what I knew. Looking at me as if I was crazy he said, "What?"

Without warning I grabbed the back of his collar and flung him forward down the stairs.

Oops!

Chapter 35

"*You* have to help me, Vito."

He was justifiably irritated. "No offense, Cesari, but don't you think this is a little insane? I don't see you or hear from you in almost six months because you don't want to have anything to do with me anymore. I run into you accidentally at Babbo last night for five minutes and you think you can just show up with some pansy-assed Brit with two broken arms and a concussion, and tell me to babysit him for you. Maybe I'm missing something here. Like the who-the-fuck-do-you-think-you-are part?"

Duncan was tucked away in one of Vito's bedrooms with an armed guard outside his door. Commandeering his Mercedes, I had dropped Cocoa off at the loft to tend to Cleo and then had brought him to Vito's apartment in Little Italy for further discussion. I had just finished interrogating him using moderately extreme techniques and then given him a bottle of Jack Daniel's with a straw to take the edge off of his pain. Because his first few answers didn't seem truthful, he now had a couple of broken toes to complement his arms, but in the end he had told all.

Cocoa was in shock when I told her what happened in the Konstandin apartment and she reluctantly accepted the short version: that I'd had some sort of premonition of what was going to happen and that's why I acted so strange in the diner. Vito was a much tougher sell.

"Vito, all I want you to do is to let me keep him here for a day or two while I deal with his father. For old time's sake, okay? C'mon, we've done much worse than this together."

That made him crack a smile despite himself. "Fine, but none of this makes any sense to me. I agree that he's an asshole and you saved that woman from him but I just don't get why he's here. Why don't you just call the police?"

"Because I don't want his father to know that I'm on to him. Right now, his son is simply off the grid. If he turns up dead or in police custody, the old man will skip out and I don't want that."

He thought that over and softened. "I guess I can wrap my head around that. So what did these poor bastards do to deserve the full wrath of Cesari?"

That's my Vito. He was coming around. "It's complicated, but they've been manipulating patient records so their insurance company doesn't have to pay out claims. People are dropping like flies because of it."

Vito snorted, "That doesn't sound very nice."

"It's not, especially if you're the one who has cancer."

Sighing deeply, he signaled that he was all in. "Fucking Cesari, I should have my head examined for helping you. You can keep him here but just for a couple of days. Understood? So, where's the dad?"

"Duncan said he's in California with his stepsister. Apparently, he owns a vineyard in Napa and is supposed to return to New York at the end of next week. I think it will work out much better if I deal with him out there. I'll also have the element of surprise on my side."

"You're killing me Cesari. One minute you're giving me this song and dance about not wanting to be in the mob anymore and the next you're flying to California to whack some guy you've never met. What's with that?"

"It's complicated. Just bear with me, all right?"

"So what happens to this guy, Duncan, when you get back? You broke his arms, not his brain. He'll still be able to hack patient records when he gets better."

"Good point. We'll work out those details on the plane. Now get your stuff."

"My stuff?"

"Of course, I can't do this alone. Your guys can watch Duncan. He's not going anywhere. He can't even stand or use his arms. Now, hurry up and pack an overnight bag. I already checked and there's a flight to San Francisco leaving out of JFK in a couple of hours. From there, we can rent a car and drive the rest of the way to Napa. You might even like it there. Napa Valley produces some of the best red wines in the world, as good or better than the French and Italians. Did you know that?"

"You're an asshole, Cesari. Did you know that?"

Chapter 36

At my prompting, Vito did quite a bit of research on McCormick Enterprises and their relationship with Unicare on the plane and in the car ride to Napa. Most of it I already knew, but had to lead Vito along gently for fear of spooking him. He wasn't, and might never be, ready to hear the full story, but I needed to bring him up to speed so we could communicate effectively. I also needed him to understand the full gravity of the situation.

He said, "This guy McCormick likes to play hardball, doesn't he?"

"Oh yeah, everybody from Unicare who signed off on the merger is either dead or missing."

He was reading from his smartphone. "It says here that during the FBI investigation, this guy Leibowitz, the CEO of Unicare, checked into some local hotel before he disappeared. The owner of the hotel originally said that the night they went missing, Leibowitz and his wife got all dolled up and told him they were going to one of the wineries for a swanky night out. A week later, he recanted and said he didn't remember anything clearly from that night at all because he was drunk. Two months later he sold the hotel for twice what it was worth and now his whereabouts are also unknown. That's not even the best part. Guess which winery the owner of the hotel initially told the FBI Leibowitz was going to."

"Stag's Leap?"

"No, the one we're going to right now. The one McCormick owns. How's that for a coincidence?"

I feigned surprise. "Wow. Well, there you go. I told you this guy Rutherford is a real menace to society. They're going to hang a medal on you for this, Vito."

We pulled into the old vineyard, parked and joined one of the tour groups. We had picked up rope, a crowbar and a couple of flashlights at a hardware store on the way and had them tucked away in a backpack. Wineries weren't big on security and no one questioned our right to carry the backpack. Most people applauded our foresight as they thought it was for carrying spur-of-the-moment wine purchases. The tour group was quite large and we easily separated from them and hid deep in the winding maze of the stone-walled cellar. It was damp, cool, and dark down there and the smell of wine in various stages of maturation permeated even our clothes and overwhelmed our senses.

Hiding behind large oak barrels, all we had to do was wait patiently. Duncan had told me that a secure door led from the tasting room to the McCormick mansion through an underground passageway. In addition to locks and bolts, there was an electronic security system guarding the door as well, but I had a plan. At 6:00 p.m., the winery shut its doors, the employees departed, and the lights went out completely.

Vito said, "Shit. I hate the dark."

"Relax."

Reaching into the backpack, I retrieved the two flashlights, handing him one. They were long sturdy Mag-Lights with six D batteries in each. The combination afforded us plenty of light as we searched around. Amongst the many things Duncan had confessed was being an eyewitness to what had happened to Leibowitz and his wife that fateful night. I hadn't told Vito this part.

"Here it is, Vito."

I pointed my flashlight down a long dark tunnel which led into a very large cavernous room lined with hundreds of oak barrels arranged in massive rows and filled with aging cabernet sauvignon. At the far end of the room there was one particular barrel marked "Rubicon private reserve," wedged snugly in its row. None of the other barrels had any markings other than dates and numbers identifying the particular vintage. This barrel was also different in that it was standing upright rather than lying on its side like all the others. It wasn't too big, four and a half feet high and three feet across at the top, but it was heavy. With great effort we were able to maneuver it out of its row where we could work on it better.

I said, "Hold my flashlight."

"What are you doing, Cesari?"

"I got a hunch about something."

I took the flat edge of the crowbar and working my around, began prying the wood top loose a little bit at a time. It was sealed tightly from the wine-soaked wood but with time yielded to my efforts. After fifteen minutes, I had worked up quite a sweat, but was ready to pop the top off.

Looking at Vito, I said, "Brace yourself."

He held the flashlight pointed at the barrel and stood very close, curious. "Don't worry about me, Cesari. There isn't anything I haven't seen."

I pulled the wood top off the barrel and we were immediately overwhelmed with the putrefying stench of decomposing flesh which practically exploded out of the container replacing the smell of wine. Dropping the cover, I stepped back in haste covering my mouth and nose with my hands. Because of his proximity, Vito took the brunt of it in the face. Gagging, he doubled over, suddenly nauseated, and began to retch off to one side. Lifting my shirt, I used it to shield me from the noxious fumes. It helped a little but I felt a little queasy too.

Looking into the barrel I saw Leibowitz and his wife literally up to their eyeballs in high-end cabernet sauvignon facing each other and partially preserved because of the lack of oxygen in the barrel. Her long blonde hair, now dyed purple from the wine, floated at the surface. His face arched upward and his teeth and skeletal jaw bone made for a grotesque smile. She still had one eye intact but the eyelid and facial skin were gone giving her a zombie-like appearance. After a minute or two the foul gases had dissipated slightly and we could breathe normally again. I helped Vito as much as I could but some things just had to run their course.

I sat down on the floor next to him and we both knew how this had to end. Vito hadn't been certain as to the necessity of it all but was now fully on board. I filled him in on the rest of the story Duncan had told me.

"Jesus Christ, Cesari. That was brutal. He invited them over to dinner and then did this? Damn, and people think I'm dangerous."

"And then he stole the guy's company from him."

"Okay, so what now? I know you got something up your sleeve."

"Well, according to Duncan the door leading from here to the estate is too secure for us to go there undetected and I believe him. In addition to cameras and security guards at the house, there are Dobermans patrolling the property. The smart move is to lure him here in such a way that he'll come alone or with minimal protection."

"And just how do we do that?"

"Watch."

I pulled out Duncan's cell phone, looked up his father's number, and sent him a text.

Boarding a plane for Napa. Things have gone terribly awry with Cesari. Says he's been in the wine cellars out there and knows everything. Urgent, check on the Rubicon to be sure. Tell Esha to grab the laptop and DO NOT let go of it for any reason. Will call as soon as I arrive. Duncan.

Vito said, "You think that will make the old man come?"

"Let's keep our fingers crossed, but I don't see how he couldn't. I just hope Esha comes too with the laptop, because if she doesn't then you and I are going to have to make yet another trip to Unicare in Boston."

His brow furrowed at that. "What do you mean by yet another trip to Unicare in Boston? I've never been to Unicare."

I hesitated. This was the wrong time for a slip-up like that. "I meant *me*, not you. *I* might have to make another trip to Unicare. Of course you've never been there, but you know, you may want to come with me if I do go. There's this really pretty girl who works there named Sarah. Rumor has it she likes to play dress up."

He liked that. "Really? Well, then that's definitely a possibility. Okay, are you sure we have everything we need?"

"I'm sure."

We turned the flashlights off and waited in the dark.

Chapter 37

*S*afely back in New York, Vito and I reviewed strategy and adjusted our game plan. I had wanted to kill both Rutherford and Esha when they arrived in the wine cellar, but Vito had gone soft on me. I had made the mistake of telling him about the girl in Boston, and with visions of Sarah plums dancing in his head, he poured forth all his nurturing onto Esha.

Give her a second chance, Cesari. She's so pretty.

This is what I have to put up with. So, we tied her up and immobilized her on the floor between the partially decomposed corpses of Mr. and Mrs. Leibowitz to give her something to think about while she waited for the authorities. I gave her twenty-four hours to publicly resign her position at Unicare and to get on a plane back to London, Bombay or whatever rock it was she had crawled out from under or I would be coming back for her. I also told her that the next time I called Unicare they had better tell me the 49th floor had been shut down completely and permanently and that every geek there had been fired with extreme prejudice.

Rutherford wasn't so lucky. We called the FBI and California State Police anonymously from the San Francisco Airport and told them that they should reopen the missing persons case file on Mr. and Mrs. Leibowitz and now consider it a double homicide. When they arrived at the winery, they not only solved that mystery but had a new one because they found

Rutherford face down, legs dangling over the side, drowned in the same barrel of cabernet that the Leibowitzs had, giving new meaning to the expression full-bodied wine. Esha wasn't talking to anybody about anything without a lawyer, and from the look in her eyes as she watched us submerge daddy kicking and thrashing in the wine barrel, I knew this was the last we were going to see of her. The Hollywood director who lived next door said he never really trusted any of them.

We were more creative with Duncan and had a local tattoo guy come up to Vito's apartment for some freelance work. After shaving Duncan's head the guy tattooed swastikas on both his cheeks fairly high up so a beard could never cover them. Then he put the words *White Power* across his chest and *Kung Fuk Yu* on his back. Content with the art work, we shot him up with heroin and dropped him off at midnight in the middle of one of the rougher gang-run sections of Chinatown wearing nothing but his underwear. He was soon discovered by a roving band of Tongs who took umbrage at his tattoos and bad attitude.

The ambulance delivered him to the Saint Matt's emergency room, severely beaten and incoherent. His broken arms were the least of his problems, as he may have suffered brain damage from being kicked in the head repeatedly after they tired of beating him with their nunchakus. Keeping an ear out for his arrival, I scrambled down to the ER as fast as I could with Esha's laptop, and using the Z1 hacked his ER visit and psychiatric evaluation.

Thanks to my efforts, he was now a well-known paranoid schizophrenic drug abuser with complex and often violent delusions. He had many ER visits in the past for drug overdose and attempted suicides and was fixated on the idea that he was the son of titled English nobility, believing he was educated at Oxford and MIT. So wrapped up was he in this delusion that he spoke always with a stiff upper crust English accent that he had developed to perfection. I was just about to close the file when I decided to add one more line to the assessment. The *pièce de résistance,* as they say. The last thing I wrote was that he was a compulsive masturbator and should never under any circumstance ever be allowed near children. I clicked enter and laughed all the way back to Vito's apartment.

I was sitting in my office now in between appointments when I suddenly chuckled out loud thinking about Vito's reaction when I told him the story.

"Vito, his psychiatrists are going to write a textbook about him if and when he recovers."

"Damn, Cesari, I'm glad we're on the same side."

"Yeah, well don't forget it. Imagine what I'll write about you in your chart."

My cellphone buzzed. "Hi, Arnie. How's it going?"

"Things are going well, almost back to normal. Tony's improving every day too. The shrinks say he's been asking for you so if you've got some time, pay him a visit."

"That's great news and I certainly will, either later today or first thing in the morning. Say Arnie, did you catch that thing on the news about the implosion at Unicare?"

"Did I ever. It's unbelievable what greed does to people. I still remember when Leibowitz disappeared. Everyone knew something bad had happened but I don't think anyone could have dreamt this up. Look, Cesari, the main reason I'm calling is that there's an old lady in a wheelchair in my office waiting room covered in unusually large diamonds and accompanied by an entourage. She dropped by unannounced and wants to make a substantial donation to this hospital, and when I say substantial, I'm thinking at least five, maybe six figures. From her appearance, my guess is six."

"Okay, well I guess congratulations are in order. Great job, Arnie."

"Thanks, but I want you to come up here, shake her hand and tell her how much you appreciate her philanthropy."

"Me? Why me?"

"Because she asked for you by name, that's why. Who knows, maybe she saw you on TV saving Tony. I really don't care. When people offer you large sums of money you generally don't ask them to explain themselves. The bottom line is this. If she's prepared to donate thousands of dollars to get a better look at the great Dr. Cesari then that's what she gets and anything else she wants from you. So come on down, practice smiling, and stop by a condom machine on the way."

Man, he was on fire. "But, Arnie, I'm in the middle of a busy office schedule."

"Not any more you're not. I called your secretary before I called you. She's rescheduling all your patients as we speak. You are now officially free."

Oh, brother. "I'll be right there."

I hung up my white lab coat, straightened my tie and primped in the mirror. Arnie's office was on the tenth floor and I hopped on the first elevator that came by. What do you say in a situation like this? Thank you ma'am, may I please have the honor of kissing your ass?

I knocked on Arnie's door and he invited me in. He stood up from behind his desk to shake my hand and introduced me to the old woman in the wheelchair covered in bling. My jaw dropped slightly as she turned toward me and I got a good look at her.

Arnie said, "Mrs. Sinclair, this is Dr. John Cesari, one of our finest gastroenterologists."

She extended her hand and I took it trying not to let my surprise show. I looked in her eyes. They were just as warm and kindly as I remembered. She said, "Hello, Dr. Cesari. You can call me Madeline."

I stood there frozen, staring at her.

Arnie said sharply, "John, how about saying hello to Mrs. Sinclair?"

"Hello, Madeline."

"Why, doctor, you're trembling. I hope you're not frightened by an old woman."

Holy shit. I really was trembling. "Of course not, Mrs. Sinclair. I mean Madeline. I—it's just that I rushed to get here when Dr. Goldstein called me. I'll be fine."

Arnie chuckled, "John, relax. Mrs. Sinclair won't bite you. Now have a seat."

"Thank you for taking time out of your day to see me, Doctor."

Sitting down next to her I said, "The pleasure is all mine, Madeline."

"John, Mrs. Sinclair has decided to make a sizable donation to Saint Matt's and I was just telling her how grateful we all are."

Not quite fully recovered from my shock, I said, "Thank you for your extraordinary generosity, Madeline. May I ask how you came to choose Saint Matt's?"

She smiled. "Why, because of you of course, Dr. Cesari. I thought that much was obvious."

I hesitated and looked at Arnie uncomfortably. He just shrugged his shoulders politely. *I don't know this woman, I don't know this woman, I don't know this woman.* Just keep saying that to yourself. I asked, "Is it because you saw me on TV helping my friend out? Because if it is, I wish to assure you that I'm not a hero. I simply acted instinctively. If I'd had time to think it through, I probably would have run in the other direction."

Arnie didn't like that and interjected, "Don't let him fool you, Mrs. Sinclair. Dr. Cesari is being modest. He would run into a burning building to rescue a kitten." You had to love Arnie. If this woman wanted a hero, then by golly he was going to give her one.

Nodding in agreement she looked at me saying, "Trust me, Dr. Goldstein, I believe you."

I was dumbfounded. This didn't make any sense. "Well, thank you both for the vote of confidence."

She turned back to Arnie. "Well, let's get down to business, gentlemen. I am an old woman and I don't have much time left. I want to put my money to good use and healthcare is a very worthy cause especially in today's cash-strapped environment and spiraling costs. So, without further fanfare, I wish to make a donation of one hundred million dollars to Saint Matt's Hospital. In addition I have already rewritten my will such that upon my death, half of all my net worth will be bequeathed to this hospital in the form of a trust in perpetuity. I won't be crass and tell you how much that is, but there is one stipulation that I must insist on, and one that I'm afraid is nonnegotiable, Dr. Goldstein."

From the look on Arnie's face, I thought he was going to faint. That was way more money than he or anyone could possibly have imagined, but here it came though, the proverbial other shoe. She probably wanted us to rename the hospital after her grandson or some distant relative.

Arnie gulped and asked hoarsely, "And what is that?"

She continued. "I want Saint Matt's to create a new department of ethics to oversee patient care, medical compliance, professional conduct and relationships between insurers, pharmaceuticals and the medical community. I want Dr. John Cesari to be the chief for life of this new department and to have broad-ranging authority to review patient records, complaints, and third party contracts as well as administrative policies and financial dealings. As chief, he is to be made a permanent board member and to be intimately involved with all hospital financial matters. All monetary contracts and relationships, even that of the CEO, are to be reviewed and signed off by Dr. Cesari. As far as I am concerned, from this day forward, he is in charge of everything and everyone at Saint Matt's Hospital."

Arnie gasped and sat back in his chair, speechless. I said, "Mrs. Sinclair, I am truly flattered, but Dr. Goldstein doesn't have the authority to agree to those conditions even if he wanted to, and believe me, I'm not worthy of this honor."

She smiled warmly as if she had asked for nothing more than some honey with her tea. "I've been around a long time, Dr. Cesari. I believe in right and wrong and I know you do too. There are too many bad people in this world and a shrinking supply of those willing to stand up to them. I know in my heart that I can count on you to always do the right thing. I know that you are a good person."

"How do you know that? We've never even met before ten minutes ago."

"Haven't we?" she asked coyly and winked.

I held my breath. This couldn't be happening. She couldn't possibly know what I'd been through. Arnie didn't like this at all but one hundred million dollars was one hundred million dollars. He said, "No need to be rude, Cesari. If Mrs. Sinclair feels like she knows you then she knows you."

She said, "No, worries Dr. Goldstein. Dr. Cesari is just bit overwhelmed by all of his new responsibilities. I trust you will present my requests to the proper governing bodies and let me know what you intend to do, but a word of advice, I will not take no for an answer."

Arnie nodded enthusiastically. "I will call all the appropriate people including the CEO and get back to you by the end of the week."

"You will get back to me tonight, Dr. Goldstein, or the offer is rescinded."

He cleared his throat. "That's what I meant. I'll get back to you tonight."

She looked at me. "Don't look so serious, Dr. Cesari. This is good news. Okay, gentlemen, I have a couple of things I'd like to give you."

She reached into a very expensive-looking hand bag and took out a thick manila envelope which she flipped onto the desk in front of Arnie. "That's a contract spelling out what my wishes are, including Dr. Cesari's new salary, and the time frame in which I expect all this to take place. My lawyers have already gone over it in great detail. If you have any questions, you'll have to take it up with them as I don't understand all that legal gibberish. I expect the CEO, you, and anyone else who is indicated in those papers to sign and return them to me no later than tomorrow morning. I'll be staying at The Plaza in midtown. If I don't receive the signed agreement from you by the time I check out, I will assume that you have declined my offer."

She was a firecracker for sure, and I was certain Arnie hadn't been spoken to like that since grade school. She reached back into the bag and retrieved a small, neatly gift-wrapped box complete with ribbon and bow. Handing it to me, she said, "This is for you, Dr. Cesari. Please don't open it until you return to the privacy of your office. You'll understand."

Both Arnie and I were stunned and at a loss for words. I murmured, "Thank you."

"Dr. Cesari, I would like to discuss the financial arrangements in a bit more detail with Dr. Goldstein if you wouldn't mind. I'm sure you have more important things to do."

Abruptly dismissed, I looked at her numbly, and stood up, holding the gift. "Thank you again for your generosity."

She touched my hand lightly as I turned to leave and I saw a tear form in one of her blue eyes. It slid slowly down her cheek. "No, Doctor. Thank you for restoring my faith in the goodness of people."

It was a strained moment. What she hinted at was undeniable knowledge of things she could not possibly know. I gathered myself to say something but found that I couldn't so I stood there looking at her.

Finally, Arnie broke the tension saying, "I'll talk to you later, Cesari."

I nodded and left them. When I reached my office, my heart was pounding, I had a headache and my legs were weak. I was emotionally exhausted. None of this made any sense. She couldn't know me. She didn't know me. It was my dream, my delusion, my vision.

I stared at the thin, six-inch-square box with beautiful gold wrapping paper on my desk in front of me. It was very light as if there were nothing inside. I shook my head. This couldn't be happening—but it was. I carefully unwrapped the present and placed the paper, ribbon and bow to one side of my desk. Opening the box, I found a small envelope and lots of delicate tissue paper. In the envelope on very expensive gold leaf stationary was a brief, handwritten note.

My Giannuzzu

Follow the Light Always

Trembling, I covered my face with my hands and took a deep breath, letting it out slowly. My eyes started to water up and I was in danger of losing it. This couldn't be happening. Collecting myself, I waded through the tissue paper, finding an unexpected object at the bottom of the box. It was Julie's gold locket that I had taken from her body, breaking the chain in the process. I had given it to Mrs. Sinclair to return to Julie's parents when I was in Boston. Just to be certain, I opened the locket and saw Julie's parents on either side, her father in his military uniform. This was the locket all right. I sighed deeply and thought it over. It was what it was.

Julie was sitting at her desk and I brought the locket out to her but before showing her I asked, "Julie, what happened to that pretty locket you showed me? The one your parents gave you for your eighteenth birthday."

She looked dejected. "I'm not sure. I haven't seen it since that day. I don't know if it was stolen or the chain just broke and it fell off my neck somewhere. I've been going crazy looking for it. I haven't had the heart to tell my parents yet. They're going to be devastated."

I put my hand in front of her and opened it, watching her eyes grow wide with joy. She jumped up excitedly, taking the locket. "How? Where?"

I smiled. "Does it matter?"

"No. No it doesn't. I can't believe it. Oh, my God. It's a miracle."

"Exactly."

The End

About the Author

*J*ohn Avanzato grew up in the Bronx. After receiving a bachelor's degree in biology from Fordham University, he went on to earn his medical degree at the State University of New York at Buffalo, School of Medicine. He is currently a board-certified gastroenterologist in Geneva, New York, where he lives with his wife of twenty-eight years.

Inspired by authors like Tom Clancy, John Grisham, and Lee Child, John writes about strong but flawed heroes.

His first three novels, Hostile Hospital, Prescription for Disaster and Temperature Rising have been received well.

About the Cat

*W*hen my black lab, Cleopatra, passed away a part of me went with her. I was that attached to her. Friends suggested I get another pet but I just wasn't ready, emotionally. About a year later, my son and his girlfriend started bringing their cat, Button, to the house.

At first, I was alarmed. I don't like cats. I never did and this one thought she owned my house. Several times, I noticed her looking at me and several times I caught myself looking at her. Then it happened. I was sitting in my favorite chair watching television and she came over and sat on the floor in front of me meowing. I ignored her and after a few minutes, she did the unthinkable and jumped onto my lap, sat down and meowed as hard as she could.

Then I did something I couldn't ever have imagined. I picked her up, kissed her and flipped her over onto her back cradling her like a baby. We sat there like that for about an hour. She purred and I cuddled. I think I am now a cat person. Damn cat.

Author's Note

Dear Reader,

I hope you enjoyed reading Claim Denied as much as I enjoyed writing it. Please do me a favor and write a review on amazon.com. The reviews are important and your support is greatly appreciated.

Thank you,

John Avanzato

Hostile Hospital

*W*hen former mob thug turned doctor, John Cesari, takes a job as a gastroenterologist at a small hospital in upstate New York, he assumes he's outrun his past and started life anew. But trouble has a way of finding the scrappy Bronx native.

Things go awry one night at a bar when he punches out an obnoxious drunk who won't leave his date alone. Unbeknownst to Dr. Cesari, that drunk is his date's stalker ex-boyfriend—and a crooked cop.

Over the course of several action packed days, Cesari uncovers the dirty little secrets of a small town hospital. As the bodies pile up, he is forced to confront his own bloody past.

Hostile Hospital is a fast paced journey that is not only entertaining but maintains an interesting view on the philosophy of healthcare. If you aren't too scared after reading, get the sequel, Prescription for Disaster.

Prescription for Disaster

*D*r. John Cesari is a gastroenterologist employed at Saint Matt's Hospital in Manhattan. He tries to escape his unsavory past on the Bronx streets by settling into a Greenwich Village apartment with his girlfriend, Kelly. After his adventures in Hostile Hospital, Cesari wants to stay under the radar of his many enemies.

Through no fault of his own, Cesari winds up in the wrong place at the wrong time. A chance encounter with a mugger turns on its head when Cesari watches his assailant get murdered right before his eyes.

After being framed for the crime, he attempts to unravel the mystery, propelling himself deeply into the world of international diamond smuggling. He is surrounded by bad guys at every turn and behind it all are Russian and Italian mobsters determined to ensure Cesari has an untimely and unpleasant demise.

His prescription is to beat them at their own game, but before he can do that he must deal with a corrupt boss and an environment filled with temptation and danger from all sides. Everywhere Cesari goes, someone is watching. The dramatic climax will leave you breathless and wanting more.

Temperature Rising

TEMPERATURE
RISING

John Avanzato

A JOHN CESARI NOVEL

*J*ohn Cesari is a gangster turned doctor living in Manhattan saving lives one colonoscopy at a time. While on a well-deserved vacation, he stumbles upon a murder scene and becomes embroiled in political intrigue involving the world's oldest profession.

His hot pursuit of the truth leads him to the highest levels of government, where individuals operate above the law. As always, girl trouble hounds him along the way making his already edgy life that much more complex.

The bad guys are ruthless, powerful and nasty but they are no match for this tough, street-smart doctor from the Bronx who is as comfortable with a crowbar as he is with a stethoscope. Get ready for a wild ride in Temperature Rising. The exciting and unexpected conclusion will leave you on the edge of your seat.

CPSIA information can be obtained
at www.ICGtesting.com
Printed in the USA
LVOW04s1651060916
503439LV00023B/567/P